O9-BUB-237

# The
# Price
## of
# Blood

## Also by Patricia Bracewell

*Shadow on the Crown*

# The
# Price
# of
# Blood

Patricia Bracewell

Viking

VIKING
Published by the Penguin Group
Penguin Group (USA) LLC
375 Hudson Street
New York, New York 10014

USA | Canada | UK | Ireland | Australia | New Zealand | India | South Africa | China
penguin.com
A Penguin Random House Company

First published by Viking Penguin, a member of Penguin Group (USA) LLC, 2015

Excerpt from *Gesta regum Anglorum—The History of the English Kings* by William of Malmesbury, edited and translated by R.A.B. Mynors, R. M. Thomson and M. Winterbottom, Volume 1 (1998). By permission of Oxford University Press.

Map illustration by Matt Brown

LIBRARY OF CONGRESS CATALOGING-IN-PUBLICATION DATA
Bracewell, Patricia, 1950–
The price of blood : a novel / Patricia Bracewell.
pages ; cm
ISBN 978-0-525-42727-8
1. Emma, Queen, consort of Canute I, King of England, –1052—Fiction. 2. Ethelred II, King of England, 968?–1016—Fiction. 3. Great Britain—History—Ethelred II, 979–1016—Fiction. 4. Queens—Great Britain—Fiction. 5. Normans—Great Britain—Fiction. I. Title.
PS3602.R323P75 2015
813'.6—dc23        2014038484

Printed in the United States of America
1 3 5 7 9 10 8 6 4 2

Designed by Nancy Resnick

For Ron and Dot
Who share my earliest memories

# Dramatis Personae

## Anglo-Saxon England, 1006–1012

### Royal Family

Æthelred II, King of England
Emma, Queen of England

*Children of the English king, in birth order:*

Athelstan
Ecbert
Edmund
Edrid
Edwig
Edgar
Edyth
Ælfgifu (Ælfa)
Wulfhilde (Wulfa)
Mathilda
Edward

## Emma's Household

Aldyth, niece of Ealdorman Ælfhelm
Elgiva, daughter of Ealdorman Ælfhelm
*Father Martin
*Hilde, granddaughter of Ealdorman Ælfric
*Margot
Wymarc
Robert, Wymarc's son

## Leading Ecclesiastics

Ælfheah, Archbishop of Canterbury
Ælfhun, Bishop of London
Wulfstan, Bishop of Worcester, Archbishop of Jorvik

## Leading Nobles

Ælfhelm, Ealdorman of Northumbria
Ufegeat, his son
Wulfheah, his son (Wulf)
*Alric, his retainer

Ælfric, Ealdorman of Hampshire

Godwine, Ealdorman of Lindsey
Leofwine, Ealdorman of Western Mercia

Eadric of Shrewsbury
Godwin, Wulfnoth's son
Morcar of the Five Boroughs
Siferth of the Five Boroughs
Thurbrand of Holderness
Ulfkytel of East Anglia

Uhtred of Northumberland
Wulfnoth of Sussex

## Normandy

Duke Richard II, Emma's brother
Duchess Judith
Dowager Duchess Gunnora, Emma's mother
Robert, Archbishop of Rouen, Emma's brother

## The Danes

Swein Forkbeard, King of Denmark
Harald, his son
Cnut, his son

Hemming
Thorkell
Tostig

# Glossary

**Ætheling:** literally, *throne-worthy.* All of the legitimate sons of the Anglo-Saxon kings were referred to as æthelings.

**Ague:** any sickness with a high fever

**Breecs:** Anglo-Saxon term for trousers

**Burh:** an Anglo-Saxon fort

**Burn:** a small stream

**Ceap:** the market street

**Cemes:** a long linen undergarment for men

**Ceorl:** a freeman, neither noble nor slave; peasant

**Chasuble:** an ecclesiastical vestment, a sleeveless mantle covering body and shoulders, often elaborately embroidered, worn over a long, white tunic

**Cyrtel:** a woman's gown

**Danelaw:** an area of England that roughly comprises Yorkshire, East Anglia, and central and eastern Mercia, where successive waves of Scandinavians settled throughout the ninth and tenth centuries

**Ealdorman:** a high-ranking noble appointed by the king to govern a province in the king's name. He led troops, levied taxes, and administered justice. It was a political position usually conferred upon members of powerful families.

**Eyas:** a falcon chick, taken from the nest for training

**Five Boroughs:** a region in Mercia made up of Leicester, Nottingham, Derby, Stamford, and Lincoln, it exercised significant political influence in late Anglo-Saxon England

**Flǽscstrǽt:** literally *flesh street*; outdoor meat market

**Fyrd:** an armed force that was raised at the command of the king or an ealdorman, usually in response to a Viking threat

**Gafol:** the tribute paid to an enemy army to purchase peace

**Garth:** a small piece of enclosed ground used as a yard, garden, or paddock

**Geld:** a tax levied by the king, who used the money to pay the tribute extorted by Viking raiders

**Gerningakona:** Old Norse term for a woman who practices magic

**Godwebbe:** precious cloth, frequently purple, normally of silk; probably shot-silk taffeta

**Haga:** a fenced enclosure; a dwelling in town

**Handfasting:** a marriage or betrothal; a sign of a committed relationship with no religious ceremony or exchange of property

**Headrail:** a veil, often worn with a circlet or band, kept in place with pins

**Hearth troops:** warriors who made up the household guard of royals and great lords

**Hibernia:** Latin name for Ireland

**Hide:** an Anglo-Saxon land reckoning for the purpose of assessing taxes

**Hird:** the army of the Northmen; the enemies of the English

**Host:** army

**Hythe:** Old English term for a wharf or pier

**Leech:** a physician

**Lindsey:** the district of eastern England between the River Witham and the Humber, in the northern part of Lincolnshire

**Mantling:** in falconry, the action of a bird spreading its wings and arching over its prey to hide it

**Mere:** a lake or pond

**Murrain:** a disease of domestic animals

**Nithing:** a pejorative term in Norse and Old English meaning "abject wretch"

**Reeve:** a man with administrative responsibilities utilized by royals, bishops, and nobles to oversee towns, villages, and large estates

**Rood:** the cross on which Christ was crucified

**Sámi:** a culture indigenous to Norway, believed to have prophetic skills

**Scop:** storyteller; harper

**Screens passage:** a vestibule just inside the entrance to a great hall or similar chamber, created by movable screens that blocked the wind from gusting into the hall when the doors were opened

**Scyrte:** a short garment worn by men; shirt

**Seel:** to sew shut the eyes of a falcon for training

**Sennight:** a week

**Skald:** poet or storyteller

**Smoc:** a shirt or undergarment

**Thegn:** literally *one who serves another*; a title that marks a personal relationship; the leading ones served the king himself; a member of the highest rank in Anglo-Saxon society; a landholder with specified obligations to his lord

**Thrall:** a slave

**Wain:** a wagon or cart

**Wergild:** literally *man payment*; the value set on a person's life

**Witan:** wise men; the king's council

**Wyrd:** fate or destiny

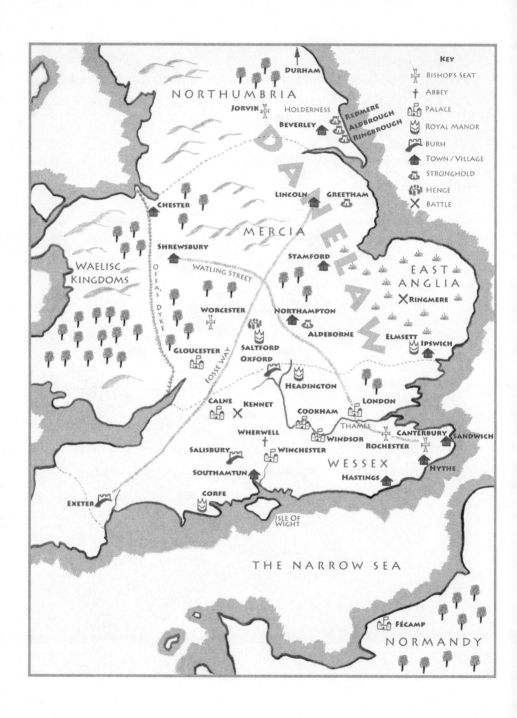

KEY

🏛 BISHOP'S SEAT
✝ ABBEY
🏰 PALACE
👑 ROYAL MANOR
🏯 BURH
🏘 TOWN / VILLAGE
🏰 STRONGHOLD
👥 HENGE
✕ BATTLE

NORTHUMBRIA

DURHAM

JORVIK    HOLDERNESS
BEVERLEY    REDMERE
            ALDBROUGH
            RINGBROUGH

DANELAW

CHESTER

LINCOLN    GREETHAM

MERCIA

SHREWSBURY

STAMFORD

EAST
ANGLIA

WATLING STREET

OFFA'S DYKE

WAELISC
KINGDOMS

WORCESTER    NORTHAMPTON    RINGMERE

ALDEBORNE    ELMSETT
                    IPSWICH

GLOUCESTER    SALTFORD
              OXFORD

FOSSE WAY

HEADINGTON

CALNE    KENNET            LONDON

        COOKHAM

WHERWELL            THAMES    CANTERBURY    SANDWICH
        WINDSOR
SALISBURY   WINCHESTER    ROCHESTER

SOUTHAMTUN                WESSEX        HYTHE

EXETER            HASTINGS

CORFE

ISLE OF
WIGHT

THE NARROW SEA

FÉCAMP

NORMANDY

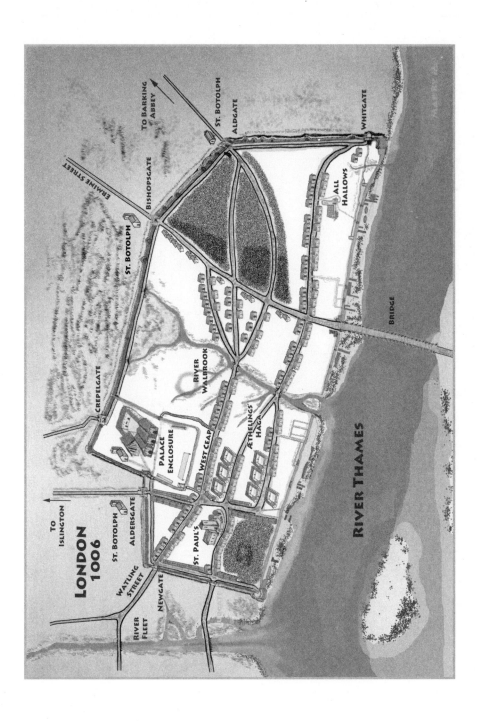

LONDON
1006

TO
ISLINGTON

WATLING STREET

RIVER
FLEET

NEWGATE

ST. BOTOLPH

ALDERSGATE

CREPELGATE

ERMINE STREET

ST. BOTOLPH

BISHOPSGATE

TO BARKING
ABBEY

ST. BOTOLPH

ALDGATE

WHITGATE

ST. PAUL'S

PALACE
ENCLOSURE

WEST CEAP

ÆTHELINGS' HAGA

RIVER
WALBROOK

ALL
HALLOWS

BRIDGE

RIVER THAMES

In the Year of our Lord 979 Æthelred, son of Edgar . . . came to the throne . . . His life is said to have been cruel at the outset, pitiable in mid-course, and disgraceful in its ending. . . .

He was hounded by the shade of his brother, demanding terribly the price of blood. Who could count how often he summoned his army, how often he ordered ships to be built, how often he called his nobles together from every quarter, and nothing ever came of it?

The evil could not be lulled to rest . . . for enemies were always sprouting out of Denmark like a hydra's heads, and nowhere was it possible to take precautions . . .

—*The History of the English Kings*
William of Malmesbury
Twelfth Century

# The
# Price
## of
# Blood

# Prologue

Shrove Tuesday, March 1006

Calne, Wiltshire

Æthelred knelt, his head clutched in his hands, bowed beneath the weight of his crown and his sins. Somewhere above, the vesper bells rang to mark the call to evening prayer, and at the very moment of their tolling he felt his limbs tremble, convulsed by a force beyond his control.

The familiar, hated lethargy settled over him, and though he strove to keep his head down and his eyes shut, a will far stronger than his own pulled his gaze upward. The air before him thickened and turned as black and rippling as the windswept surface of a mere. Pain gnawed at his chest, and he shivered with cold and apprehension as the world around him vanished. Sounds, too, faded to nothing and he knew only the cold, the pain, and the flickering darkness before him that stretched and grew into the shape of a man.

Or what had been a man once. Wounds gaped like a dozen mouths at throat and breast, gore streaked the shredded garments crimson, and the menacing face wore Death's gruesome pallor. His murdered brother's shade drew toward him, an exhalation from the gates of heaven or the mouth of hell—he could not say which. Not a word passed its lips, but he sensed a malevolence that flowed from the dead to the living, and he shrank back in fear and loathing.

Yet he could not look away. For long moments the vision held him in thrall until, as it began to fade, he became aware of another figure—of a shadow behind the shadow. Dark, indistinct, shrouded in gloom, it hovered briefly in the thickened air and then, like the other, it was gone.

Released from the spell, he could hear once again the pealing of the vesper bells and the murmur of voices at prayer, could smell the honeyed scent of candles and, beneath it, the rank stench of his own sweat. The golden head dropped once more into cupped hands, but now it was heavy with fear and tormented by a terrible foreboding.

**A.D. 1006**  This year Ælfheah was consecrated Archbishop; Wulfheah and Ufegeat were deprived of sight; Ealdorman Ælfhelm was slain . . .

—*The Anglo-Saxon Chronicle*

# Chapter One

March 1006

Near Calne, Wiltshire

Queen Emma checked her white mare as it crested a hill above the vast royal estate where the king had settled for the Lenten season. Behind her a company of thirty men, women, and children, all of them heavily cloaked against a biting wind, rested their mounts after the long climb. In front of her, in the middle distance below the hill, the slate roof and high, gilded gables of the king's great hall dwarfed the buildings and palisade that encircled it. The hall marked their journey's end, and Emma looked on it with relief, for it was late in the day and her people were weary.

As she studied the road ahead, a single shaft of sunlight broke through the clouds massed in folds across the sky to slant a golden light upon the fields below. The furrowed land shimmered under a thin film of green—new shoots that promised a good harvest in the months to come, if only God would be merciful.

But God, Emma thought, seemed to have turned His face against England. For two years now, promising springs had been followed by rain-plagued summers so that food and fodder were scarce. This past winter, Famine and Death had stalked the land, and if the coming season's yield was not bountiful, yet more of the poorest in the realm would die.

She had done what she could, distributing alms to those she could reach and adding her voice to the faithful's desperate pleas for God's mercy. Now, as the golden light lingered on the green vale below, she prayed that her latest assault on heaven—the pilgrimage she had made to the resting places of England's most beloved saints—might at last have secured God's blessings on Æthelred's realm.

She glanced around, looking past the horse litter that bore her son and his wet nurse to find her three young stepdaughters. Wulfhilde, just eight winters old, was asleep in the arms of the servant who rode with her. Ælfa sat upon her mount slumped within the folds of her mantle. Edyth, the eldest at twelve, stared dully toward the manor hall, her face drawn and pale beneath her fur-lined hood.

Emma chided herself for pushing them so hard, for they had been on the road since daybreak. She turned in her saddle to lead the group forward, but as she did so the wind made a sudden shift to strike her full in the face. Her mount sidled nervously, and as she struggled to control the mare another fierce gust pushed at her like a massive hand that would urge her away.

She felt a curious sense of unease, a pricking at the back of her neck, and she squinted against the wind, searching for the source of her disquiet. On the mast atop the manor's bell tower, the dragon banner of Wessex heralded the king's presence within. He would be there to welcome her—although not with anything resembling love or even affection, for he had none of either to give. Æthelred was more king than man—as ruthless and cold as a bird of prey. Sometimes she wondered if he had ever loved anyone—even himself.

She did not relish the coming reunion with her lord, but that alone did not explain her sudden sense of foreboding.

As she hesitated, her son began to wail, his piercing cry an urgent demand that she could not ignore. She shook off her disquiet, for surely it must be her own weariness that assailed her. She nodded to her armed hearth troops to take the lead, and then followed them down the hill.

When she rode through the manor gates she saw a knot of retainers making for the kitchens behind the great hall, one of them carrying the standard of the ætheling Edmund. She puzzled over his presence here while a groom helped her dismount. Edmund had accompanied his elder brothers Athelstan and Ecbert to London in February, charged with the task of repairing the city's fortifications and the great bridge that straddled the Thames. All three of them were to remain there until they joined the court at Cookham for the Easter feast. What, then, was Edmund doing here today?

The anxiety that had vexed her on the hill returned, but she had duties to perform before she could satisfy her curiosity. She led her stepdaughters and attendants into her quarters, where she found a fire blazing in the central hearth, the lime-washed walls hung with embroidered linens, and her great, curtained bed standing ready at the far end of the room. Three servants were setting up beds for the king's daughters, and a fourth stepped forward to take Emma's hooded mantle and muddy boots.

She slipped out of the cloak, then looked about the chamber for the women of her household who had been sent ahead and had, she guessed, supervised all these preparations.

"Where are Margot and Wymarc?" she asked, still unnerved by that moment of unease on the heights above the manor.

Before anyone could respond, Wymarc entered the chamber with a quick step, and Emma, relieved, drew her into an embrace. They had been parted for only a week, yet it seemed far longer. Wymarc was a bright, comforting presence in her household—and had been since the day they left Normandy together for England. Four years ago that was— four years since Emma stood at the door of Canterbury Cathedral as the peace-weaving bride of the English king, with Wymarc looking on from only a half step away.

She had missed Wymarc this past week.

"Margot has taken Robert down to the millpool," Wymarc said, "to look for ducklings." She shook her head. "It is a marvel that a woman of her years can keep pace with my young son, yet she does it."

Emma smiled, imagining Margot, as small and cheerful as a wren, walking hand in hand with a child not quite two winters old. Children, though, had ever been the center of Margot's world. Healer and midwife, she had been Emma's guide since birth—and the nearest thing to a mother that Emma had in England.

She glanced at Wulfa and Ælfa, who were already shedding their mud-spattered cyrtels for fresh garments.

"The girls will be glad to see Margot," she said. "Ælfa took a fall this morning and wants a salve for the cut on her knee. And Edyth"—she nodded toward one of the beds where Æthelred's eldest daughter was curled up tightly, knees to chest—"yesterday she bled for the first time and she's feeling wretched, of course, and swears that she's ill. She'll listen to no words of reassurance from me, but I expect that Margot can persuade her that she's not about to die."

At this the expression in Wymarc's usually merry brown eyes grew guarded, and the warning glance she cast toward the girls told Emma that something was wrong but that an explanation would have to wait until they could speak privately.

She changed quickly into clean stockings, linen shift, and a dark gray woolen cyrtel, then she drew Wymarc aside.

"What is amiss?" she asked, taking the silken headrail that Wymarc was holding out to her. "Is it something to do with Edmund? I saw his bannermen as I came into the yard."

"I pray it is not true," Wymarc whispered, "but there is a rumor that one of the æthelings has died in London." She clutched Emma's hand. "Emma, I do not know who it is."

The headrail slipped, forgotten, from Emma's fingers. She stared at Wymarc and had to will herself to breathe. Edmund had been with Athelstan and Ecbert in London. Was it possible that one of them was dead?

*Holy Mary*, she prayed, *let it not be Athelstan.*

She had been on God's earth for nineteen summers, had been wife and queen for four of them, and had born a babe who was heir to England's crown. In all that time she had loved but one man and, God forgive her, that man was not her royal husband but his eldest son.

Clasping her hands together to stop their trembling, she pressed them against her mouth and shut her eyes.

"God have mercy," she whispered, then looked to Wymarc. "I must go to the king."

Her thoughts flew back to that moment on the hill above the manor and the foreboding that had shaken her. Had she sensed some trouble in the air then—a portent of loss greater than she could bear to imagine?

*Sweet Virgin*, she prayed again, *let it not be Athelstan.*

She took long, slow breaths and walked with a measured step to disguise the fear that clutched at her heart, to try not to think of how wretched the world would be if Athelstan were not in it.

Nodding to the guards at the entrance to the great hall, she slipped inside. Torches flamed in their sockets along the walls and a fire roared in the central pit, but the vast chamber, which should have been busy with preparations for the evening meal, was all but empty. Æthelred sat on the dais in his great chair with Edmund kneeling before him. The king was bent forward, his silver-streaked, tawny hair contrasting with his son's darker, disheveled locks. The king's steward, Hubert, stood to one side, dictating something to a scribe; a gaggle of servants hovered nearby looking frightened.

Filled with dread, Emma walked silently and swiftly to the dais and sank into the chair placed beside the king's. Æthelred did not even mark her entrance, so absorbed was he in what Edmund was saying. Edmund's face, she saw with despair, was wet with tears, and she forced herself to listen to him in silence, swallowing the urgent query that was on her lips.

"It came on suddenly, and he was in agony from the start," he said in a voice laced with grief. "The leeches gave him a purgative, but that only seemed to make him worse. They bled him, to try to release the evil humors, but even I could see that they thought it was futile. A corruption had taken hold inside, they said, and only a miracle would spare him. They tried to dose him with poppy juice to ease his pain, but what little he swallowed he spewed back again. It was as if some devil would not allow him any succor, would not even let him sleep. His suffering was terrible, my lord. He did not deserve such torment."

Edmund's voice broke, but he took a breath, mastered his grief, and went on.

"On the second morning the bishop arrived with the relics of Saint Erkenwald and a clutch of priests. They prayed for a miracle, but by midday I was begging God to put an end to his agony." He drew a heavy breath. "That prayer, at least, was answered. I am come to you straight from Ecbert's deathbed, my lord. Athelstan insisted that you hear it from one of us and no other."

Emma dropped her head into her hands, unable to keep back her tears. She mourned for Ecbert, and she grieved for Athelstan, who had lost his dearest companion. Yet even as she wept for pity, she murmured a prayer of thanks. Athelstan was alive.

"Why do you weep, lady?" Edmund's harsh voice flayed her. "Your own son thrives, does he not? And Ecbert was nothing to you."

She looked into the grief-ravaged face of her stepson, unsurprised by his words. At seventeen he was a grown man, but even as a youth he had regarded her with resentment and suspicion.

"I am no monster, Edmund," she said. "I grieve for Ecbert as I would for the death of any of my husband's children."

"Ecbert would not want your—"

"Edmund." Æthelred's voice silenced his son.

For once Emma was grateful for the rigid control that the king wielded over his children. She had no wish to wrangle with Edmund. Not today.

The king was gazing into the middle distance, his eyes unfocused and empty.

"On what day," he asked, "and at what hour did Ecbert die?"

"Two days ago," Edmund replied. "Shrove Tuesday, just before vespers."

Æthelred closed his eyes, and the hand that he lifted to his brow trembled. Emma could only guess at what he was feeling. Anguish for the suffering of his son? Anger at a pitiless God? She wanted to comfort him, and she would have reached out to touch his arm, but his next words checked her.

"I beg you, lady, to leave us to our grief. Send my daughters to me. I would tell them of their brother's death."

It was as if he had struck her a physical blow—a terse reminder that she was an outsider, a foreign queen who could be beckoned or dismissed at the king's whim, like a bit of carved wood on a game board.

Without another word, she left the hall.

Grieving and wounded, she returned to her apartments and, as the king had bid her, sent his daughters to him. Then she drew her son from his nurse's lap. Edward nuzzled contentedly against her shoulder, happily fingering the thick, pale braid of her hair. As she paced restlessly about the room, finding comfort in her son's warm, milky scent, Edmund's words and the venomous look he had turned upon her played in her head like a bad dream.

His anger, she feared, was directed as much toward her son as toward her. She had watched it grow and fester for more than a year now— ever since Æthelred had named Edward heir to his throne. In disinheriting the sons born to him by his first wife, the king had pitted all her stepsons against her child. Brothers against brother; a host of Cains against her tiny Abel.

Athelstan, for her sake she suspected, kept his brothers' resentment in check. But how long could he continue to do so?

Royal brothers had been murdered before this for the sake of a crown. Æthelred himself had been but ten summers old when his half brother, King Edward, had been slain. No one had been punished for that murder. Instead, certain men close to the newly crowned young Æthelred had prospered.

How many powerful men, she mused uneasily, had interests that would be ill served if her son should one day take the throne? How many of the elder æthelings' supporters could be called on to dispose of a troublesome half brother for the benefit of the sons of Æthelred's first wife?

The thought turned her limbs to liquid, and she had to sit down. She rested her cheek against Edward's bright silken hair and held him close. He was her treasure, her whole reason for being. His life was in her hands, and Ecbert's death was a reminder that even for a royal son, life was perilous.

"I promise you," she whispered, "that I will protect you from all your enemies." Then she thought of Athelstan, alone in London and grieving for his brother, and she added, "Even those whom I love."

# Chapter Two

March 1006

Calne, Wiltshire

The next day dawned sunless, heavy with the threat of rain. As Æthelred performed the prescribed rituals of mourning for his dead son, his mind was filled with thoughts as black as the sullen skies—thoughts that sprang not from grief, but from rage.

Grief, he told himself, was a sentiment of little use to him. Better to howl than to weep. Better to channel his fury toward a pitiless God and the vengeful shade of a murdered king than to mourn for the innocent dead.

Both heaven and hell, he was certain, had cursed him—the bitter fruit of ancient sins. He had witnessed the murder of his brother, the king; had raised neither voice nor hand to prevent it; had taken a crown that should not have been his. For these wrongs his brother's cruel shadow continued to torment him, despite all that he had done to lay the loathsome spirit to rest.

Ecbert's death was yet another sign that Edward's hand—or God's—was raised against him. Shrines and churches, prayers and penance had not bought him peace. He was still dogged by misfortune.

Now he understood that the price of forgiveness was far too high. God and Edward demanded his kingdom and his crown, and that was a price he would not pay.

As he knelt within the cold heart of the royal chapel, he made a solemn vow. He would defy heaven; he would defy hell, too, and anything else living or dead that sought to break his grasp upon his throne. For he was of the Royal House of Cerdic. Never had his forebears relinquished their claim to kingship until the moment that each took his final breath, and neither would he.

If a king was not a king, then he was nothing.

By midafternoon the storm had dissipated, but when the household assembled for the day's main meal Æthelred still seethed with a brooding rage that he directed toward the God who had turned against him. He took his place upon the dais and nodded brusquely to Abbot Ælfweard, seated at his right hand, to give the blessing. A commotion at the bottom of the hall, though, drew his attention to the screens passage. There, a tall figure stepped through the curtained doorway. Cloaked all in black and with the long white beard of an Old Testament prophet, Archbishop Wulfstan strode with measured step toward the high table.

Here, then, Æthelred thought, was God's answer to his earlier vow of defiance. Like some carrion crow, Wulfstan—Bishop of Worcester, Archbishop of Jorvik—had come to croak God's Word at him.

Like the rest of his household, he stood up as the archbishop advanced. But Wulfstan's progress was pointedly slow, and he leaned heavily upon his crosier as he made his way to the dais, sketching crosses in the air over the bowed heads of the assembly.

The old man was weary, Æthelred thought, unusual for Wulfstan, who usually had the vigor of a rutting stallion. A vigor that he dedicated to his king's service, he admitted grudgingly, as well as to God's. What was it that had driven him so hard today? Was it Ecbert's death, or did he bring news of some further calamity?

Emma, he saw, was already rounding the table to present the welcome cup before kneeling in front of the archbishop for his blessing. Wulfstan passed his crosier and then the cup to a waiting servant, took the queen's hands in his, and bent his head close to hers to speak a private word. Æthelred watched, irritated. Wulfstan had always been Emma's champion; indeed, most of England's high clergy had been seduced by his pious queen.

Beside him Abbot Ælfweard, who knew his place well enough, scuttled off the dais to make way for his superior, and Æthelred knelt in his turn as the archbishop offered a prayer over his royal head. When the prelate had cleansed his hands and the prayer of thanksgiving had been said at last, the company sat down to eat.

After glancing with distaste at the Lenten fare of eel soup and bread that was set before him, Æthelred pushed the food away and turned to the archbishop. May as well hear what the man had come to say, he thought, and be done with it.

"Do you come to console me, Archbishop?" he demanded bitterly. "Do you bring words of comfort from the Almighty that will recompense me for the death of a son?"

Wulfstan, too, pushed aside his bowl.

"I bring no consolation, my lord, for I have none to give," he said, and there was not even the merest hint of compassion in the archbishop's cold gaze. "*Thus says the Lord,*" he went on, "*your sons shall die and your daughters shall perish of famine. None shall be spared among them, unless you repent of the wickedness of your hearts.*" His gray eyes glinted in the candlelight like chips of steel, fierce and bright. "I am come, my lord, because I am afraid—for this kingdom and its people." He paused and then he added, "And I fear for its king."

Fear of God's wrath. Of course—it was Wulfstan's favorite theme, the wickedness of men and the need for repentance. But God used men to flay those whom He would punish, and it was the men whom Æthelred feared, although he did not say it.

"Your kingdom is mired in sin, my lord," Wulfstan's cold, implacable voice went on, "and even innocents will suffer for it. The death of the ætheling and the famine that we have endured—these are signs from the Almighty. God's punishment will be inflicted on us all, from the king to the lowliest slave, and no one will escape judgment. If we are not penitent, God will destroy us."

Æthelred gritted his teeth. He had tried penitence, but over and over God had spurned his prayers and his offerings of recompense. His brother's hideous wraith still walked the earth—how else if not by God's will? Let others turn to the Lord for succor; he would not. Let Wulfstan batter heaven with his prayers—such was his episcopal duty. Mayhap God would pay heed to *him*.

He toyed with a bit of bread, listening with half an ear as Wulfstan gravely catalogued the sinful deeds of the men and women of Worcester. Adultery, murder, pagan rituals, and the miserliness of tight-fisted nobles ranked high among them, but Æthelred had no interest in the petty sins of Worcestershire folk.

"What of your northern see, Archbishop?" he asked when Wulfstan paused for breath. "What black sins, exactly, do the men of Northumbria have upon their souls?"

Wulfstan's hard eyes—a zealot's eyes in a grim face, he thought—fixed on his own.

"*The Lord said to me, from the north will come an evil that will boil over on all who dwell in the land.* The prophet Jeremiah gives you warning, my king, and you would do well to heed his words."

Æthelred closed his eyes. *Jesu*, but the man maddened him. He spoke of prophecies and warnings, but what further calamity did they presage?

Scowling, he tossed his bread to the table.

"I could heed your prophet far better if you would make his message plain to me," he growled. "What mischief is brewing in the north and who is behind it?"

Wulfstan steepled his hands and rested his chin thoughtfully upon his fingertips.

"The men of the north have little love for their king." He shook his head. "They are wary even of their archbishop. It is true that unrest is brewing in Jorvik, but I cannot say who is behind it."

Cannot? Æthelred wondered. Or will not?

"What of my ealdorman?" he asked. "How does he treat with the men of Northumbria and the Danelaw?" Ealdorman Ælfhelm's commission was to bend the damned rigid northerners to the will of their king, but he had long suspected that the man's activities in Northumbria had been far more self-serving. Get close enough and Ælfhelm's actions stank more of scheming and guile than of vigorous efforts at persuasion.

Wulfstan's thin lips seemed to grow thinner still. Whatever Ælfhelm was doing, the archbishop did not approve.

"I am told that he has the ear of the northern nobles," Wulfstan said, "although what passes between them I do not know. Lord Ælfhelm does not confide in me."

No. Ælfhelm was not the kind of man to confide in an archbishop. But Wulfstan clearly knew something about the ealdorman that he was reluctant to reveal. Sensing that there was more to come, he waited, and eventually Wulfstan spoke again.

"I urge you to speak with Lord Ælfhelm on these matters, my lord. I, too, will take counsel with him at the Easter court, for I have reason to believe that some men in the north consort with pagan believers and evildoers from foreign lands. They must be brought to heel through fear of God's wrath and the punishments sanctioned by law."

Æthelred grunted his agreement to Wulfstan's advice, but his thoughts lingered on the foreign evildoers the archbishop spoke of. He would like to know more about them and their dealings with the men of Northumbria, and perhaps with Ælfhelm himself. He would get nothing else from Wulfstan, he knew. The archbishop had never been one for details.

As for his ealdorman, he had grave doubts about Ælfhelm's ability to bring the men of the north to heel. Or perhaps it was willingness that was lacking. Although Ælfhelm was the most powerful and wealthy of England's magnates, he wanted more power still, and he would use every means at his disposal to get it. That meant alliances with those who bore some malice toward the Church or the Crown, and there were certain to be many such men.

So what alliances was Ælfhelm forging? His elder son had been wed years ago to a girl from the Five Boroughs; the younger last spring to a widow with lands along the River Trent. Each marriage had extended the ealdorman's influence northward, and now he had but one child left unwed—Elgiva, his beautiful witch of a daughter.

And witch she certainly was, he knew from experience. When he had first wearied of his Norman bride, Elgiva had kept him spellbound for many a month. Her father had been behind that, he was certain. And Ælfhelm was likely using Elgiva now to snare some powerful ally among the disgruntled lords of the north. To what purpose he could not say, but he could make a very good guess. The men north of the Humber had never liked bending the knee to southern kings. It would take little to push them into betraying the oaths they had made to the House of Cerdic.

Betrayal. That might very well be the evil that Wulfstan's prophet saw boiling over the land.

He glanced down at the gathering before him, to where the queen's women sat at a table just below the dais. Ælfhelm's troublesome vixen of a daughter should have been among them, and when he could not find her he breathed a quiet curse. When Wulfstan had been drawn from the table by a cluster of priests, Æthelred turned to Emma.

"Where is the Lady Elgiva?" he asked.

Emma's green eyes considered him with innocent surprise. "I presume she is still in Northampton, my lord. You gave her leave to attend the wedding of her cousin Aldyth to Lord Siferth of Mercia."

*Christ*, he had forgotten. But that had been a month ago, when the court had been at Sutton and Ælfhelm's estate but two days' ride away. Since then the queen had gone on pilgrimage, and the court had moved here to Wiltshire.

"So she never joined you on pilgrimage?" he asked.

"No, my lord. I expected to find her here upon my return."

He frowned. "I should have been told that she was still in Northampton." Ælfhelm had had his she-whelp with him for a month. Christ alone knew what mischief they were up to. He glanced at Emma. "Wulfstan suspects that there is something amiss in the north. I'll wager half my kingdom that Ælfhelm is at the bottom of it and that Elgiva may have a role to play in his schemes." *Jesu*, it might indeed cost him half his kingdom.

Disgusted with himself, his queen, his archbishop—and with God more than all the rest—he stood up, calling for a light bearer to lead him to his chamber. He would send a messenger to Ælfhelm tonight commanding his entire family's attendance at the Easter court. The ealdorman's response would direct his next move.

As he stalked from the hall, he ignored the men and women of his household, for his gaze was turned inward as he considered all that the archbishop had said, and all that he had hinted. Wulfstan's counsel may not have given him much insight into Ælfhelm's mind, but he had other tools besides the archbishop—other eyes watching whatever events might be unfolding in the north. He would discover what treachery Ælfhelm and his offspring were plotting, and then he would find a way to stop it. He would strike, he vowed, before his enemies and their foreign-born allies could tear his kingdom away from him.

# Chapter Three

March 1006

Aldeborne Manor, Northamptonshire

When Elgiva learned that a messenger had arrived bearing missives from the king to her ealdorman father, she did not wait for a summons to the hall to hear the news. Such a summons, she knew, might never come. Her father liked to flaunt his power by being niggardly with information.

So, with a servant girl at her back bearing a cup and a flagon of mead strong enough to loosen even a giant's tongue, she entered the great hall, where her father had been meeting with men from his various estates. Reeves, grooms, armorers, huntsmen, and their underlings—perhaps a score of men all told—stood in groups about the chamber waiting for an interview with their lord.

Whenever her father was in residence the hall was peopled almost exclusively with such men, and he would not suffer her to stay among them for long. Since she had returned here from her cousin's nuptials, he had kept her mewed up, out of the sight of these fellows in case someone should look at her with covetous glances.

In his zealous regard for her chastity her father seemed to have forgotten that once, hoping to gain greater influence over Æthelred, he had turned a blind eye while she had been the king's leman for near a year. No doubt he had expected, as she had, that the king would set aside his Norman bride and wed *her*. But Emma and the bishops had persuaded the king that his queen could not be easily disposed of and, to Elgiva's father's fury and her frustration, the king's ardor toward her had cooled and she had gained nothing from the dalliance but a few golden trinkets.

Since then Æthelred had shared his bed with an assortment of favorites whose kin were far less prominent than her own, while she was kept like a caged bird under the queen's watchful eye. And now, even worse, she was spending her days and nights here, fettered by her father's far too rigorous protection.

As she made her way through the crowded chamber she searched for her father and found him standing in a narrow beam of sunlight that spilled through one of the hall's high, glazed windows. She tried to gauge his mood from the expression on his face, but it told her nothing. Like his temper, his countenance was ever cold, dangerous, stone-hard, and grim. He was a fearful man to look upon—his face seamed and roughhewn, as if it had been carved from rock that had been cracked and broken. His black hair, coarser than hers but just as thick and curly, was shot through with skeins of white, and the once-black beard was mottled with gray. He was not a gentle man, as likely to greet her with a cuff as with a kiss, although he would welcome the honey wine readily enough.

She took the brimming cup from the servant and, walking boldly forward, she offered it to him.

"Good day, my lord," she said, casting a slantwise, inquisitive glance at the parchment in his hand that bore the king's seal.

Her father took the cup, drank deeply, fixed her with a steady gaze, and said—nothing.

She waited, silently cursing him for this little show of power over her. He knew what she wanted, yet it amused him to make her wait upon his pleasure.

He drank again, then wiped his mouth with the back of his hand and waved the parchment at her.

"I suppose, daughter," he said, "that you wish to learn what news the king has sent me, eh?" He bent toward her with a sneer. "Trust me, lady, it is of no consequence to you." He tossed back the rest of the mead and held out the cup to the servant for more.

Elgiva winced. She had brought the mead to loosen his tongue, not addle his wits. Her father was difficult to deal with when he was sober. He was impossible when he was drunk.

"Yet it is news," she said, careful to keep her voice mild despite the seething anger his bullying always sparked in her. "I would be glad to hear it." She smiled at him, but he responded with his usual scowl.

"The king's second son has died," he said, carelessly tossing the parchment to the floor.

She stared at him, willing his bald statement to be a lie even as it echoed in her head. She had thought to wed an ætheling—either Athelstan or Ecbert—for it had been foretold to her that she would one day be queen. How else could that come about if not by an alliance with either the king or one of his sons? But the king, tied as he was to his whey-faced queen and her half-Norman brat, had gone beyond her reach. And now, if her father spoke true, Ecbert, too, had been taken from her.

"I don't believe, it," she whispered. "He was well enough at Christmas. What happened to him?"

"The missive does not say." He shrugged. "The king has sons enough. He'll not miss this one overmuch."

"Even so, it will mean a dismal feasting at the Easter court." Still, Athelstan would be there and would perhaps need consolation in the wake of his brother's death.

"That, too, is of little consequence to you," her father replied, "for neither you nor I will be attending the feast at Cookham, although it seems the king desires our company. We must disappoint him, I fear, but I will send your brothers in my place."

He had surprised her again. To ignore the king's summons to the Easter council was likely to raise suspicions in Æthelred's already suspicious mind. Why do such a thing?

"My brothers can hardly take your place, my lord," she said smoothly, "as you are his most prominent ealdorman, and their counsel can hardly measure up to yours. Besides, why should we not attend the gathering? The queen will have been looking for me to return to her household for some weeks now, and by—"

"Are you so eager to return to your royal keepers?" he snapped. "Now that I've prized you from the court, I see no good reason to take you back there again. You are my property, Elgiva, not the king's, and I'll not have my plans for you disrupted because Æthelred decides to take you into his bed again or to marry you off behind my back."

"What plans?" she demanded. This was what she had feared for some weeks—that he had kept her here because he intended to put her to some use that suited his purpose, without caring in the least what she might want.

"You will learn that when the time is right," he said. "Until then I will keep you close by my side because I have learned that I cannot trust anyone else to watch over you."

She glared at him, and he glared back at her, confident, she supposed, that he had kept her blind and deaf, as helpless as a newborn kitten. But he was wrong about that, for she knew more about his affairs than he imagined.

"I am aware of your frequent dealings with northerners, my lord," she hissed, "and I've heard that even men from across the Danish sea have been in this—"

In an instant he had slammed down his cup and grasped her arm with all the strength of a man well used to wielding a sword. She found herself thrust into a corner out of sight and hearing of the men in the hall.

"If you cannot watch your tongue, girl, I shall cut it out for you," he snarled. "And while you're about it, keep that inquisitive little nose of yours out of my business. I promise you, I look forward to the day when I hand you off to your husband and you become someone else's problem."

"And that day would be when?" she spat at him. "Soon, I think, for I am twenty summers old and you must use me before I am too old to be considered a prize for any man!"

"You are no prize now, sullied as you are by the king's lust." He gave her a shake, and then, to her astonishment, he grinned. "But have no fear, daughter," he said jovially, his words slurred and indistinct. "Your betrothal is all but settled. In the end, you will thank me."

He stumbled against her, and she realized that the drink had done its work and more. He would be less careful now about what he said.

"Who is it then?" she demanded. "Who am I to wed? I will go to him gladly, so long as you have not sold me to some brute of a Dane."

The words were barely out of her mouth before he'd clamped a hand at her throat.

"I told you to keep your mouth shut!" he snarled. "Get you back to your chamber, now; I've no more to say to you."

He thrust her away from him and, her mouth set in a grim line, she left the hall.

Her father had not revealed everything, but he had said enough.

He had done the unthinkable—betrothed her to some filthy Danish warlord, some savage with a great deal of gold who wanted to buy a noble wife and rich properties in England. What had been the bride price, she wondered, that her father had demanded for her? Whatever the settlement, it would prove worthless, for she would marry no Dane. She had watched them rape and murder her old nurse, and her father well knew how much she hated and feared them. If he tried to force her into a marriage with one of those brutes, she would murder him with her own hands.

But it would not come to that. The king's messenger must still be here, for he would eat and rest while a fresh mount was readied. If she could just get to him, she could put a stop to this marriage herself.

She sent the maidservant—her father's eyes and ears, she was certain—to the larder house with what remained of the mead. Inside her own chamber she went to the coffer that held her most precious belongings, unlocked it, and withdrew a handful of coins. It should be enough, she guessed, to enlist the services of the royal messenger and to purchase the silence of any of her father's grooms who might be about.

Fearing that she may already be too late, she made her way swiftly to the stables.

The king's man, she saw with relief, was still there, checking the girth of his mount while a young groom clutched the bridle and spoke soothingly to the gelding. There was no one else about.

She went up to the boy holding the horse, whispered, "You did not see me here," and pressed a coin into his palm. "Understand?" He grinned and nodded, and she added, "There's more of that for you if you make sure that no one enters the stable while I am here."

He scurried to the door, and she left him to watch the entryway while she turned to the courier. The man did not even glance at her, clearly in a hurry to be off. She stepped to his side and whispered with some urgency, "I am Lord Ælfhelm's daughter. I would have you carry a message to the king."

"Aye, lady," he said, his eyes still trained on his task. He continued to busy himself with the saddle straps, and she was tempted to snatch his hand and force him to attend to her. There was no need, though. A moment later, apparently satisfied at last with his mount, he finally turned to face her. "What is it then?"

Now she hesitated. What if she could not trust him? What if he simply strode into her father's hall and repeated to him everything she said?

She studied his face. He was young, barely more than a gawky lad, fair-haired and smooth-faced. Now that he was looking at her, his eyes glimmered with interest and, she thought, admiration. Surely he would be sympathetic to the plight of a woman under the thumb of a cruel father. And even if he betrayed her, no punishment that her father could inflict on her would be worse than a Danish marriage.

"You must tell him," she said, gazing at him earnestly and willing her eyes to fill with tears, "that my father has betrothed me against my will to a Danish lord, and that I beg the king to help me, for only he can stop the alliance. Tell him too that my brothers are in my father's confidence, and the king must not trust them." She took the man's hand and placed four bright silver pennies there. "Can you do that for me?"

His eyes widened when he looked at the coins in his hand. She had probably given him too much, but she did not care. If he did as she asked, it was silver well spent.

"I will give him the message, my lady," he said, quickly slipping the coins into the purse at his belt, as if he feared she might ask for some of them back.

"Can you remember all of it?" she asked.

"I have it here," he said, tapping a finger to his forehead. "The king will have it in three days' time; I give you my word."

He nodded to her, and she stepped back as he mounted his horse. Keeping to the shadows of the stable, she held her breath as she watched him ride toward the manor gate. If the gate wards should stop and question him, he might give her away, however unwittingly. But they waved him through, and she expelled a little sigh of relief. She pressed another coin into the filthy hand of the stable lad and, satisfied that she had disrupted her father's wretched scheme, she returned swiftly to her chamber.

The matter was in the king's hands now. He would be furious when he learned what her father was planning, of course—would likely impose a fine or confiscate some of his properties just for considering such a move.

Her brothers would likely suffer the same fate. In truth, she wasn't certain that her brothers were aware of her father's plans. But if she had accused them falsely, what did it matter? They had treated her badly for years upon years, and now she would have her revenge.

She wanted all of them punished, but especially her father. For far too long he had kept her from his counsels, had plotted her future with never a thought for her interests and desires. He had treated her like a fool instead of recognizing that she could be of far more use to him if he would but confide in her. She would make him see that she was not without resources, make him regret that he had so badly misjudged both her wit and her willingness to bend to his will.

# Chapter Four

March 1006

London

A procession of heavily laden carts was making its way from the Thames bridge toward the East Ceap. Athelstan nudged his mount past it, grimacing at the noisy clatter of wooden wheels on graveled street. It was just past midday, the sun had burned away the mist that frequently hovered over the river, and London was, as usual, crowded as well as noisy.

And stinking, he thought, as he was forced to wait for another cart, laden with baskets of fish, to turn into the side gate of one of the city's larger hagas before he could make his way into Æthelingstrete.

A sennight ago, when Ecbert's coffin had been borne along this route to St. Paul's Abbey, the streets had been quiet. The ground had been more river than road that day and the air thick with fog and mist, but the men and women who had lined Æthelingstrete to watch the somber procession had stood in silence—a mark of respect for his brother that still moved him.

It had been ten days since Ecbert had died, yet a dozen times on each of those days he had found himself turning to speak to the brother who had been his near constant companion for as long as he could remember—only to discover yet again that Ecbert was not there. He wondered if he would ever become accustomed to that emptiness. Certainly he had tried. He had thrown himself into his work, overseeing the building of a new wooden tower on the London side of the bridge; it exercised his brain and body well enough, but it did little to fill the void that Ecbert had left behind.

He rode beneath the wooden archway that marked the entrance to what the Londoners called the Æthelings' Haga—usually an apt description, although since Ecbert's death and Edmund's immediate departure for Wiltshire, he had been the only ætheling in London. That was apparently no longer the case, he concluded, eyeing the lathered mounts in the yard. Edmund must be back.

He left his horse with a groom and moments later he entered the hall, where he found his brother waiting for him, still cloaked and grimed from travel. Edmund was seated at a table with an ale cup in his hand, and he wore an expression forbidding enough to keep the other men in the hall—slaves, men-at-arms, and trusted companions—at a healthy distance.

Even on a good day, Athelstan knew, Edmund could be forbidding. He had always been burly, but now, at seventeen, he had outstripped all his brothers in height. Athelstan couldn't even remember the last time he'd won a wrestling match with Edmund. It had been years ago.

Going on looks alone, men took care not to cross Edmund.

*The dark, silent one*, their grandmother, the dowager queen, had named him. *They are always the most dangerous. When he speaks, you would do well to listen.*

At the moment Edmund was staring into his ale cup as if he could read the fate of the world there and he had just discovered that the world was about to end.

"You look like hell," Athelstan said, sitting down opposite his brother. And no wonder, considering the tidings he had borne to the king. "How bad was it?"

Edmund took a long pull from his cup, then set it down and stared at it morosely.

"He wanted to know every detail," he said heavily, "so I had to relive it in the telling." He took a breath and ran a hand through the thick brown hair that set him apart from his Saxon-fair brothers. "One can't blame him, I suppose, for wanting to make certain that all had been done for Ecbert that could have been." He drained his cup, then pushed it away from him. "*She* came in while I was answering his questions. Hung on every word. Pretended to grieve for Ecbert. As if anyone would believe that she would mourn the death of one who might have stood between her son and the throne." He scowled at Athelstan. "I am mistaken," he corrected himself. "You would believe it."

"Leave off, Edmund," he said wearily.

Emma had ever been a sore point between them. To Edmund she was not a living, breathing woman but a tool of her ambitious brother, the Norman duke Richard, and so a threat to all the sons of the king's first marriage. And as for *him*—but he thrust the thought of Emma away from him. She was on his mind far too often as it was.

"Was the king satisfied that we had done all we could to save Ecbert?" *Had* they done all that they could to save their brother? The question had been nagging at him like a toothache and would not go away.

"Do you mean does the king blame you for Ecbert's death?"

Edmund's penetrating eyes probed his own, and Athelstan admitted to himself that this was exactly what he'd meant. As the eldest ætheling he had always shouldered responsibility for his brothers' welfare, at least when they were together. He had also been burdened with most of the blame whenever their father found fault with them.

He made no reply, though, and Edmund shook his head.

"Ecbert's illness and death were no fault of yours, Athelstan, and the king knows that. When will you allow yourself to believe it?"

"I keep asking myself if there was something more—"

"The answer is no," Edmund said. "He was treated, he was blessed, he was shriven, and he has gone to God. Now you must let him go." He leaned across the table and his dark eyes were insistent. "You cannot bring him back."

Athelstan rubbed his forehead with his fingertips. Edmund was right. He could not bring Ecbert back from death; could not change his wyrd. Yet since Ecbert had died, he had been unable to rid his mind of words that he had long tried to forget.

*A bitter road lies before the sons of Æthelred—all but one.*

That prophecy had been uttered two years before, within the shadow of a pagan stone dance by one who was said to be able to read the future. They were dismal words that he had repeated to no one. Why tell others a thing that he wished he had never heard himself? Even if he had shared the prophecy with Ecbert, it would not have changed anything; nor would it change Edmund's fate, whatever it might be, if he were to speak of it now.

So he remained silent, and when he looked again at his brother he saw that there must be something more on Edmund's mind, for he was tapping his fingers nervously against his empty cup while he chewed on his lower lip. When Edmund did not speak, Athelstan prodded him. "What are you not telling me?"

"It's just that . . ." Edmund frowned, glanced away, then seemed to make up his mind about whatever was troubling him. "Ecbert's death did not surprise the king. He already knew. When I entered the hall he looked up at me and nodded, as if he had been waiting for me. Before I said a single word he asked, *Which of my sons is dead?* Not sick or injured, but dead. He knew. I have been trying to explain it to myself all during the long journey back, but I cannot make sense of it. How could he have known?"

Edmund's question hung in the air between them, and Athelstan was uncertain how best to answer it. Not with the truth, for the king had forbidden him to speak it.

*The king is troubled in his mind.*

It was Archbishop Ælfheah who had first alerted him to his father's secret torment. And then he had witnessed it himself—had seen the king cower, gray-faced with horror from some invisible threat. Afterward, when his father was himself again, he had spoken of seeing signs and portents of disaster.

Had he, then, been given some warning of the death of a son?

*Jesu.* He did not want to believe it, did not even wish to discuss it with Edmund. To do so was to tread perilously close to what he had been forbidden to reveal.

"For fifteen years," he said, "the kingdom has suffered one blow after another. Viking raids, lost battles, murrains, flooding, famine—it is no wonder that the king looks for calamities. And rumor, as you know, travels on the wind."

Edmund gave him a dubious look.

"Aye," he said slowly. "Rumor. That may explain it." Then his face took on the shuttered expression that hid what he really thought.

Edmund would let it go for now, and Athelstan hoped that there would never be reason to speak of it again.

"While we're on the subject of tale-telling, then," his brother went on, "you should know that Archbishop Wulfstan arrived while I was at Calne. He bent the king's ear for the space of a long meal, and whatever news he brought from the north, the king did not like it."

That was no surprise. When their mother had died, the northern links that their father had forged through that marriage had been broken, and no measures had been taken to restore them. The northerners felt far more loyalty to one another than to a distant king who all but ignored them.

"There may be rebellion stirring among the Mercians and Northumbrians," he said, "and Ealdorman Ælfhelm is likely up to his neck in it. The northerners' allegiance to the king is no stronger than a chain made of straw." And what would his father do to stem that unrest? Another massacre, like the one on St. Brice's Day three years before, when so many Danes in England had been put to the sword?

"If our father had taken Ælfhelm's daughter to wife instead of Emma," Edmund growled, "there would be no trouble in the north. We need a more binding alliance with Ælfhelm or with one of the other northern lords to keep them loyal to us rather than to their Danish brethren across the sea. It should have been forged long ago."

"A marriage, you mean."

"*Your* marriage," Edmund said, "to Ælfhelm's scheming daughter, yes. It's what the girl and her father have wanted since before you could grow a beard and not, as you know, because of your comely face and bright blue eyes."

Edmund was right about that. Elgiva, she-wolf that she was, had tried to worm her way into his bed for political gain—drawn to his

status as heir to the throne. When that had failed she had opened her
legs for the king instead, who used her as any king would. Despite that,
he would take her to wife if it would ease the situation in the north—
and if there was a chance that the king would approve. Which there
was not.

"The king," he said, "will never allow it."

"Then you must do it without his permission."

"*Sweet Christ*," he muttered. "You know how the king would regard
that. He would think that I was making a bid for his crown. I might gain
the allegiance of the northern lords, but the king would see it as the
blackest treachery. It would rip the kingdom in two."

"Then you must reason with him. Convince him of the necessity of a
marriage alliance with Ælfhelm's daughter!"

"And you think he would listen to me?" Athelstan barked a bitter
laugh. "When has he ever heeded any counsel that I have offered? For
twenty years he has followed no one's counsel but his own, and I have
not the art to frame my words in a way that would convince him that
they sprang from his own mind."

"You have to try, Athelstan," Edmund insisted. "*We* have to try, and
we won't be without support, I promise you. Ælfmær in the west and
Wulfnoth in Sussex would welcome it. Most of the southern nobles
would understand the necessity of such a move. At the very least, let us
broach to Ælfhelm's sons the idea of a marriage, and see what kind of
response we get. We will have wagered nothing."

He could guess the likely outcome of that. If his father heard of it, he
would deem it a conspiracy led by his two eldest sons. The king already
mistrusted him; this could only add to his suspicions.

Yet Edmund was right. Something must be done to prevent Ælfhelm
from stirring up trouble in the north. Despite the king's wrath, for the
sake of the kingdom he and Edmund would have to take the risk and
raise the possibility of a marriage. He did not see that they had a choice.

# Chapter Five

March 1006
Calne, Wiltshire

The springtime sun was westering when Æthelred, satisfied with the day's sport, beckoned his falconer. Before transferring his prize gyrfalcon from his own leather-clad arm to the keeper's, he spoke a few soft words to the bird. The hawking season was nearly done, and this one had earned his summer's rest.

All his raptors had done well today—seven cranes brought down. Clean kills, every one.

As he mounted his horse, one of his retainers gave a shout and pointed to a rider who had just topped a nearby ridge and was moving slowly toward them.

"Someone from Calne," Æthelred said, "although whatever news he brings does not look to be urgent."

Soon enough he saw who it was—Eadric of Shrewsbury—another kind of raptor that he had loosed months ago and who was now come back to the lure. What prey, he wondered, had Eadric brought to ground? He had set the young thegn a delicate task, and now he was about to find out if he had been successful.

He gestured to his men to follow at a distance while he spurred his horse toward Eadric. The journey back to the manor would take the better part of an hour, and he and Eadric had much to discuss.

As he drew near to the younger man, he studied Eadric's handsome, bearded face with its thin, sharp nose and high brow. He'd chosen wisely with this one. Eadric's dark good looks inspired trust, and he radiated a pleasing charm that worked on women and men alike.

At a glance, no one would guess how very dangerous he was. Eadric, he'd found, was the perfect tool—efficient, reserved, thorough, and, when necessary, casually ruthless.

"I hope you met with success," he said as Eadric fell in beside him. "Word has reached me recently that Ælfhelm is planning to bestow his daughter upon a Danish warlord. Can you confirm it?"

"Indeed, my lord," Eadric replied. His eyes, black as a raven's wing, met Æthelred's with brutal frankness.

"You're certain?"

"Aye. For some time now, a man who serves Lord Ælfhelm has been carrying messages back and forth across the Danish sea. It is always the same man and he always takes ship from Gainesborough. That was where I spoke with him but seven days ago."

"And he told you who is to claim Elgiva and all her lands?"

"He told me what he knew—that she is to wed someone very close to the Danish king."

Æthelred gnawed on his lower lip. For the right price, a man might admit such a thing even if it were not true. He wanted assurance, beyond any doubt, that Ælfhelm was planning such an alliance. The man's vague excuse for missing the Easter court because of pressing matters in Mercia rang as false as a whore's promises of love. Still, he wanted to be sure.

"How can you be certain that he told you the truth?"

"I bartered the life of his wife and her two whelps for the information," Eadric said. "It took a little bloodletting to get him to speak, but he cooperated eventually. And when, after the first babe was dead and I could get no more out of the vermin but howls, I felt certain that he had told me everything he knew. I had to kill them all, of course, in the end."

Æthelred grunted. Treachery carried a high price.

"How long, think you, before Ælfhelm's suspicion is aroused?"

Eadric shrugged. "Some weeks, at least. Anyone who asks after them will be told that they took ship for Denmark and have not returned."

"Good," he said. It gave him time to strike before his prey grew wary. "This marriage must not go forward."

His greatest fear was that, with a Danish warlord at his side and with the support of King Swein, Ælfhelm would grow bold enough to attempt to wrest all the land north of the Humber from English rule. It had happened before. Fifty years ago Eric Bloodaxe had styled himself King of Jorvik, and although the upstart Viking had been driven from his makeshift throne, the memory of that Norse kingdom on English soil was still fresh and alluring in the minds of the men of Northumbria and northern Mercia. How they chafed under the rule of the ancient kings of Wessex!

"Will you bind the lady to someone loyal to yourself instead?" Eadric asked, his eyes alight with interest. "Someone who will stand with you against any Danish assault?"

Bind her! Æthelred allowed himself a grim smile. He would like to bind Elgiva in chains and shut her in some island tower so that he would never have to think on her again. She was like a lodestone that her father was using to draw men of iron into his plots against his king. Even now, in Eadric's question, he could hear the man's unspoken yearning to be the one to claim the lady's hand—and wealth. But to wed the cunning Elgiva to any man with a thirst for power was to create yet another enemy.

He should have wed the girl himself, bound the restless northerners to him with blood ties as he had done with his first marriage. But he had chosen instead to forge an alliance with the Norman duke. He had taken Emma to wife hoping to deprive Danish raiders of the friendly ports that welcomed them along the Narrow Sea within striking distance of England's coast. He had sealed the alliance by giving Emma a crown and a son—all for naught. His southern shores were still beset by Vikings, while in the north men plotted against him.

"There is no man," he said at last, "with whom I would trust the Lady Elgiva." He had a sudden vivid memory of Elgiva's little bow of a mouth and the things that she could do with it—an agreeable memory, but alarming as well. "She is ambitious and shrewd," he muttered, "and she would harry her husband until he set all of England at her feet."

"Then can you not place her in a convent?" Eadric suggested. "Bestow her lands on the nuns at Shaftesbury or Wilton?"

"Her father would never agree to such a fate for his precious daughter. And if any man had a mind to wed her, convent walls would not prevent it. My own father got two children on a nun. No, a vow of chastity and even abbey walls made of stone would not deter a man determined to claim such a prize, and they certainly would not stop a Danish warlord."

Both men rode in silence for a space, then Æthelred gave voice to the purpose that had been forming in his mind from the moment that he had received Elgiva's plea for deliverance from a Danish marriage.

"Ælfhelm has become too powerful," he said. "He has forged a web of conspirators throughout Mercia and into Northumbria. Nay, not a web but a hydra, and I must sever every head if I am to put an end to the plots. Were you able to learn the names of the men who have been a party to this enterprise?"

And for the first time, Eadric disappointed him.

"Forgive me, my lord, but I could not," he said. "Surely, though, Ælfhelm's sons must know his plans."

Æthelred nodded. He would discover what the sons knew when they joined the court at Easter. His more immediate concern was Ælfhelm. He must be dealt with efficiently and—for now—in secret.

"Did you learn aught else from your Gainesborough messenger?"

"He carried nothing in writing. I could only wring from him the words he was meant to deliver to Ælfhelm: *Look to Lammas Day.*"

Lammas Day. August first, when men would be busy with the harvest and reluctant to answer a call to defend villages and fields that were not their own.

Still, it was months away. There was time yet to sever the bond between Ælfhelm and the Danes.

"Ælfhelm has ignored my summons to the Easter council. I would have you make certain that he never attends another one." He cast a quick glance at Eadric, who was cocking an interested eyebrow. "You are newly come into your inheritance," he continued, "and Ælfhelm is your ealdorman. Feast him. Flatter him. Invite him to your hall and make sure he brings his daughter with him."

He glanced again at Eadric's face, but—as he'd expected—he saw no shadow of hesitation or distaste.

"What of the girl?" Eadric asked.

"Take her, but do not harm her. It was she who warned me of her father's treachery, and that has earned her some grace. I will have to send her away from England, to Hibernia perhaps, where she is less likely to stir up mischief."

Although, he thought with a frown, even in Hibernia the lady could be a threat. He would have to give more thought as to how he would provide for Elgiva. The fates of her father and brothers, though, were now sealed. The hydra that threatened him would lose three of its heads, at the least.

# Chapter Six

Holy Saturday, April 1006
Cookham, Berkshire

The day before Easter was meant to be one of silent reflection and prayer. At least, it was for some, Emma thought as she sat in isolated state beside the king and looked out upon the subdued company that had assembled for the Holy Saturday repast. It was not so for England's queen, nor for those of her household who must cater to court guests and prepare the great feast that was to be held on the morrow.

Although she would not show it with even the slightest gesture, she was weary from the stresses of the past week: from welcoming the highborn of England to the year's most important gathering; from pondering an endless string of requests from abbots and bishops who sought her patronage; from answering the multitude of questions posed by attendants, stewards, and slaves; and from the hours of almsgiving on Maundy Thursday and the interminable rituals of Good Friday.

But it was more than exhaustion that made her muscles stiffen and her stomach clench, more even than the hunger brought on by the string of fast days that made up Holy Week.

Beside her, Æthelred sat robed in a mantle of deep blue godwebbe that shimmered in the candlelight like a dragonfly's wing, but his face was dark with suppressed anger. She could only guess at the source of his displeasure, for he rarely confided in her. Instinctively, though, she felt it must be rooted in fear and so she, too, was fearful.

Æthelred was most dangerous when he was afraid.

The king was a man of dark moods, and she thought she had grown used to them. But this most recent ill humor seemed heavier than any she had yet seen. She had told herself that it was because of Ecbert's death, still raw in all their minds, especially after yesterday's mournful Good Friday service, with its vivid reminder of death's agonies. But although this brooding had begun with Ecbert's passing, she felt that something else was feeding it, and that the storm brewing within Æthelred could erupt at any time into cataclysm. Anxiety made her neck ache, as if she bore a leaden chain across her shoulders.

Reminding herself that it was fruitless to dwell on something she could not remedy, she turned an appraising eye on the sons of the king, most of whom she had not seen since Christmas. The three youngest had arrived earlier today, boisterous and jocular when they entered the royal apartments until they caught sight of their father's thunderous face.

Edgar had grown like a wheat stalk in a matter of months. He was thirteen now, and his face had lost the roundness of boyhood. His long hair, pulled straight back from his forehead and bound behind his neck with a woven silver band, had darkened to the color of honey. A sparse beard covered the point of his chin, and that gave him something of the look of Athelstan. He was nearly as comely as his eldest brother, too, with blue eyes that were turned upon the king just now with sober speculation. Not quite a man yet, Edgar, but serious for his age.

Far more serious than the brighter-haired Edwig, who, at fifteen winters, should have been the more responsible one. There was a carelessness about Edwig, though, and she had sometimes glimpsed in him a callous disregard for others that she did not like. He and his elder brother Edrid—the two of them so near in age and looks that they could be taken for twins—served along with Edgar in the retinue of Ealdorman Ælfric, and attended the king only on the high holidays and feasts. Even when they were children she had known them but little.

She watched as Edwig took a stealthy swallow from a leather flask at his belt—some strong liquor, she guessed, forbidden on this holy night, when only watered wine would be served in the king's hall. Afterward he waved away some protest from his frowning, twinlike brother, Edrid, who was clearly the good angel to Edwig's bad.

She glanced at the king to see if he had witnessed Edwig's transgression, but Æthelred's brooding gaze was fixed upon the two eldest æthelings, Athelstan and Edmund. They stood to one side of the fire pit at the center of the hall, deep in conversation with two men whose faces she could not make out until one of them turned and the firelight flickered on a handsome, chiseled cheek and black, curly hair.

And then she knew them—the sons of Ælfhelm, who had arrived without their sire or their sister, Elgiva. Æthelred would surely read treachery in their absence. Did he know, though, with certainty, of some perfidy that Ælfhelm might be planning? Was that the cause of his foul mood?

"I think, my lord," she ventured, although she had little hope that he would respond, "that you are troubled by the absence of Elgiva and her father."

"I am troubled by a great many things, lady," he replied, his voice laced with sarcasm. "Would you care to have me enumerate them?"

But she refused to respond in kind.

"If it would give you ease, my lord," she said.

"Nothing will give me ease except death, and I have no desire for that as yet. Not for myself, in any event. What if I were to tell you that I think my sons are consorting with my enemies? What would you say then to give me ease?"

His words chilled her, and she glanced again to where Athelstan was speaking with apparent urgency to the sons of Ælfhelm. She placed her hand upon the king's arm and said gently, "You judge your sons too harshly, my lord. They are never your enemies."

There were those, she knew, who would counsel her to speak ill of her stepsons—that as the king's esteem for them lessened, his regard for her own child must increase. As queen and mother of the heir, they would say, it was her task to put forward her own son and so garner greater status for him and, through him, for herself.

Yet she had no wish to turn Æthelred against the elder æthelings, and that was self-serving, too, in its own way. For she believed that if Æthelred should die while her son was still a child, the witan would place a warrior king upon the throne—someone who could wage war against England's enemies. It would be Athelstan who would rule the kingdom; Athelstan who would hold her fate—and that of Edward—in his hands.

When that happened, her world would change utterly, and how was she to prepare for it except by cultivating the goodwill of her stepchildren for Edward's sake? Æthelred's tally of years was forty winters long now—many years longer than the men of his line who had come before him. And with each year that passed, the tension grew more pronounced between an aging king who could not relinquish one jot of control and the grown sons who were eager for advancement and responsibility—especially Athelstan.

She felt as though she walked a sword's edge between them—the king who was her husband, and the ætheling she could not help but love and whom she defended at her peril.

"My sons," Æthelred said, "covet my crown, and would take it from me if they could find a way to do so." He nodded toward the group near the fire. "Even now Athelstan is garnering support from the sons of Ælfhelm for his claim to the throne."

She looked again to where Athelstan's fair hair showed golden against Edmund's darker locks and the black curls of the sons of Ælfhelm. The king could not possibly read what matter they were discussing any more than she could. But she knew that although Athelstan might oppose his father at the council table, he would not reach out his hand betimes to take the throne. He had given her his pledge on that, and she trusted him to keep it. Æthelred had enemies, she did not doubt it—too numerous to count. But Athelstan could not be numbered among them.

"My lord," she said, weighing her words carefully, for if the king suspected her feelings for his son, it would do Athelstan more harm than good, "you do your son an injustice. Should he raise his hand against you it would weaken the kingdom, turn the men of this land one against another. Athelstan must know this, and I think he would do nothing that would place this realm in such peril."

"Would he not?" Æthelred asked bitterly. "Lady, there is much that goes on, within the court and without it, of which you know nothing. It were best you keep your mind upon matters of your household and the schooling of my daughters. Leave my sons to me."

He stood up abruptly and left the dais, disappearing into the passage that led to his private chamber. A moment later, she saw a servant hurry to the group at the fire and escort them from the hall, following in the king's wake. She did not like the look of that.

She beckoned the king's cupbearer to her, a red-cheeked boy of ten whose father was the lord of several large estates within her dower lands near Exeter.

"Take a flagon of wine to the king," she said, placing a silver penny in his palm as he bent to fill her cup, "and linger in the chamber in case he should have need of you. Tomorrow you shall tell me, and no one else, all that you hear."

The boy nodded and left. Emma rose from the table to mingle with the men and women in the hall, but her thoughts were still directed toward the chamber of the king. Æthelred was correct when he said that she did not know everything that went on at court.

Still, she knew a great deal, and in Æthelred's court, knowledge was power.

# Chapter Seven

Holy Saturday, April 1006

Cookham, Berkshire

The king's chamber was alive with light—banks of candles turning the night to day and reminding Athelstan that his father did not like the dark.

The king was afraid of shadows.

But his father feared other things as well, and there was suspicion in the hooded blue eyes that swept over the four of them: Ufegeat, Wulf, Edmund, himself. He felt like a warrior in a shield wall, but without benefit of either shield or blade.

Did the king suspect that they had been speaking of Elgiva and a marriage alliance? Was that why they had been ushered in here? If so, he was going to need the tongue of an angel to convince his father that his only intention was to save the kingdom, not steal it.

There was a long, heavy silence while a cupbearer slipped in and filled the goblet that stood on the table beside the king's great chair, and then the silence was broken by the tread of boots and the creak of leather. Six of the king's retainers, handpicked to do his bidding and ask no questions, filed into the chamber. Two of them stepped forward to flank the king. They were men whom Athelstan knew well, but when he probed their faces, they did not meet his eyes.

His palms began to sweat. He had often been called to answer to his father for what the king considered misdeeds, but there had never been armed men at his back before. He looked a question at the king, but his father's eyes were fixed on Ælfhelm's sons. Following that glance he saw a fine sheen of sweat on Ufegeat's forehead, and next to him Wulf's face was so pale that it looked to be carved from wax.

A thin shaft of fear sliced through him, and he cursed under his breath. There was some undercurrent here that he could not read, something to do with the sons of Ælfhelm and, likely, their father. He recalled now what Edmund had told him in London about trouble in the north, and recalled as well the many rumors that had sifted through the hall like smoke today—rumors about Ælfhelm's absence from this gathering that, like a fool, he had not heeded.

It would not surprise him to learn of some treachery that the ealdorman was planning. For a long time now he'd had his own doubts about where the man's true loyalties lay, although he had never been able to prove anything. If the king had discovered that Ælfhelm and his sons were plotting some move against him, then he and Edmund might well be deemed guilty by association.

Anxiously he watched his father, who rested an elbow on the arm of his chair, fingered his beard thoughtfully, and addressed Ufegeat.

"I would know," the king said slowly, "what it was that you and my sons were discussing in the hall."

His tone was not threatening, but Athelstan knew his father, knew that it was a ploy—a swordsman's feint to disguise a second, far more lethal, thrust. He stepped forward to give his own explanation, but the king raised a hand to stop him.

"I wish to hear it from the son of Ælfhelm," he said.

Ufegeat cleared his throat, and the noise of it was loud in the chamber's tense silence.

"The æthelings," he said, "broached the subject of a marriage alliance with my sister. They wished to know if we would support it."

"My lord," Athelstan began, but his father's quelling hand silenced him yet again. He cast a nervous glance at Ufegeat.

"And what was your response to my sons' proposal?"

"My first question, my lord," Ufegeat said, "was whether you would agree to any such betrothal. I reminded your sons that it breaks with custom for an ætheling to wed while his father still lives."

There was censure in his voice—disapproval of anything that might defy the king. Athelstan glared at him, but Ufegeat ignored him.

"Indeed, it does break with custom," the king said. "But you have another reason, do you not, for rejecting such a proposal? Is not your sister already pledged?"

And there was the second sword thrust. Stunned, Athelstan gaped first at his father, then at Ælfhelm's sons to see their response. Ufegeat's face had become a blank wall. Wulf, though, looked like he was going to be sick. Was it true, then? And if it was, who had bargained for Elgiva's hand?

"My lord," Ufegeat said stiffly, "I cannot say what arrangements my father may have made regarding my sister. He does not apprise us of every plan that he undertakes."

"No," the king said, his face thoughtful. "Perhaps not. A wise father does not share all his secrets with his sons."

His eyes, hard and mocking, flicked toward Athelstan, who flinched as the barb struck home. His father had a great many secrets that he kept from his sons.

The king turned to Ufegeat again. "Yet your sister appears to know something of your father's intentions," Æthelred observed. "Surely you do not expect me to believe that Ælfhelm would confide in his daughter and not in his sons?"

Ufegeat shrugged. "Elgiva is but a woman, with a woman's desires and a meager understanding of the affairs of men. She longs to wed, to be sure, but I cannot speak to what fantasies she may have spun from the whispers of servants and from her own feverish imagination. I certainly will not be held to account for it."

"Ah, but you will, my lord," the king said, his bland voice belying the threat in his words, "as will your father and this brother of yours." He raised his hand and the guards took hold of Ælfhelm's sons.

Ufegeat resisted, struggling against his captors until one of them cuffed him about the face.

Staggering, his mouth bloody, Ufegeat cried out, "We are guilty of no crime, my lord. You cannot prove that we have done anything wrong."

"Yet I deem you guilty of treachery against my throne," and now the king's voice was sharp as steel, "and in this I am your only judge." He gestured to his retainers. "Take them."

Athelstan watched, his gut churning, as the king's men dragged Ælfhelm's sons from the chamber. They were not gentle. Ufegeat and Wulf tried to protest and were silenced with vicious blows.

When they had gone he turned to stare at his father, who was still flanked by two of the guards and who was eyeing him now, wolflike, as if taking the measure of a rival.

Would he and Edmund be dragged off as well, locked away until his father decided on their punishment? And if so, for what? He still did not see what Ufegeat and Wulf had done that was so wrong.

"What is their crime?" he asked.

The king reached for the wine cup at his side, drank deeply, then set the cup down so hard that the sound made Athelstan flinch.

"Ælfhelm has betrothed his daughter to a Danish lord," his father said, "and they were privy to it. You saw their faces."

If it were true, it would explain the ealdorman's absence from court as well as his sons' terror at being hauled before the king.

"Are you certain?" he asked.

"The lady herself sent me word, insisting that her brothers could not be trusted." His father's voice was sardonic. "Is that good enough for you?"

"My lord," Edmund said, "there must be a blood alliance between your line and that of Ælfhelm. It will garner you the support of all the Mercian nobles against any other—"

"Support for *me*?" the king cried. "And what guarantee can you give that they would not support whoever weds Ælfhelm's bitch?"

There it was again—that suspicion that always lay like a wide gulf between them.

"We have sworn our allegiance—to you and to Emma's son," Athelstan protested. "We are not traitors."

"Aye, so you say," his father scoffed. "But actions speak louder than any vow! You would have conspired against me with Ælfhelm's sons had they not had schemes of their own in hand! If what you intended was in *my* interests, Athelstan, why did you not speak of it first to me?"

"And what would you have said to such a plan?" he demanded. "You would have humiliated me by saying it was foolish, then you would have accused me of disloyalty. What must I do, my lord, to convince you that I am neither a fool nor a traitor?"

He glared at his father, struggling to quell his rising anger, for he knew very well that there was nothing he could do. The king scowled back at him, but before either of them could speak again, Edmund stepped between them.

"My lord," he said, "we are certain that Elgiva is the key to securing allegiance in the north." Athelstan almost laughed. His brother was beating a dead horse, and in any case, Elgiva was not really the issue here. "If you would but agree to—"

"I will not reward treachery!" his father thundered. "And I will not be tutored by my sons!"

"No!" Athelstan shouted back, frustration overcoming caution. "Nor by anyone else! You refuse all advice! Why is that? Are you so confident in your decisions, my lord? Was it not you who chose to make Ælfhelm the ealdorman of Northumbria? Yet now you are not so pleased with that decision. How are you to undo it? You cannot legally strip him of his lands and his powers unless you can prove—"

"I am the king!" His father thrust himself to his feet as he bellowed the words. "And I am the law!"

He glared at them, and Athelstan, staring into his father's livid face, despaired. His father would never listen to him, not while he felt so threatened.

"What will you do?" he asked, although he feared to hear the answer.

The king waved a dismissive hand as if weary of the conversation, then took his seat again. Closing his eyes, he massaged his forehead, and for some time said nothing. He looked tired, and it seemed to Athelstan that every year of his long reign was etched upon his face.

After some moments his father muttered, "A hunter does not wait for the boar to charge before throwing the spear." Then he looked at Athelstan and growled, "I have done what is necessary. Now, leave me. I would be alone."

Athelstan felt Edmund grasp his arm to urge him away, but he was not yet ready to leave. He wanted to know what his father would do to Ufegeat and Wulf. Ælfhelm would not sit idly by while the king held his sons captive, nor would the other lords take their arrest lightly. They, too, had sons.

"My lord—"

"Get out, Athelstan, before I set the guards on you!"

He did not doubt that his father would be as good as his word, so he shut his mouth, bowed stiffly, and followed Edmund out of the chamber and back to the hall. There was no music ringing through the high roof beams, no scop reciting a tale, no rumble of voices. This was Easter Eve, when Christ was in the grave and all men were to reflect on the suffering and death He had endured for their sins. The Winchester bishop stood upon the dais reading a sermon to the assembly. Athelstan paused only long enough to cast a swift, reassuring glance toward Emma, whose eyes—full of questions—met his. Then he followed Edmund, threading his way through the hall and out the door.

When they were alone, standing next to one of the clay ovens still warm from the day's baking, Edmund muttered several colorful curses, then said, "You should have just made off with the girl and wed her."

Athelstan barked a mirthless laugh. "If I had, I would be with Wulf and Ufegeat right now, probably in chains. And God knows where Elgiva would be." He frowned. "Come to that, I wonder where she is. With Ælfhelm, I assume."

"Or with her new Danish lord, whoever that may be," Edmund suggested.

"If Elgiva betrayed her father's plans for her, she clearly has no desire to marry whoever it is." Athelstan recalled the haggard look on his father's face near the end of their interview. *I have done what is necessary,* he had said. What was it, exactly, that his father had done? "I'll wager that the king has already taken some action against Ælfhelm," he said. "I wonder what mischief he's set in motion, and what trouble is likely to come of it."

At midnight Æthelred stood in the darkened church among his family and his court. A line of priests bearing glowing tapers—symbols of hope and resurrection—made its way through the nave. But as he watched the candlelight begin to blossom around the altar, something flickered at the edge of his vision, some movement in the shadows that lingered outside the light. His eyes were drawn toward that darkness, and there his dead brother—a dark wraith amid the shadows—stared back at him with black intent.

Pain crawled up his arm and into his chest, and he clutched his shoulder to ease it. Beside him, Emma reached out a hand, but he shrugged it off. This enemy was his alone—a burden he could share with no one, least of all his queen. It had already taken two of his sons, and it sought to sunder him now from those who were left.

He cursed it under his breath, and as if in response the shadow faded, taking the pain with it, and he drew a long, grateful breath.

Released from his brother's malignant spell he sought and found Athelstan and Edmund, their youthful faces lit by the tapers in their hands. His thoughts swept back to the events of an hour before and to his sons' protestations of loyalty. He put little faith in them. Athelstan, he did not doubt, was laying the foundation for his own rule in England. It was what *he* would do, were he in Athelstan's place.

Ambitious sons, he reflected, were like wild horses that had to be kept in check—with force, if necessary. It had not come to that yet, but it would. His dead brother's vengeful shade would likely hasten the day.

And when it came, he told himself, he must never flinch. He must do whatever was needed to hold on to his kingdom, even if it cost him his sons.

# Chapter Eight

Easter Monday, April 1006
Western Mercia

Elgiva shivered as she peered into the gloom of the little manor chapel, saw that it was empty, and stepped inside. She did not like churches, but she needed a place to think, and this was as good a place as any to take refuge from unwanted company and from the sudden chill breeze that was scrabbling across the manor yard.

Pulling her cloak tight about her, she gazed up at a portrait of Saint Peter that had been elaborately painted on the chancel wall. The saint's right hand was raised in benediction and in his left he held a magnificent silver key. A golden halo encircled his head, and in his white-streaked hair and beard she could make out a marked resemblance to King Æthelred.

Had the man who drew this, she wondered, ever seen the king? More to the point, she thought, as she began to pace the chapel's floor, was *she* ever likely to see the king again?

The gloom seemed to deepen around her as she forced herself, once more, to face the truth. Even if the king had sent someone to rescue her from the living death of a Danish marriage, no one would think to look for her in a stronghold on the western edge of Mercia. Yet here she was, despite her protests that she was unwell and that she should not be made to travel so far to attend some wretched noble's Paschal feast.

"You are well enough," her father had barked. "And I have business with Eadric."

Yes, she thought bitterly, business that involved hunting and drinking and the swearing of oaths, none of which had anything to do with her. This Eadric—newly come into his father's estate—was a man of some substance now it appeared. Her father likely wished to bend the new man to his own purposes, to forge another solid link in his chain of alliances. It was a worthy enough goal, she supposed, although she knew there was some larger purpose behind it that her father, curse him, kept from her. As for Eadric, she guessed that he had invited them here in order to court the favor of his powerful overlord.

And still, none of it had anything to do with her.

She passed through a shaft of light that speared down through a high window, and the sudden dazzle drew her mind back to last night's gathering in Eadric's brightly lit hall. If his purpose in urging her father's sojourn here had been to impress, Eadric had succeeded. Yesterday's feast had been lavish, and he had shown her father great honor. He had even been gratifyingly attentive to her, which had mollified her somewhat for the arduous journey across Mercia that she had been forced to make in order to get here.

In truth she had found the young thegn's manner to be so charming that she wondered why she had taken so little note of him before this. Black-haired, with a neatly trimmed beard, tawny skin, and dark eyes, he had the look of an outlander, although his family had been settled in Mercia for hundreds of years. Or so he said. She had caught a flash of cunning in his glance that had made her suspect he was not entirely to be trusted, which only intrigued her the more.

She had dreamed about him last night, had meant to tell him so this morning, but all the men had ridden out to hunt. It was vexing to find herself alone here but for a few servants, reduced to staring at the painted walls of a wretched little church while she waited for the bell to ring for the midday meal.

She completed a circuit of the chapel to find herself in front of Saint Peter again, and she scowled at him, for he was a reminder of the king's indifference to her plight. She was about to turn away when a hand clamped over her mouth and an arm clutched her tight at the waist, pulling her against a hard male body. She struggled to escape but could not move.

"It is Alric," a voice whispered urgently in her ear. "Do not cry out! Your father is dead, lady, and you are in grave danger. This has all been an elaborate trap, and if you wish to escape you must come with me now before it is too late."

For a moment she stood frozen, paralyzed by terror and indecision. Alric was one of her father's thegns, and one whom she trusted. But what he was telling her was monstrous! Impossible!

"Lady, we must fly!" He turned her about so that she was looking into his face. His familiar, mocking smile was gone, and there was fear writ plain in his wild eyes. "Will you trust me?"

And she knew then that she had little choice. She nodded, and at once he snatched her hand and pulled her toward the door. He halted there briefly, glancing to the hall and then the stables before leading her out and around the corner of the building. Two horses stood there, saddled and tethered. He helped her to mount, and as she clutched the reins she heard, through the fog of shock that had settled over her like a shroud, the winding of a distant horn.

"That will be Eadric and his men returning," Alric said. "A stroke of luck for us because they'll have opened the gate. There is no time to lose. Stay close behind me, and do not stop for anything. Are you ready?"

She hesitated, for she was not ready, not for this. She wanted to pelt him with questions, to curse, to howl, but the grim set to his face kept her mute. At her nod he spurred his horse, and she followed him, charging toward the open gate from behind the cover of the church wall.

The few servants in the yard scattered away from them like frightened geese. The gate ward, though, stood his ground at first, waving his hands frantically until he dove sideways to avoid being trampled by Alric's mount. She followed Alric through the yawning gateway and up a track that led away from the sound of the horn winding yet again, closer now than it had been before.

He led her on, clearly pushing the horses hard to put as much distance as possible between them and, if he had told her true, the pursuit that soon must follow. She could not ask any of the questions that flooded her mind, nor could she still the words that echoed in her ears like a tolling bell: *Your father is dead.*

It seemed to her that the whole world had just gone mad.

## Easter Monday, April 1006
## Cookham, Berkshire

Emma stood alone atop the new wooden rampart that had recently transformed the king's Cookham estate from manor farm to fortified burh. In the grounds below her, tents and pavilions lay in neat rows, lit by firelight and by the shimmer of a half moon that glowed in the clear night sky. From a nearby tent she could hear a woman singing softly, soothing a whimpering child to sleep. In her own apartments, hidden from her sight just now by the massive bulk of the great hall, her own son was tucked into his cradle beside Wymarc's little Robert. Edward had been sleeping when she'd left him, watched over by Wymarc and Margot and Hilde.

Æthelred's daughters had been there too, and it was the sight of the two older girls, Edyth and Ælfa, whispering and giggling, their heads drawn close, that had driven her to seek a few moments alone. They had reminded her so of herself and her own sister, Mathilde, when they were children.

And there had been news today of Mathilde—of her death in Normandy. *Struck down by a fever at Christmastide,* her mother's letter had said.

She had wept for her sister; Margot—who had guided them both into the world—had grieved with her, rocking her as if she were a child again.

Poor Mathilde. Even as a girl she had been plagued by fevers and agues; half her days, it seemed, spent abed. And now she had lost her final battle.

"How is it that I did not know?" she had asked Margot. "We were once so close. I should have felt it in my blood and my bones that she had left this world."

Yet she had not known.

Now she gazed into the night, remembering other times and other places. Just like Æthelred's daughters, she and Mathilde had been born a year apart, had shared beds, lessons, and duties. They had looked to each other for friendship and counsel; had quarreled, wept, and forgiven. Until her marriage had separated them forever.

It was Mathilde who should have come to England and been crowned Æthelred's queen, for she was the elder. But their mother had deemed otherwise, and so Emma had wed a king and, a year later, Mathilde had become the bride of a Frankish count. Had she ever found happiness in that life? Emma had longed to know, but although she had sent letters, begging for some word from her sister, there had been no reply from the Countess of Blois.

The younger sister's royal marriage had been too great a blow for the elder sister to forgive. There would be no forgiveness now.

She began to walk, her eyes misted with grief. She halted, though, when she realized that she was not alone, that in front of her a man stood beside the parapet, looking out through an opening toward the dark plain that led to the river.

"You should go within doors, lady," he said. "The night is cold, and you would not wish to catch a chill."

It was Athelstan's voice that came to her through the darkness, offering advice that she would heed if she were wise. But tonight she was not wise, and the mere sound of his voice drew her to him.

Athelstan, too, she guessed, was weighted with grief.

She had not spoken to him yet of Ecbert's death, for there had been no opportunity to share a private word. Now, burdened with her own sorrow, she longed just to be near him.

Going to his side, she gazed out toward the rushing, moonlit river, and she drew in a long breath, for her heart ached for both of them.

"I have wanted to tell you before this," she said, "how much I grieve for the loss of your brother." That grief was bound up now with her sorrow at the death of her sister, but she would not burden him with that news tonight.

"There is no need for you to speak of it," he said. "I know what is in your heart."

She studied his face, the half that she could see just visible in the moonglow. Did he truly know what she felt? His brother Edmund had not believed that she could grieve for Ecbert, and for some time now she had been afraid that Edmund's distrust of her, like some foul contagion, had spread to Athelstan as well. But in the next moment, when he turned to face her, the look he cast upon her dispelled all doubt.

"I am not Edmund," he said gently, answering the question she had not spoken.

She looked into eyes filled with such sorrow and longing that she was suddenly frightened. How she wanted to reach for him, to draw him into her arms and console him as a sister might.

Yet she dared not offer him that comfort, for it was not a sister's love that she carried locked within her heart.

"No," she said softly. "You are not Edmund. Forgive me for doubting you."

She very nearly touched him then, nearly placed her hand upon his arm where it lay so close to hers there on the palisade. But she resisted the temptation, turning instead to look out toward the river, knowing that she should go inside as he had urged her, yet unable to bring herself to leave him.

In the darkness she was reminded of another time that they had been alone together—when they had both succumbed to temptation. When desire and passion had overwhelmed wisdom and duty and solemn vows.

She had been shriven of that sin long ago, had promised God that she would sin no more. But the human heart, she had learned, was a thing not easily governed. And although she had thought that tiny bit of her was nothing more than a withered relic locked inside a casket of gold, now she felt it yearning for this man at her side.

After a time it was Athelstan who broke the uneasy silence between them.

"Your son appears to be thriving," he said, "and my father does not yet mistrust the boy. I envy him that."

She heard the pain in his voice, sharp as a knife, and she did what little she could to blunt it.

"Edward is too young yet to disturb his father's peace of mind," she said. "The king reserves most of his displeasure, I fear, for the son who stands closest to the throne." She knew what had occurred in the king's chamber on Easter Eve, for her young spy had dutifully reported the angry words that Æthelred had flung at Athelstan that night.

He gave her a sour smile. "Nothing I do, it seems, will earn for me my father's good opinion. Since he cannot bear the sight of me, I shall return to London tomorrow. Let him make of that whatever he likes."

She bit her lip, afraid for him. The king was uneasy on his throne, and because of that the sons of Ælfhelm lay in chains tonight, under heavy guard.

"Your father is suspicious because you do not attend him," she insisted. Why could he not see that? "When you are absent from court for months at a time he imagines that you are working against him in secret. Athelstan," she whispered, pleading with him, "do not return to London yet. Stay with your father. Break bread with him. Hunt with him. Partake in his councils. You cannot win his confidence if you are not with him."

He kept his eyes focused on the distant darkness and did not meet her gaze.

"I leave for London at first light," he said, as if she had not spoken. Then he turned to her, and the passion that flared in his eyes seared her to the depths of her soul. "You know why."

Yes, she knew why. For a moment they stared at each other. They did not touch or speak, but she read in his face all the longing and despair that she knew he must see in hers.

"Go to your chamber, lady," he said softly, "before we give my father good reason to distrust us both."

# Chapter Nine

Easter Monday, April 1006
Western Mercia

Elgiva could not remember ever being so cold. She rubbed her arms for warmth while Alric fumbled with flint and steel to light a fire. They were in a crumbling hovel of wattle and daub—a swineherd's shelter she guessed, although she could not tell where. She had lost all sense of direction once the sun had gone down, but until then Alric had led her along narrow tracks, mostly through wide swathes of forestland. Sometimes, when they came to a clearing and she looked to her left, she could see the dyke that marked England's border with the Wælisc kingdoms.

She edged nearer to Alric and the fire pit, away from the horses that he had insisted on bringing into the shelter with them, the two of them grooming the beasts with straw as best they could even before he would turn his hand to lighting a fire. She watched him coax the spark into life, a thick shock of brown hair falling over his eyes as he worked. What little she could see of his face, shadowed with a day-old beard, was pale and grimly set. His hands, as he fed twigs to the tiny flame, were trembling.

He was cold, too, then. Not from the night chill, though, any more than she was.

As the flames began to lick at the bits of wood and the stacked turf, he placed their saddles on the ground at the fire's edge so that they made a kind of bench. He motioned for her to sit and she did so, wrapping her mantle about her and holding her hands to the smoky fire. She watched him take off his sword belt and lay it close. Then he sat beside her, handed her a skin of water, and from a satchel drew a half-eaten loaf and a block of cheese to share between them. She realized suddenly how thirsty she was, and she took a long drink of water.

Once, years before, she had traveled rough like this, when she and her brother Wulf had fled from Exeter with the Danes at their backs. They'd had a large group of armed men as escort then, had been well provisioned, too, for it was high summer and the land was bountiful. The Danes had been no more than a distant threat.

That had seemed like sport compared to this. She hadn't been so afraid then.

She looked at the dry bread in her hand, but her stomach recoiled at the thought of food. She could think only of her father, and that he was dead.

Earlier, when they'd been forced to stop for a time to allow the horses to rest and graze, she had flung a question at Alric about what had happened. But he had clasped a hand over her mouth, listening for sounds of pursuit, hissing for silence. She had been frightened before, but it was worse after that, and she had swallowed all her questions.

Now, though, she had to know. However bad it had been, she had to know.

"How was my father killed?" She was hunched over, staring into the fire, bracing herself against whatever she was about to hear.

Beside her, Alric shifted forward as well.

"He took an arrow in the chest."

"An arrow!" She straightened, gaping at him. "But he was hunting. It might have been an accident." This could all be a misunderstanding. Her father might even still be alive. She could leave this stinking hovel in the morning and go back to Shrewsbury, discover how her father fared.

"It was not just your father," he said, then took a long pull from the water skin, set it on the ground, and wiped his mouth with his sleeve. "It was all your father's men, too—his falconer, his grooms, the four hearth companions, and the two retainers who rode with him. All of them dead."

She stared at his face, sculpted into harsh angles by the firelight. No accident, then. And no chance that her father was still alive. The hope that had flickered in her mind shuddered and died, and she recalled Alric's words in the chapel, that it had been a trap.

"Yet you escaped," she whispered. "How?"

"I was late to the hunt, still mead-drunk from last night's feast. When I awoke, the others were gone, but I knew they planned to loose the falcons on the heath below Shrewsbury. So I rode that way, thinking to join the hunt. I was still in the woods when I heard the shouting and realized that something was wrong." He drew a breath, grimacing at whatever picture was in his mind. "By the time I reached the forest edge, your father and the others lay on the ground in a wide clearing with arrows in their guts. Eadric and his men were already inspecting the bodies, making sure that—"

He stopped abruptly, glanced at her, and began again.

"It was an ambush, and Eadric must have planned the whole thing. His archers had been hidden among the trees and they turned the meadow into a killing ground."

She imagined how it must have been—horses and men confused by the onslaught of arrows, men cursing, crying out in pain, and after that, silence. In the end, it probably hadn't been a feathered shaft that killed her father, but a knife or a sword blade. And still she could not believe that it was true. It seemed unreal, like a tale told by a scop who would change the ending to suit her if she commanded it.

But Alric wasn't finished.

"The bastards never saw me," he spat. "They were too bent on stripping the bodies and keeping the hounds from—" He cursed, then snapped his mouth shut. "I went back to the manor to find you. I climbed the palisade easily enough, but I would have been hard-pressed to know where to look if I hadn't seen you going into the chapel."

She closed her eyes. She was trembling so hard that her teeth were chattering, and she clasped her hands tight, trying to focus—not on what had happened, but on what she must do next.

"I must get to my brothers," she said between shallow breaths. "I have to tell them what Eadric has done so they can demand a wergild. The king has to make Eadric pay for this."

But Alric was shaking his head.

"Nay, lady," he said, "Eadric would never have done this thing unless the king himself commanded it. Æthelred must have discovered the plots that your father was hatching with the Danes. He wanted your father dead. Eadric will be rewarded, not punished, for this day's work."

She felt suddenly dizzy, the walls around her spinning so that she had to drop her head to her knees to make them stop. This was Æthelred's response to the message she had sent him. But she had never dreamed that the king would do something so savage. To cut down the premier ealdorman of England was an act that spoke of a hatred so fierce it was not likely to stop there.

And her brothers were with the king.

"What will he do to Wulf and Ufegeat?" she whispered.

"If they are still alive," Alric said, "I doubt they will be so for long. You cannot help them, lady. You must look to your own safety."

Suddenly the day's events became too real, and she rocked forward and back, hands against her mouth to stifle the wail that was swelling in her throat. She felt Alric's arms go round her, and she gave herself up to the terror of what she had set in motion. She had wanted her father punished, but not like this.

Why had the fool chosen to wed her to a Danish lord? It was a decision that made no sense to her, and now they must all pay for it. Even she must pay for it.

That thought made her pull away from Alric and wipe her eyes with her hands. She would not weep for her father. Had he treated her better he would still be alive, and she would not be here now.

*You must look to your own safety*, Alric had said. And he was right. She was still alive. And although the world around her had changed utterly, she was still who she had ever been—the daughter of Ealdorman Ælfhelm, granddaughter of Wulfrun of Tamworth, and descendant of Wulfric the Black. She had lands and she had money, and there were men who would help her if she could but get to them.

"My father's thegns in Northampton will protect me from the king," she said. "You must take me there."

Alric snorted. "That is exactly where Eadric and the king will expect you to go. There may already be king's guards posted at the gates of your father's manors, and by tomorrow they will be hunting for you all over Mercia."

Of course; her father's estates would be watched. Likely she could not even get a message to the men who might be of most use to her. In any case, many of her father's closest allies would be with the king at the Easter court, and so at risk themselves.

She had no way of knowing how hot the king's vengeance would blaze, or how far. If Æthelred should find her, what would he do to her? Would he murder her as well? Or would he merely imprison her, cast her into some black cell where she could never be found? He would certainly not wed her to any of his sons.

Yet that was where her destiny lay, she was certain of it. She had been promised that she would be queen, although how she was to make that come about she could not see. Not yet.

"I must get as far away from Æthelred as swiftly as I can. Go where he cannot reach me." She must find a protector—someone with men and arms who would not be afraid to use them against the king if need be.

"Then you must go either west into the Wælisc lands," he said, "or east to the Danelaw."

"Not west," she said. "I would be still within reach of Eadric, and I have no kinsmen there to protect me." She must go into the Danelaw, then. They had little love there for Æthelred—or so her father always said. Whom could she trust, though, to resist the lure of gold if the king should put a price upon her head? She ran through the list of her father's allies, and then she had the answer. "We will go to Thurbrand," she said, "to the Lord of Holderness."

Thurbrand had never been tempted by anything that Æthelred could offer him. She had once heard her father call him an old pirate, and chide him for shunning the rewards given to those who attended the king. But Thurbrand had vowed that he wanted neither the rewards nor the responsibilities that bending the knee to Æthelred would gain. So he remained in his fastness on the edge of the Danish sea, plotting against his English enemies in Jorvik, paying lip service to the House of Cerdic, and governing his people like a half king.

"We'll have to take a ship, then," Alric said, "for we could not hope to make it across Mercia with the king's men after us. At first light we'll go to Chester. The harbor there will have any number of vessels readying to make sail, and we can buy passage aboard the first one we find."

"How long will it take us to get to Holderness?"

He shrugged. "Impossible to say. Much will depend on the weather and on how quickly we can get passage on ships bound where we wish to go. It may take us months, and if it does, what does it matter? It will do you no harm to disappear from England for a time. Let Æthelred wonder what has become of you."

That prospect cheered her. She would be the missing piece on the game board that was England. They would probably search the abbeys for her, and the king would grow frantic when he could not find her. It was hardly recompense for her father's murder, but it was a beginning.

"We must get word to Thurbrand," she said, "that I am making my way there. Can it be done?"

"Yes, but"—he held up her hand and the gold and gems that covered each finger glittered in the firelight—"it may cost you some of these baubles."

He turned her hand over and ran a fingertip across her palm, and she was astonished by her response—desire shimmering through her like summer lightning, the heat of it easing her fear. Her body remembered Alric well, it seemed, for he had pleasured her like this before, years ago, and she was sorely tempted to lose herself in the sensations that she knew he could arouse in her. But once she set her foot on that path there would be no going back, and she had no wish to knock at Thurbrand's gate with Alric's brat in her belly.

She clasped his hand between her palms and held it tight.

"I am your lord now, Alric," she said, "and I expect you to serve me as you served my father." He could rape her if he wanted to, she supposed. She would not have the physical strength to resist him, and even if she did, where was she to run? Her father had trusted Alric, though, had been generous with him; she hoped that she could do the same. She released his hand, slipped a ring from her finger, and placed it in his palm. "You have done well by me today," she said, "and I give you this as a pledge of far greater favors to come. Will you protect me until we reach Holderness?"

She watched him closely, saw the cocked brow and the speculative look in his eye. Had any woman ever refused Alric's attempt at seduction? Likely she was the first.

He nodded, and pocketed the ring.

"I am your man, my lady," he said, "to Holderness and beyond, if need be."

"Good." She held up her hands. "The rest of these baubles we will use to get us there. And in Chester you will buy me a fine tunic and breecs. The king's men will be looking for a woman and a man, not a young lord and his servant."

They settled themselves to sleep then, on either side of the fire. For a long time, though, she lay awake, staring into the dying flames and pondering her future. If her brothers were dead, there was no man now who could command her except the king. And once she slipped free of whatever net Æthelred might throw out to snare her, she could claim her estates and marry. She could marry any man she wished.

She closed her eyes, and as she let herself drift toward sleep she wondered where Lord Athelstan was. She wondered if he realized just how valuable she could be to him.

**April 1006**
**Near Saltford, Oxfordshire**

Athelstan halted his horse beside the standing stone that pointed skyward like a gnarled finger. In the shallow valley in front of him, beyond the ring of stunted oaks, he could see the circle of stones and the figure seated at its center, waiting.

It was not too late to turn back; not too late to make his way to London as he had intended when he left his father's hall. Even now he did not know if he had come here of his own free will or if he had been drawn by some force that he did not understand.

He knew only that he was afraid—for himself, for the king, for England.

A succession of grim possibilities had been coursing through his mind for days now in an endless, looping string. Any move that his father made against Ælfhelm might split the kingdom. Any action that he himself might take to avert such a split would add to the suspicions his father was already nursing against him. Any hint of discord between the king, his sons, and his thegns would bring Viking raiders to their shores like wolves drawn to a bleating lamb, and that might well destroy England altogether.

Below him, the woman seated beside the fire did not look up, but she must know that he was here. He could not shake off the sensation that she had called him—that she had some answer to give him, if he could but ask the right question.

That, too, made him afraid.

Above him the sky darkened, then brightened again, as clouds drifted across the face of the sun.

The sky was of two minds, he thought, just as he was. But he'd come this far already, three days' ride in the wrong direction.

So he swung off his horse and led it down the hill, leaving it to graze while he walked into the circle to take his place across the fire from the seeress. As they regarded each other for a long, silent moment, it crossed his mind that she had suffered some wasting sickness, for her face was thinner than he remembered, her nose as sharp and pointed as a merlin's beak, and her skin creased with lines that had not been there two winters ago. He glanced past her, to the daub and wattle hut that was her dwelling. When last he was here he had left behind a purse of silver, but she had clearly not spent it on her comforts.

Finally she broke the silence.

"Twice before this you have come to me, lord, and twice you left here doubting the truth of the words I spoke to you. Will this time be any different?"

How did she know that he had doubted her? Perhaps it was not such a difficult thing to divine, though. No man wished to believe in a future that was bleak.

"Mayhap it depends on the question asked and the answer given," he replied.

She nodded. "Ask your question, then, lord, and I will give what answer I can."

He paused, and as he looked into her eyes the question that he would pose came to him at last.

"Is it possible for a man to change his fate?"

The black eyes flashed at him, or perhaps he was merely seeing the flames reflected there.

"Every man's wyrd is set, my lord, for it is the fate of every man to die. That end is inescapable."

"That end, yes," he agreed. "But there is far more to any man's life than just the leaving of it. Is there only one path that a man must follow to his life's end?"

"One path only," she said. "Yet not every step upon that path is carved in stone."

It seemed to him that her words were a riddle set within a maze.

"Then how," he asked, "can anyone read a man's future?"

She dropped her gaze from his, frowning into the fire.

"The future of any man's life is not a path that runs along a plain, my lord, but one that follows a trail over mountains and chasms that are hidden in mist. Sometimes, for a brief spell, the mist clears, and one who has the gift can see the way. Can you change the path? No. But no one, not even the most gifted, can perceive at a glance every valley or every mountaintop that a life will follow, nor every other life path that crosses it along the way." She looked into his eyes again. "You have not asked me about the thing that concerns you the most, I think. There is something far greater than the fate of a single life that troubles you."

That much was true. It was not his wyrd that mattered, or his father's. It was the fate of England that he would know.

He made no answer, but she spoke as if she had read his thought.

"Then I will give you this answer to the question that you do not ask. Whether the thing that you desire is within your reach or not, failure is only a certainty if you do not strive to grasp what you would have."

So. He must do whatever he could to preserve the kingdom, no matter the cost. Yet she would not promise him success, only certain failure if he did not make the attempt. What, he wondered, would be the price that he must pay?

"And if I give you my hand now and ask you to tell me my future, what would you say to me?"

She dropped her eyes to the flames again, and her voice was a mere whisper.

"What I would say to any man, for I have searched the fire and smoke again and again these many months, and what I see is ever the same."

He waited for her to speak, and when she seemed disinclined to go on, he prodded her.

"What is it?" he demanded. "What is it that you see?"

She lifted her gaze to his, and he thought she tried to smile, but her eyes were filled with tears.

"I see fire," she said, "and smoke. There is never anything else."


## April 1006
## Cookham, Berkshire

The imprisonment of Ælfhelm's sons led to angry clashes between Æthelred and his ministers. Throughout Easter Week while the council sessions continued, Emma observed the discord and the king's response to it with growing dismay. Æthelred went nowhere without a ring of trusted warriors close about him, but the presence of armed men in the hall merely added to the tension that charged the air like lightning about to strike.

She was not present on the day that Lord Eadric of Shrewsbury strode into the hall with a dozen men at his back to report that Ealdorman Ælfhelm was dead. She heard about it soon enough, though. His bald statement set the court buzzing. The king declared that Ælfhelm had been punished for his treachery against the Crown, and immediately ordered Ælfhelm's sons sent in chains to the fortress at Windsor. For safekeeping, he insisted.

This led to more unrest among the men of the witan. They demanded an accounting of Ælfhelm's crimes and the crimes of his sons, but the king steadfastly refused to enumerate them. It was enough, he claimed, that he knew what they were, and even his bishops could not move him to say any more. At this Lord Æthelmær of the Western Shires grew so irate that he retired from the king's council altogether, saying he would rather spend the rest of his life in an abbey serving God than continue paying court to an unjust king.

Emma had met with the man and tried to dissuade him from taking a step so drastic and irrevocable. He had listened to her arguments with grave respect and courtesy, but in the end she could not sway him from his decision. The next morning he had left Cookham with his sons and more than fifty warriors beside. The king never even tried to placate Æthelmær and sent no word of Godspeed, but Emma had watched the company ride away with misgiving.

And all the while there was an endless flurry of rumors about Elgiva, who seemed to have disappeared from the earth altogether. Some claimed that she was dead, but Emma gave those stories no credence. Elgiva was alive, she was certain. The Lady of Northampton had somehow slipped whatever snare Eadric had set for her, and that had merely goaded him into redoubling his efforts to capture her. He'd even sent men to the convents that were scattered throughout England—a fruitless endeavor in Emma's opinion, despite tales that Elgiva had been seen at Polesworth, at Shaftesbury, and at Wilton. Elgiva, she knew, would never willingly place herself within the confining walls of a nunnery.

She had said as much to Wymarc as they walked together one morning beside the river. Pausing for a moment to look up, into the wide blue expanse that was uncharacteristically free of clouds, she had wondered aloud, "Where under this English sky is Elgiva? And what is she doing?"

"She's a temptress, isn't she?" Wymarc had replied. "She'll have used her looks and her cunning to persuade some fool of a man to give her shelter."

Emma thought that all too likely. But to whom would Elgiva turn for help?

"Let us hope," she said, "that she has gone to ground and stays well hidden." Preferably outside England's borders, where her wealth and connections would not tempt one of Æthelred's ambitious thegns or, God forbid, an ætheling, to wed her.

Such an alliance, even now, with Ælfhelm dead and his sons imprisoned, would have its advantages. She imagined Athelstan fettered to the beautiful, scheming Elgiva—and abruptly she pushed the thought away. The king would never agree to it, and to attempt it without his blessing would mean catastrophe—father and son irrevocably divided and, far worse, a kingdom in chaos. Athelstan would never take that step.

He must not.

"I doubt you need worry about Elgiva," Wymarc said. "She's crafty as a cat. Toss her in the air and she'll land on her feet every time."

Yet Emma worried. As relieved as she was that Elgiva was no longer in her household, she had no wish to see her at the side of an ætheling or of some northern warlord, but neither did she wish her to be at the mercy of Eadric and his hounds.

When the council session ended, most of the nobles set out for their homes—fled, Emma thought—eager to get away from the king's fierce, suspicious gaze. Two of the Mercian magnates, though, were ordered to remain. They were the brothers Siferth and Morcar, kin by marriage to Ælfhelm and the first to plead with the king on behalf of Ælfhelm's sons. Æthelred claimed that he wished them to advise him in the search for Elgiva, but everyone knew that the men were hostages to the king's fear of Ælfhelm's supporters. The two men could not plot against him if they were at court, under his so-called protection.

Siferth's young bride was Elgiva's kinswoman, Aldyth. She was fifteen winters old, and tall for her age, quite the opposite of Elgiva, who, Emma reflected, was elfin in comparison. Everything about Aldyth was large—mouth, hands, feet, even her teeth. Yet she was not unattractive. The large eyes beneath her dark brows were beautiful, and her skin was fair and smooth. She had a lovely, wide smile—when she did smile, which had not been a frequent occurrence of late.

When Aldyth had first arrived at court, just before Easter, she had been shy and exuberant all at once. With the arrest of her cousins though, her excitement had turned very quickly to bewilderment. And when word came of her uncle's death and Elgiva's disappearance, her bewilderment had turned to horror and fear.

Emma had done what she could to shelter her from the rampant speculation about the fate of her cousins and from the cloud of suspicion that had settled upon her husband and his brother. It was Hilde, though, Ealdorman Ælfric's granddaughter, who had taken charge of Aldyth, just as she had once taken charge of the king's young daughters when she was no more than a child herself.

They sat together now, Hilde and Aldyth, on one of the fur hides that covered the floor, keeping watch over Edward and Robert, who seemed determined to explore every corner of the chamber. From her place at the embroidery frame under the high window, Emma watched them and smiled. Hilde had grown into a lovely young woman, her hair in its long braid the color of honey. She was the same age as Aldyth, but she seemed years older somehow. Perhaps that was due to the responsibilities she had shouldered in the royal household, Emma thought. Or perhaps it was because she had lost both of her parents when she was so young, her mother to sickness and her father to the king's vengeance. Hilde was smiling now, though, as Aldyth spun a wooden top before the delighted eyes of the two bairns.

Edyth, who was seated with her sisters beside Emma, looked at the group on the floor and scowled.

"Can we not get some servants to take the children so these ladies can help us with this altar cloth?" she asked, her tone surly. "The design is intricate and it is likely to take us years to finish it."

"This is a gift from the royal family to Archbishop Ælfheah," Emma replied, "and therefore we should be the ones to work the embroidery."

She frowned at Edyth, who had been discontented with the entire world, but mostly with Emma, for some weeks now. The king's eldest daughter was clearly gnawing on some grievance, but Emma had yet to determine in what way she was at fault.

She saw Edyth about to make another protest, but before she could say anything one of the household slaves, a boy of about eight, raced into the chamber and straight to Emma's side. Without waiting for permission to speak, he cried, "There is word from Windsor that the lords Wulfheah and Ufegeat have had their eyes put out!"

The needle slipped from Emma's hands, her gaze drawn immediately to where Aldyth and Hilde sat frozen, their faces ashen. They stared back at her with horror in their eyes until Aldyth collapsed forward, wailing as if she'd taken a mortal blow. Instantly Margot was at the young woman's side, wrapping a comforting arm about her while Wymarc swept a protesting Robert from the floor.

Emma grasped the young slave by the arms and pulled him toward her. He was new to the court, still raw and untutored, sold into slavery during the worst of the famine when his parents could no longer feed him. He had meant no harm. He had only been eager to tell her the news, but a slave who could not hold his tongue was of no use to her.

"You are never to speak in my presence until I give you permission to do so, whatever the message you carry. I shall punish you if you ever burst into my chamber like that again. Do you understand?"

He nodded, his eyes wide and frightened.

"Good," she said, drawing him still closer. "Now, tell me," she said more gently, for his ears alone, "what else do you know of their fate?" She cast another quick glance at Hilde and saw with a pang that the girl's face was wet with tears as she clutched a whimpering Edward to her breast and stared pityingly at Aldyth. Hilde's father had suffered this same cruel punishment, had even survived it, although he'd spent the rest of his life in exile, consumed by bitterness and hatred. Hilde had known him only in the weeks before he died—a twisted wreck of a man. This news, Emma thought, must bring back all the anguish that his young daughter had felt for him. Swallowing the hard knot of pity in her throat, Emma turned back to the boy and asked urgently, "Do the prisoners still live?"

"I know not, my lady," the boy whispered, clearly frightened by the distress he'd caused.

"Go and see if you can discover it," she said, "and bring me word."

"Yes, my lady," he said, remembering to bow before he scampered off.

Emma drew in a long breath and stood up, considering what to do next. Aldyth still sat on the floor, wrapped in Margot's arms and sobbing with sorrow or with terror—likely both, Emma thought. The girl certainly had good reason to be afraid. She belonged to a family that had earned the king's enmity, and there was no telling how far Æthelred would carry his vengeance. If he should send men here to take Aldyth away, even she would not be able to stop them.

All work on the archbishop's altar cloth had ground to a halt. Edward was crying despite Hilde's efforts to soothe him. Aldyth was distraught, and Edyth was frowning at her while her younger sisters stared at the weeping girl with frightened eyes.

"Hilde," Emma said, taking Edward from her and pacing with the light, bouncing step that usually quieted him, "please take the younger girls outside for a walk." That would remove them from this turmoil and give Hilde a task that would hopefully take her mind from painful memories.

But it was Edyth who stood up and began to herd her sisters toward the chamber door, saying, "I will take them."

"I wish you to stay, Edyth," Emma said. "I may need your assistance." Edyth was old enough now to begin to learn how to deal with a court crisis.

"And I wish to go," Edyth said, her voice taut as the string on a bow. She paused beside Aldyth and said, "You should not weep for those men. They were my father's enemies. He would not have punished them had they not deserved—"

"Be silent!" Emma said sharply. In an instant she had thrust Edward into Hilde's arms and, drawing Edyth aside, she hissed, "Edyth, you must show compassion for this girl. Her cousins have been horribly punished, her uncle is dead, and whatever they may have done, she must be very frightened. She is all but a hostage because of them."

"If she has done nothing wrong," Edyth replied, "then she need not be afraid. My father will not harm her. Why do you not tell her that?"

Emma wanted to weep with frustration. "I cannot tell her not to be afraid," she said, "because things are not as they should be. Everyone is frightened, tempers are raw, and I cannot speak for the actions of anyone." Least of all the actions of the king.

"But it is your duty to defend my father," Edyth persisted, her face growing flushed and angry. "Only you will not, because you hate him."

Emma stared at her. Where had this come from?

"You are mistaken, Edyth," she said coldly. "I do not hate the king."

"Yes, you do," Edyth insisted, her voice rising. "You hate all of us. You only care about Edward and no one else. My brother Edmund says that you will not be happy until all of us are dead."

Emma slapped her almost before Edyth finished speaking. The girl glared at her for an instant, then turned and fled the chamber.

Still stunned by the poison of Edyth's words, Emma let her go. Her heart, though, was filled with misgiving. When had Edyth begun to resent her? At the time that she and Æthelred had wed, his daughters, all of them so very young, had accepted her almost as if she were an elder sister. Whatever suspicions the king's sons may have harbored against her, his daughters had warmed to her. Clearly that had changed, at least where Edyth was concerned.

Had it started with Ecbert's death, or did it go even further back, to the birth of Edward?

She put her fingertips to her temple and rubbed them against the pressure that had begun to pulse there. *Dear God*, she should have expected this. She should have prepared herself to face it, for it had to come sooner or later—this chafing between them. The girl was mature enough now to understand that her prestige had been lowered when her father had wed a Norman bride and given her a crown that Edyth's own mother had never been granted. Edward's birth could only have added to Edyth's resentment. Edyth was ambitious. As she grew older, she would likely demand a role that held some influence within the court, and until she got it there would be no peace between stepmother and king's daughter.

She looked at the others in the room—all of them upset and afraid. The younger girls were most frightened of all, she suspected, because they would not understand what tensions lay behind the little drama they had just witnessed.

She nodded to Hilde to take Edward and his half sisters away, then she drew Aldyth to the bench along the wall and sat beside her. Even as she murmured words of consolation, though, she brooded on the king's eldest daughter. She would have to find a way to reassure Edyth, win her over somehow; only she was at a loss as to how to go about it.

Edyth was too proud ever to admit that she could be in the wrong. She shared that trait with her father.

And was the king wrong about the guilt of Ælfhelm and his sons? Perhaps not; but the cruel measures that he had taken against them and his silence about their crimes could only breed discontent among men whose loyalty was already strained. If the summer brought dragon ships to England's shores, would the men of England unite under their king, or would they turn to someone else to protect them?

Once more, her thoughts flew to Elgiva, who was as capable of treachery and deceit as her father and brothers. Where was she, and what kind of vengeance might she even now be plotting against the king?

A.D. 1006    Then, over midsummer, came the Danish fleet to Sandwich, and they did as they were wont; they barrowed and burned and slew as they went.

—*The Anglo-Saxon Chronicle*

# Chapter Ten

July 1006

Cookham, Berkshire

The midsummer sun was at its height as Athelstan rode with Edmund and a dozen of their hearth guards along the Camlet Way toward the royal manor at Cookham. The road here, just north of the bridge that crossed the Thames near Shaftsey, cut through a forest of oaks, and he was grateful for the cooling shade. As they neared the river the trees thinned, and a horn blared from the walls of the burh that guarded the crossing.

Good, he thought, the guards are vigilant. He counted fifteen of them on the palisade. His bannermen, riding at the head of his company, signaled to them, they signaled back, and the wail of the horn faded. Casting a critical eye on the fortified structure perched on the island midriver, he noted that two new watchtowers had been added since last he was here.

"It looks like Ealdorman Ælfric has been strengthening the shire's defenses," he said to Edmund. His brother made no reply, and Athelstan, irritated, scowled at him. "Edmund, something's been eating at you all day. Are you going to tell me what it is, or are you going to continue to keep me in suspense?"

Edmund scowled back at him, but finally he broke his sullen silence. "How much will you tell the king about what you've been doing?"

It was a fair question, and one that Athelstan had been asking himself for weeks as he met with thegns all through the Midlands in an effort to stem their outrage over Ælfhelm's murder. He had told them that

Ælfhelm had been consorting with men close to the Danish king. He had done what he could to convince them that his father had been forced to move against the ealdorman, but he had not been able to defend the king's tactics—the ruthless butchery of Ælfhelm and his sons. When pressed he had vowed that if he were on the throne, he would be far more open and even-handed in his dealings with his nobles than his father had been.

It was a promise not likely to endear him to the king, should he hear of it.

"Are you afraid that I will end up like Wulf and Ufegeat?" he asked Edmund. Poor devils. They had been mere pawns in their father's dangerous game, yet they had died miserably in a dank and fetid stone cell, their wounds, it was rumored, gone untreated. Siferth and Morcar, it seemed, had been granted possession of the ravaged bodies of their kinsmen for burial, and they had borne witness to the consequences of the king's wrath. Word of it had spread through the realm like wildfire.

"Aren't you afraid?" Edmund turned the question back at him.

"Yes," he growled, "I am. The king sees enemies everywhere and I am hardly invisible. But if he demands an accounting from me, I will give an honest answer. Someone has to speak openly to him about the uncertain temper of his nobles."

Edmund was silent for a few moments. Then he said, "The king's enemies *are* everywhere. Our northern border is under attack by the Scots, and the king's spies have warned that the Danes will strike before summer's end—God alone knows where. I think he was right to make an example of Ælfhelm. He has made it clear that he will punish treachery and disloyalty. It used to be that gold and lands and preferment were enough to keep men loyal. No longer, though. In times such as these, fear of punishment may be the only thing that will compel men to cleave to their king."

"But he is a weak king, Edmund, and no warrior. If the men inside his realm turn against him, it is because they fear he cannot protect them from the enemies who press us from outside. Mark me, there is a storm coming and we are ill prepared to meet it. *Jesu*, with Ælfhelm dead there is no longer an ealdorman in Northumbria or in Mercia. Who will organize the defense if the Danes strike the towns along the Trent or the Ouse?"

"Eadric of Shrewsbury, judging by the trust the king has placed in him lately."

"Eadric!" Athelstan snorted. "He is a henchman, not a warrior."

"Warrior or not, he is better than no leader at all," Edmund countered.

As to that, Athelstan had his doubts. What they needed was time—time to consult over the leadership of the northern shires, time to bring in the harvest, time to prepare and stock the burhs for defense. He had begged the churchmen he had spoken with to pray for time so that they could gather strength to meet their enemies.

But as Edmund said, there was already fighting along the border with the Scots, and he feared there was an ill wind blowing across the Danish sea. The one thing that the people of England did not have was time.

They were over the bridge now, the island behind them, and the gates of the palace rose ahead, reinforced, he noted, by a triple guard. Within the walls all was clamor and mayhem, far surpassing the everyday comings and goings of servants, retainers, and men-at-arms. He had difficulty guiding his mount past men sorting through piles of arms and equipment, women and children scurrying from building to building weighed down with bundles, and grooms loading horses and pack mules.

The king's household was preparing to move, but there was nothing orderly or methodical about these preparations. Something was wrong, something more pressing than the Scots' invasion of far-off Northumbria.

He and Edmund dismounted, tossed their reins to a groom, and went into the hall. Here, too, all was chaos, except for a table full of scribes who sat writing furiously on wax tablets. Instructions from the king to his royal thegns, Athelstan guessed. He paused to address a steward who was hurling curses at a trio of slaves that was frantically packing silver candlesticks and goblets into chests.

"What is amiss?" he asked.

"Danish ships have been sighted at Sandwich, my lord. We've not been told yet where we are to go, but word has come down that we are leaving on the morrow."

Athelstan glanced at his brother and knew that they were thinking the same thing. Time had just run out.

Inside the royal apartment, the king sat at a central table with a small circle of advisers about him. Athelstan, flicking his gaze around the chamber, found Emma in an alcove lit by a bank of candles. Her Norman priest, Father Martin, stood at a writing table beside her, his stylus moving swiftly across the parchment laid out before him.

Emma must have heard them enter, for she looked up just then and their eyes met, and held, and the silent communion that was both torment and consolation flashed between them. Then she looked away, and he turned his attention to the men around the king. His younger brothers were there, as was Ælfric, Ealdorman of Hampshire. Bishop Ælfheah was there too, and then he corrected himself, for the man who had been bishop of Winchester was now archbishop of Canterbury—one of the wisest appointments his father had ever made. There were several lesser lords among the assembly as well, and he noted with misgiving that Eadric of Shrewsbury stood at the king's right hand.

With Edmund right behind him, he made his way through the men gathered about the table. The king drew his gaze from a roughly drawn map that covered most of the table to frown at them and, to Athelstan's surprise, gestured them to come closer.

"I had not thought to see you here," his father said, "but your arrival is timely. You've heard?"

"Yes," Athelstan replied. Apparently it took the threat of a Viking army to win him his father's regard. He peered at the map. "How large is their force?"

"Sixty ships, curse them. Near two thousand men. They have already begun to move west from Sandwich." He expelled a breath and sat back heavily in his chair. "I had not expected them to come so soon," he murmured. "I thought we had another month at least."

"Is it Swein who leads them?" Athelstan asked.

"No, but that is the only good news," his father said. "With the harvests not yet in we will be short on men and on food stores. *Christ!*" He ran his hand wearily over his eyes. "We shall have to fortify the burhs across Wessex and strike at them piecemeal, harry their flanks like midges in a swamp."

Athelstan glanced at the faces around the table and found there little relish for this plan. It was what they had done for years, and for years it had been a tactic that had led to failure. What they needed to do was to bring a massive army against the shipmen and beat them back into the sea, but England was ill prepared for such an endeavor. Any army they could raise would be composed for the most part of men whose hands were more used to grasping the handles of a plow than the hilt of a sword, while their enemies would be fierce Danish shipmen who were weapon-trained and battle-ready.

Athelstan turned to the archbishop. "If they strike at Canterbury, will the city be able to hold against them?" he asked.

"Our walls are in good repair," Ælfheah replied, "so we can withstand them for some days."

Athelstan nodded. "Likely they have not come to lay siege but to strike quickly and grab whatever is not nailed down. It is the smaller towns and abbeys of Kent and Surrey that will be vulnerable if the raiders sail westward"—he moved his finger along the line that marked England's southern coast—"and if they decide to strike to the north it will be the towns along our eastern shores at risk."

The king was frowning at the map. "I will call out the forces of Mercia and Wessex, all the men who can be spared from the fields and even many who cannot. Their commanders will meet me at Windsor to organize the defense, but it will take time for them to gather. Meantime we must get fighting men into the burhs in the southeast as soon as may be. The Danes will not stray far from their ships, so we should strive to keep them confined to the coast." He turned to Ælfric. "How many of your house guards are here with you?"

"Thirty men, my lord, all well armed and mounted," the ealdorman replied.

"Good. You will lead them to Rochester and summon the fyrd of Kent to you there. You will have to scour the countryside for whatever provisions you need."

Ælfric nodded, and the king turned to Eadric. "You will go north into Mercia, muster whatever force you can there, and come to me at Windsor as soon as you may. Athelstan, you will ride with the queen's Norman retainers to Lewes and summon the men of Sussex. Provision them however you can. Take Edrid and Edwig with you. Edmund, you and Edgar and your men will escort your sisters and the queen to Winchester and take charge of the fyrd there. Do not attempt to meet the shipmen in a pitched battle."

That last order was directed to all of them, but Athelstan found the king's faded blue eyes looking intently into his own and he knew that it was meant for him more than anyone else. His father judged him too eager for battle. In this instance, his father was probably right.

"If the Danes approach," the king continued, "you should have plenty of warning. Gather the villagers and their livestock into the burhs and defend them there. For now we can do little more than try to minimize the damage."

*Minimize the damage.* Athelstan had to swallow a curse, for this was not the time to question a policy that his father had followed for twenty years. *Jesu!* It near maddened him that once again the best outcome that they could hope for was to confine their enemy to the coast. Three years ago that tactic had failed utterly, and the Danish army had thrust its way into Wiltshire. Two years ago the shipmen had pillaged and burned fifty miles into East Anglia. How far would their enemy strike this time? How many towns would be ravaged?

*Dear God.* If they could do no more than minimize the damage, then they were defeated before they'd even begun to fight.


Emma had listened to the king's commands with growing dismay. His decision to entrust her son into Edmund's care without the benefit of her Norman house guards to protect him filled her with foreboding, and now she rose swiftly and approached the king.

"My lord, I would speak," she said, and the men around him gave way so that she could kneel beside his chair.

She was risking his displeasure by daring to appeal to him in front of his council, but she had no choice. To trust her son to Edmund's care would be to take a far greater risk.

"What is it?" he snapped.

"I would go with you to Windsor, my lord," she said. "I cannot be seen to cower in Winchester like a nun behind cloistered walls while the king and his sons face this threat. My place, and that of our son, is at your side. I beg you, husband; do not send us away from you."

She saw the surprise on his face, and then the frown as he considered her words. He would not imagine the real reason behind her request—that she feared what Edmund might do if she and her son were in his power. Only Athelstan would know what was in her mind, and she risked a quick glance in his direction and saw him scowling at her. He would think her fears were groundless; but Athelstan trusted Edmund, and she did not.

"A war council is no place for a woman," Æthelred objected.

"My lord king." Archbishop Ælfheah was standing beside her, and now she felt the gentle pressure of his hand upon her shoulder. "The queen's request bears some merit. At Windsor you will meet with many nobles whose lands will be under no immediate threat from the Danes, and they will not be eager to take up arms. Some of them may even bear you ill will. If your nobles see that your sons have taken the field and that the queen herself stands firmly by your side during this time of trial, it can only help your cause."

He did not mention Ælfhelm, but Emma guessed that the name was echoing in all their minds. She did not doubt that the new archbishop had dispensed more than a few blistering words of condemnation into the king's ear over Ælfhelm's slaying at Shrewsbury. And when the council session began this morning Ælfheah had made no secret of his conviction that the arrival of the Danes was God's punishment for the king's treachery toward his ealdorman.

Now she called down a silent benediction upon Ælfheah and held her breath as she waited for the king's decision. At last he waved an impatient hand at her.

"Whether you go to Windsor or Winchester makes little difference to me, but I will ride at dawn. If you wish to attend me to the war council, then make certain that you do not delay my departure, for I will not wait for you."

"Thank you, my lord," she said. "I shall be ready."

She rose to her feet and left the chamber, leaving Father Martin to finish the correspondence they had begun together.

As she strode through the great hall she heard someone call her name, and when she paused and turned, she saw that Archbishop Ælfheah had followed her from the king's chamber.

"I would speak with you, my lady, if you can spare me a moment."

"Of course," she answered as they left the hall and entered the shade of the covered walkway that ran the length of the building. She paused there and touched his arm. "Thank you, Archbishop, for convincing the king to grant my request. It means a great deal to me."

Ælfheah had ever been a friend to her, as well as to the king and to his sons. As they stood face-to-face, his wise gray eyes kind, she could see the worry in the frown that creased his forehead. Of course he was worried. The Danish raiders were heading west from Sandwich, and Canterbury was directly in their path.

"Your request was a shrewd one, my lady," he replied, "and courageous. Your mother, I think, would have done the same were she in your place." He placed his hand upon hers and smiled. "Indeed, she is the reason I wish to speak with you, for as you know I am recently come from your brother's court."

"My mother is well, I hope," Emma said quickly. Ælfheah had brought her several letters from her family, and she had read nothing in them to alarm her.

"She is well, yes," he assured her. "I think she may outlive us all. She is a formidable woman, and in the short time that I spent in her household I developed a great admiration for her. Your brother is wise to look to her for advice and assistance."

"He places great trust in her," Emma said. Once, she had thought to play the same role, of adviser and confidante, to her husband, the king. Æthelred had quickly disabused her of that idea.

"She has skills that make her particularly valuable to Richard. I happened to observe an audience that your brother held with an envoy from the Danish king." Her alarm at hearing this must have shown on her face, for he added quickly, "Normandy's cordial relations with Denmark are, in some ways, to our advantage; nevertheless, the king will hear no word of the envoy from me. What I found of most interest in the exchange, though, was that your mother acted as interpreter. She can speak to the Northmen in their language, and as I listened I wondered if that gift had been passed to her daughter."

She looked away from him, not knowing how to answer, not wanting to lie to a man she trusted and admired. But she had kept her knowledge of Danish as secret as she could. Margot and Wymarc knew; and Athelstan, who had guessed her secret years ago. There were two others: Swein Forkbeard and his son, who had held her captive one wretched summer's day that had seemed to last an eternity. She had not been able to stop herself from cursing them in their own tongue.

She looked into Ælfheah's face again, and knew that in hesitating she had already given him an answer.

"I see," he said. "The king does not know, I take it. But my lady, this skill of yours may be of use to him should he need to negotiate with our enemy! It could earn you a place at his side if—"

"It could also earn me the enmity of those who would accuse me—and my brother—of sympathizing with the Danes." It was what Edmund would believe of her, if he knew. It would be like handing him a weapon to use against her and against her son. "Although you might not speak to the king of my brother's dealings with that Danish envoy, Archbishop, others will."

His eyes now were grave and she did not wish to hear whatever he was about to say. She did not want this man to think badly of her.

"I recognize the risks," he said, "but I beg you to give me your trust in this matter. Give me leave to reveal your secret if I see the need to do so. It will not be done lightly, I promise you."

She hesitated again.

She trusted the archbishop, of course, but in the world of the court, knowledge was power. Whoever learned her secret from him would hold mastery of a kind over her, just as Ælfheah did now. Nevertheless, this man was one of the wisest at court, numbered among the king's oldest friends and most trusted counselors. It would be wrong to hinder him from using all the tools at his disposal for England's benefit, should he have need of them.

"I give you my leave," she said. Perhaps the situation might never arise. And if it did, she must hope that she could find a way to use it to her advantage.

"I will guard your secret with my life," he said, taking her hand and clasping it between his own. "I give you my oath on that." For a long moment he searched her face, then he smiled. "You are very like your mother, Emma, and you are wise, I think, beyond your years. Should you ever again need me to intercede with the king on your behalf, you have but to ask." He made the sign of the cross on her forehead, whispered a blessing in Latin, then squeezed her hand. "Now I will take leave of you, for both of us, I believe, have much to do."

She parted from him to hurry toward her quarters, for he was right—she had a great deal to do if she was to leave with the king at first light. As she walked she pondered all that Ælfheah had said to her.

She believed that her mother would have approved of her request to accompany the king to his battle council. But if Gunnora had ever done such a thing—and Emma suspected that she had—it would have stemmed from her desire to support her husband and to stand beside the man she loved. In that, she and her mother differed.

Her own decision was more a matter of expedience. She was the mother of the heir, and so she must, perforce, be the king's ally. But it was a bitter alliance, for there was no affection and little respect between them.

He used her body at his whim, but in the four years that she had been wed to him he sought neither her company nor her advice. Her presence at his council table would not change that. Nevertheless, she would learn a great deal and, most important, Edward would be with her, and far out of the reach of his half brother Edmund.

*Sweet Virgin.* She wished that she could trust Edmund as Athelstan did. Certainly she admired the loyalty he showed his eldest brother and she even respected Edmund's determination to see Athelstan inherit the throne. But he was far too much like his father, and that was the cause of her mistrust.

She could not dismiss the fear that, like Æthelred, Edmund would not balk at murder to accomplish his ends.

# Chapter Eleven

August 1006

Holderness

Riding along a narrow track in Alric's wake, Elgiva guided her horse across a shallow stream, one of several that had flowed across their path today. A heavy fog hung in the air, thick as a woolen veil. As she wiped her wet face yet again, she decided that the people of Holderness must be all but invisible. She had seen a few scattered villages early on, their fields planted in long strips of rye or oats; and there had been the occasional flock of forlorn-looking sheep barely discernible through the mist. But for the most part this seemed to be a vaporous land, eerie and empty, as if everything alive had been sucked out of it.

Already she hated it, and she was determined to leave this miserable place as soon as ever she could.

Bored, because there was little of interest to see, she reflected on the events that had brought her here. It had taken far longer than she could have anticipated—nearly four months when she tallied the weeks together. Alric had found them a ship in Chester the very day they had entered the town and, tucked among bales of leather and tuns of salt, they had set sail with the morning tide. That ship had taken them only as far as a port belonging to one of the Wælisc kingdoms, and they had been stranded there for—how long had it been? Two weeks? Three? However long it was, it had seemed longer, stuck in a fishing hamlet that was nothing more than a scatter of shabby crofts beside the sea. When they at last found another vessel to carry them farther south, it reeked of fish.

Then Alric had found a trader hauling tin from Cornwall to Southamtun—a port much too close to Æthelred's royal city of Winchester to suit them, but they had no choice. There the weather had turned against them, and she had lost count of the days she spent penned up, this time in the guest chamber of a squalid harborside inn, fearing that if she stepped outside someone from the court might see and recognize her. That was where she'd learned of her brothers' torture and death, and she hoped never to see that foul place again in her life.

When at last the winds allowed, they had boarded a vessel bound for Hythe, and there caught another ship that carried them past the Isle of Thanet to East Anglia. There were three more ships after that, traders like the others, each one, it seemed to her, less seaworthy than the one before. None of them had afforded protection from sun or wind or rain, and the only seat she'd ever had was the small, wooden chest that Alric had purchased before they left Chester that held her cyrtel and undergown.

Her men's garb had kept her safe enough from the shipmen, although she had seen more than one brute cast covetous eyes on her fine woolen cloak. Alric's ready knife, she felt certain, had kept any thieving hands at bay, but nothing could protect her from the stench of the pitch and fish oil that permeated the ships. Nor could anything dispel the fear and sick dread that rose in her throat whenever a sudden squall battered them.

She had learned to avoid eating anything in the hours before they boarded, but how she hated the motion of the waves! They were always the same, heaving the vessels with such force that she had to keep her mouth clamped shut to keep from spewing bile. Even now, although the water roads were behind her, the rhythm of her horse's gait made her stomach churn.

At least there had been welcome news last night when they had debarked at last at Beverley. King Æthelred had taken up arms against a Danish army that was ravaging somewhere in Wessex. She hoped that it was true. She hoped that a Danish axe would find him and gut him. It was because of Æthelred that her father and brothers were dead, because of him that she was riding across this miserable flat bog of a land.

A damp breeze tugged at her cloak and clawed uncomfortably at her legs, for she was still clad in a man's tunic and breecs. Her neck was cold too, for her thick hair was braided and tucked into a boy's woolen cap. As she pulled her hood over her head for warmth, Alric hissed a warning and brought their horses to a halt. The sound of hoofbeats echoed from somewhere ahead of them, growing louder as whoever was out there came nearer. Alric drew his sword. Now she heard horses behind them as well, and afraid that the king's men had tracked her down at last, she searched wildly about for someplace to hide. But there was not even a rock or tree visible in this barren wasteland. She snatched the small knife from her belt, clutching it so tightly that her palm hurt. Then she could do nothing but wait.

The noise from two companies of men grew louder, competing with the terrified beating of her heart. Her mount began a nervous skittering, and she pulled hard at the reins to steady it as riders burst through the drifts of fog. In a moment she and Alric were surrounded, and it was only when he called out a greeting in what she thought was Danish that she was able to catch a shallow breath, for now she recognized Thurbrand among the riders.

He was as massive as she remembered—tall, wide-shouldered, barrel-chested, with a broad face framed by thin black locks. His beard was full and wild, and she shuddered to think what might be living in it. But his cloak was clasped with an intricate brooch of gold, and its fur trim rippled as he touched his fist to his shoulder in a gesture of greeting.

"You certainly took your time getting here," he growled at Alric. "My men have been shadowing you ever since you left Grimsby, keeping an eye out, you might say. We had king's men nosing about last month— mean-spirited bastards asking questions about a black-haired beauty." He turned to look at her then, and she saw his eyes travel from her bound breasts down to her toes. "My men sent word that you were garbed as a boy. I could hardly credit it, having seen you in your father's hall." His mouth twisted in a leer. "I see I was wrong." He turned his horse to face back along the track from which he'd come. "But we must hasten. There are folk awaiting us at Ringbrough."

It was hardly the courteous greeting she had looked for, but she had no chance to rebuke him. A moment later she found herself riding swiftly through the mist with armed horsemen on either side of her. She cursed under her breath. How could she have forgotten what a brute Thurbrand was? He had all the courtesy of a boar, and now that she'd seen Holderness, she would not be surprised to discover that he was not only uncivilized but half-mad as well.

Her decision to come to him for help seemed far less wise in this light, but it was too late to do anything about it. She could only wonder uneasily who was waiting for them at Ringbrough, whatever Ringbrough may be.

As it turned out, Ringbrough was a small manor—far smaller than she had expected. It was set within a palisade among fields of rye bordered by a forest of oak and ash. There was a hint of salt on the breeze, and she guessed that they must be very near the sea. The afternoon was far advanced as they entered the compound through a narrow wooden gate guarded by armed men. When she heard the latch close behind her she could think of nothing so much as a trap springing shut, and she felt a sudden tremor of apprehension.

As Alric helped her from her horse, she glanced toward the center of the yard, where a timbered hall—half the length of her father's—stood flanked by smaller buildings. It was not long, but it was tall, with a high, curved roof ornamented with soaring crossbeams carved in the shape of beasts gaping with fierce, open mouths, like the monsters on the prows of dragon ships. She did not like the menacing look of that hall, and when Thurbrand grasped her elbow and would have led her inside, she wrested her arm away and rounded on him.

"Why have you brought me here?" she demanded. "I've heard my father describe the massive stronghold of the mighty Thurbrand. This is not it."

"Aye, that's so. But what we do today must have few witnesses, and those only men that I can trust. Get you in."

Now her fear was as wide as a river in flood.

"I will not," she snapped, "until you tell me what you are about." And likely not even then, if she could help it.

"Lady Elgiva," he growled, taking her arm again and pushing her toward the open door, "I stand here in your father's stead. You have nothing to fear."

Yet she was afraid, for she saw her father's hand in this, reaching out from the grave to bring her to ruin. She was afraid that some bastard of a Dane was waiting in there for her, and that the marriage she had tried so desperately to avoid was about to come to pass. But she was not strong enough to resist Thurbrand, who simply dragged her through the doorway as if she were made of straw.

Inside, the far end of the hall was lit by thick candles set on a trestle table, where four men sat laughing and drinking. She did not recognize any of them, and she turned around to look to Alric for help, but there was only darkness behind her. As Thurbrand propelled her toward the strangers their talk and laughter died, and she felt their gazes burn her skin. She was thrust none too gently onto a stool next to one of them. Volleys of words shot back and forth among the men, but she understood nothing.

When a servant appeared from the shadows to set a cup before her, she reached for it eagerly and took a long swallow, then coughed as the liquid burned its way down her throat. It was beor, a drink more potent than wine or mead, but she was thirsty. She wiped her streaming eyes, then drank some more while she peered at the faces around the table and considered her options. The usual tricks for cozening a man would be of no use to her here. She did not want to charm them but repel them. And if her men's clothes and the stench from a week's worth of travel filth did not do it, likely nothing would.

She decided that the fellow seated directly across from her must be their leader, for he was covered in gold. There were gold rings on his fingers and arms, and a heavy gold chain hung about his neck. Well, if he was to be her husband, he appeared to be rich enough to suit her, but, *Jesu*, he was ancient. Still, he might well die soon, and that would be an advantage.

His long hair, tied back in the Danish fashion, was stark white, and his face was so seamed and weather-worn that she was reminded of the chalk cliffs that she had seen on the southern coast. His black eyes scanned her as if he were calculating her worth, and when she arched an insolent brow at him, one corner of his mouth lifted, as if she'd amused him. He flicked a finger, and Thurbrand pulled the hood and woolen cap from her head, releasing the long braid that fell to her waist.

"Do not touch me, you whoreson," she snarled, batting his hand away. "Who are these men? I came to you in trust and you have betrayed me."

"No betrayal, lady," he said smoothly. "I am merely completing the bargain that your father agreed to."

"But I did not agree to it!" She stood up, knocking over her stool and glaring at him.

He responded by striking her so hard that she lost her balance. She would have fallen but for the man who occupied the stool beside hers. He caught her, and she heard him shout something at Thurbrand. But the blow and the beor made the room spin, and she was only dimly aware that in the moments that followed, her hands were clasped hard between a man's calloused palms and more words were spoken that she did not comprehend.

"It is done," she heard Thurbrand say then. "Greet your husband, lady. His name is Cnut."

She looked up into eyes as dark as those that had bored into her from across the table. But these eyes belonged to a far younger man—younger even than she was, she guessed. His beard, like his hair, glinted copper in the candlelight while those dark eyes considered her with a steady, solemn gaze. He slipped a fat gold ring from one of his fingers and placed it upon one of hers. She studied the ring and dredged up a smile for him.

Then, still smiling, she spat in his face.

Elgiva could not say how long it took for her head to finally clear from a haze of confusion, anger, and beor. She remembered being bathed and clothed in a clean shift of white linen. Now she was alone, her hair combed and plaited, and she was lying on a curtained bed that was strewn with furs. Despite the fire that burned on the small hearth in the center of the chamber, she was cold. She sat up and, wrapping one of the furs around her shoulders, noticed a cup on the table next to the bed. She picked it up, sniffed it, and tasted it. The liquid inside was hot—an herbal infusion of some kind, sweetened with honey. She sipped it gingerly as she tried to make sense of what had happened to her.

She appeared to be in a woman's bower—the rafters above her head intricately carved with flowers and birds, and painted in bright hues. The linen hangings that covered the walls were embroidered with sailing ships and sea monsters. A loom stood against one wall, and next to it several coffers were stacked one atop another. She wondered idly what they held, but she was too tired to get up and inspect them. Instead she lay back upon the pillows and saw that some fool had scattered flower petals there. *Jesu!* Did they think a few blossoms would placate her for having to spread her legs for a filthy Dane?

That was what she would be forced to do, assuming her hazy memory was correct and she had actually been wed to that youth in the hall. There had been no priest to bless the nuptials, but that made no difference. Whoever he was, he could claim her as his handfast wife once he'd bedded her. No doubt he would set about that soon enough.

The chamber door opened slowly and she sat up, expectant and wary. A woman entered, perhaps several years younger than she was, thin as a stick, with flaming hair that hung in plaits to her waist. Her green woolen cyrtel was belted with a silver chain, and she wore strings of amber beads around her neck.

Someone of status, then.

Another woman slipped into the room behind the first. This one would be a servant or slave, for she was gowned in a shift as gray and plain as dirt, and she moved as silently as a shadow. She went to a stool in the corner and, pulling a spindle and wool from a basket, she began to spin.

Like one of the Norns, Elgiva thought, one of the mystical creatures that the Norse believed in, who spun the thread of fate for each living being. Even as she thought it, the woman looked up with an expression so dark and knowing that Elgiva instinctively flinched and looked away.

She is but a slave, she told herself, and no Norn. There is nothing to fear from her.

She turned instead to the woman in green, who was still hesitating near the door.

"Who are you and what do you want?" The question was probably

pointless. She'd heard nothing but Danish spoken since she'd arrived in
this miserable place.

"I am Catla," the young woman whispered. She looked nervous, her
eyes enormous and her skin pale as milk. "I am wife to Thurbrand, and
he has bid me attend you until your lord comes." She smiled weakly and
gave her head a little shake. "I cannot abide the hall when the men
get . . ." She waved her hand helplessly.

*Dear God.* This waif was hardly a match for the bearlike Thurbrand.
He must chew her up and spit her out daily to make her look so frightened. But at least the girl spoke English and might be able to tell her
something useful.

"Sit here, then." Elgiva gestured to the bed but she could not bring
herself to smile. She was still too furious at the trick Thurbrand had
played on her. "I won't bite you. Tell me of the man they've foisted on me.
Do you know who he is?"

The girl came closer but she did not sit down.

She reminded Elgiva of a fawn or a rabbit, frightened of its own
shadow.

"He is Cnut, lady. Son of Swein, son of Harald, son of Gorm." She
recited it as if she were a skald about to begin a tale, or as if it had been
beaten into her.

"Swein," Elgiva repeated. "Is that the man I saw in the hall, clad all in
gold?"

Catla gave a quick nod. "He landed on Lammas Day, and he was
furious when he did not find you here. It's as well that you arrived today
because by tomorrow he and his son would have been gone."

Elgiva closed her eyes. Another day, and she would have escaped this
fate. How the Norns must be laughing at her.

When she opened her eyes again, Catla was gesturing toward the
caskets that stood beside the loom.

"King Swein bid me tell you that everything here is yours. The bed,
the hangings, everything in the boxes you see there, even Tyra"—she
nodded toward the gray woman with the spindle—"belongs to you. She
will be your body servant. They are all morning gifts from Cnut."

But Elgiva was no longer listening, for the words *King Swein* had struck her ears like a thunderbolt. She thrust herself from the bed and crossed the chamber to lift the lid of one of the coffers that stood against the wall. It was filled with silver—rings and chains, cups and plates, crosses, candlesticks, and medallions. She turned to another coffer and inside she found golden arm rings, enameled necklaces, finger rings set with precious gems—a Viking hoard of gold and jewels.

She knew now, who it was that she had wed. She was the handfast wife of the son of King Swein of Denmark. It must be. She had never heard of any other king named Swein, and the wealth in these chests argued that she was the bride of a king's son.

She closed her eyes, remembering the prophecy of her old nurse, Groa.

*You will be a queen, and your children will be kings.*

She had always believed that she must marry Æthelred or one of his brood for that to come true. It had never dawned on her that there might be another way. But there was, and this was it. This marriage was an alliance that would inspire northern lords like Thurbrand, men dissatisfied with the kingship of Æthelred, to pledge themselves to the warrior king from Denmark—and to his son. Æthelred might one day find himself ruler of only the southern half of England, while Swein held all the rest.

And someday, when Swein died and Cnut was crowned king after him, she would be queen beside him.

How long had her father been negotiating this marriage? And why had the fool not confided in her, not told her that it was Cnut she was to wed? She would have helped him, not betrayed him. If he'd had the good sense to trust her with his great secret, he might still be alive and her brothers would not have been tortured and left to die.

Her father, damn him, had wasted all their lives.

The sound of voices outside brought her bitter musing to an abrupt end. She made it back to the bed just before the door was flung wide and the room filled with drunken men. Two of them carried torches, and when one of them stumbled toward the bed, she cried out for fear he would fire the hangings. But he righted himself and she saw that it was Alric, ogling her and grinning like an idiot.

She scrambled to the top of the bed and pulled the furs up against her breasts, making the men howl with laughter. Catla, the little coward, slipped out the door like a shadow, but Elgiva knew that for her there would be no escape. She was wed to Cnut, and his kinsmen had come to watch him plough his furrow and plant a babe in her belly. *Jesu*, if they expected to find blood on the sheets afterward they were in for a disappointment, for she was no virgin.

She glanced at the king, who was staring at her wolfishly, his mouth set in a leer. Would they kill her in the morning because she was no maid?

No. They needed her to claim the allegiance of her kin.

She had no more time to think about that, for Cnut had come to the foot of the bed and he was surveying her with eyes that showed no trace of drunkenness. He pulled off his tunic and skinned his breecs away as the men cheered and pounded their feet on the floor—for encouragement, she supposed. But Cnut was naked now, standing tall in the torchlight that gleamed on his skin, and judging by the way his rod stood at attention, the encouragement was hardly necessary.

Well, she was not going to just sit here like a stick of wood, like a frightened little Catla.

She drew her feet under her, stood up on the mattress, and slowly walked its length to face her husband. A shout of anticipation went up from the men, and Cnut eyed her warily, perhaps thinking she might spit at him again. But she knew who he was now, and she had no qualms about consummating this marriage. She put her arms around his neck and kissed him, drawing his tongue into her mouth. He responded by slipping his hands beneath her shift and pulling her roughly against him. Beneath the pounding of blood in her ears she heard the howls of the men as Cnut guided her back down to the mattress.

He sheathed himself inside her and she wrapped her legs about his hips, moving to the rhythm that he set. His thrusts were quick and hard and deep, and it did not take long. Well, what was she, after all, but a prize to be plundered? When he collapsed on top of her the Danes sent up a roar. The slave, Tyra, came forward, and for an instant their eyes met and held. Elgiva felt her skin prickle under that knowing gaze, and she breathed a sigh of relief when Tyra drew the curtains around the bed and that cold glance was hidden.

They were alone after that, and as she lay spooned against Cnut beneath the furs, he murmured to her in Danish. She did not understand him, and she was glad when he finally fell asleep, his hand cupped possessively over her breast. She was uncomfortable in his arms, though, and in spite of her weariness she lay awake far into the night. She tried to conjure up her future, tried to imagine herself in a great hall wearing a golden circlet, but the only images that rose in her mind were the faces of her father and her brothers, who stared at her with cold, accusing eyes. At last she fell asleep, and she dreamed of a woman in gray who sat spinning, and the golden thread that fell from her fingers shriveled into dust.

The next day, gowned in her own shift and cyrtel, and bedecked with some of her bridal gold, she followed Cnut through the hall to the dais, where King Swein waited to greet her. Alric, looking haggard after last night's celebration, fell in behind her, whispering that he had been commanded to act as interpreter.

Cnut took her hand, standing at her side as Swein pinned her with those black eyes of his, eyeing her belly as if he had the power to discern whether Cnut's son was already growing there. She resented that look and resented the way this marriage had come about, although she was satisfied enough with her husband—assuming that, in the end, she got what she wanted.

"I wish to know," she said, not waiting for the Danish king to speak first, "when King Swein will take the crown of England as his own."

She watched Swein's face as Alric translated her question, and she thought she caught a flicker of amusement in the king's eyes.

"When you give Cnut a son," the reply came back, "blending English blood with Danish, I will wrest the crown from Æthelred. Your father's death stalled our preparations, but we will begin again. You have but to do your part."

She nodded. It would do, for now. She would complete her part of the bargain. After all, even the whey-faced Emma had finally produced a son. Surely she must be as fecund as Emma, although—the alarming thought fluttered into her mind—she had not conceived in the months that she had slept beside the king.

She reminded herself, though, of the prophecy that Groa had sworn to her was true, that she was destined to wear a crown, destined to bear sons who would be kings. So it was foretold and, therefore, she assured herself, no power on earth could prevent it.

**Windsor, Berkshire**

Æthelred paced his inner chamber as he waited for Emma to respond to his summons. It was late and he was weary but, *by Christ*, he would not face another night in his bed alone. His dreams were a torment, filled with phantoms—the dead come to haunt him. His brother, his mother, even his father had troubled his sleep for a week. Their faces, decaying and putrid beneath golden crowns, hovered over him, as if they would warn him of some coming disaster. Last night it had been Elgiva, beautiful and naked, riding him hard until suddenly she was no longer Elgiva. It was her father whose dead weight pressed upon his chest and whose rough, bearded mouth covered his own, drawing all the breath from his lungs until he woke, crying out in terror.

The menace of that nightmare still clung to him, yet it offered a glimmer of hope, for it could mean that Elgiva, too, was now rotting in some unhallowed grave.

So far, she had not been discovered in either Mercia or Northumbria, and he dared to hope that some mischance had befallen her—the last of Ælfhelm's brood of vipers.

Alive, wedded to some powerful Danish lord, she could be a threat—a rallying point for Ælfhelm's disgruntled northern kin.

Dead, she could do no more than haunt him.

He paused at his worktable to finger a pile of scrolls and wax tablets that bore news from Kent, where the Danes continued to burn and plunder. His fyrds were doing exactly as he had ordered, shepherding his people into the burhs to protect them. From within the safety of their fortress walls, though, they had to watch as their homes were torched and their livestock driven away. They were powerless to stop it, for they had not the numbers to confront the better-armed shipmen and their savage leader—some bastard, he saw scrawled on one of the tablets, named Tostig.

Was Tostig the warlord who had sought the hand of Elgiva? She had been promised to a Dane. What if that marriage had already taken place? What if she was still alive and this Tostig had taken her as prize? Might he not hunger for a far greater treasure than he could plunder from the villages and towns of Kent? Might Elgiva not goad him into seeking a crown?

All the more reason to hope that Ælfhelm's daughter was dead.

He looked up as the door to his chamber swung open to reveal Emma, clad in her night robe. She was as beautiful as the day he had first seen her—perhaps more so. Her pale hair hung in a long braid over her shoulder and her complexion was as smooth and fair as marble. She regarded him with those startlingly light green eyes—not the downcast eyes of a maid but the thoughtful, knowing gaze of a woman and a queen, and for once he was comforted to see her. He was weary of struggling against phantoms; surely she would serve as armor against them. When he buried himself inside her, the lingering horror of Elgiva's succubus must fade.

He poured mead into cups for both of them, then gestured toward the table and its pile of tablets.

"You may as well read those."

She sat at the table, and as she read through the reports he studied her face. She looked anxious, and he wondered if it was because of the Danes harrying his realm or some small thing having to do with Edward. Motherhood had softened Emma in a way that puzzled him, for maternal affection was far outside the realm of his experience. His own mother had been cold, had seen him as nothing more than a stepping-stone in her rise to royal power. She had ground him beneath her feet like so much chalk. And as for his first wife, she had barely glanced at her offspring once they'd left her body. *God's plague upon women for the sin of Eve*, she'd called them.

Emma, though, delighted in her son, and was unwilling to be parted from him for very long. That was inconvenient, and it would have to change. Not that he would make an issue of it just yet, but he could not allow Edward to be so closely tied to his mother's girdle. God willing, he would get her with child again soon—maybe even tonight. Put another babe in her belly and it would be easier to wean Edward from her side. Certainly it helped that while she was here she spent much of her time in his hall, listening to the debates over the English response to the Danes, or consulting with the churchmen and nobles who had answered his summons. It meant that she had little time to spend with her son, but that, he knew, was a double-edged sword. For she was taking this opportunity to make allies among his counselors, and he did not welcome any division of loyalties within his hall.

He must get her with child soon. Emma's place was beneath him, on her back, not among the council of the wise.

A knock sounded at the door, and when his steward entered he was carrying yet another missive that must be dealt with.

"It is from Jorvik, my lord," Hubert said, "from Archbishop Wulfstan."

Æthelred muttered a curse. There had been an ominous silence from the north since the Scots king had laid siege to Durham. To receive news from Wulfstan now, after a week of dark dreams, boded ill.

He sat down, steeling himself for catastrophe.

"Read it."

Hubert broke the seal and unfolded the parchment.

"*Archbishop Wulfstan, lupus episcopus, to Æthelred, Rex Anglorum, greetings and apostolic blessings,*" Hubert read in his reedy voice. "*I write in haste to advise you that Uhtred of Bamburgh has defeated the Scots host at Durham.*"

At last, Æthelred thought. He could claim a victory instead of a rout.

"*King Malcolm escaped with his life,*" Hubert read on, "*but the greater part of his army was slaughtered. By command of Lord Uhtred, the heads of the slain Scots were placed as trophies upon the ramparts of Durham. By this you will perceive that Uhtred is a fierce and merciless warrior. Ignore him at your peril. If you do not make use of his battle skills, others surely will.*" Hubert looked up. "That is all, my lord."

Æthelred snorted. "If Uhtred were here now I would set him against the Danish scum that are ravaging Kent." He waved a hand at Hubert. "Compose a suitable reply. I will look at it in the morning." As Hubert left, he turned to Emma and found that her face was still troubled despite the good news from Jorvik. "What ails you?" he asked. "Can you not rejoice in our enemy's defeat?"

"My lord," she said, "I have had news from my brother Richard that I—"

"No!" he barked, slamming his cup onto the table. "Do not weary me with your Norman concerns tonight! I would savor the good news from Durham a while longer before you burden me with whatever your brother would have you lay across my back." He stood up and took her arm to lead her to the bed. "Get you under the sheets, lady. That is where your duty lies tonight."

He tugged off her wrap and watched as she drew her night rail over her head. The tight set of her mouth told him that, as usual, she was in no mood for bed sport. She would submit to him for duty's sake, to fulfill her royal obligation and no more.

There had been occasions, though, when she forgot herself and twisted away from him, snappish as one of his hounds in heat. The bedding was better then. Perhaps, he reflected as he covered her body with his, it was strife between a woman and a man that bred sons.

Now, though, she opened herself to him with placid disinterest, and that bored him. He finished quickly and lay, spent, on top of her, sated yet unsatisfied. The memory of Elgiva's grotesquely changing face still lingered in his mind. When he finally rolled off of Emma she sat up, obviously intending to return to her own chamber. He clasped her arm to prevent her.

"You will stay with me tonight," he said. "Of late I have been waking in the dark hours, and I may have need of you later. In the meantime"— he ran his fingers along the smooth swell of her breast—"as I do not wish to sleep yet, you may as well tell me your Norman news."

She pulled the sheet up to her chin, but he dragged it off again. It had been some time since she had spent a night in his bed and her body was like one of his estates—he felt the need to survey it occasionally to make sure that all was in order. And indeed, he decided, Emma's body was very much in order. She was golden in the light from the candles that still burned in their brackets along the walls. As he made his inventory of breasts, of belly, and of the pale thatch between her thighs, he felt his cock stiffen again.

"My lord," she said, "Richard writes that King Swein of Denmark is resupplying his father's forts."

He frowned and stilled the idle movement of his hand at her breast.

"The camps, you mean? Where Harald trained his armies?"

"Two of the camps, at any rate," she said. "The Danish king has sent out a call for warriors."

He stared at her for a heartbeat, reading the worry in her eyes, then got out of bed and filled his cup again.

"Swein's northern kingdoms are full of landless young thugs," he said, "who need occupation. One way to keep them from turning against their king is to train them and then loose them somewhere else. The army pillaging in Kent right now is likely there with Swein's blessing." He studied his wife, rival emotions warring in his mind—satisfaction that she'd brought him this information, and annoyance that she'd come by it at all. Emma's sphere of influence was widening—to his benefit, for now. But what else might she know that she used for her own purposes? After all, peace-weaving brides straddled two realms, and who could say which allegiance proved the strongest? "How did your brother come by this knowledge?"

"One of his bishops visited the new church at Roskilde and returned with word that the Danish king has sworn to thrust you from your throne. It was rumored that he made oaths, my lord"—her voice was insistent now—"both to Odin and to Christ." The green eyes probed his face. "What will you do to stop him?"

"Stop him? *Christ!* We cannot stop the vermin that are even now crawling over our fields and villages. Write to your brother that I am grateful for the warning, but I must slaughter the wolves in my house before I try to confront the enemy at my door."

Nevertheless, the news was worrisome. Was this the threat that his black dreams portended? That Swein, who had allied himself to both

God and the devil, was building an army for the sole purpose of destroy-ing England?

He could well believe that Swein's army, borne on a perilous tide, would one day reach the English shore. It would not make landfall soon, perhaps not for years, but it was coming. And unless, as his queen urged, he found some way to stop it, that great army and the man who led it would seek to destroy him.

A.D. 1006   Then the king ordered out all the population from Wessex and from Mercia; and they lay out all the harvest under arms against the enemy; but it availed nothing more than it had often done before. Then, about midwinter . . . was their army collected at Kennet; and they came to battle there . . .

—*The Anglo-Saxon Chronicle*

# Chapter Twelve

"It will not be long now."

Archbishop Ælfheah's words were all but lost in the constant roar from thousands of voices, and Emma had to strain to catch them. She stood with him upon the high parapet of a burh that crowned a barren hill near the village of Kennet. A handful of women from her household and a scattering of priests who traveled with the archbishop attended them. Behind them, in the belly of the stronghold, the women and children from the village and nearby farms clustered around campfires beneath makeshift shelters, awaiting the fate of husbands, fathers, and sons. At intervals along the ramparts, armed men from the local fyrd kept watch, and far below them, in a valley between the downs, two armies prepared to face each other in the gray light of a winter afternoon.

She shivered within her fur-lined cloak, for the mild weather had turned bitter overnight, and the sky was hung with clouds that threatened snow.

Her Norman hearth troops were out there on the field of battle, thirty men who were well trained and well armed, part of the company led by Athelstan. She could see him with his bannermen beside him, urging his men into position.

*Sweet Virgin*, she prayed silently, *keep him safe.*

Looking toward the crest of the long, low hill that bordered the valley on the left, she could just make out the king astride his horse, surrounded by armed and helmeted riders—the retainers who would spirit him to safety if, God forbid, the battle should be lost.

In the valley itself, men were forming into line after line, the English with their backs to her, and although from this distance she could not be certain, the Danes seemed to have more lines than the defenders.

"There are too many of them," she heard someone mutter as, impossibly, the shouting grew louder. "God has abandoned us."

"Never doubt the Lord!" Ælfheah's rebuke was swift and fierce. "Cling to Him, and He will not abandon us!"

Yet many in the realm, Emma thought, had begun to believe that God had done just that. Throughout the late summer and fall, the shipmen had pillaged and plundered, hampered by the English but never deterred from their grisly business. Englishmen died, their women were raped, their children dragged off for the slave markets. In November an early snowfall had driven the shipmen across the Solent to Wight Isle, and so the English defenders, who had done little more than harry their enemies, had gone back to their homes.

But just before midwinter the weather had turned mild and the Danes had struck again, moving so swiftly that the only warning beacons to be lit were the villages that they torched as they passed. Now, as the shipmen threatened the rich abbeys and estates of Berkshire and Dorset, the king had been stung into action. He had gathered a well-armed force of English nobles and their retainers to sweep the Danes back to the sea. But the Danes, too, were well armed. And *sweet Virgin*, there were so many of them!

She could hear another sound now, beneath the roar of voices—a low rumbling that turned into a rhythmic beating as swords banged against linden shields and men, shouting, worked themselves into battle madness.

"Now it begins," Ælfheah murmured.

And as the priests around her began to chant a psalm, Emma felt a snowflake graze her cheek.

A great shout went up from below as the space between the two battle lines disappeared in a thunderous crash when shield wall met shield wall. She held her breath, sweeping her gaze from the men on the ground who fought behind shields that seemed to offer pitiful protection, to Athelstan, mounted now and heedless of the spears and arrows that flew from the Danish host.

She saw men in the shield walls fall, but each line held steady as men stepped from behind to fill the gaps. There was a constant, grinding roar like the sound of waves smashing against rocks, and above it the clang of metal as swords clashed against ring mail and helms. There were screams, too, high-pitched, heartrending shrieks from the injured and dying.

Beside her, Ælfheah continued to pray, but she could do no more than watch, teeth clenched in horror at the spectacle of human carnage taking place below. The shield walls did not break, but the English gave ground while the Danish line moved inexorably forward, careless of the wounded they trampled beneath their feet.

It seemed to her that for long moments she did not even breathe, as if time were suspended for everyone except for the men who cursed and fought and died on that valley between the hills. Suddenly she saw a gap yawn on the right side of the English line and the Danes were swarming through it. English horsemen pounded toward the breach, but the snow was falling in earnest now, driven by a northern wind, and she could no longer find Athelstan among the defenders.

At the center of the English line the shield wall broke again, and like a flooding tide the Danes surged forward. Englishmen, those who could, turned and ran, impeded by the rear line that attempted to stand firm behind them, and her gorge rose as she saw fleeing men struck down from behind and trampled by Danes wielding long-handled axes.

She wanted to look away but she could not, for she was desperate to find Athelstan in the chaos. Her eyes were streaming with tears and she had to wipe them to be able to see at all, but try as she might she could not find him, blinded as she was by her tears and by the thickening fall of snow.

And then, all in a moment it seemed, it was over. The Danes, watching their enemies flee, raised a wild, victorious cry that made her blood run cold, and she understood, far too clearly, what men meant when they spoke of holding the slaughter field.

Along the parapet there were wails of despair from the priests, and curses from the men-at-arms. Women were weeping, and on the distant killing ground, the Danes set about scavenging the dead and wounded for weapons and plunder.

She continued to stand, unmoving, searching for Athelstan until at last, peering through the sheet of snow, she caught sight of him on the ridge from where the king had watched it all. Athelstan was safe, then. He was whole and unharmed, and she thanked God for that. But even as she whispered her prayer of thanksgiving, she looked again at the field of battle where the snow was mounding on the bodies of the dead and the wounded. Already the Danes were on the move, returning to their camp somewhere in the forest to the east, where their women and their plunder waited.

"What will they do now?" she asked.

"Celebrate their victory, I should imagine," Ælfheah said. "But this storm is a blessing for us. It will drive them back to their ships by the swiftest route, for their first concern now will be shelter, not plunder. And," he continued heavily, "they will send an emissary to the king to demand tribute—a bribe to encourage them to depart in the spring. However much they demand, after this the king will have no choice but to pay it."

So, she thought, in the spring the shipmen would return to their homeland, where King Swein Forkbeard was building another army, or so her brother claimed. One day it too would cross the sea to wreak vengeance on England, and all of this would be repeated yet again.

She stared down at the battlefield, where folk were moving among the English bodies: women who searched for sons or husbands, men who would carry the injured to the church at Kennet. And she swallowed the bile in her throat and turned to descend the ramparts. There were wounded men to be tended, and there would be work for many hands, even the hands of a queen.

**A.D. 1007**   In this year was the tribute paid to the hostile army; that was, 30,000 pounds. In this year also was Eadric appointed ealdorman over all the kingdom of the Mercians.

—*The Anglo-Saxon Chronicle*

# Chapter Thirteen

June 1007

Ringbrough, Holderness

Elgiva, seated at the table beside Cnut, pushed away a plate of fresh cheese that had been placed in front of her. The slimy look of the stuff disgusted her, and the smell was even worse. *Jesu!* She hated the babe in her belly for sickening her like this, although the midwife had said it was a sure sign that she carried a boy.

And her child must be a boy. She had done everything she could to guarantee it—from arousing Cnut first thing in the morning when, everyone knew, men were most virile, to clenching her fists tight when he entered her—a practice that one of the women in Thurbrand's household swore had resulted in her six sons.

She frowned, recalling several times over the winter and spring when she had lain with Cnut and she had so lost herself in the pleasure of their coupling that she forgot to tighten her fists. And there had been the days when he had taken her not just in the morning but at night, and even at midday. What if the babe had taken root at the wrong time? What if it was not a boy?

She would not know the answer to that for months yet, not until Yuletide if she could believe her slave woman, Tyra, who claimed to have knowledge of such things. Now Elgiva knew only that she was sick, already eager to be quit of this burden, and that the long months until she was released from it seemed to stretch into eternity.

A servant appeared at her side and placed a plate of boiled eels next to the cheese, and she put a hand over her nose and mouth, willing back the nausea. Cnut, after a quick glance at her, picked up the eels, thrust them at the servant, and demanded a loaf of bread and a bowl of wild strawberries. Elgiva doubted that she would be able to eat those, either, but at least they would have no stench to make her gag.

She supposed that she should thank her husband for his thoughtful gesture, but she did not. She was too furious even to speak to him. Now that he'd gotten her with child he was about to desert her, would leave for Denmark on the morrow's tide. His father had summoned him, and Cnut was eager to go. The only reason he was still here was because he had been so determined to see her well and truly pregnant before he left. That was the duty his father had set him, and Cnut, she had discovered, set great store by doing his duty.

Granted, it was a duty that they both relished. Her young husband was an exuberant lover who, to her surprise, could make her desire him even when she was tired and ill tempered. Unlike King Æthelred, who had bedded her solely for his own gratification, Cnut was not content unless he had aroused her. Or perhaps it was just Cnut doing his duty. For although their bedding gave them both pleasure, it was, at its core, a duty. Now she would be pent up here in Holderness like a brood mare while Cnut pursued other duties elsewhere. And because he was a man she had no doubt that he would fill the vacant place in his bed with whomever came to hand.

Irritated by that unpleasant thought and defeated by the sight and smell of food, she was about to quit the table when she saw Alric striding toward the dais, and her heart gave a surprising little leap. He had been away for months, and she realized suddenly how much she'd missed him—how dull the hall had seemed without him.

"Alric," Cnut greeted him with pleasure, "come sit, and tell us your news."

Elgiva called for more food as Alric took the bench across the table from them and helped himself to bread and strawberries. She watched his face, so pleasing with its even features and with that shock of brown hair that fell just above his right brow. He must have felt her eyes on him, for he flicked a glance at her and in that instant something flashed between them that set her skin tingling. It was still there, then, she thought—that attraction that had always shimmered between them, a banked fire, all the more beguiling because it had never been allowed to blaze.

Cnut was oblivious to it. His mind was fixed on Æthelred and Wessex, and he pelted Alric with a hail of questions. Reliable accounts of events occurring beyond Holderness were all too infrequent and Alric, who had pledged his allegiance to Cnut on her wedding day, had been sent south to gather news. She wondered if, once Cnut was gone, Alric would transfer his allegiance back to her again. She would have to make sure that he did, for she would have need of men about her whom she could trust.

She listened to his report, concentrating hard because the Danish did not yet come easily to her. As Alric unfolded his tale of the English geld payments to Tostig and of the political appointments that Æthelred had made in the spring, she glanced at Cnut, who was frowning. What must he be thinking? Surely he must see that he should follow Tostig's example. Rather than take ship for Denmark on the morrow he should urge his father, King Swein, to bring his armies to Holderness. Æthelred was weak! Now was the time to attack.

She said as much to him when they were alone in their chamber, but he dismissed her arguments.

"I will leave in the morning, Elgiva, as I intended from the first."

He pulled on a heavy wool tunic, preparing to go to the dock, where he would oversee the final provisioning of his ship. His calm determination infuriated her, but she forced herself to rein in her anger. It was easier to bend Cnut to her will with pleas rather than demands.

"But do you not see that this news changes everything?" she asked. "Æthelred has rewarded Eadric—the man who murdered my father— by making him ealdorman of Mercia. Will you stand by and let that butcher's advancement go unanswered?" She looked into his face for a sign that she had moved him, but he only looked irritated.

Of course he would do nothing about Eadric, she realized. Not yet. Not until a Danish king sat on England's throne, for it was kings who dispensed reward and punishment. If what she really wanted was to keep Cnut at her side, then she must find a better argument.

"What if Eadric and the king discover where I am?" She allowed tears to well in her eyes, placing herself in front of him so he could see her distress. "What do you think they will do if they learn that I am carrying your child—the grandson of the Danish king? Will you not stay here to protect your wife and son?"

"We have been over this road before," he said. "You will be in Thurbrand's care, guarded in his stronghold by his retainers. My presence would make no difference either way. I have done all that I can to ensure your safety. If you are afraid, then come with me to Denmark."

But she would not leave England. This was where her destiny lay. This was where she must one day be queen. If she left, she might never return. Indeed, she feared that Cnut might never return.

"What if you do not come back?" she asked. "If some mishap befalls you, how will I even—"

"Do not beckon misfortune," he snapped at her. "I have promised that I will return, and I will do so."

"But why must you go at all when there is such opportunity here?" she demanded. "You heard Alric. Æthelred has paid Tostig and his shipmen thousands of pounds of silver to leave his realm in peace! He is not prepared for battle."

"Nor are we! The ships are not ready, our alliances have not been forged, and my father is loath to leave Denmark in my brother's hands. You do not understand the complexity—"

"I understand that Eadric is ealdorman of Mercia! I understand that Uhtred, who is the mortal foe of your ally, Thurbrand, has been made ealdorman of Northumbria! I understand that if you do not strike soon, all England will be allied against you, because Æthelred is weaving a net of noble warriors to keep you out!"

"Æthelred will not succeed." He crossed the room to snatch up his cloak from the bed. "My father has been laying plans to conquer England for years. Nothing will prevent him from doing that. But he will not strike before he is ready."

"Yet he risks all by waiting." And why, she thought, must Swein be the one to grasp the crown of England? Why should it not be Cnut?

"The greater the risk, the greater the reward," he said, throwing the cloak over his shoulders and pinning her with a hard look. "What you need, lady, is patience."

"I have no patience," she replied, "and I did not wed your father, I wed you." He was fumbling with the clasp at his throat—a sign, she hoped, that she had reached him at last, that her words had unsettled him. She placed herself directly in front of him again, pushing his hands away and swiftly fastening the golden ring herself. Then she clutched the fine wool with both hands, and concentrating hard to get the words right, to make sure that he understood her meaning, she whispered, "Why should you wait for your father? Summon your shipmen, and I will summon my kinsmen. Together we will take Northumbria before Æthelred can gather an army against us. You will be the king of the north and I will rule at your side. After that, we will bring Mercia to its knees, then Wessex. *We* will do it. Not Swein."

She looked into his face, eager and expectant. He was comely, this youthful husband of hers—and she could not say that about many men in Holderness. His muscular shoulders graced a wiry frame that towered over her, for he was so tall that his chin and coppery beard touched the top of her head. She willed him to bend and kiss her, to forget everything but his desire to please her. She wanted him to conquer England for her and lay it at her feet.

But the look he turned on her was cold. "I owe all that I have to my father. My allegiance and obedience go to him first, above all others. Even above you, Elgiva."

He grabbed her wrists, thrust her hands away from him as if he could not bear to touch her, and then he left her without even a farewell.

She considered calling out to him, or going after him to try to mend the breach between them, but she could not bring herself to bend to him in that way and, besides, it would do no good. She would never be first with Cnut; he had made that plain enough. He may be her husband, but before that he was Swein's son.

Defeated, she went to her bed and lay down, curling her body around the child in her belly. She had been unwise to try to turn him against his father. He would never forget it, and he would never forgive her for it. In trying to bind him to her, she had merely succeeded in pushing him further away.

She closed her eyes, feeling wretched and sick and stupid. After a little while, though, she sat up and, settling her chin against her knees, she tried to think. All was not lost, she decided. Cnut would do his duty by her, of that much she was certain, and their son would be a bond between them. The child's birth would bring his father back to her, and then everything would change. Swein's hold on his son must weaken when Cnut had a son of his own, and her own influence would be that much stronger.

It was true that she would have to be patient, but she need not wait for Swein to die to get all that she wanted. She need only wait for the birth of her son.

October 1007
Winchester, Hampshire

"Ange will want a carrot, Edward," Emma said. "I hope you brought one with you."

It was late afternoon, and she and Hilde were walking briskly toward the stables, each with a firm grip on one of Edward's small hands. He was nearly three winters old now, and they were playing one of his favorite games, lifting him over the puddles on the path so that he crowed with delight.

As she breathed in the scent of ripe fruit that wafted from the nearby orchard, Emma whispered a brief prayer of thanksgiving. England had been at peace this summer, and after three years of dearth, the harvest had been plentiful. The Viking army that had wreaked such havoc the year before had abandoned Wight Isle to its fishermen and seabirds— the war leaders content with the huge tribute paid by the king. This past summer they had not returned, so perhaps God had finally heard the pleas of the English. Perhaps, too, her brother's warnings of planned invasions by the Danish king were groundless.

Perhaps her son would grow up in a kingdom at peace.

She looked down at the small, fair-haired head beside her as Edward, on his own feet for the moment, pulled his hand free and patted the leather pouch strapped to his belt—a recent, treasured gift from the king.

"Ange's carrot is here," he said.

She laughed and took his hand again. "Then I am sure that you will be most welcome."

"Will my father's horse be there too?" he asked. "The black one?"

"Yes, the king's horse will be there."

And even the big black one, as Edward called him, would be placid enough just now to take a gift from a boy's small hand, for the king had ridden to the hunt this morning.

It had been a family party for the most part, excepting Lord Eadric, who had been in constant attendance upon Æthelred since December. She wished that he would go back to his lands in Shropshire, for she could not like the man. Behind his dark good looks and honeyed words she sensed a calculating mind and an emptiness of soul that chilled her.

It should have been Athelstan, not Eadric, at the king's side today, she thought unhappily. But there had been a heated argument between father and son when Æthelred first announced that he would appoint Eadric as ealdorman of Mercia. After that quarrel even Edmund had not been able to dissuade his brother from leaving the court, and so they had not seen Athelstan since the Easter gathering.

It worried her, this widening gulf between Athelstan and his father while the king depended more and more on his new ealdorman. Eadric was a man who could charm at will, yet whenever she listened to him speak she felt as if the world tilted slightly—as if the earth was not quite firm beneath her feet. Every instinct warned her that Eadric was not a man to trust, that there was another face behind the one that he showed the world. Which of them, she wondered, did the king see?

When they reached the stables and stepped inside, she heard a girl's laughter. Glancing around for the source she spotted a couple embracing in a shadowy corner—a lovers' tryst, apparently. She might have been amused except that the girl was Edyth, and no matter who the man was, the little game they were playing had to be stopped.

"Go see Ange," Emma said to her son, who trotted off happily with Hilde. Then she frowned at the couple in the shadows. "My lord," she said, aiming the words like stones at Edyth's companion.

He unwrapped himself from around the king's daughter, turned, and bowed. She caught her breath, struck by the sensation of the earth shifting, and wishing that she had something harder than words to throw at him. Eadric and Edyth! Here was something she had not suspected. She thought back to today's hunt. Had there been glances, touches that she had not seen? Was she so blind? But she could recall nothing, no sign of an attachment between them.

"Leave us, my lord," she commanded. "Edyth, you will stay."

Eadric glanced once at Edyth, bowed again to Emma with all the grace and self-assurance of a preening cat, and made his exit. Emma turned to her stepdaughter, who was looking offended when she should have been abashed. *Sweet Virgin*, did the girl not even realize how she had compromised herself?

"What is it?" Edyth's voice was tart with impatience.

Emma managed to control the anger that was making her blood pound. She could imagine the argument that was going to ensue, and although a byre might be a fitting place for it, she did not trust herself to deal calmly with Edyth just now.

"We will not speak of this here," she snapped. "Go to my chamber and wait for me."

With a smirk that made Emma want to slap her, Edyth stalked out of the stable, head held high. As Emma watched her go, she called to mind that other Edyth, the fair-haired little girl who had once begged her for stories and had brought kittens to show her. How she missed that child! This Edyth, who was all sweetness and deference with the king, was as obstinate and intractable as an ill-bred colt with her.

She drew in a long breath, voicing a prayer for the patience she was certain to need for the confrontation to come. The last time they had battled, Edyth had been the winner. Just after Christmas she had pleaded with her father that she was too old to stay in the queen's chambers with the younger children. She had insisted that as she was nearly thirteen and Ælfa nearly twelve, they should have their own quarters.

Unmoved by Emma's arguments against it, Æthelred had granted Edyth's request.

When she reflected on her own girlhood, Emma could not recall a moment when she had not been under the strict supervision of someone else—her mother, her nurse, her sister, or her brother's wife. It had seemed to her a grave mistake to allow Edyth so much freedom, but the king never paid enough attention to his daughter to see the headstrong, surly Edyth that she had come to know.

She would have to tell him about Eadric, and it would be neither easy nor pleasant, for Eadric was golden in the king's eyes. Nevertheless, that gilding would be somewhat tarnished once the king realized that the ealdorman had cast covetous eyes and hands on his daughter, and that was all to the good.

Emma found Edyth waiting for her, seated in a ribbon of sunlight, industriously embroidering a length of delicate silk. The girl's mouth was still set in that irritating smirk, but Emma schooled herself to be patient.

"I wish to discuss what you were doing in the stable," she began.

"What?" Edyth said, not looking up. "Kissing Eadric?"

So much for patience, Emma thought. She reached down and snatched the embroidery frame out of Edyth's hands.

"You are making light of it," she snapped, "but surely you understand that you must be circumspect in your behavior toward all of the men of the court. As the king's daughter, you are not free to show favor to any man—especially in that way—no matter what your personal inclinations and no matter how much he may importune you." She had no doubt that Eadric was the moving force in this. "However strong the temptation, Edyth, you absolutely cannot give in to it. You must give me your word that what happened today will not happen again."

Edyth folded her hands and looked up at her then, her back straight as a board.

"I can make no such promise," the girl said, "and I confess that I do not understand your concern. Surely my father has told you that Lord Eadric and I are to be wed at Yuletide."

There was a look of amusement and triumph on her face, and Emma felt yet again that her world had suddenly shifted.

"That cannot be," she whispered.

"Has he not mentioned it, then?" Edyth asked, although Emma could tell from the bold look on Edyth's face that she was well aware that the king had said nothing to her of a betrothal. "Ælfa, too, will be wed at Yuletide. To Lord Uhtred. It is all arranged."

Blow upon blow, Emma thought, and this one worse than the first. It demanded all her composure not to recoil from it. Ælfa to marry! The girl was so quiet and shy that she seemed far younger than her twelve winters. To wed her to a man like Uhtred was akin to mating a rabbit to a wolf.

No. It had to be a lie. The ealdorman of Northumbria was not even free to marry. It was impossible!

"Lord Uhtred already has a wife."

"Yes," Edyth agreed. "He has gone to Jorvik to rid himself of her. It should not take very long, as my father particularly desires that it be accomplished quickly." She stood up and smiled. "May I be excused, my lady? I wish to return to my own chamber now if you have nothing more to say to me."

For a moment they faced each other, and it seemed to Emma that the seven years' difference in their ages suddenly contracted to nothing. She could think of a thousand things she wished to say to the girl—first and foremost to beware of Eadric, to hold herself somewhat apart from a man whose ambition might outpace his abilities.

But Edyth was to wed Eadric. She could not separate herself from him, nor would she wish to do so. The girl desired this marriage. Her exultation at having won such a prize as Eadric was writ plain across her face. She would see only the man's charm and his high standing with the king—and Edyth idolized the king. She must believe that marriage to Æthelred's favorite could only increase her value in the eyes of her father, a man who for years had paid no heed to his daughters. Edyth, who hungered for her father's attention and respect, would hope to earn that through this alliance. It would give her greater status at court, and she could expect to wield far more influence with the king as Eadric's wife than she ever had as Æthelred's daughter.

More than that, it would give Edyth the opportunity to step out from under the shadow of a queen—perhaps even to step in front of her. For Edyth, like Eadric, was ambitious.

"And what would you have said to the king had he consulted you about Ælfa's marriage to Uhtred?" Margot's bright eyes had lost none of their intelligence as she aged, and now Emma's old nurse pinned her with that familiar, discerning gaze. It was late, the young ones were asleep, and Emma finally had a free moment to discuss the king's marriage plans for his eldest daughters.

"I would have told him that Ælfa is too young to marry anyone, least of all Uhtred," she said.

"Such a response would have earned you little gratitude, I think," Margot observed. "The king is not concerned, Emma, with what is best for his daughters. He is concerned with what is best for his kingdom."

Margot was right, of course. Daughters were expendable—political game pieces on a vast board that covered all of Christian Europe. Emma's own marriage to Æthelred had been negotiated by her elder brother with little thought given to what her life would be like as Æthelred's queen.

And in truth, she understood her husband's thinking. Although England's royal daughters had often been wed to foreign princes, Æthelred was concerned with matters closer to home. He needed to do whatever he could to solidify his hold on the northern shires. He had made Eadric ealdorman of Mercia and now would bind him with blood ties through this marriage to Edyth. They would be a formidable couple, both of them hungry for power.

But it was Ælfa's fate that made her heart ache. She was prettier, sweeter, more biddable and more loving than her elder sister. And she was so young, barely twelve winters old, while the fierce Earl Uhtred, who decorated his fortress with the heads of his enemies, was nearly as old as the king. Uhtred, who had already rid himself of his first wife, was taking steps to dismiss the second. Ælfa would be the third, and with each marriage the man had garnered more lands, more wealth, and greater power. Now he would wed the daughter of the king, and it did not matter to him that she was but a child, and a fragile one at that.

"I think that the king is more concerned with what is best for Æthelred than with what is best for England," Wymarc observed.

"As to that," Margot said, "for him they are likely one and the same. But the queen knows that. I expect that there is something else about all this that worries you, my lady."

Emma frowned, hesitating even to put it into words. But she needed to unburden herself because she was weary of struggling with her fear by herself.

"The king," she said, "did not seek my counsel in this matter of his daughters. He should have included me in his decision making. At the very least he should have informed me of his plans for the girls. His daughters have neither mother nor grandmother to take their part. As Æthelred's queen, that responsibility—that privilege—is mine."

"The king's children had no mother even when their mother was alive," Margot replied gently. "She played no part in their upbringing, and they knew only caregivers and attendants. That was what the king wanted, and what he still wants. They are pawns to him, not children. Now that he has two families, he is perfectly willing to play them one against the other, and you will be caught in between. His son Edmund has been wary of you from the start, and Edyth, it seems, has come to resent you." She reached out to place her hand on Emma's knee. "Have a care, my lady. I have watched you try to mother the king's children, but you are throwing your heart against a stone. Look to your own child, and be on your guard. Æthelred will be jealous of the bond between you and Edward, and I fear he will one day do his utmost to break it."

Emma was silent, her gaze lingering on her sleeping son as she pondered Margot's warning. She could not imagine a day in her life that did not in some way revolve around Edward, for he was all the world to her. To Æthelred, though, he was—like the other children—no more than a game piece in the palm of a king, to be used in ways she could neither predict nor prevent. And this, she knew, was what lay at the root of her fear.

She went to her son, and as she bent to kiss him, murmuring a prayer for his protection, a servant appeared with a summons from the king.

Reflecting bitterly that there was but one task that Æthelred deemed suited to his queen, she threw on a shawl and, leaving her son in the care of others, she left her chambers to spend the night in the king's bed.

### December 1007
### Aldbrough, Holderness

It was raining. To Elgiva it sounded as if rocks were landing on the roof's wooden shingles, so loud that it was like a pounding inside her head. She screamed, partly to clear her brain of that drumbeat, but mostly because Cnut's child was trying to rip her apart. She did not believe in any god, but if one existed, surely he was a man. No goddess would sit back idly and allow women to go through this.

She was surrounded by so many attendants that she thought she must suffocate, but she managed to draw another gasping breath as the pain eased. They would not let her rest, though. They forced her to walk, even in the trough between contractions, even when she had begged them to let her lie down for just a little while.

"The child will come more quickly if you stay on your feet," they promised her.

And so she walked. She distracted herself from the pain by counting off the reasons that she hated Cnut Sweinson. First, because he was a man. Second, because he had planted this thing inside her. Third, because he was still cowering in Denmark at his father's side in spite of all her urgent messages that he come to her to lay claim to his son.

Every time she had sent another envoy across the sea, Thurbrand had laughed at her.

"Birthing is women's work," he had said. "Cnut knows that. Your entreaties will only provoke him and, trust me, lady, he will not heed you."

The response to her pleas had always been the same. *Lord Cnut will come when he can.* The last message had come from Swein. *Send word when you bear a son*, the messenger had said. She had slapped the servant who relayed it, and that, too, had made Thurbrand howl with laughter.

As the night dragged on the pains became more frequent, so that she had little time to think any more about Cnut. Her mind focused inward and she was consumed by the agonizing demands of childbirth until the dawn silvered the edges of the closed shutters, and all she wanted was to see her ordeal ended.

"Push!" Tyra was urging her to do what she was already doing with all her might.

She was naked now, propped on the birthing chair, sweating from her labor and from the heat that radiated from the fire pit and from the clutch of women who surrounded her. She bore down hard once more, then shouted with triumph as she felt the sudden gush of something large and solid between her thighs. Cnut, damn his eyes, had a son at last.

She went limp with the release, but almost immediately they made her push some more for reasons she was too weary to question. She complied, and when some other thing had been expelled from her, they bathed her swiftly, then helped her to her feet and guided her to the bed. They gave her a cup of warm ale and butter, and she drank it greedily, listening with satisfaction to the infant's lusty cry and the women's excited gabbling. She was exhausted, but far too elated to sleep yet. Besides, there was something else she must attend to first.

"Catla," she called out, beckoning to Thurbrand's mouse of a wife. "You must send word to Cnut. Say that he must come to me as soon as can be to acknowledge his son."

"But Elgiva," Catla's whisper was little more than a squeak, "your child is a girl. You have a beautiful daughter. Look at her!"

Catla drew aside and one of the women came forward with a squalling bundle in her arms.

Elgiva stared at the thing, but she made no move to take it.

"You lie," she whispered. "I bore a son. I must have a son."

No one answered her, and the only sound in the room was the wailing of the girl child who could not be hers, who must be some changeling they were trying to foist upon her. She flung away the ale cup and put her hands over her ears to shut out the sound.

God! Could they not find a way to silence the creature?

But they were all frozen, staring at her, gaping, and it seemed to her that this was a nightmare and she was attended by madwomen.

"Take it away!" she screamed. "Get it out!"

She wanted to throw something at them, but she was too weak. She could only curl herself into a tight ball of misery and weep for her lost son, until at last the nightmare ended and she fell asleep.

When she woke, it was to face the bitter knowledge of utter failure. The chamber was empty but for Tyra, who sat beside the fire, hands busy with her spindle. Elgiva ignored her, gazing dry-eyed into the darkness of the soot-blackened rafters high above her bed. She was hungry and desperately thirsty. Her breasts were so engorged that even the weight of the coverlet was agony. And it was all for nothing. All that work and pain, all those months of discomfort for nothing! For that was exactly what a girl child was worth to her.

The men of the north would not be persuaded to renounce their oaths to the English king, to pledge themselves to Swein and Cnut, unless they were guaranteed that another royal line—sprung from the bond between the Danish king and the northern nobility—would take its place. For that she needed a son.

All that day and for three days after, she refused to see anyone except Tyra, who brought her food and drink and who bound her leaky breasts. On the fourth day she had tired of self-pity. She rose from her bed, allowed Tyra to dress her, threw on a heavy cloak, and went outside. Walking was still difficult for her, but she made her way slowly, unhindered by anyone. She left Thurbrand's enclosure and took the eastward path that led to the cliff above the sea. It was a familiar route, for she had walked this way many times to search the horizon for Cnut's ship.

Catla, she knew, was following her. Probably the girl feared that she would throw herself from the high headland, although how Catla thought she could prevent it, Elgiva could not begin to guess. But she had no desire for self-destruction. She merely wanted to stand in the wind, to feel it buffet her, to make her feel alive again.

She came to the cliff edge, to the end of the only world that she had ever known. The sea was the color of steel, and from the horizon to the middle heavens, loops and swirls of cloud were massed in a huge bank of scarlet and black that was strikingly beautiful.

She was aware of Catla beside her now, and she said, "I will not jump, you need not worry. I have faced calamities far worse than this and they have not defeated me. Have you sent word to Cnut that he has a daughter?"

"It has been done, lady, but . . ." Catla's voice dwindled to nothing, and Elgiva wanted to scream at her to grow a spine.

"What is it that you would tell me?" She looked into the white face beside her. The girl was weeping, her nose wet and red, and all of a sudden she knew what it was that Catla could not bring herself to say. "The babe is dead, then."

"She was thriving," Catla mewed, "but this morning the wet nurse could not waken her. It was as if her spirit just slipped away in the night."

Elgiva turned her eyes back to that wall of cloud hanging over the sea. The wind gusted against her so that her cloak swirled and her eyes watered, and for long moments she was silent, watching the play of cloud and light.

"The child's death is of no consequence," she said at last. "It was a girl, and what use have I for a girl? Cnut needs a son, and now he must come back to England to give me one."

But she recalled the cold look that her husband had cast upon her before he went away, and her heart faltered. She frowned at the sea and the sky that lay between this kingdom and the land of the Danes. The mountainous clouds had shifted so that they looked no longer beautiful but ominous, a looming darkness riddled with fiery light; and suddenly she was afraid.

Without a son to draw him, Cnut might never return. She would be left alone here—a forsaken concubine with no man, no child, and nothing to cling to but her bitter hatred for Æthelred and for his whey-faced Norman queen.

A.D. 1008  This year bade the king that men should speedily build ships over all England; that is, a man possessed of three hundred and ten hides to provide one galley or skiff; and a man possessed of eight hides only, to find a helmet and breastplate.

—*The Anglo-Saxon Chronicle*

# Chapter Fourteen

September 1008
Corfe, Dorset

A thelstan settled into a corner of one of the wide, cushioned benches that lined the walls of Corfe's royal lodge. A servant placed a cup of ale close to his hand, and several dogs ambled over, one of them nosing his booted foot before flopping against it with a grunt. A thin haze of smoke from the fire pit hung just below the roof thatch, and the hall smelled pleasantly of wood smoke and roast meat. On the walls, deer hides and antlers hung as mute testaments to the lodge's purpose and to the wealth of game on this Isle of Purbeck.

He stretched, rotating his right arm before him as he tried to ease muscles unused to the demands of a hunting bow. The summer had been uneventful, thank God, and this refuge peaceful—at least until his brothers and their companions had descended upon it like a pack of young wolves. For the moment, though, tired from stalking deer in the hills, the men were relatively quiet, and he thought there could be no better place to spend a dank September afternoon.

He was fond of this hall, in spite of its sordid history of treachery and murder. He did not know the exact spot where his uncle, the sainted King Edward, had been slain. His father could have shown him the place, but he had not set foot here since the day Edward died, and it was the king's distaste for Corfe that made Athelstan value it all the more. His memories of this place were unsullied by his father's glowering presence or by the memory of a king who had been murdered decades ago.

His brothers felt the same, and it had become their retreat, a place where they could spend time together with their companions.

By common consent no women were allowed—not even servants, although there were girls aplenty in the nearby village, always eager for royal companionship and a little silver. He suspected that his youngest brother was enjoying the embrace of some willing maiden right now, for Edgar had stopped at one of the houses in the village as they'd passed through, waving the rest of them to go on without him. He would have his pick of the girls, to be sure. With his even temper, comely face, and liberal hand, Edgar was even more popular around here than the martyred king who drew pilgrims and their purses to the village church dedicated to him.

He picked up his cup and slugged back a mouthful of ale, wiping his lips afterward with the back of his hand as he eyed each of his younger brothers in turn. Edmund, who liked to keep his ear to the ground and who paid well for information, stood with a group of men near the fire, his dark head cocked to one side. He glanced now and then toward the door, but for the most part he seemed to be listening intently to what was likely some nugget of local gossip. If it were useful, Edmund would share it with him later.

Off to one side of the hall, Edrid and Edwig had cleared a space on the sleeping platform and were throwing dice with half a dozen companions. He watched their gaming for a while, frowning when Edwig rose to his knees, leaned toward one of his men, and began to cuff him sharply about the face. His victim did not even attempt to fend off the blows—Edwig was an ætheling, after all—and Athelstan was about to put a stop to it when Edrid ordered his brother to leave off. Edwig laughed uproariously and turned back to the game, nearly falling off the platform as he did so because he was filthy drunk.

*Christ*, he'd been drunk for days. The fact that he'd managed to stay astride a horse this morning was a testament to either his skill or his luck, neither of which could be counted on forever. Drunk or sober, Edwig took great pleasure in needling men until he'd driven them past caution and almost invariably to violence. Twice now the king had paid wergild for beatings that had ended in death. Edwig, though, would not always be able to count on his father or his brothers to get him out of trouble. One day, thought Athelstan, he would come to a bad end.

That thought brought to mind the words of the foreboding prophecy that he had succeeded in muting but that nevertheless still rang in his memory. True words or not, he reflected, Edwig's road would surely be a bitter one if someone did not throttle some sense into him. Although, at seventeen, it was likely already too late.

His musings were interrupted when a man came through the screens passage and addressed Edmund, who, Athelstan suddenly realized, must have been watching for him. A moment later the newcomer made his way purposefully to Athelstan's bench. It was Wulfnoth of Sussex, one of the king's thegns. He had been traveling hard, for his boots and cloak were mud-spattered, and the face beneath his short thatch of gray hair was lined with weariness.

Athelstan nodded to him, noting that the hall had suddenly cleared until only his brothers and an ancient, trusted servant remained. Old Osric busied himself fetching stools and more ale, and Athelstan took another pull from his cup to fortify himself against whatever his brothers and Wulfnoth were about to spring on him. As he swallowed he glowered at Edmund.

What was he up to now? Surely this was not about Elgiva again; the girl had not been seen for two years, and if she had any sense at all she was tucked up in some safe haven in the lowlands across the sea. Wulfnoth could have nothing to do with *her*.

Could he? Was it possible that he had found her in Sussex somewhere, hiding under their very noses?

Muttering a curse under his breath he sat up a little straighter and wished he were with Edgar, happily whoring in Corfe village.

"It appears," he observed ruefully, "that someone has called a council."

"Stinking waste of time, councils," Edwig slurred. He had propped himself against one of the hall's columns, ale cup in hand.

Athelstan was impressed that Edwig could stand up at all. "Should we not wait for Edgar?" he asked.

"I have sent for him," Edmund replied. "Wulfnoth, here, represents a number of the southern lords. He wishes to speak of Eadric."

Not Ælfhelm's daughter, then. *Thank God.*

"Ah, the infamous Eadric," he said, raising his cup to Wulfnoth, who, everyone knew, detested Eadric. *Jesu,* they all detested Eadric, but Wulfnoth had more reason than most. "The man who was promoted to ealdorman above at least one other far more deserving candidate." he said, nodding toward Wulfnoth, who scowled, "and whose influence with the king appears to be growing daily. My sister's adored husband and my father's darling. What more is there to say about Eadric?"

"That he is as vile a piece of murdering, thieving scum as ever fouled your father's court."

"Oh, that's harsh," Edwig sneered. "Surely there's been someone at least as bad in, what, thirty years?"

"Not that I can recall, my lord," Wulfnoth growled. "Eadric's actions have convinced a great many men that your father's rule has lasted well past its appointed time. There are prayers offered daily that God will gather the king to His bosom as soon as may be and thus rid us of Eadric."

"It's the first I've heard of it," Edwig said brightly. "Shall we all say amen?"

"Shut up, Edwig," Athelstan said. He turned to Wulfnoth. "I have avoided my father's councils all summer, since my opinion is rarely consulted and always ignored. What is Eadric up to now?"

"Your father has put him in charge of the fleet," Wulfnoth answered. "He is taking ships."

Athelstan leaned forward, suddenly more alert. This was a wrinkle he knew nothing about. The king had ordered all of his thegns to build ships—some lords having to build as many as ten, depending on how much land they owned. It was something that he had been urging his father to do for years as part of their defense against the Danes, but it was only when Eadric had raised the idea at this year's Easter council that the king agreed to it. By then Eadric had brought in shipwrights from Normandy, offering their services to the English magnates at three times the normal rate. By next spring, England would have a massive new fleet, and Eadric would be very, very rich. Some might call it unscrupulous. Eadric merely called it good business.

"What do you mean, he's taking ships? The vessels that the king ordered built cannot possibly be completed yet."

"Not the new ships. Eadric has sent armed men into the ports of Kent and Sussex carrying writs demanding that all seaworthy ships be turned over to him, at sword point if necessary."

"To what purpose?" Athelstan asked.

"To patrol the coast through the winter, they say, although everyone knows that the Danes would never risk sending an entire fleet across the sea during the winter gales. Our ships are all forfeit to the crown, which means, of course, to Eadric. If we want to replace them, we've got to build new ones."

"Using Eadric's shipwrights," Athelstan said.

"Exactly. He's bleeding us dry and growing fat at our expense. If a man does not have the silver to pay for building more ships, Eadric will gladly take land instead. The bastard will own properties all over Kent and Sussex before he is done."

"He sounds brilliant," Edwig blurted. "Here's what we do. We take all the silver and gold in the kingdom, give it to Eadric, and when next the Danes come raiding, we tell them to plunder *him*. Problem solved."

"This is no subject for jest, lord," Wulfnoth snapped. He turned to Athelstan. "The king has placed Eadric in charge of our coastal defenses. Aside from the fact that he is getting rich off the appointment, he knows as much about ships as a swineherd. None of the men in the southern counties want to trust their defense to Eadric, and they are questioning their oaths of loyalty to the king. They fear that his dependence on Eadric is the result of a mind weakened by age. I've heard men say that if someone else does not seize the reins of power, the king will place them in Eadric's hands, and then we are surely lost."

Wulfnoth locked his eyes on Athelstan's, and the message in them was easy to read. The men he spoke for wanted a new king.

But to unseat a king, one must have an army.

Athelstan felt all their eyes on him now. They had thrown him a challenge as if it were a banner, and they were willing him to pick it up and run with it. But where did they expect him to go? How many of them would follow him toward what was certain to be the edge of a cliff?

Years ago he had thought to raise an army against his father—a wild, desperate desire borne of youth, frustration, and rage. He had learned caution since then. *Jesu!* Just having this conversation imperiled them all.

"So you wish to persuade the king to abandon his reliance upon Eadric," he said. "Urge him to trust in someone more to your liking. Compel him by force, if necessary. Let us consider that option." He set down his cup and addressed himself to Wulfnoth. "According to you, Eadric controls the fleet and all of Mercia. Ealdorman Uhtred controls Northumbria, and Ealdorman Ælfric most of Wessex. They owe their lands and titles to the king, and they will do whatever he commands. Therefore, any man who thinks to defy the king, perhaps even lay claim to the throne, will have more than two-thirds of the fighting men in the realm pitted against him. How is he to win? Or perhaps you are come to me because you think that if I ask politely, my father will just shrug and hand over the crown?"

"He'll never do it," Edwig said. "Have to fight him for it. Scary prospect."

Athelstan ignored him. "Wulfnoth, I understand your fears, but the situation is not as dire as you seem to think. When the shipbuilding is completed we will have nearly two hundred vessels to patrol our shores. That alone may be enough to deter any enemies who think to attack us, no matter who is in command of the fleet. Even Eadric. God willing, we won't have to fight at all."

"I told you he wouldn't like it," Edwig said.

"Edwig, shut up!" Edmund barked. "Athelstan, you have not heard—"

"My lord," Wulfnoth interjected angrily, "I have taken the temper of men all over England, not just in the south. They are afraid to trust a king who listens to the poison that Eadric whispers in his ear. They fear for their titles and their lands. They have not forgotten the murder of Ælfhelm and his sons."

Athelstan raised a quelling hand.

"Ælfhelm was a traitor," he said. It galled him to have to defend his father's action against Ælfhelm, but the past could not be undone. And to encourage these men in any move against the king was unconscionable.

"That may be so," Wulfnoth admitted, "but Ælfhelm was killed before he was given the chance to answer his accusers."

"His accuser was the king and his crime was treachery," Athelstan snapped. "My father's method of dealing with Ælfhelm was unwise; nevertheless I am convinced of the man's guilt." He glared at Edmund, who knew as well as he did that Ælfhelm had been conspiring with the Danes. Edmund had even regarded their father's brutal response with guarded approval. To Wulfnoth he said angrily, "Have a care what you say now, my lord, for we are perilously close to treason ourselves. Do you trust the king so little that you would break your oaths to him and raise your sword against him? For that is what this must come to."

Edmund raised his hands in a calming gesture. "It need not lead to a battle," Edmund said. "The nobles and their ships are to meet at Sandwich in the spring. If we can gather enough men to our cause we will be in a position to challenge Eadric, wrest control of the ships from him, and strike a bargain with the king."

Athelstan shook his head. "It sounds very neat, Edmund. Very civilized. But you have forgotten one significant detail: The king is not one to bargain with his nobles."

What was it the seeress had said to him when last he saw her? *Strive to grasp what you would have.* What he would have was a kingdom entire, but it would likely break into pieces if these men were allowed to follow through with their plan.

"My lord, we are desperate," Wulfnoth insisted.

"Well, I am not." He stood up abruptly. The others rose as well and the dogs at their feet, alarmed, scattered. "Until I am desperate, I will not take up arms against my father. Nothing that you say, my lord, will shame, goad, or coerce me into doing so. There's an end to it."

Edwig laughed. "You fools. You have not bribed him yet. Offer him the queen, and he might reconsider. *Christ*, offer *me* the queen, and I will challenge the king myself."

Athelstan had had enough. He turned and smashed his fist into Edwig's sneering face, watching with satisfaction as his brother spun to the floor, senseless. Then he turned to Edmund.

"We are finished here," he said. "And I find that this hall is no longer to my liking."

As he stalked toward the door he rubbed his bruised fist. He did not regret the blow, although Edwig's taunt had been very close to the truth. He would, indeed, try to take his father's crown if he thought that, by doing so, he could win the queen as well. But he had once laid such a plan at her feet, and she had forced him to see what madness it was. England—all of it—would be his one day, but he must bide his time until the crown fell into his hands. He would not steal it.

In the yard he found that Edgar, accompanied by the two men sent to fetch him, had just dismounted. Snatching the reins of Edgar's horse he hoisted himself into the saddle.

His brother looked up at him in surprise. "What is amiss?"

"Ask Edmund." He pointed to the two hearth guards. "You men are with me," he said, and swung the horse toward the gate.

He would go to Wareham, he decided. There he would get very, very drunk and wipe from his mind all thought of his brothers, of Eadric, and of the king. Emma, he knew, would remain, for he had found no elixir that would wipe *her* from his thoughts. *Jesu!* Had he not tried? In mead halls, on the practice field, in the arms of other women? And still she haunted him.

One time only they had yielded to passion, and it had left them shattered and despairing; for Emma was bound by oath to his father and not to him, and she would not break her pledge.

He had let her go, as she had asked him to. Yet she was with him still; would be with him always.

And he could not say if it was a blessing or a curse.

He led his companions away from the lodge, down a track that meandered back and forth across the face of the hill. They had reached the lane at its foot and had nearly left Corfe behind when one of the men called out and pointed back up toward the top of the steep, turf-covered slope.

Edgar was riding down the side of Corfe Hill, clearly intending to cut them off.

"Hold," he said. "It appears that my brother wants a word."

He suspected that Edgar, ever the peacemaker, would try to persuade him to return to the hall. But he would go to hell before he would give Edmund and Wulfnoth another shot at him.

He scowled as he watched his fool of a brother navigate the steep slope—without a saddle and far too fast—grinning with delight at his own daring. Edgar would not be grinning if his mount stumbled, Athelstan thought.

And then, to his horror, the horse did stumble. One leg buckled and the great head went up as the steed lost its struggle for balance and took a hideous fall. Athelstan, cursing, leapt from his mount and ran. He dropped to his knees beside Edgar, who lay chest-down with his head twisted at an impossible angle amid stones spattered with blood.

A few steps away the horse lay screaming and thrashing, and only when the terrible shrieks ceased did some part of his mind register that one of the men must have slit the poor creature's throat. He was too stunned even to weep, and could only stare in misery at Edgar's face and its expression of mild surprise.

Unbidden, the words of prophecy rang like a knell inside his head: *A bitter road lies before the sons of Æthelred, all but one.*

"You fool," he whispered. "Edgar, you God damned stupid young fool!"

And then he wept, paying no heed to the two men who stood beside him, silent and helpless. At last he reached out and closed Edgar's eyes, then ordered the men back to the hall for help. He waited alone beside his brother's body, murmuring prayers that were as much for himself as for Edgar; for how, in God's name, was he to tell his father that another prince of England had met his death at Corfe?


October 1008
Elmsett, Suffolk

Emma lay curled upon her bed beneath a thick woolen coverlet—awake but resting. Beside her, Edward was bunched on his tummy, fast asleep, his rump in the air and his face all but hidden by silky blond curls. For the moment it was just the two of them, cocooned together as if there were no one else in the world.

Outside the manor walls a fog hung wet and heavy, as it had for the

past week, caught like a spider's web among the branches of the surrounding elms that gave this place its name. The mist colored every hour
of daylight the same pale gray, and it seemed to her that time itself had
been arrested—sun and moon forever stilled.

She had miscarried again. It was the second time since Edward's
birth that her womb had emptied itself of its tiny burden almost as soon
as she had realized it was there. The event had not been so painful as the
first time, but the emptiness beneath her heart was like a wound that
would not heal.

Next to her Edward stirred a little, and as she looked at him—so
defenseless as he slept—her love for him swelled until love and loss overwhelmed her, and her eyes filled with tears.

What if something should happen to this son of hers? How would
she continue to live? The priests advised her to petition the Almighty to
keep Edward safe; but although she offered prayers to God and gifts to
His Church, she did not trust the Lord in this. It seemed to her that He
was far too careless when it came to children. Should she ever lose Edward, only another child would bind her to this earth. So she begged the
Virgin daily for another babe. Yet with each failed pregnancy, she felt
more closely tied to her son and more desperate for another child, for
she knew that she could not keep Edward with her forever. Children
never stayed.

She closed her eyes, recalling the dashing, sixteen-year-old Edgar,
and the moment when Athelstan had entered his father's hall bringing
news of his brother's death. He had knelt at the king's feet, his face gray
with grief as he told the wretched tale of Edgar's headlong plummet
down Corfe Hill, and she had wanted to take him in her arms, to offer
him the solace that he so clearly needed. But even to say a small measure
of what was in her heart would have revealed too much. It had taken
every reserve of strength she had to remain motionless and silent at the
king's side, and when Athelstan's eyes strayed, just once, to hers, the pain
she saw there had made her weep, not for Edgar, but for Athelstan.

Æthelred, though, had heaped abuse upon his son, cursing him,
blaming him for what seemed to her could only have been an accident—
an act of that all too careless God. Athelstan had knelt there, impassive

and silent, accepting the blame, head bowed under the torrent of anger and condemnation. She had been forced to listen, mute and miserable, and only too aware that anything she might say would make matters worse.

When the king had run out of words and ordered Athelstan from the chamber she had longed to follow him, to offer some consolation that might offset the bitterness of his father's accusations; but her duty was to the king, and he had need of her. He had mourned then as a king mourns—angry, offended by fate, raging at God. He had threatened to tear down the buildings at Corfe and burn the village to the ground, swearing that because his brother and now his son had met violent deaths there, the place must be accursed.

She had listened to his fury, silently pitying him, for she knew that his words sprang from a terrible dread. Of the seven sons of Æthelred's first marriage, Edgar was the third to die. It was not Corfe that was accursed, but the king and his sons—or so the rumors went. The whispers could be heard in the dark corners of the king's halls and, she supposed, in market squares and in villages all across the land. News of this death would only add fuel to the ominous mutterings. Æthelred himself believed them, and she saw the fear of it gnawing at him. Some days were worse than others, for he would start and stare into space, transfixed, as if he could read some horrible future there. He was like a bird caught in a snare, struggling blindly against an inexorable fate. He was afraid of what the deaths of his sons portended, she guessed; afraid that the royal line of Cerdic would fade into oblivion.

It had crossed her mind that day to tell him that she was with child, but some good angel had kept her silent. Instead she had prayed for poor Edgar and wept for Athelstan, and when her husband sought to deny his own mortality in the dark hours of the night, she had given him her body—an act of compassion, for once, rather than odious duty.

The next morning when father and son had left together for the great abbey at Ely to pray for Edgar's soul, Æthelred had been unaware that she was with child. Nor, in the days that followed, did she send him word that she had miscarried. He would have seen it as further proof of God's disfavor—that his seed withered even in the womb.

On the bed beside her, Edward heaved a little sigh and woke, snuggling close to plant baby kisses on her mouth and chin. Their idyll was curtailed, though, when his nurse entered the chamber and announced that Father Martin had arrived from Northumbria and begged an audience. Edward was carted off to be fed and cosseted while Emma sent for Margot to help her dress, assuring her that after three days of rest she was fit enough to speak with the priest.

"He will have news of Ælfa and Hilde," she said as Margot, protesting that she should not stir herself yet, brought her a blue woolen cyrtel.

It had been nearly a year since Father Martin and Hilde had been among the party that had escorted twelve-year-old Ælfa to her new husband's lands in the north. Poor Ælfa. On the day of her wedding feast she had tried to hide her fear, but it had been obvious to Emma that the girl was terrified of her new husband—hardly surprising, given that Uhtred was a fierce man and a warrior with, as far as she could tell, no hint of tenderness in his nature. In the days leading up to the ceremony she had tried to counsel Ælfa, but Edyth, for many months in complete control of her younger sister and newly wed herself, had usurped that task. All Emma's efforts to speak with Ælfa were rejected, and she could only watch the nuptials with foreboding.

The next day, when Ælfa had appeared beside her new husband, she had looked wan and listless. Something had deserted her in the night—some spark of youthful hope had fled and left but a husk behind. There had been no opportunity to speak with her, though, for the party left immediately for the north. Emma was consoled by the fact that Hilde, who had attended the king's daughters for years, would be one of Ælfa's household. Hilde would surely be a help to the girl, and a confidante if she needed one.

Father Martin had traveled with them, ostensibly to make pilgrimage to the shrines in the north, but also to listen, to watch, and to gather news of anything that might be of particular interest to Emma. His messages, though, had been scarce and, when they did arrive, all too brief. Now she was eager to speak with the priest, for Hilde had sent word that Ælfa had given birth to a daughter, and Emma wished to know more.

When he entered the chamber she offered him wine and urged him to a seat on the bench close beside her. He looked well, in spite of what must have been a long, weary journey down the length of England. He had taken the time to exchange his traveling clothes for a tunic of finely woven black wool, plain but for the cross that hung from a silver chain about his neck. The intervening months since she had seen him last, she observed, had taken a toll. There were a few streaks of white in the straight gray hair that lay, flat and thin, upon his head, and his clean-shaven face looked more weathered than she remembered. When he had sipped some wine and assured her that he had been well fed in the kitchens, she asked him about Ælfa.

Father Martin pursed his lips, gathering his thoughts before he responded.

"The birth was difficult," he said at last. "Hilde believes that the girl will never have another child."

Emma exchanged a glance with Margot, who shook her head and sighed. Emma knew what Margot did not say, for it was what she herself believed. Ælfa had been too young to wed, too young and too small to bear a child.

"And Uhtred?" she asked. "Is he gentle with her?"

Father Martin hesitated, then said, "Ælfa is content with her lot. She loves the child dearly, and Uhtred is often away."

He had sidestepped her question, but she did not press him. His silence told her as much as any words could convey.

He went on to speak of the fortress that was now Ælfa's home, a forbidding place almost completely surrounded by a churning sea, forlorn and windswept but, according to the priest, with a kind of fierce beauty. He spoke of the folk who lived in the north, and of how in their minds Uhtred was more their king than Æthelred, for Uhtred's ancestors had ruled Northumbria for as long as Æthelred's forebears had ruled in Wessex. Their kin ties were to the lord they knew, not some monarch in the distant south who, even if he were to appear among them, would be eyed with suspicion.

Emma pondered this for a moment, recalling her own father's annual sojourns through Normandy to see his people and to be seen by them—something that Æthelred had never done. "The king is making a grave error," she said softly, half to herself. "The people of England must know and recognize their ruler, else how can he inspire their loyalty and trust?"

"You are right, of course," the priest said, "yet the king's father, Edgar, instituted a system of governance that has worked well now for many decades. As long as his administrators are capable and loyal, the farther reaches of the kingdom can be governed from anywhere—from the palaces at Calne or Winchester or London, it does not matter."

"If," she said, "the administrators are loyal." Ealdorman Ælfhelm had forfeited his life because of his treachery. It had been two years since Ælfhelm's death, yet the tension that his murder had stirred among the elite of England had not abated. From what she had seen and felt at the council sessions it had only increased, even among the nobles of the southern shires.

Father Martin nodded gravely, then set his cup aside and looked at her speculatively, his face creased with concern. "My lady, I think that I may have found a trace of Elgiva in Holderness," he said, "but I could not follow the rumors to their source, and so I cannot be sure if there is anything there at all."

Emma leaned forward a little. She would be glad to learn that Elgiva was alive, although she was not, by any means, eager to see her return to court.

"Go on," she said.

"Before I made my way south, I lingered for several days at the abbey in Beverley. There I heard tell of an apparition—a dark-haired woman— that first appeared in the wastelands near the sea some two years ago."

Two years ago. When Ælfhelm had been killed, and Elgiva had disappeared with no trace.

"An apparition?" she echoed. "Has no one spoken to this phantom then?"

It was perhaps no more than a fanciful tale, but such tales were sometimes rooted in fact.

"Not that anyone will admit to. She has only been seen from a distance, and never in daylight. The story is that she is under a spell, and that at dawn she turns into a black swan that nests in the meres on the eastern edge of Holderness." He raised a skeptical brow.

"And you think it may be Elgiva that is hiding there, in the wilderness?" She tried to imagine Ælfhelm's daughter biding in some nameless village on the edge of England, living like an anchorite or a wild woman, but the image would not come. Elgiva was too fond of luxury, and far too proud of her lineage to submit to such a life.

"I tried to look into the matter," Father Martin went on. "When I left Beverley I rode toward the coast, but I didn't get far—turned back at the very first village I came to by a band of armed riders. They wore no badges, so I do not know who they answered to, but they were following orders from someone, I'm certain. They were pleasant enough. No threats exactly—just friendly advice." He smiled ruefully. "They told me that there were brigands abroad, and if I rode any farther east I'd likely be murdered or, if I was lucky, robbed of my horse and belongings and left to find my way to shelter, naked and on foot. They were so concerned for my welfare that they escorted me back to Beverley and well along the southern road. When I asked them about the dark-haired phantom, they scoffed. They said it was a mad tale spun by one of the local women who had too fond a taste for ale."

"That is far more believable than a spellbound swan," Emma observed.

"But not, I think, the truth," Father Martin said. "My lady, I later learned that the Lord of Holderness is a man named Thurbrand. He governs his people much like an ealdorman, but although he pays mouth homage to Æthelred, it seems that he has little love for the king. He has even less regard for his new ealdorman, Uhtred, for their families have quarreled over land and power and cattle for generations." His brown eyes fixed on hers and he continued, "Thurbrand, I understand, was ever a friend to Elgiva's father."

Emma was silent for a moment, studying the priest and considering his words.

"So it could be," she said at last, "that this Thurbrand is indeed harboring Elgiva." Not in some wild refuge, then, but in the hall of a great lord.

"I think it could be," he said. "The question is, what's to be done?"

What, indeed, was to be done? Every action or inaction had its consequences. Elgiva's father and brothers had paid for their treachery with their lives, but her properties remained untouched. They were administered by her kin in the expectation that she would one day return, an heiress and an obedient subject of the king. Perhaps, when enough time had passed, that was exactly what Elgiva would do. She had once been the king's darling, and Emma suspected that he might not be indifferent to Elgiva's charms should she set out to beguile him again.

But the king was not the only one to consider. Ealdorman Eadric had the king's ear now, more so than any other subject in the realm. If Eadric should discover Elgiva's hiding place, he would certainly use her in some way for his own purposes. Or he might quietly kill her.

She had little love for Elgiva, for the woman had ever been her enemy and rival. But she had no desire to see her fall into Eadric's hands. If Elgiva had indeed taken refuge with this Thurbrand, why betray her? Whose purpose would it serve? Not her own, as far as she could see.

"There is nothing to be done," she said to Father Martin, "except to keep this knowledge to ourselves. To speak of it would only cause discord, whether the dark lady is Elgiva or not. Whoever she is, her presence in Holderness has gone unremarked by Eadric and his men. I am content to leave her be."

If it was Elgiva, let her stay with this Thurbrand of Holderness. If she was far from the seat of power, she could do no harm.

Long after Father Martin had left, though, Emma's thoughts lingered upon what he had said, and at last she unburdened her heart to Margot.

"What think you, Margot?" she asked. "Am I wise to keep silent about Elgiva, assuming it is Elgiva?" She stood up to pace the room, thinking aloud. "Perhaps I should send someone to discover if there is any truth to this tale of a dark lady."

"Even if it is true," Margot said thoughtfully, her hands busy with her embroidery, "it is not Elgiva that the king fears, is it?"

"No," Emma replied. "It is the man whom she might wed. Certainly not this Thurbrand, who, if Father Martin's source is correct, appears to be content with his own wife and is not like to raise an army against the king."

"And as there was no mention of a Danish lord biding with this swan lady, where's the harm?" Margot asked.

No harm at all, Emma thought, except—

There was one man she could think of who might be tempted to wed Elgiva and, with the backing of her lands and men and gold, challenge the king for his throne. If Athelstan knew where Elgiva was hidden, might he not attempt that very thing?

She did not know, and she saw no reason to place temptation in his way. For surely, she told herself, it was the possibility that Athelstan might try to seize the throne that she feared, and not that he, as his father had years ago, might fall under the spell of the Lady Elgiva.

November 1008

Redmere, Holderness

The palest glimmer of dawn light had begun to creep into her chamber when Elgiva woke to the delicious sensation of fingertips brushing along her naked hip then sweeping down toward her inner thigh. She turned over, reached for the man lying beside her in the great bed, and placed her hand lightly against his cheek.

"Again?" she whispered.

He did not answer, but began to suckle her breast, using hands and mouth to arouse her until she thought she must cry out with her need for him. But he was in no mood to hurry, and he teased and tormented her until she pleaded with him, and at last he entered her, moving from a languid to an urgent rhythm until waves of pleasure broke over her and his own release quickly followed. When he eased himself from her, she lay in his arms and studied his face in the dim light.

"I wish that you did not have to leave today," she whispered.

"Bid me stay, and I will."

Her dark hair lay spilled upon the pillows around them, and he toyed purposefully with a coil of it. She knew this game. He was a devil, tempting her to grant her own wish and compel him to stay. But they had gone over the plan yesterday for hours, and the necessary preparations had all been made. It would take him months to speak to every man on the long tally of her father's former retainers, spread as they were across a wide swath of Mercia and the Five Boroughs. Yet the task must be completed before King Æthelred's great gathering of ships at Sandwich in May, and it must begin before the household stirred this morning and someone blundered into her chamber.

"I wish that we could stay here forever," she said, tracing his lips with her finger, "but there is very little time for you to accomplish all that you must do. The sooner you leave, the sooner you will return to me."

He grimaced in mock despair before delivering one last, lingering kiss.

"Much as it grieves me, I shall do as my lady bids," he whispered, then slipped from her bed.

She turned over to watch him dress, admiring the play of muscle beneath naked skin.

"Tell me again, Alric," she said, "what you intend to say to them."

"I will say," he replied, pulling on woolen breecs, "that you are alive and well, but that you must remain in hiding because the king would have you as dead as your father and brothers. I will suggest that if they are foolish enough to keep their pledges of loyalty to Æthelred, he will reward them with betrayal—their lands forfeited, their families torn apart." Sitting down beside her he pulled on his boots. "I will assure them that Ealdorman Eadric is a butchering liar and that they should be as wary of him as they would an adder about to strike."

She sat up and rested her chin upon his shoulder. "But you must go about it slowly. Take your time. Make certain that they trust you before you reveal anything, and then do it sparingly and reluctantly. Say nothing yet of Cnut or Swein, or even of Thurbrand." Thurbrand, the bastard, was like her father—unwilling to recognize that a woman could do more than produce babies. As far as he was concerned, her role was to open her legs for Cnut and keep her mouth shut. If he knew what she and Alric were doing, he would be livid. "We must not give the game away before it is begun, and my husband, it seems, is not yet prepared to keep all his promises to me."

She had given up begging Cnut to come to her, and instead had sent messengers to his royal father with whatever news she could garner. It was meager, to be sure, but it might be of some use to him, and it was her way of reminding the Danish king that he had sworn that he would one day take Æthelred's crown.

Alric, boots in place, turned to face her. "I am to sow mistrust and discontent, without drawing too much attention to myself."

She nodded, satisfied.

"You have it exactly. When Swein does come, we want the men of the north reluctant to take up arms against him." She bit her lip. Swein must come. And Cnut must come before that, and very soon. She needed a son. "It would seem," she said, thinking aloud, "that in my husband's absence I must be the one to lay the foundation for his rule. Perhaps one day he may even appreciate my efforts."

He took her hand and whispered, "I have no doubt, my lady, that he will build upon your work; but I suspect that he will never appreciate you as you deserve."

He kissed her palm, and when he released her, she removed from her thumb a golden ring engraved with her name.

"Use this as a token that you have been sent by me," she said, placing the ring on his smallest finger. "It was a gift from a faithless king, and it is fitting that we use it to undermine his people's trust in him. Have a care, though, who sees it. Eadric has spies everywhere."

He nodded and, getting to his feet, threw on a fur-lined hooded cloak and bowed low before her. He looked every inch the royal emissary, and she nodded her approval.

When he left her, slipping from her chamber as quietly as a wraith, the chilly room seemed to grow even colder. She lay back down among the bedclothes and began to compose in her head the messages that she would send to Swein and to Cnut, urging them to bring their army to England. Would any words of hers, though, move them to action? It had been more than a year since Cnut had sailed to Denmark. She could not even remember what he looked like but for his height and his fiery hair.

She closed her eyes, conjured Alric's image with no effort at all, and smiled. Cnut had been away too long, and after so many years of playing at seduction with Alric—a game that had always ended in a draw—she had at last decided to give in.

It was possible, she supposed, that she would regret taking him as her lover, but she did not think it likely. Alric knew as well as she did that his future success depended on her, and that hers depended upon Cnut. The son of the Danish king was their key to power, and when her husband returned to her bed, Alric would not complain.

She drew one of the furs around her and, leaving her warm bed she went to one of the large coffers that stood against the wall. The key to this one she kept on a chain about her neck, and now she used it to unlock the great chest. The prize she pulled from it was a highly polished wooden box that fit in the palm of her hand. Opening it she considered the four chambers within—a large one, and three smaller ones—and the red, black, and white glass beads that they held. Tyra's instructions, when she had presented her with this gift, had been precise. Starting on the first day of her courses, she must each day put a red bead in the large compartment until her bleeding ceased. Then she must daily place a white bead to join the red.

"When Cnut returns to you," Tyra had said, "the white-bead days will be most important, for on those days you will be most likely to conceive a child."

After the white beads had all been moved to the larger chamber, the black beads, marking the days when no man's seed would grow within her, must be placed there in their turn.

Elgiva bit her lip. This morning the largest compartment held all the red and white beads as well as a scattering of black. She took another black bead from its nest, placed it in the larger chamber, shut the lid tight, and replaced the box and locked the coffer.

If the beads could be used to help her conceive, then it stood to reason that if used contrariwise they would keep her belly from swelling while her husband was across the seas.

If Tyra's beads should prove faulty—the thought of what might happen then sent a shudder through her as she scurried back to her bed. But Tyra had assured her that the beads would work, and she had come to trust her sullen slave about such matters, as did everyone else, it seemed, in Holderness.

"She is a Sámi woman," Catla had told her, "taken from her homeland in the far north. She has the gift of foretelling."

Elgiva knew nothing about the Sámi people, but she had watched Tyra cast the rune sticks, and the watching had raised gooseflesh along her arms. It seemed to her that Tyra read more than just the markings carved on those yellowed bits of bone. She read hearts and minds, too, as if every face she looked at had been scored with runes that only she could see.

"Do you ever lie to people?" she had asked Tyra once. "Tell them what you believe they want to hear instead of what you have read in the runes?"

It was the only time she had ever seen fear in the Sámi woman's eyes.

"My gift is from the gods," Tyra had answered her. "I dare not lie, for to abuse such a gift is to risk the gods' vengeance."

So, Tyra was a truth teller as well as a rune reader—and because of that, Elgiva considered her perhaps the most valuable of all the gifts that Cnut had given her.

She lay back on her pillows and listened to the sounds that had begun to filter into her chamber from the yard outside—youths drawing water, women stirring up the kitchen fires, the murmur of voices speaking English as well as Cnut's Danish tongue. They were her people now, part of her household and this holding that she rented from Thurbrand—an excellent use of Cnut's silver as far as she was concerned. She could wish that it was farther away from the dwelling of Thurbrand and that mouse, Catla, but she might one day have need of Thurbrand's fortified walls.

There were men who continued to search for her. Now and then someone would appear in one of the nearby villages asking questions, and Thurbrand would send a party out to deal with them. Only a few weeks ago a Norman priest had come as close as Beverley, and she had been alarmed when she heard of it, for she feared that it was someone sent by Emma.

But Tyra had cast the rune sticks and had told her that she need fear no priest.

The woman had said nothing about kings, though, or their henchmen, and Elgiva had no doubt that Æthelred and Eadric wanted her dead.

**A.D. 1009**  This year were the ships ready, that we before spoke about; and there were so many of them as never were in England before, in any king's days, as books tell us. And they were all transported together to Sandwich; that they should lie there, and defend this land against any out-force.

—*The Anglo-Saxon Chronicle*

# Chapter Fifteen

April 1009

London

I t was nearing noontide when Æthelred took his place beneath the royal canopy set close beside the Thames. He acknowledged the greetings of the nobles and prelates who clustered about the dais, and when he was seated he beckoned to Edmund and Edyth to take the chairs on either side of him. He spared a glance at a second pavilion that had been erected for the queen.

Emma, however, had sent word that she was unwell and would not be present today. She must be ill indeed, he thought, to forgo such an important occasion. It was unlike her. The boy was here though, young Edward, with his playfellow to keep him entertained, as well as a small mob of the queen's attendants to keep the boys from venturing too near the water's edge.

Shielding his eyes against the sun he looked to the river and nodded with satisfaction. Most of the inhabitants of London, it seemed, had turned out for the blessing of the ships. They thronged the shore on both sides of the Thames and crowded along the railings of its massive wooden bridge, shouting and waving, tossing flowers and leafy garlands onto the shimmering surface of the water. Hundreds had clambered aboard the ferries and barges that normally plied the river but that today served as viewing stands for the central event.

In the middle of the channel, bright sails billowing and banners snapping, thirty of his newly built warships were maneuvering into position, preparing for the moment when the tide would turn and carry them past his pavilion and eastward to the sea. Not since the time of King Alfred had so many warships filled the Thames. Yet this was only a fraction of the fleet that would gather next month at Sandwich. From there they would guard his coasts, able to intercept and engage any fleet that threatened his realm.

It would be a massive, floating safety net, built by his thegns and blessed by his bishops, yes, but ordered into existence by him. As he drank in the sight of the mighty ships he felt his heart swell with pride. This was the answer to the dark dreams that had filled his broken nights. How many times had he wakened in the silent hours to find the cold, piercing eyes of his dead brother's wraith gleaming at him from the shadows—a midnight companion that terrorized him still?

But not today. There was no place in the brightness and glitter of this day for the shade of a dead king, and the only anxiety that gnawed at him now had to do with his eldest son. Athelstan, who should have been standing here beside him, had left the city. The rest of his sons were at their posts—Edmund and Edward here, and the other two aboard their assigned ships. Athelstan, though, had left London last night after yet another quarrel about Eadric.

And so, on a day when he should have had no cares to mar his triumph, he was forced to consider what devilry his son might be stirring up.

He glanced at Edmund, who was silently observing the activities on the water. Edmund and Athelstan had ever been close, but recently there had been a chill between the brothers—or so Edyth had advised him. Something had occurred at Corfe last fall, she had suggested, perhaps something to do with Edgar's death. Whatever it was, it seemed to have placed a wedge between his two eldest sons.

That was likely all to the good, he mused. If there was a breech between the brothers, he might be able to make use of it.

He had long suspected Athelstan of working against him in secret, of forging alliances that he might one day use against his king and father. *Christ!* Even in public his eldest son had ever been ready to argue against his decisions, and in council he had been far too quick to voice objections. Last night's outburst against recent powers granted to Eadric was only the latest skirmish in the long battle between them. If Athelstan was entertaining any thoughts of moving against him—or against Eadric, for that was far more likely—Edmund might well be privy to them. And what better time to glean information from Edmund than now, when the brothers were at odds and this one perhaps less guarded about revealing whatever he may know or guess about the actions of the other?

He did not lift his gaze from the river, but murmured to Edmund, "I'm told that when Athelstan set out from London last night, he went north. Did he tell you where he was going?"

Now he chanced a quick look at his son, seeing the dark brows furrow and the eyes narrow as Edmund squinted into the sunshine.

"He will meet us at Sandwich, my lord," Edmund replied, tight-lipped.

The gathering at Sandwich was set for late in May, some three weeks hence. And Edmund had not, in fact, answered his question.

"He was not riding toward Sandwich, Edmund," he growled, "and I would know where he will spend the intervening time." He hesitated, still uncertain as to where Edmund's true loyalties lay. Would he speak the truth, even if he knew it? Edmund might lie if he thought it necessary to protect his brother. "I am concerned for Athelstan," he added. "I fear that he may be playing some dangerous game, one that he will come to regret."

He shifted his eyes toward Edmund again and, noting that his son was no longer looking at the ships, followed Edmund's gaze to where young Edward stood pointing at the colorful sails upon the water, his face lit with boyish delight.

"What kind of game would you play, my lord," Edmund asked, "if your father named the infant son of a foreign bride his heir?"

Æthelred snorted. "Does Athelstan fear Edward so much? A child with few supporters?"

"Few?" Edmund echoed. "At your command, my lord, your nobles have pledged to accept Edward as your heir. Even if most of them disavow that oath in the time to come," he lowered his voice, "there are many powerful men who would be eager to see Edward inherit your throne. The brother of your Norman queen, I think, would like to extend his reach beyond the Narrow Sea should the opportunity arise. And," he said, even more softly, "there are men of influence here in England who would seek even greater power by controlling the regency of a young king."

There was no mistaking this barely veiled reference to Eadric. They were jealous of Eadric, these sons of his, and that suited him well enough. Jealousy among his family might be dangerous, but it had its uses.

"I am far more concerned with what plots are brewing now than in those that may surface after my death," he growled, impatient with Edmund's skill at avoiding his question. "I will ask you again. Where is your brother?"

"I do not know, my lord," Edmund grunted. "I am not in his counsels." He looked toward Edward again and said, "I am surprised that the queen is not here today."

"She is ill." Æthelred dismissed the subject of Emma with a flick of his hand.

Edyth, seated on his left, now bent her head close to his. "The queen's illness is cause for joy, my lord," she whispered. "She is with child and has known it for some weeks. I wonder that she has not yet told you."

On the bridge, Archbishop Ælfheah, garbed in a brilliant gold chasuble, his miter rising above the heads of the white-robed priests who surrounded him, raised his arms to invoke the blessing. In the ensuing silence, as the archbishop intoned the prayers, Æthelred digested Edyth's words.

She was right. If the queen was with child, he should have been told immediately. She'd had plenty of opportunity, for he saw her almost daily, so why had she not done so?

He fingered his beard as he tried to encompass the mind of his queen. Perhaps she feared that her condition would give him an excuse to bar her from a seat at his council, and of course it would. He would take advantage of it immediately. Let her stay sequestered in the queen's apartments, where she could not meddle in the affairs of his kingdom. Too many people looked to her for favors and privileges, usually churchmen and usually at his expense; he would be glad of an excuse to put a stop to it.

His eyes fell again upon young Edward, and he watched as the boy bowed his head in an attitude of prayer that was somewhat belied by his incessant fidgeting from one foot to the other.

He had never wanted Edward to remain at court under the influence of his Norman mother. Now that Emma was with child again, he could at last pry her son from her side. He would send Edward to one of the abbeys and have him schooled in disciplines far removed from the political lessons that his mother would instill in him. Let them make a priest of him, perhaps even a bishop, so that he could one day be of use to an English king. That had ever been the plan he'd devised for the boy. Despite naming Edward as his heir, he had never intended that the child should actually rule. It had been merely a move to bedevil his eldest sons and to garner the goodwill of Emma's brother Richard.

Later today he would speak with the abbot of Ely about taking the boy north with him, for he must strike before Emma could think of some way to prevent him. It would be just like his lady wife to set her favorite bishops or, God forbid, Archbishop Ælfheah against him to compel him to leave the boy in her care.

The archbishop appeared to have finished his interminable blessing, and now a choir of monks from the abbey at the West Minster began to sing a Latin hymn. Priests posted all along the bridge rail used leafy branches to fling holy water onto the ships clustered below. Soon the ceremony would be over, the tide would have turned, and London's ships would begin to move with it, eastward toward the sea.

And still, despite his pleasure at the sight of the ships and his satisfaction at having determined the disposition of his youngest child, Æthelred toyed with his beard and wondered where his eldest son had got to and what mischief he might be planning.

Two days after the king's new ships sailed to join the rest of the fleet at Sandwich, one of London's dense fogs wrapped an enormous, wet paw around the city, a grip that only seemed to tighten as the morning progressed. Emma was content to be within doors on such a day, especially here; for the London palace was the newest and finest of all the royal dwellings. Over the past three years, Æthelred had spared no expense in rebuilding and refurbishing what had once been a fortress housing a Roman army. The result was wondrous.

Her own apartments were constructed of wood above a lower floor of mostly Roman stonework that had been repaired and reinforced. She had housed her Norman hearth guards in the lower hall, while the spacious chambers on the upper floor accommodated her household of nearly thirty women and children. In the queen's chamber there were windows, narrow and high, with panes made of thick glass instead of horn. Even on days like this, light spilled through them like a radiant waterfall.

This morning she was seated on a low, cushioned bench, with a small book on her lap and a boy on either side of her. The book's pages were filled with drawings of strange creatures that thrilled her young companions, although Emma found them unsettling and ugly. What was it about monsters, she wondered, that was so appealing to little boys?

She turned a page, composing a tale to fit the image that greeted her of a headless man whose enormous eyes, nose, and mouth gaped at her from below his shoulders. By now he was a familiar sight, for this book was a favorite, and she drew her story from bits and pieces of previous tales.

From time to time she glanced toward the others in the chamber who were listening while they worked. Wymarc, Margot, and Wulfa were clustered on benches in the center of the room, fingers and needles busy. The altar cloth that they were hemming was all but finished, and Emma considered it one of the most beautiful that had been produced in her hall. Made of bloodred silk and trimmed with a wide band of cloth of gold, the central ornament was a golden rood that she had embroidered herself with painstaking care. With every stitch she had whispered a prayer to Saint Bride, the patron saint of infants, imploring her protection for the child growing within her. On the morrow she would tell the king that she was again with child, and she would carry the cloth herself to St. Bride's Church before she left with the court for Sandwich.

She had just ended her tale with a desperate fight to the death between two fierce monsters when a servant entered to announce the arrival of the king's steward, Hubert, who followed only a half step behind him.

"Good day, Hubert," she said, as he made a perfunctory reverence and then stood solemnly before her, hands folded. She eyed him warily, this dark-robed, weasel-faced little cleric, for they had little liking for each other. Hubert had served the king faithfully for decades as private scribe, casual counselor, and, she had reason to believe, household spy. His appearance in her chamber meant that he bore some message of import from the king; and from the smug expression on his face she suspected that she was not going to like what she was about to hear. "There is nothing amiss, I hope," she said.

"The king bids you to prepare your son for a journey, my lady. He is to leave for the Abbey School at Ely within the hour."

She felt Edward, beside her, give a little start of surprise. She was surprised as well, and frightened; but she would not allow Hubert to see it.

"What you ask is impossible," she said, with far more compsure than she was feeling. "It will take far longer than that to prepare my son for so arduous an undertaking. If I am not mistaken, it must be a journey of at least five days to reach Ely."

"The necessary preparations have all been completed, my lady. You need only supply the boy with whatever clothing he must have on the journey. The king trusts that he's given you sufficient time for that." He wore the confident expression of a man who has just made a winning throw of the dice, and she knew that she was beaten.

She looked toward Margot, who slipped from the room and would return in a moment, Emma was certain, with a handful of servants. Margot knew as well as she did that there could be no fighting the inevitable. The command that she had so dreaded had come at last. The king would take her son away from her, and she could do nothing to prevent it. Why now, though? And why with such dispatch? It felt like a punishment, although she suspected that it was nothing more than Æthelred carelessly flaunting his power. He would not, though, have it all his way.

She swallowed what felt like a tide of grief and apprehension that was rising in her throat. She must not frighten Edward. For his sake she had to remain calm, had to make him view this as a huge adventure.

She wrapped her arm around her son and hugged him to her side.

"Well, Edward," she said lightly, "the king has given us an order and we must obey it. You are too old now to study with only Father Martin to help you, so you will go to a great abbey, where you will have many teachers."

His face, though, was clouded with doubt.

"Are you not to come with me?" he asked.

She ran her fingers through his blond curls, imagining him at Ely, alone and frightened, without any familiar faces about him, without her there to care for him. Then she banished the picture, for if she dwelt on it she would weep, and that she must not do.

"I cannot come, my love," she said. "But I am sure that the king will send a grand company with you, with banners and men-at-arms, just as if the king himself were going. Now, here is your nurse to help you choose the things that you wish to take with you. Wulfa and Robert will help too."

Edward's small face puckered with distress as he slipped off the bench, but he did not cry.

"May I take this book?" he asked her gravely.

"Of course," she said, closing the book and handing it to his nurse.

When the children were gone she turned again to Hubert.

"Who is to attend Edward on the journey?" she asked. At least it would not be Edmund. He had already left for Sandwich.

"The bishop of Elmham and the abbot of Ely will take responsibility for him. They each have large retinues, and they are assembling at St. Paul's, where the ætheling is to join them. The king wishes his son to wait upon him in the great hall before his departure."

She nodded, waited until the chamber door had closed behind the steward, then rose from the bench, restless and angry. There was a great deal to do, for she would not send her son to Ely without attendants from her own household. She bid one of the servants to fetch Father Martin and turned to Wymarc, who had come to her side and now took her hand.

"You knew this had to come," Wymarc said.

"He is not yet five winters old," she replied bitterly. "He is too young to understand why he is being sent away, and I will not allow him to be alone among strangers." Why had she not prepared for this?

Because, she told herself, she had not wanted to face it, even in her mind. Now she must find a way to deal with it in the space of an hour.

She looked into Wymarc's eyes and saw her own grief reflected there. She saw understanding, as well, and resignation. Wymarc had already guessed what was in her mind.

"You wish Robert to accompany Edward," Wymarc said. She drew a breath. "Yes, of course he must. Edward will need a companion."

Emma squeezed her hand. Wymarc had surmised some of it, but not all.

"I wish you both to go," she replied. "It will be to Robert's advantage to continue at Edward's side, and you must attend both our sons. Take lodgings somewhere near the abbey, and send me word of Edward as often as you can. Father Martin must go as well; he will be welcome within the abbey precincts." She paused, casting about in her mind for what else must be done. "Some of my Norman hearth guards will accompany you, and Edward must have a body servant who can see to his needs, someone we can trust. Young Lyfing, I think."

It was all happening too swiftly. She felt as if she were being buffeted by a windstorm, helpless in the grasp of something she could not control. She studied Wymarc's face, as familiar to her as her own, then pulled her into a long embrace.

"I shall miss you," Emma whispered. "I cannot guess how long we may be parted, but Edward must have someone nearby he can turn to should he have need of comfort. Stay as close to him as you can."

"I will," Wymarc said. "He is like my own son. You know that."

At last they drew apart, and brushing a kiss against her friend's brow Emma said, "Make haste. You have very little time."

Wymarc nodded, and when she was gone Emma pressed her fingertips over her eyes in an effort to compose her face into something resembling equanimity before going to assist Edward. When she took her hands away, she found that Margot was at her elbow with a cup of wine in her hands.

"Drink just a little," Margot said. "It will calm you, and that is how Edward must remember you."

She took the cup, obediently swallowed once, twice, then handed the cup back to Margot with a grateful smile.

"I want you to wrap the crimson altar cloth in a length of waxed wool," she said. "It must go to Ely with Edward. I do not know what gifts the king will send as compensation for sheltering our son, but the abbot will expect recompense from me as well."

She could not send Edward empty-handed. Indeed, she would make certain that the abbot was beholden to her. The silken altar cloth embroidered in gold would be but the first gift of many. St. Bride's would have to wait.

An hour later, on the steps of the chapel near the west gate, Emma gathered her son into her arms to bid him farewell.

"I will give you our special kiss," he said, his arms about her neck.

She nodded and closed her eyes as he planted kisses on her forehead, her eyelids, her lips, and the tip of her nose.

"God bless you," Edward said, just as he always did when he bade her good night.

"God keep you safe," she answered, although she was not certain that God could be trusted in this.

Edward was lifted up and settled, like Robert, in front of one of her Norman retainers. Wymarc rode behind them, and as the company set out, she raised a hand in farewell. Emma watched, dry-eyed, as they disappeared into the mist. Then she went in search of the king.

He was still in the great hall, where he had taken leave of Edward, surrounded by clerks and attendants, finalizing arrangements, she imagined, for the upcoming ship gathering at Sandwich. She sidestepped Hubert's attempt to head her off and went straight to the dais, where Æthelred was seated at a table littered with documents.

"I have followed your command regarding my son, my lord," she said, "but I would know why you insisted on sending Edward away in such a cold, heartless manner. It was cruelly done, and I wish to know your reasons."

Her words silenced every other voice in the hall, but she did not falter. Let them all listen. Perhaps they were as curious to hear the answer as she was.

"You are distraught, lady," he said without even bothering to meet her gaze. "I will discuss your concerns with you later."

"If you will look at me, my lord, you will see that I am not distraught. I am merely curious. I think, as your queen," she said, emphasizing the title, "I deserve an answer."

He did look at her then, and with the slightest flick of a finger he cleared the room of observers. That gesture was a signal of his power, utilized so casually that one might almost believe that he was not aware of how intimidating it was. But Emma knew the king, and she knew that every word and gesture had a purpose. He was reminding her that although she may be queen, her powers were merely a reflection of his own and of Edward's as his heir. And now Edward was gone.

"Are you distressed, lady, at losing your son?" he asked. "Or perhaps it is your son's apparent eagerness to leave your side that you find so upsetting."

The words were meant to cause her pain, and her first instinct was to retaliate. But she had no weapon to use against him. She could not torment him with his son's lack of feeling for him, because Æthelred cared nothing for that. He desired only that his children should fear him, and in that he had succeeded all too well.

"Instead of taunting me," she said, "you should commend me for raising my son to obey your commands without question. I still wish to know why you felt it necessary to send Edward away with so little warning."

"I have been told," he said, idly perusing one of the documents in front of him, "that you are with child. How is it that you have been so unmindful that you have not shared with me such joyous news?"

So someone had betrayed her. Stunned, she opened her mouth to answer him, but he waved her to silence.

"It is no great matter," he went on. "Now that Edward is gone, you will be able to direct all your energies toward preparations for the coming birth. To that end, you are excused from attending my councils—indefinitely."

"My lord, I only wished to be certain—"

"In three days' time I will depart for Sandwich. You and your house-hold will remain here in London, and until I set out on my journey south you are forbidden to enter my hall or my chambers unless you are summoned. I want no more outbursts such as this. Is that clear?"

"No," she snapped, "it is not clear. I am not your prisoner and nor am I a child, yet you would treat me as one. If you do not wish my counsel then I must hold my tongue, but to bar me from the court is to imply that I have committed some crime when I have done nothing wrong. Why must we be always at odds? What is my offense?"

She already knew the answer. She had offended by shouldering the responsibilities of a queen when he wanted nothing more than a bed mate. Æthelred wanted all preferments, all decision making, all power in his hands. He wanted no rivals near his throne—not his sons, not his nobles, and certainly not his queen.

"Yes, lady," he said, "it seems that we must be always at odds. Would you know why? Because against my will I was made to give you a crown, yet that gift has not satisfied you. I have granted you lands and wealth, and I have named your son my heir, and those gifts, too, have not quenched your thirst for influence. You desire to master me, and I will not be mastered. I will use you as it suits me, and just now it suits me to keep you in London while you await the birth of your child."

He was watching her now, waiting for her to make a misstep. She did not care. He had already taken her son and barred her from the court. What more could he do to her?

"And if I should wish to leave London?"

He shrugged. "Go where you please; but if you think to follow your son to Ely, you had best think again. You may have a few bishops in your palm, Emma, but the abbot of Ely belongs to me and he has his orders. You will not be welcome there." He picked up a handful of documents. "Hubert!"

She stared at him a moment longer, but he had already dismissed her from his mind. Even to try to cajole him now would be pointless. She made her way back down the length of the hall, numb with shock at how he had turned his twisted reasoning against her.

She had kept her own counsel about the child for fear that she might miscarry, little thinking that someone else would guess her condition and apprise him of it—Edyth most likely. Æthelred, with his suspicious mind, saw only cunning and, *Jesu*, she knew not what else, in her silence. Now he was using her pregnancy as an excuse to keep her from the court, something she had not anticipated. The child she so longed for, that she had prayed for, was to be her undoing. Her place at the king's side, that she had spent years carving for herself, was forfeit. He would dismiss her from the channels of power and information.

Worse even than that, he would keep her from her son; if she did nothing else, she must find a way to rectify that.

She placed her hand upon her belly. It would be six months, at least, until this child made its way into the world. Until then there was little that she could do.

Six months, she told herself, was not so long a time.

But there was little comfort in that thought. For in the life of a boy not yet five winters old, six months would be an eternity.

# Chapter Sixteen

June 1009

Kent

Athelstan and a company of fifteen men rode from Canterbury along the southern leg of Watling Street toward Sandwich. On either side of the muddy, pitted road, the flat terrain alternated between long fields of ripening grain, tracts of dense woodland, and broad meadows where newly shorn sheep huddled together for warmth.

It was nearly twilight and the sky spattered rain—a parting gift from the fierce storm that had struck two days before. The foul weather had forced them to shelter for two days in Rochester, and now they were trying to make up for lost time, with little success. The gale's fierce winds had flung tangles of branches and the occasional uprooted tree across the road, so that they had to halt frequently to clear a path through or around the debris. Athelstan chafed at their slow progress, but there was nothing to be done about it. He was already many days late, and a few more hours would make little difference.

When at last the company topped a rise and Athelstan saw Sandwich below him, the rain had stopped although the skies were still threatening. He surveyed the harbor that skirted the town on three sides, searching for a forest of masts. They were there, but far fewer than he had expected. Forty, maybe fifty ships were anchored in the wide, sheltered channel. There should have been three times that many.

He had reckoned that the fleet would not sail until mid-June at the earliest, so the absence of so many ships puzzled him. The crews were new to their captains and to one another. Some of the men were likely even new to the rowing benches, and surely they would not have taken so many vessels into the open sea so soon, even for purposes of training the crews. So where in God's name were the ships?

He led his company through the tent city that had sprung up around Sandwich to house the men who would crew the fleet, their numbers diminished now by more than half, he guessed. Inside the town gates the dwellings were all newly built, freshly thatched and painted, for Sandwich had been destroyed utterly in the Viking raids three years before. Whatever havoc the recent storm had caused had been cleared away and, no doubt due to the king's presence, the town appeared orderly and peaceful. The nobles who would dine with the king tonight had begun to gather outside the entrance to the royal hall. Athelstan skirted that group and made instead for a nearby pavilion where Edmund's banner tossed fitfully in the breeze that swooped in off the water. Directing his men to set up his own lodging near Edmund's, he dismounted and went into Edmund's tent.

His brother was speaking with two of his household guards, but he waved the men away the moment that he saw Athelstan.

"Where in Christ have you been?" Edmund demanded. "The king is suspicious as hell."

"I went into Mercia," Athelstan said, "looking into Eadric's affairs." He nodded in the direction of the harbor. "What's been happening here?"

Edmund pointed him to a stool, and a servant appeared with water and a scrap of linen. He began to scour the travel grime from his face and hands as he listened to his brother.

"We've had more trouble than you could possibly imagine," Edmund growled. "As soon as the king arrived here, Eadric's lout of a brother Brihtric accused Wulfnoth of plotting rebellion."

Athelstan froze, water dripping from his face. In his mind, blazing like a warning beacon, was the memory of the damning interview with Wulfnoth at Corfe.

"*Jesu*," he cursed. "How did Wulfnoth answer the charge?"

"He did not answer it," Edmund said, pulling up another stool and facing him. "It would have been his word against Brihtric's. I expect Wulfnoth believed that he would be murdered no matter what he said, so he fled. Took twenty ships and their crews with him. More than five hundred men that the king could ill afford to lose."

Athelstan swore again. Wulfnoth and his men were unquestionably among the best-trained shipmen in England. Their loss dealt a massive blow to the entire fleet.

"It gets worse." Edmund's voice was grim. "Wulfnoth took it into his head to raid along the Sussex coast for supplies. He and his crews hit royal storehouses mostly—helped themselves to food and arms, and cut down anyone who tried to stop them. When that news reached us, our worthy fleet master, Eadric"—he sneered the name—"insisted that Wulfnoth be brought back, dead or alive. The king agreed, and Eadric told his brother to take as many ships as he needed to do the job."

Athelstan had been drying his hands and face as he listened, but now he tossed aside the towel and gave Edmund his full attention. "How many did he take?"

"Eighty of our best ships."

"He took eighty ships to capture twenty, and the king allowed it?" Athelstan gaped at his brother, incredulous.

Edmund offered him a cup of ale, but he waved it away.

"Brihtric argued that the Sussex men's skill at ship handling would give Wulfnoth a strong advantage," Edmund said. "He insisted that without superior numbers he would have no hope of capturing his quarry. Five days ago they set sail, and we've had no word from them since. We had a hell of a blow here two nights back, the worst the locals have ever seen. Christ alone knows how they fared in that. The king has sent men overland to scour the harbors all along the southern coast in search of news."

Athelstan was silent, digesting it all. It was the accusation of rebellion that worried him the most. Wulfnoth may have been accused by Brihtric, but surely it was Eadric who was behind it. Could Eadric have somehow learned of Wulfnoth's meeting with all the king's sons at Corfe?

"Did Brihtric accuse anyone else?" he asked.

"Not in my hearing. God only knows what he suggested to the king in private. But you and I know that Wulfnoth's only crime, until now, was his hatred of Eadric."

"That's crime enough in the king's eyes," Athelstan said, "and in running away the fool has condemned himself of far worse." He ran a hand through his hair, frustrated, maddened, and, he had to admit, afraid of what action the king might take now. "We've little hope of turning the king against Eadric after this, and even less chance of saving Wulfnoth's hide. We'll be lucky if he doesn't bring us down with him."

Edmund took a long swallow of ale, wiped his mouth with the back of his hand, and muttered a curse. "This is my fault, Athelstan, for summoning Wulfnoth to Corfe last fall. I may be able to right things, though, if I tell the king what happened there—that I encouraged Wulfnoth, but that you refused to have anything to do with his plan."

Athelstan stopped his pacing to scowl at his brother.

"Do that and you'll likely turn the king's mind against both of us. No. There is advantage in having him continue to think well of you. Besides, we cannot even be certain that he knows what happened at Corfe, bar Edgar's death. This may all be guesswork." Pray God he was right.

Edmund grunted, and Athelstan took it as agreement, albeit grudging.

"What did you learn about Eadric in Mercia?" Edmund asked.

Athelstan grimaced. "That Wulfnoth was right when he claimed that there is little love for Eadric there. He is a heavy-handed administrator, assessing taxes and fines far higher than those in Wessex or Northumbria, and keeping more than his portion. His wealth has increased at the expense of a great many thegns, many of them Ælfhelm's kin who already had good reason to hate him. They call him Eadric the Grasper."

He would have said more, but one of Edmund's men-at-arms drew aside the leather flap at the tent's entrance and announced, "Riders have been spotted, lord, coming north from Eastry."

"They may be bringing word of the fleet," Edmund said. "If they've taken Wulfnoth, it could mean disaster for us."

"With eighty ships in his wake, I don't see how Wulfnoth could have escaped," Athelstan replied. "But we've no choice except to go and hear the news. I will not make Wulfnoth's mistake and run before I've had a chance to defend myself."

Æthelred stalked into the hall on the heels of his bannermen and took his place upon the dais, flanked by his archbishops, his ealdormen, and his daughter. Edyth greeted him with an obeisance and a dazzling smile, and he grunted with approval. The girl acquitted herself well enough in the queen's absence. His only regret at leaving Emma sequestered in London was that he had not been able to rid himself of her any sooner.

After rinsing his hands in the bowl before him, he nodded to Wulfstan, and as the archbishop intoned the blessing Æthelred glanced over the bowed heads of the magnates of England gathered there, gleaning what he could from the way they had aligned themselves. Feuds, bargains, marriages, and plots, he knew, often sprang from gatherings such as this.

He noted that the bearlike Thurbrand, whom he had at last managed to lure from his dank lair in Holderness, had placed himself between Morcar and his brother, Siferth. That boded ill, surely. They had all three been close to Ælfhelm, and he did not trust them. Who could say what their lingering outrage at the ealdorman's death might spur them to do? Sooner or later that trio would have to be dealt with, but he had not yet determined how best to go about it.

Edrid and Edwig, he saw with approval, were seated near Ealdorman Ælfric. The old man would keep a close watch on them. He searched for Edmund and Athelstan and found them standing off to one side of the hall. His eldest son, it seemed, had arrived within the past hour without, happily, the show of force that he had half expected his son to bring with him. Although he had forged a plan for dealing with that eventuality, it was a relief not to have to set it in motion. If Athelstan had been contemplating some action in consort with Wulfnoth, then Eadric's timely intervention had scotched it for now.

He had discovered long ago that the key to controlling his realm was to keep his enemies separate from one another so that they could not unite and bring a significant force against him. A weak nobility made for a strong king. Athelstan would have to discover that for himself one day, if he aspired to the throne.

For now his son stood with his eyes fixed expectantly on the door. Æthelred followed his gaze and saw three men, wet and travel-stained, huddled near the screens passage, waiting for the prayer to end. He placed a hand on Wulfstan's shoulder to silence him, nodded to the men in the passage, and watched with everyone else in the hall as one of the men strode forward, limping with every step.

"That is Sitric, my lord," Eadric whispered in his ear. "He is thegn to my brother Æthelnoth. He looks like he's been in a brawl."

Sitric, who was little more than a youth, was filthy. His long, fair hair was tangled and knotted, and his broad face bore a bruise below one eye and a weeping gash that ran from his ear to his chin. Watching him limp forward, Æthelred steeled himself against whatever wretched tale the man was about to inflict upon him.

When the young man reached the dais, he dropped to one knee and bowed his head.

"Rise," Æthelred said. "What is your news?"

Sitric's eyes flicked to Eadric before he said, "Evil tidings, my lord. Brihtric is drowned, along with many of his men, may God have mercy on their souls."

It seemed to Æthelred that the hall darkened, as if half the torches had suddenly gone out. The men at the tables began to shout, cries of dismay mingled with disbelief, and he raised a hand that did little to quell the din.

"Silence!" It was Eadric who roared the command.

When it had been obeyed, Æthelred drew a heavy breath. There was worse to come. He could read it in the man's face, could feel it in the thickening air. "Go on," he said, dully. "I would hear it all."

"It was the storm, lord," Sitric said, and his voice trembled as he spoke. "We tried to outrun the bastard, hoping to reach safe harbor at the Camber, there in the haven behind Winchelsea's great shingle bank. But the winds carried us past the channel entrance, and then we were at the mercy of the gale. The sea swallowed at least a dozen ships, and the rest were driven hard toward the shore, smashing one against the other.

Lord Brihtric's ship was one of those that went down with all hands." He hesitated, his mouth working, and at last he ground out, "We lost, all told, nearly four hundred men to the sea."

Cries and curses again split the air. Æthelred gaped, unbelieving, at the man cowering in front of him, and then from the youth's mouth came the words, "There is more to tell, my lord."

Eadric called once more for quiet, and although Æthelred wanted nothing more than to strangle the fellow into eternal silence, he nodded to him to continue.

"Æthelnoth bade us drag what ships we could salvage above the waterline, even those that were badly damaged. He intended, once the storm abated, to enlist the aid of the men of Winchelsea to make repairs. We followed his commands as best we could, hampered by rain and wind, and by a blackness that must have come straight from hell. When we could do no more, we found what shelter we could in the lee of a low ridge that runs behind the beach there."

Now he drew another long breath, and Æthelred's sense of foreboding increased.

"We did not know," Sitric said, "that Wulfnoth's fleet had made it into the Camber haven before the storm hit. When the storm abated, and while we were still sleeping, the traitors sailed from the haven, torched our ships, and set out westward with a good wind in their sails." He took a breath and let it out again in a sob. "We could not save the ships, my lord. I am sorry. The ships are gone. They are all gone."

His last words came on a wail that was echoed by the men gathered in the hall. It sliced through Æthelred's body like the point of a spear, and his knees gave way so that he crumpled into his chair, grasping the table for support as he went down. He did not bother to search the shadows for his brother's shade, for he felt its presence like an unseen hand upon his heart.

One hundred ships lost and countless men either drowned or fled. This was Edward's cursed work, and God had allowed it for He was merciless in His vengeance. Time, treasure, and lives all wasted. His enemies, the living and the dead, were bent on his destruction, and every effort he made to defend his kingdom came to nothing.

He reached out to Wulfstan, who stood beside him, silent, for once, as if he had been turned to stone.

"You are God's servant," he said to his archbishop. "You must find a way to placate the Almighty. His face is turned against us, and if you cannot win His mercy, then we are all lost."

A.D. 1009   The king went home, with the alder-
men and the nobility; and thus lightly did they forsake
the ships . . . Thus lightly did they suffer the labor of all
the people to be in vain; nor was the terror lessened, as
all England hoped. When this naval expedition was
thus ended, then came, soon after Lammas, the formidable army of the enemy, called Thurkill's army, to
Sandwich . . .

—*The Anglo-Saxon Chronicle*

# Chapter Seventeen

Athelstan guided his mount through London's crowded, noisome streets, and brooded on the circumstances that had landed him here on a bright summer's morning: The king's despair at the destruction of his mighty fleet; Eadric's cunning in attaching all the blame for the disaster to the banished Wulfnoth and the dead Brihtric; the witan's insistence that the remaining ships return to London; and finally his father's surprising decision to place him in charge of the forlorn and decimated fleet. So while the king and court had limped off to Winchester to nurse their shattered nerves and blighted expectations, he had sailed up the Thames yestere'en with forty ships, charged to protect this city from whatever force might emerge from the Viking harbors across the sea.

But *good Christ*, he thought. They were taking a terrible risk! With all of the fleet anchored here, London would indeed be well protected, but it left the southern waters all but undefended. If the Danes should attack—and he had no doubt that they would strike, and soon—they would once again have their pick of weak coastal targets, from Canterbury to Exeter. The English could only hope that the forces ranged against them would be small and ill trained.

That seemed to him a forlorn hope. He could see no reason why some Danish warlord, or even King Swein himself, would not return with another great army to wrest what gold and silver they could from

Britain. For the Danes it had become a way of life, and surely the news of the destruction of the English fleet must have reached the Danish ports by now. The Northmen would be climbing all over one another in their eagerness to board ships and set sail to plunder England.

He skirted the eastern end of the extensive, walled grounds of St. Paul's and picked his way through the crowded stalls of the West Ceap. Some distance to his right he could see the palisade that surrounded the royal palace and the single English treasure that he coveted. It seemed incredible to him that after years of avoiding his father's court and the temptation that was Emma, he was now charged by the king with her protection. If God meant to test him by putting the queen so firmly in his grasp, then God was a fool, for he would surely fail the test. He had tried to banish her from his mind, had taken other women in order to forget the one woman he could not have, but it had been an exercise in futility. He loved her still, unrepentant and unashamed, God help him.

Not for the first time, he wondered why Emma was still in London rather than in Winchester awaiting the arrival of the king. Why, for that matter, had she not attended the ship meet at Sandwich? Edyth had been there, accorded a privileged seat near the king. Surely that should have been Emma's place. He had been troubled by her absence at the time, but the catastrophic events at Sandwich had driven all else from his mind.

He pondered it now, though, searching unsuccessfully for an answer as he passed the reeking butchers' stalls of the flæscstræt. For a time his mount, made fractious by the smell of blood, demanded all his attention, but soon enough he turned onto the wide lane that ran toward the Aldersgate and the northern road. Moments later he was riding between the square stone towers that marked the entrance to the palace.

Ahead of him, on the broad track leading from the hall and royal chambers to the workshops and stables beyond, Emma stood on a mounting block beside her white mare. She was gowned in a robe of tawny wool that hung loose from her shoulders, and, seeing her profile limned by sunlight, he found the answer to the riddle he had posed himself.

The queen was pregnant, and that alone, he thought, was reason enough for her to forgo the rigors of a journey to Sandwich.

As he drew near she looked up and met his gaze. For an instant her studied reserve vanished and her face brightened in welcome. For an instant she was his alone. The silent acknowledgment of it flashed between them like quicksilver before it disappeared, and she assumed a far more solemn mask for the benefit of the servants and men-at-arms hovering about her.

He greeted her with matching formal courtesy and asked where she was bound.

"Out of the city to St. Peter's," she said. "The abbot is building a Lady Chapel to house a relic of the Virgin, and has invited me to inspect the progress he's made. I could go another day, my lord, if you have pressing business with me." She looked at him uncertainly. "Or would you care to accompany me?"

So he rode with her small company, slowly, through a gathering crowd, back around St. Paul's and toward the Ludgate. Emma smiled and nodded to the folk who cheered lustily while several of her Norman guards distributed alms. Sometimes, he noted, the guards would stop and say a few words before depositing coins into eager palms.

Emma, he realized, was seeking the good opinion of the Londoners not just for herself, but for her Normans as well. His brother Edmund would have denounced this as devious and somehow sinister. He saw it as politic and farsighted. But then, he and Edmund never agreed on anything where Emma was concerned.

There was little opportunity for conversation as they passed through London's western gate and out beyond the scattering of houses and shops that perched outside the city wall. Once they crossed the Fleet, though, the number of folk lining the road dwindled to nothing. As they passed fields of ripening grain he answered the questions that Emma posed about the events at Sandwich, and told her of the charge he had been given to organize London's defense despite whatever suspicions his father harbored against him.

"The king must still place great trust in you," she observed, "if he has given all of London into your care."

"I suspect it is just the reverse," he said, "and that my father has placed me in charge of London precisely because he does not trust me."

She frowned at him. "I do not understand."

"The king knows that whatever the temper in the rest of his realm, the men of London are fiercely loyal to him. The wealthiest landholders and merchants within the city are his thegns, and he has granted them rights and privileges that can be found nowhere else in the kingdom. I expect he is confident that nothing I could say or do would turn the Londoners against him, and so he has placed me here, where I can do him no harm. As for the city's defense, what is left of our fleet is now anchored in the Thames below the bridge. Those forty ships will likely deter our enemies from attempting to reach London. Their presence alone guarantees the city's safety, no matter who is in charge of its defense."

They rode in silence for a little, then she said, "And are you so certain that there will be an attack? The Danes did not come last summer. Mayhap they will stay away again."

"We can hope for that," he said, "but by now they will know that our fleet has been destroyed." He shook his head, wishing that he could be more sanguine. "They will come, and soon. There is nothing we can do now to stop them. People are afraid, and the king most of all."

"But not to London," she said softly, "because of the fleet anchored here. Where then?"

He frowned, for he had been trying to puzzle that out himself for days.

"Sandwich again, perhaps. The town and its walls have been completely rebuilt since Tostig's army burned it three years ago, but it is not an easy place to defend. The Sussex coast is vulnerable as well, because when Wulfnoth fled he took a great many of the Sussex defenders with him."

"What of the regions north of London? Is it possible they may strike the fen country?"

"No place is completely safe," he said, then looked hard at her. "What is your interest in the fens?"

She frowned into the distance, as if she could see some invisible threat there.

"The king has sent Edward to the abbey at Ely for schooling," she said.

"Ah," he breathed. "I did not know." He should have guessed that it had to do with the boy, that Edward was not in London, else he would have been at Emma's side even now.

"There are many tempting treasures at Ely," she said, "and a king's son would not be the least of them if he should be discovered there."

"Perhaps so, but the abbey is protected somewhat by the fens themselves. There are watchers on the coast, and the monks would have adequate warning of an attack that would allow them to flee. Edward is well guarded, is he not?" He knew almost nothing of his half brother, and that was intentional. The child was a maddening reminder of his father's claim to Emma's body.

"He has his own retinue, yes."

"I expect they will keep Edward safe, and that you need not fear for him." He meant to reassure her, but when he glanced again at her ripening figure, a sudden, hot streak of bitterness knifed through him. "There will be another child in his place soon, I see."

For a heartbeat, then two, she made no reply, but he saw her face harden and her mouth settle into a thin line. Even before she spoke, he knew that he had blundered.

"One child can never take the place of another, my lord," she rebuked him, her voice cold as steel.

He cursed under his breath. He had spoken from despair and jealousy; had not considered how his words could be willfully misinterpreted by a mother who has just been parted from her only child. Snatching the bridle of her horse, he brought both mounts to a halt.

"You know that is not what I meant," he said. "Do not purposely misunderstand me, Emma, I beg you. If you wish me to keep my distance while I am in London, you must say so. But do not invent reasons to push me away."


Emma gazed into piercing blue eyes that regarded her with an emotion she hardly dared name. It had been many months since she had studied his face, and now she noted the changes that time and events had wrought there. He had watched two of his brothers die, had been through battle and seen men butchered all about him. It seemed to her that he looked older than his years, and that he had already shouldered some of the cares that would come with the burden of a crown.

She was aware that in the distance, back along the road toward London, her retinue had come to a halt, leaving her sequestered, for courtesy, with the son of the king. She could speak plainly to him here, overheard by no one. But what was she to say? Was she to speak of his grief at the loss of his brothers? Of her bitterness toward the king and her fear for her son? Was she to tell him of her desperate need for someone to talk with and confide in?

No. She could say none of those things, and perhaps he was right. Perhaps she was inventing reasons to push him away, for almost as strong as her fear for Edward was her fear of the power that Athelstan would have over her, should she allow him to take it.

She drew in a breath and said, "I am a reviled queen, my lord. I have neither the strength nor the will to push away a *friend*."

She placed such emphasis on the last word that he could not miss her implication.

The blue eyes flashed, searching her face as if he would read all that was in her mind. At last he spoke in a voice raw with passion.

"I will never be anything less than your friend, Emma," he said, "and I would be far more than that, if you would but let me."

His words hung in the air between them, potent as wine, dangerous as a naked blade. She dared not give him the response that he so clearly wanted, for along that road disaster waited for both of them. Desperate to step away from what she feared was an abyss she said, "Be my protector, then, and my adviser, for I have great need of both."

For a moment he said nothing, and then the dangerous light in his eyes was quenched.

"As you wish, my lady," he said, his tone curt.

He released her bridle and they resumed their progress toward the West Minster, in what she felt was a brittle and stony silence. When she could bear it no longer, for she had great need of his counsel, she said, "My lord, I believe we have a mutual enemy in Lord Eadric. It would be helpful to me to learn what you know of him. Many in London now call him the Grasper. Do you know of this?"

"I have heard it, yes," he replied, "and the name is more than apt. He is using his position as ealdorman to enrich himself at the expense of those whom he should protect."

To her relief he seemed to have shrugged off his ill humor, and now he continued in the same thoughtful tone that had marked their earlier conversation.

"My father places too much trust in the Mercian ealdorman, and I would to God I knew how to wean the one from the other. But Eadric has my sister Edyth in thrall, as I am sure you know. If the king is not listening to Eadric, he is listening to Edyth, and what one says the other repeats like a litany." He grimaced. "I suspect that Eadric was behind the accusations made against Wulfnoth at Sandwich."

He described a meeting at Corfe the previous autumn between the æthelings and Wulfnoth—a private council arranged by Edmund. It occurred to her that if it had never taken place, Edgar would still be alive and Wulfnoth would still be in England. The king's great fleet would not lie at the bottom of the Narrow Sea.

Edmund, it seemed to her, had much to answer for, but she did not speak her thoughts aloud. Although she believed Edmund to be her enemy, even she had to admit that the consequences of that meeting were far from what he had intended.

Athelstan went on. "I think that somehow Eadric learned of Wulfnoth's visit to us at Corfe. Eadric could not know what was said, but he must have suspected that Wulfnoth was planning a move against him. It would not matter to Eadric that I refused to agree to the plan. The meeting itself suited his purpose—to accuse Wulfnoth of treachery and so rid himself of an outspoken enemy." He shook his head, frowning. "It's another indication of Eadric's growing power, that he has spies even among my servants."

Even, perhaps, among the æthelings, she thought. She sifted through her memories of Athelstan's youngest brothers. She had seen little of them in the first years of her marriage, for Edrid and Edwig had been youths then, fostered away from court. Even now she saw them only rarely, at high feast days. Edrid, the more likable of the two, had some of Athelstan's charm, although she suspected he did not have his eldest brother's self-confidence. Edwig, though, had earned a reputation for casual cruelty.

It would not surprise her to learn that he had thrown in his lot with Eadric.

"Yet none of this," she observed, "explains why the king placed his trust in Eadric in the first place. Can your father not see that Eadric's counsel is rooted in a thirst for power?"

"In that, Eadric is no different from any other of the king's thegns," Athelstan said thoughtfully. "I think that, as is his custom, my father has somehow tested Eadric's abilities and loyalty, and Eadric passed the test. The king does not fear his ambition, and so he trusts him in ways that he does not trust his own sons."

Or his queen, Emma thought. Æthelred would not allow her even to raise their son. She was meant only to bear royal children, not to influence them. That would be Eadric's counsel to the king and no doubt Edmund's as well, for he had never trusted her. In their minds she would ever be a hostile queen, a Norman and the pawn of her brother. Their own ambitions prevented them from even imagining that she might want nothing more than to give her son the skills that he would need to manage a kingdom, to ready him for whatever role God ordained for him.

It was something she could not hope to accomplish if she and her son were barred from the king's presence. How long, she wondered, must they endure such an exile?

The babe within her moved, reminding her that she was an expectant mother as well as a wife and a queen. She must find a way to reconcile all her roles, but for now her duties as child bearer must come first. Athelstan had assured her that Edward would be safe in East Anglia, and for now she would be content with that. But once this child was born, she must find a way to bring Edward back to her side and, for good or ill, insinuate herself again into the inner circle that advised the king.

She glanced again at Athelstan. He, too, must find his way to the king's side; and he must learn to accept that Æthelred would always, always stand between them.

# Chapter Eighteen

July 1009

Holderness

The shadows were long as Elgiva rode with Tyra, Catla, and a handful of hearth men along a muddy track toward her holding at Redmere. She had been away since yestermorn, and now, as the palisade came into view, she wondered if her husband had at last found his way to her hall.

It had been five days since Catla, seeking shelter from the storm of shipmen who had descended upon Thurbrand's manor, had brought word of Cnut's return to Holderness.

"The hall is crowded with men," Catla had complained. "It's no fit place for women or children, so Thurbrand has given me leave to come to you."

Elgiva had snorted at this. She'd rather have two shiploads of men underfoot than the mewling Catla and her brace of brats. She had tried to send them straight back home, but for once Catla had proved surprisingly obstinate.

"I can help you make ready for your husband's arrival," she had pleaded. "Surely he will come tomorrow, and there is much to be done."

Reluctantly, Elgiva had allowed her to stay. She had consulted briefly with Alric before dispatching him to Jorvik until she should send for him again. Then she and Catla between them had supervised a flurry of baking, roasting, and brewing, had set women to scouring the bench hall and men to mucking out the stables.

Cnut, however, did not come on the morrow, nor the two days

after—apparently preferring Thurbrand's company to hers, Elgiva thought resentfully. Never mind that she had been awaiting his return to England for two years. Never mind that it was she, not Thurbrand, who had sent Alric to her father's allies to stir up hostility toward King Æthelred and his bloody-handed henchman, Eadric. Never mind that Cnut had neglected his duties as a husband so that she had no son while, as if to spite her, that rabbity Catla had given birth to two boys as disgustingly hairy as their father.

So, determined that she would not endure another agonizing day of watching for her husband's appearance at her gate, she had left Redmere. She had ridden north, to the village of Rodestan, where, Catla had assured her, she would see a great wonder.

"In the center of a clearing there is a tall stone," Catla had said, "placed there by giants who once ruled this land."

Tyra had pursed her lips at hearing this.

"Not giants, my lady," she said, "but men. The Old Ones, who are no more than memory to us now, raised such stones to honor their gods."

Elgiva had wondered how it was that Tyra was so certain of this, for when she saw the great stone for herself she was far more inclined to believe Catla's tale of giants. A single shaft, as thick as a man could measure with his arms outspread, and as wide across as three brawny men placed side by side, pointed high into the sky. Curious, she had walked up to the thing and into the shadow it cast. Immediately she felt chilled, as if she'd walked into a bank of snow. She backed away, seeking the sunlight again, certain that there was something here beyond her understanding.

Tyra, though, had stood long in that shadow, her hand upon the stone, as if drawing power from it, her head cocked as if listening.

Elgiva had watched her and wondered what it was that the Sámi woman heard and felt. Did she pray to the Old Ones as Christians prayed to their saints? Was there knowledge trapped within the stone that Tyra pulled into herself somehow?

Could such a skill be taught?

One day she would ask those questions, when she and Tyra were quite alone. Now, though, she led her company toward her steading over the uneven, marshy terrain, following paths that had become familiar to her in nearly three years of exile from England's heartland.

How she hated this place, Holderness. She yearned to go home, to Mercia and the low hills of Northamptonshire, to escape from this wretched world that seemed to hold nothing but water, sky, and the scattered farms of men who called Thurbrand lord. Perhaps soon she could do so. Perhaps Cnut's arrival meant that Swein's conquest of England had begun.

Long before she reached the manor gate a lookout, one of her own men, hailed her. Cnut and a small retinue, he said, had arrived midday. Elgiva smiled. So, Cnut had come looking for her and had been forced to wait. She hoped it made him impatient and ill tempered, because it was just what he deserved.

Delighted with this small victory she drew a deep breath to dispel the tension and ill humor that knotted her stomach. She needed Cnut. She needed his ships and his army and his protection. And she knew from experience that it was far easier to manage a man with smiles than with scowls.

Once inside the palisade she dismounted and handed her reins to a groom. As she did so, her husband, ale cup in hand, stepped through the door of the hall and stood beneath the eave, showing not the least sign of impatience. Their eyes met and held, and the swift, unexpected rush of desire she felt as she gazed at him unsettled her. It was as if her body, unbidden, responded to some memory of his touch. For a moment she could not move, but could only stare at him.

Cnut seemed more formidable than she remembered. His thin frame had filled out, and his shoulders seemed broader beneath the fabric of his scyrte and tunic. His thick red hair was neatly trimmed, and a smudge of coppery beard shadowed his face. In place of a cloak he wore a gray wolf pelt around his shoulders, and there was gold at his neck and wrists.

His black eyes, the crescent of skin beneath them dark with weariness, never left hers, but he said nothing. He seemed to be waiting for her to make the first move. Yes, Cnut would do that, mindful of his status as Swein's son. So she forced her limbs into action, dropping into a deep reverence before him and greeting him in his native tongue.

"My heart," she said, "is gladdened at the sight of you, husband."

She smiled at him and saw one eyebrow quirk up, his face registering both surprise and approval as he reached for her hands to draw her upright.

"Much as I wish to believe that, lady," he said, his voice low, "after so many months away from your side I hesitate to take from you even what is rightfully mine."

"You wrong me by doing so, my lord," she said and, standing on her toes and grasping the wolf pelt to draw his head down to hers, she kissed him full on the mouth. He responded by flinging his cup away and pulling her close against him and returning her kiss with gratifying urgency.

The men about them whistled and howled, and Cnut murmured against her ear, "Where is your bed?" She laughed and pointed toward the sleep house, where even now she saw her servants herding out Catla's squalling children. Cnut slipped an arm beneath her knees and swept her up, across the dooryard and into the chamber where a fire crackled on the hearthstones and the bed curtains yawned wide. He kicked the door shut and laid her on the bed. Then, heedless of garments, stockings, and boots that kept them from touching skin to skin, he took her with the same impatience that she remembered from their wedding night, devouring her the way a starving man wolfs down bread.

When the passion was spent, all too quickly it seemed to her, she tugged off his boots, tunic, and trousers. Then she stood before him and slowly divested herself of every scrap of her own clothing until he was aroused again. This time they pleasured each other slowly and, she thought with satisfaction, most thoroughly.

Sated at last she lay beside him, her head nestled against his shoulder, an arm and a leg draped across his naked frame, and a thousand questions running through her mind.

"Why did you stay away so long?" she chided him. "We could have spent many days and nights like this if you had but returned to me. What kept you from my side?"

He drew her close and murmured, "I could not come any sooner. Surely you must have known that."

"I knew only that you were across the sea. Is Swein's hall at Roskilde so far away that in two long years you could not find your way to my bed?" She had no idea where Roskilde was, or even where Denmark was, except that they were beyond an expanse of water that was not so vast that a man could not cross it if he was minded to do so.

"Would you have me give you an accounting?" he asked, with just the slightest edge in his voice. "I was at Roskilde for only a few weeks. Then I went to one of my father's fortresses for a year. After that I went to Wendland and spent a season raiding in the Baltic with a band of Jomsvikings. This past winter I was with them in Wolin. And yes, they are all a great distance from here. I had little news of England and almost no word of how it was with you." He paused and drew a breath. "Only that you had given me no son."

She heard the accusation in his words and, stung, she snapped, "I might have given you a son by now, my lord, had you but come to me. Were there so many women to service you in your fortresses that you had no need of your wife? How many brats did you leave in your ships' wake?"

His eased his arms from her to tuck his hands beneath his head, and immediately she felt the subtle distance he'd placed between them. Realizing her mistake and silently cursing herself for a fool she pushed her irritation aside.

"But you have come now," she said, "and you have brought warriors to conquer Æthelred's northern shires, have you not? Where are the rest of your men? You will need a massive army to subdue Mercia and Northumbria no matter how well trained your followers. Surely Swein will be bringing a great force for this."

He studied her in silence for a moment, then sat up, swinging his legs over the side of the bed so that his back was turned to her. "My father is in Denmark," he growled. "I have come here to see my wife, to get her with child so that when I have a son I can better sway the Mercians and Northumbrians to my side. The conquest of England will take planning and patience if it is to succeed. All of that takes time. Elgiva, you know this."

"But now is the moment to strike!" she insisted. She sat up among the bedclothes, and kneeling behind him she wrapped her arms about his neck and whispered, "England is weak and her fleet destroyed. Have you not heard that news?"

"I have heard, and it makes no difference," he said grimly. "England is not yet weak enough! There are still many who will take up arms against an invading force, and the firm hold that the king and his sons have on Mercia and the north will not easily be loosened."

"There are also many men in Mercia who will turn against their king," she assured him. "They will welcome you."

"You cannot be certain of that."

"I can, for some have already made pledges to me."

He turned, alert and frowning, to grasp her by the arms. "Who has? Who knows that you are here?"

"No one knows that I am in Holderness, but I have sent messages to some of my father's allies and kinsmen in the Five Boroughs. I know that there are many more who will give you their pledges of—"

"You little fool!" he snarled, shaking her so that she blinked at him in surprise. "Who do you think will keep such a pledge when the king holds a sword to his throat? If Æthelred discovers you, all our plans will be at risk." He threw her back against the pillows. "You will send no more messages! Time enough for that once your child is born."

She glared at him, rubbing her hands against her bruised arms. He was the fool, she thought, to so casually dismiss the alliances that she'd been building for him.

"What makes you think that the birth of your son will make so much difference?" she sneered.

"By itself, it will not. We must also have more ships, supplies, arms, and men, all of which will take time to acquire. We will need a mountain of silver as well, and England itself will provide that. There is a fleet massing on the southern coast even now. When we have bled Æthelred's kingdom just a little more, my father will be ready to make an end of it."

"So in spite of all that I have done, you will not make a lethal stroke against Æthelred until I bear you a son," she said, her voice laced with scorn, "or until your father's ships are ready, or until you have amassed a mountain of silver, or until the stars fade into darkness and the sky—"

She bit back her words as he rose from the bed and strode to where his clothes were piled. Pulling on his breecs he said, "I have but a few days to spend with you, lady, until I take my ship to join the rest of the fleet." He snatched up his tunic and boots. "Will we spend our time snarling at each other? Is that how you would have it?"

She bolted up from among the pillows. "What do you mean, a few days?"

But he was gone even before she'd finished asking the question.

Only a few days? Why had he bothered to come at all, then?

She fell back against the cushions, still furious. Closing her eyes she called to mind the box and the counting beads devised by Tyra. Red and white had been used up for this month and now only the black remained.

She ground her teeth in vexation. Even if Cnut were to stay for a sennight, she could not hope to conceive his child, although it would be useless to tell him that. He would never believe it. The workings of a woman's body were mysterious and frightening to men, and if a wife's belly failed to swell it was God's will or a curse. And it was always the woman's fault.

Yet she needed a son, so either she had to keep her husband by her side, or . . .

She opened her eyes and stared into the shadows above her.

If she wished to outwit the men who held her future in their hands, then she must put Tyra's beads to their proper use. Next spring she must give birth to a son. And if it was Cnut's or another man's, who in this miserable northern wasteland would be able to say?

**August 1009**
**Canterbury, Kent**

On the fourth day after Lammas, a Viking fleet was spotted off the eastern coast of Kent, making for the harbor at Sandwich. From the coast watch on the Isle of Thanet to Canterbury to Ledesdune to Fæsten Dic to London, the beacons blossomed one after another, warning of impending disaster.

When Athelstan heard the news, he set out for the southeast with his hearth troops to learn what he could of the enemy's movements. Three days later the company paused at the crest of a thickly forested hill and gazed down upon Canterbury.

"Holy Mother of God," Athelstan murmured.

He had never seen so massive a force. How many? Three thousand? Four thousand? Far too many for the Kentish levies to withstand.

In the distance, Canterbury was a ring of fire. The hamlets and farms that lay outside the city's walls had been torched, and smoke stained the sky for as far as he could see. With any luck, most of the folk who had dwelt there had made it inside the safety of the walls along with their cattle and goods. But their fields, ripe for harvesting, were at the mercy of the voracious army that surrounded the city.

Canterbury, with its cathedral and its churches, would be a rich vein of gold if the attackers could find a way to breach its walls. Even if they could not, all of Kent lay at their feet, ripe for plunder, for the men of Kent could not withstand them.

Immediately he sent three of his men to Cookham to report what they had seen to the king. Leaving a dozen warriors behind to shadow the enemy and keep him apprised of their movement, he made for Rochester, where the local fyrd had gathered in response to the beacons.

"You have not the numbers to make any kind of stand against this army," he told their leaders. "You will be able to do little more than harry the foragers they send out, but that you must do as best you can."

He felt helpless against such a sizeable force. Even if the king called out the entire nation, an army could not reach Canterbury in time to save the city. And after they had overrun Canterbury, where would they turn next?

He made his way back to London, already thinking how best to prepare its people for war.

**September 1009**

**London**

Emma, heavy with child, stitched tiny flowers in gold thread onto the blue silk gown that was meant to grace the statue of the Virgin at Ely Abbey. Pausing for a moment, she glanced about at the twenty or so women gathered this morning in her outer chamber and reflected that they would put a hive of bees to shame. Margot, with the assistance of the abbess and three nuns from Barking Abbey, was pawing through an assortment of herbs that the good sisters had culled from their recent harvest. Five noblewomen from Sussex, who had come here for refuge from the Danish army, had their hands full trying to keep up with their children as they tumbled about the floor like puppies.

Given the bleak news from Sussex, Emma had no doubt that others like them would soon be seeking shelter in the city, and she had already sent messages to some of the prominent women in London, asking for their aid. Several had responded by arriving this morning with offers of lodging, and now they were busying themselves with needlework as they regaled the Sussex women with gossip.

It was all about keeping their minds off of what was happening in the south. She tried to keep her own attention focused on their conversation, but she could not avoid dwelling on the events of the past four weeks.

It was just after Lammas Day that Archbishop Ælfheah and many of the Kentish nobles had found themselves trapped inside Canterbury by the massive Viking army that had surrounded the city. With no hope of relief, the archbishop had bartered three thousand pounds of silver for the safety of his people, their lands, and their crops.

Satisfied with that prize, the shipmen had left Canterbury and Kent relatively unmolested, and Emma had prayed with the rest of England that they would leave the country altogether. Instead they sailed south, following the route that, in June, Æthelred's great fleet had taken to its utter destruction. The Northmen had better luck. The weather held fair and word arrived in London that as soon as the ships passed the Rother estuary that marked the boundary between Kent and Sussex, the burning began again. Lewes, Arundel, Dean, and Bosham had all been hit.

And that was as much as she knew today, some of it gleaned from the women who had come to her for refuge, some of it from London's Bishop Ælfhun, but most of it from Athelstan, who had met with her nearly every day since the Danes had first been sighted.

She had been grateful for the constant stream of news that he brought, for she heard nothing from the king, who remained in Winchester. But it was not just gratitude that she felt. In these past weeks the old companionship that the two of them had shared years ago had sprung once more into being, far too sweet a thing to last, she knew, even had it been chaste. Her feelings for Athelstan, though, were far from chaste. Even now she felt the heat rise in her cheeks just from thinking about him and, distracted, she started when a servant appeared suddenly beside her to whisper that Athelstan requested audience and awaited her in the palace chapel.

She hesitated, considering whether she should beckon Margot to accompany her. She had taken pains to avoid being alone with him during their sojourn here in London—a necessary precaution that he had never questioned. If he wished to see her alone now, there must be good reason. She set aside the blue silk with its golden flowers and, pressing her hand against the mound of her belly, she pushed herself to her feet and left the chamber.

The deserted chapel was cool and dark, lit only by the sanctuary lamp and by the dim light that filtered through thick panes set high in one wall. Athelstan, who stood facing the altar, turned as she approached him, his brow knit with worry.

"I am sorry to draw you from your women," he said, "but there is news from the south that I did not wish to speak of in front of them."

She held her breath, certain that it must be bad, else he would have announced it in her chamber.

"Tell me," she said.

"The shipmen have settled on Wight Isle, and the king fears that they will winter there as they have in the past. From that base they can strike our market towns and abbeys without warning and bleed us to death. He has called his counselors from all across England to meet him at Bath in mid-September to determine what to do."

"And you among them, of course," she said. "When must you leave?"

"If I attend the council," he said, "I must leave tomorrow at dawn."

She heard the indecision in his voice, and she shook her head.

"My lord," she said, "you must attend the council. This is a command from the king. You have no choice."

He waved her words aside.

"You are Æthelred's queen," he answered her, "awaiting the birth of his child. No one would question it if I remained here to grant you my protection."

She looked into his eyes and what she read there worried her as much as it comforted. He would defy his father if she asked it. But she could not ask it. Athelstan was needed elsewhere. For weeks now, while she remained in the comfort and security of this palace, in the south men were beaten or murdered, their wives and daughters raped, children taken for slaves, and entire families left homeless and destitute. The king needed every tool at his disposal to deal with the enemy.

"The king would question it," she reminded him. "I cannot bid you stay when he bids you go. And London, as you have told me yourself, is well defended, no matter who is in command."

"Words spoken before I saw the size of the Danish force," he said with a frown. "They have enough ships to strangle this city, should they choose to do so, without ever coming to battle. They already control the port at Sandwich, and now their fleet is moving toward the Solent. Our coastal trade is already suffering. If they should send ships to blockade London they may very well starve us out. To leave you alone and unprotected—"

"It is not their intention to starve us," she protested. "It would take · too long. They strike swiftly and move on. It is what they have always done."

He ran a hand through his hair and began to pace.

"This army is vastly different from the forces we have faced in the past, even the force that Tostig led against us two years ago. Their commander is a man named Thorkell, and if even half of what is said of him is true, he is as skilled a warlord as any we have yet seen. His army is not made up of thugs recruited from alleyways and docksides. These men are seasoned fighters. The question is: What do they really want? What does Thorkell want?"

"Whatever it is," she said, "he is searching for it in the southern shires. The people there need your help." She reached for his hands, clasping them tightly in her own. "The king needs your counsel. Go to him. That is where your duty lies." She gazed at him—at the golden hair, the eyes far bluer than any others she knew, the tender mouth framed by the trim, fair beard. She would keep this memory of him safe in her heart, against the time when he was far away.

For a long moment they looked one upon the other, then slowly he drew her into his arms so that her head rested against his shoulder. For several heartbeats she allowed him to simply hold her while she drew strength from the shelter of his embrace. It was a moment stolen from time, and she wanted to savor it, for she did not know if there would ever be another like it.

"It is not London I fear for," he whispered, "it is you. Promise that you will send me word if you have need of me."

"I promise," she said, lifting her head, willing herself to draw away from him, for it was perilous to remain even a moment longer clasped within his arms. But in the next instant his mouth found hers, and instead of pulling away she returned his passionate, lingering kiss with all the yearning that she had kept locked within for so long.

When at last he released her, he brushed his lips against her hand, and then he was gone.

Emma pressed her fingertips against her brow, for her head ached from the effort of keeping back her tears. She had been right to send him away, she was certain of it. But *dear God*, it was going to be so hard to face each day knowing that she would not see him, would have no word of him. She took a deep breath and for a time she did not move, comforted somewhat by the silence and the peace of the chapel.

One by one the people she loved—Edward, Wymarc, Father Martin, Hilde, and now Athelstan—had been forced to leave her. She did not know how she was to bear this last leave-taking, although she had always known that it had to come. Athelstan owed his duty to his father, the king, not to her.

Gently she caressed her swollen belly, fearful lest her grief hurt the babe, reminding herself that, although so many had left her, she was not alone. The child was always with her, and Margot, too, would never leave her side.

She took a deep breath and swallowed hard against the knot of anguish that lingered in her throat. There were others, too—women who even now were gathered in her chamber, anxious and frightened. Their losses were far greater than hers, and her place now was with them.

She left the chapel to return to them, with little to offer in the way of comfort other than news of what the king was planning to do. She doubted that it would help them much, but it was all she had to give.

A.D. 1009    And everywhere in Sussex, and in Hampshire, and also in Berkshire, they plundered and burned, as their custom is. Then ordered the king to summon out all the population, that men might hold firm against them on every side . . . On one occasion the king had begun his march before them, as they proceeded to their ships, and all the people were ready to fall upon them . . .

—*The Anglo-Saxon Chronicle*

# Chapter Nineteen

October 1009

Salisbury, Wiltshire

thelred stood alone upon the rampart of the hilltop fortress and squinted up at the blank sky. The sun was hidden behind a roof of cloud, but he judged that it was near midday. In the still air, the smoke from thousands of campfires fingered skyward, and almost as far as he could see, the plain below was blackened by a vast army. His army. And now that Eadric had at last arrived with his levies, his force numbered more than three thousand strong. His heart swelled at the sight of them. He had beckoned, and they had come. Such was the power of a king.

Their banners proclaimed their territories and allegiances—Wessex, East and West Mercia, Northumbria, East Anglia—each fyrd well separated from its neighbors with guards in place to keep men of one region from savaging those of another whenever ale scattered their wits.

Armies were like packs of hunting dogs, he reflected, liable to attack anything that crossed their path if they were not kept leashed. Most of the levies had been waiting here for weeks, and tempers were short and violent.

Which was exactly how he wanted them, now that the enemy was nearly within their grasp.

The Danish shipmen, led by that whoreson Thorkell, had done just what he had feared. They had ravaged from the Isle of Wight north through Hampshire and into Berkshire like a killing tide, taking whatever they could carry and burning what was left. His own army had been forced to wait until their numbers were strong enough to confront the bastards, and meantime the people of England could do little more than pray.

And so they had prayed, ordered to their knees by decree of his archbishops—a pointless exercise unless he could back those prayers with steel. If he could but keep the men in his ranks from turning on one another for a few days more, he would unleash them upon the Northmen as they returned to their ships.

He cast one last glance at the ordered rabble below him, then made his way down the palisade steps and, flanked by two hearth guards, crossed the green to his pavilion. Just inside the entrance to his tent he halted, assailed by a multitude of impressions as he contemplated the handful of men gathered within.

Athelstan, his face a grim mask, stood at a table between his brother Edrid on one side and Uhtred of Northumbria on the other. They were intent upon a strip of parchment spread out before them—a rough sketch of Uhtred's battle plan, he supposed. Athelstan would welcome the coming conflict, for he was eager to avenge every burned village and plundered abbey. He was like a young wolf, bristling with outrage that, for now at least, was aimed at England's enemies. Whether he could be trusted to follow orders remained to be seen.

Another of his cubs, Edwig, hovered near his brothers, oblivious to everything but the ale cup in his hand. He swayed unsteadily, no doubt lost in some drunken dream and unaware that the archbishops Ælfheah and Wulfstan were eyeing him with disapproval. The young fool would prove utterly useless at today's council, but at least he wasn't off somewhere brawling in the mud.

Ulfkytel of East Anglia stood with Godwine of Lindsey and Leofwine of Western Mercia, the three of them arguing vehemently and pointedly excluding Ealdorman Eadric, who watched them from a half-dozen steps away with feral, catlike eyes.

There should have been two others here, but he had already sent Edmund and Ælfric to Winchester, with as many men as he could spare—a necessary precaution in case the Danes attempted an assault on his royal city.

That left him with this lot—all of them as surly and fractious as the men in the camps below. He could smell the tension streaking between them, acrid as lightning. Yet these were the men whom he must chivy into doing what he needed done, despite the fact that one of them was a useless wastrel, another a son he could not completely trust, and the rest of them as ready to turn on one another as they were to slaughter Danes.

"Uhtred!" he barked, covering the length of the pavilion in a few swift strides and taking his place behind the council table. "What do your scouts tell you about the enemy's numbers?"

The men had followed him to the table and, like him, they looked to Uhtred, waiting to hear the answer.

"Near four thousand, my lord."

Larger than his own force. They would be at a disadvantage from the start.

"How will an English force of three thousand defeat a Danish force of four thousand?" Leofwine snarled.

"We were outnumbered three years ago at Durham," Uhtred replied, "and we butchered the Scots. We can—"

"At Durham," Eadric interrupted, "you crushed the Scots between your forces and the city walls. They couldn't escape. Here, we don't have the walls, we don't have the numbers, and we don't have the—"

"Peace!" Æthelred said, scowling at Eadric. "Listen to the plan that Uhtred has devised, and then I will hear your counsel."

While his son-in-law laid out the battle plan, he studied the faces around the table, weighing their reactions. Their allegiances would come into play now, and it would take all his skill to persuade them to work together. For years he had nursed their petty rivalries to keep them from banding against him. Now, though, he needed them to act with one purpose.

When Uhtred had finished, Eadric spoke into the silence.

"I am not willing to place my levies beside those of Lindsey," he said, "unless Godwine can assure me that his men will stand firm and not slink away the moment they see the Danes approaching."

So it begins, Æthelred thought, as Godwine began to shout and he was forced to raise a hand for silence.

"Eadric," he snapped, "do you question the valor of Godwine's men?"

"I question their loyalty," Eadric replied. "I have lately come from Lindsey, and there is some devilry brewing there. Someone has been stirring up anger against you, my lord, and the men there cannot be trusted."

A chorus of shouts rang out at this, but Æthelred paid them little heed, for inside his head a single name burned—Elgiva.

If she was indeed alive, could she be sowing disloyalty among the men of Lindsey—men who had once sworn allegiance to her father and brothers?

"I am told"—he heard Eadric's voice as if it came from a great distance—"that Lord Godwine did not arrive here with his full levy. That some refused to fulfill their oaths to fight."

Æthelred snapped his mind back to the men around him. He looked at Godwine. "Is it true?"

"I came with all the men that I could muster," Godwine spat, "and at the appointed hour. My lord, we have been stranded here for weeks while Eadric dragged his feet in the north. Because of him we are forced to fight our enemy with the sea at our backs and after they have already ravaged three shires."

"Because of me," Eadric insisted, "the king perceives the peril that you would have kept from him. My lord king, I would counsel you to rethink the wisdom of this battle. Do you wish to hazard the fate of your kingdom on a single throw of the dice, outmanned as we are and with the loyalty of our forces in question? Better to let Thorkell and his men return to their ships and sail back to Denmark. We have little to gain by stopping them and much to lose if we should fail."

Æthelred wanted a moment to consider all that had been said. He raised a hand for silence, but Athelstan ignored him.

"Why should Thorkell return to Denmark?" his son demanded. "Why should he abandon the cow he has been milking for two months? His army has ravaged unhindered because we have been too few to withstand such a mighty force. Now that we have the numbers to meet him in battle it would be madness not to move against him."

"And if our king should fall in this battle," Eadric countered, "then you, my lord Athelstan, would be quick to take your place upon the empty throne, would you not?"

Æthelred saw his headstrong son lunge for Eadric, saw Uhtred thrust himself between the two men. He shouted for his hearth guards, but even they could not prevent Athelstan from wrenching a hand free to jab a finger at the ealdorman.

"You watch your tongue, you bastard," Athelstan shouted. "I will see you—"

But Æthelred had heard enough. He slammed his fist upon the table to silence them all.

His head was pounding, and he felt as if a weight was crushing his chest. He glowered at the men around him, each one in turn—until he met one who should not have been there. His brother's face stared at him from among his counselors—a malignant smile playing on his bloodless lips.

He flinched backward at the sight and spat a curse. Fingers of ice began to creep along his arms, and his legs trembled. He had to clutch at Ælfheah beside him to keep from falling.

Edward had done this. Edward had sown discord among his war leaders and Edward would bring disaster upon them all. This battle was what his brother wanted, and now he understood that if he were to commit to it, the outcome would be disastrous.

Steadying himself, he placed his hands upon the table and glowered at his brother's bleeding face.

"We will not bring the Danish host to battle," he snarled. "Let the shipmen pass unchallenged. Let them take their plunder and go."

There was a pounding in his ears now, and beneath it he heard cries of outrage and protest. Athelstan's voice, though, pierced through the roaring in his head.

"This is madness!" his son shouted. "The men, the arms, the provisions, all have been gathered here for the purpose of bringing the raiding army to battle. Yet now you ask us to stand aside and let them go to their ships? Shall we bow to them as they pass, lord king? Should we offer to help them carry their plunder, or would you have us feast with them before they take ship?"

He would have cuffed his son, but he hadn't the strength. He closed his eyes to rid himself of his brother's foul presence, but when he looked again the grotesque thing still hung there before him.

"Get him out of here," he shouted at the guards. "Get them all out." He pointed at Eadric. "You will stay."

While the tent was cleared he continued to glare at Edward's wraith, watching as it faded into nothing. Still, his head pounded like thunder and his stomach griped him. When a servant approached with a cup of wine he backhanded it to the ground. "Get out!"

Someone had brought him a chair and he slumped into it as Eadric rounded the table and dropped to one knee beside him. Eadric's expression was carefully bland, although Æthelred did not doubt that he must be wondering what ailed his king. Let him wonder.

"Now you will tell me," he ordered, "what you would not say in front of the council. What is happening in Mercia?"

"There is unrest in the Five Boroughs, in Lindsey and in scattered areas throughout Mercia. I cannot discover who is behind it."

"You cannot?" he snapped. "*Christ*, what use are you then?"

"I crave your pardon for failing you in this, lord king."

Eadric's expression was remorseful, but Æthelred saw something else there, too—some hint of further knowledge that Eadric had not yet shared.

"What is your counsel then?" he asked.

"I have none. Athelstan, though, is well liked among the northern magnates. He may be able to advise you."

At this Æthelred looked more sharply at his ealdorman, for there was an accusation buried in his words. "Are you saying that my son is courting the favor of the northerners? How? He has been in London since June."

"Someone is courting them, my lord; I cannot say who it is. Godwine and Leofwine must know something, although I'll wager they want to keep any word of it from reaching you."

Æthelred studied the smooth, comely face before him, looking for any sign of deceit. He knew that Eadric had no great love for either Godwine or Leofwine. Or for Athelstan, come to that. But the ealdorman's countenance showed only concern. "Why should they keep it secret from me?" he asked.

Eadric shrugged. "No ealdorman wishes to be perceived as impotent, my lord, and unable to quell unrest within his province. Or perhaps"— he hesitated an instant, then continued—"perhaps these men are at the very root of it. Or it may be that they know who is behind it yet are unwilling to intervene. If it is one of your sons who is sowing trouble, they may be looking to the future, and so covertly supporting him." Eadric frowned. "Or they may yet have ties to Ælfhelm's daughter. Elgiva is still out there somewhere. She has little love, sire, for either you or for me, and she is skillful at getting men to do her bidding."

Yes, Elgiva could be very persuasive. She had held even him in thrall until he had wearied of her. What might lesser men not do at her behest? If she was alive, her place of refuge remained a mystery, one that he would see resolved before he raised his hand against his counselors or his sons.

"You will return to the Five Boroughs," he said to Eadric, "to Siferth's estate. His wife may know something of her cousin, so linger there for a time. See if you can persuade her to tell you what she knows. Go to the estates of Godwine and Leofwine as well. You may learn something there. They were close allies of Ælfhelm." And now he recalled the face of Ulfkytel, who had stood between Godwine and Leofwine at the council. "What do you know of Ulfkytel?" he asked. The man had served him well in the past, but if Godwine and Leofwine were false, then Ulfkytel might be false as well.

Eadric was silent for a time, his expression thoughtful. At last he said, "Ulfkytel is a fierce war leader—near the equal of Uhtred. I think he will not easily be swayed from his oaths of loyalty."

Æthelred understood the question that Eadric did not voice. Who held Ulfkytel's loyalty? "We must make certain of his allegiance," he said slowly.

He had one more daughter to spend. Wulfhilde was—how old? He could not remember. Surely she must be of an age by now to wed. She would make a fitting bride for Ulfkytel. In return for a royal daughter and her dowry, Ulfkytel must help him stem the tide of disaffection that was seeping across his kingdom. And if Elgiva was at the root of it, then Eadric must find her and put a stop to it.

When prodded by the point of a sword drawn by one of his father's stone-faced hearth guards, Athelstan had turned and stalked out of the tent. He had waited near the entrance, though, to watch the others leave—all but Eadric, who had remained inside with the king. Eadric—the man of the hour and the only man the king listened to or trusted. Or believed.

He wished to know what the king was discussing with Eadric, but the tent flap was down and the two guards merely glared at him, unmoving. Frustrated, he left, making for his own tent. He had not gone far when his brother Edrid and Lord Uhtred fell into step beside him.

"The king is a fool," Athelstan snarled, "and I am an even greater one." He had let his temper rule him, while Eadric had remained calm and merely outfaced him.

"Aye, my lord," Uhtred agreed. "You should learn to keep your mouth shut around your father; he seems not to value your advice."

"Yet he insists that I attend his council."

"That is because he fears you," Uhtred replied. "Did you not see his face in there? He looked as if he was seeing the devil incarnate, and he was staring straight at you! What mischief have you been up to that so terrifies the king?"

Athelstan glanced at the big ealdorman from Northumbria. They'd come to know each other somewhat these past weeks, and to his surprise he'd grown to like Uhtred. The man was no beauty, and he could be crude as hell, but his men loved him and he was no more self-serving than anyone else on the king's council.

"I went north in the spring and asked questions about Eadric," Athelstan said. "My father must have learned of it."

Uhtred's eyes locked on his as if he read far more in that sentence than the words conveyed.

"Oh aye," Uhtred grunted, "and you let it be known, I'll warrant, that you bear no love for the king's darling Eadric. Do you and your father agree on anything?"

"Not that I am aware of," Athelstan said with a bitter laugh.

Uhtred nodded, and they walked in silence for a few steps. Then Uhtred said, "You were right about one thing back there." He gestured with his thumb, back toward the king's pavilion. "The ship rats will not leave England anytime soon. Eventually the king will have to fight them or bribe them, no matter what Eadric counsels."

"What do you think, Uhtred," Edrid asked, "could we have won a battle?"

Uhtred shrugged. "Who knows? Would Godwine's men have deserted, and if they had, would it have made a difference? The outcome of a battle rests on luck and leadership as much as on the numbers on either side. But Godwine was right when he said we should have stopped the shipmen before they raided all the way up into Berkshire. It was Eadric's delay that forced us to wait. I wonder if his late arrival was merely cowardice, or if it was treachery."

"It was treachery," Athelstan said, the realization suddenly dawning on him. "Eadric came here determined to avoid a pitched battle because, win or lose, it would be to his disadvantage. If we won, it would be you, Uhtred, who would reap the glory because you laid out the battle plan. If we lost, the king would blame his council, including Eadric, and so Eadric's influence would be lessened. He could not risk either of those outcomes, and so he had to find a way to prevent the battle. Eadric is brilliant. And he is a complete and utter villain."

"There must be a way to pry him from the king's side," Edrid insisted.

Uhtred snorted. "Forget him, lad. He's a worm. It's this piece of Danish offal, Thorkell, that we must fear. He'll be laughing all the way to his ships now, rejoicing that we've not attempted to get in his way. Mark me, he'll strike somewhere else before this is over, and I want to know where."

Athelstan halted as the truth of Uhtred's words struck him. A pitched battle against a similar-size force was the last thing that Thorkell wanted. Instead he would look for a rich target that he could bleed into submission, as he had done at Canterbury. The English army was too close to Winchester to make that city an attractive target, and that left only one other.

"He will go to London," he said. London, where Emma was trapped, awaiting the birth of her child.

"It is what I would do," Uhtred agreed. "The question is when will he go? Will he wait out the winter months on Wight?"

"No," Athelstan said. "He has ravaged along this coast already, and our own army has depleted most of the harvest in Dorset. He has too many mouths to feed to remain here."

Uhtred grunted. "Yet our army cannot move until his does, and his ships will get him to London faster than we can walk it, unless God sends a storm to swallow his fleet."

Uhtred was right, and Athelstan could imagine what would happen next as if it had been written down for him. Thorkell's unbloodied, unchallenged army would sail northward, soon, while the good weather lasted. They would make for the Thames and for London, where Thorkell would try to starve or cripple or beat the city into submission.

"London has plenty of good men," he said, "but they need to be warned."

"Then you'd better warn them," Uhtred growled, "because the king won't do it. He's deceived himself into believing that the shipmen will be happy with the plunder they've taken and will scurry home." He placed a meaty hand on Athelstan's arm. "But don't go yourself, man! If you go haring off to London without the king's leave, it will be another sin added to your tally. Eadric is with your father right now, likely trying to poison his mind against you, so play the good son for a few more days. Give him the lie. Send your warning, and let London look out for itself. You'll get there soon enough."

Uhtred stalked away, and Athelstan, with Edrid still beside him, made for his own quarters.

"What are you going to do?" Edrid asked anxiously.

"Send messengers to London," he snapped. Uhtred was right. He must play the good son, and, in any case, his presence in London would make no difference. It was the warning that mattered; so he would send it, and follow as soon as he could.

# Chapter Twenty

November 1009

London

The rain began to drum on the slate roof of St. Botolph's Aldgate as the priest intoned the final blessing. Emma, kneeling below the altar amid nuns, priests, and London's noble elite, bowed her head and whispered a last, fervent prayer for the English people. When she stood up and made her way through the congregation and into the porch, Bishop Ælfhun drew beside her and placed a restraining hand upon her arm.

"Wait until the rain has eased, my lady," he said. "The shower will pass soon enough."

But she could not wait. The milk in her breasts had turned them to stone, and in the palace on the other side of London her daughter would be howling with hunger.

She smiled at the bishop and patted his hand.

"I am well defended against the weather," she said. Her woolen head-rail was fastened tight beneath her chin, and now she pulled the hood of her fur-lined cloak over that. "Come to the palace as soon after midday as you can. I have summoned the local reeves as well to discuss what more must be done to maintain order within the city."

It had been five days since word arrived that enemy ships had sailed into the mouth of the Thames. Their appearance had not been unexpected, because Athelstan had sent a warning that London might soon be under siege. The exact number of ships was still under debate, though—some said fifty vessels, others swore there were five hundred.

The shipmen had set up camps on both sides of the river and had systematically begun to ravage farm holds and villages for food and supplies. They had pillaged grain stores from Tilbury to Shoebury and had herded scores of cattle and sheep into their camps.

They would not be leaving anytime soon.

In a matter of days the Aldgate had been flooded with streams of people seeking the shelter of London's walls, and that tide had only increased with each passing day. This morning she had come to pray at the little church just beyond the eastern gate and to see for herself what the conditions were like for those fleeing from the savagery of the Danes. She could not cower behind her palace walls. The people had to be reassured that she was in their midst.

Now she stepped into the downpour and nodded to her grooms to assist her into the saddle. Her bannermen moved forward, setting a measured pace, their standards limp in the steady rain. Three priests followed her, chanting a litany. She murmured the response to the prayer automatically as she scanned the road and the broad wastelands on either side, awash with water, mud, and refuse.

Here, between London's eastern gate and the Walbrook, makeshift shelters had been erected to house those who had fled their farms and villages. They had carried with them their children, their household goods, their animals, and their terror. They had carried tales of disaster, as well, rumors that had been winging through the city for days like shreds of burning thatch.

*The king has lost a great battle in Hampshire.*

*The king and his sons have been killed.*

*Canterbury and Winchester have been torched and burnt to the ground.*

The more outrageous and unbelievable the report, the more it was repeated. Yet the truth, she reflected, was bad enough.

She had not yet reached the Walbrook when the rain stopped as abruptly as it had begun. Beyond the bridge the road was lined with people who took up the response to the litany, and like a distant rumble of thunder the sound of it swelled and echoed.

*Ora pro nobis.* Pray for us.

Emma pulled back her hood and gravely studied the faces around her—hollow-eyed men, haggard from sleeping rough; children with their mouths agape; monks and nuns; matrons cloaked in furs; old women dressed in little more than rags. The only thing they had in common was the fear that she could read in their eyes.

It was the women with infants at their breasts, rocking from side to side to comfort their babes, who broke her heart. Her own breasts ached for her daughter. Like these women, she had a helpless child who was completely dependent on her. Like them, she was afraid of what terrors the future held.

Her thoughts drifted to the king's eldest daughter, Edyth. Barely sixteen winters old, she was pregnant with her first child and was even now at Headington for her lying-in. Emma wondered how childbirth would change Edyth, for she was certain that it must. She hoped that motherhood would soften her stepdaughter, and that the breach that gapped between them would be healed.

When at last she rode through the palace gate, she was alert for the sound of Godiva's crying. At five weeks old, her daughter was not the placid babe that Edward had been. The child was fretful and restless no matter what attempts were made to pacify her. Margot had insisted that some babes cried more than others, but it had not relieved Emma's fear that something was wrong. Abbess Ælfwynn had advised that because Emma herself was distressed by the Danish attacks, her milk acted upon her infant like a poison.

"You should give the child to a wet nurse with a sanguine humor," Abbess Ælfwynn had said. "You are overburdened with cares and you are passing your distress to the babe."

But Emma had resisted this advice. The only peace she had was in the moments when she held Godiva to her breast. Her daughter's eyes, colored the deep blue of the marsh flowers that Emma recalled from her summers at Fécamp, would fix on hers with an unblinking gaze. This respite never lasted long, for the baby would invariably fall into a heavy sleep that always ended too soon, and once more the piercing wails would echo through the palace halls.

The heaviness and breast pain that Emma was feeling now told her that Godiva should be awake and hungry and crying for her mother.

So why, she asked herself as she dismounted before the queen's hall, was the palace so quiet? Her heart in her throat, she ran up the stairs leading to her chamber.

## Redmere, Holderness

Shielded against the November chill by a heavy, woolen cloak, Elgiva picked her way along a muddy path that ran beside a trio of beehives. She had nearly completed her round of inspection—past the mews to the kitchens and brew house, behind the hall to the stables, down by the craft houses to the weaving sheds, through the orchard, and back to the women's quarters.

It had taken most of the morning, but she did not begrudge the time it cost her. She would be imprisoned within doors soon enough when the winter set in, and then time would move slowly indeed. Her reeve regarded her intrusion into his territory as a slight to his abilities, but she never gave any heed to his injured glances. Besides, she enjoyed it when she caught the men watching her with moon eyes while their women—well, she didn't care about their women.

She sniffed with pleasure at the sweet scent of malt and yeast that wafted toward her on a light breeze. Then the wind changed and brought with it the stench from the slaughter pens, where the butchering of the aged livestock was nearly finished. The smell made her gorge rise, and she hastened away from it, following the path through the apple orchard to the manor's central yard and there she halted.

The garth was no longer hers. It had been usurped by a ship's complement of Danes who were garbed in mail and armed with shields and blunted swords. Ten of them had paired off to hack at each other under the watchful eye of their war leader while their companions shouted encouragement or abuse.

The din they were making brought back evil memories. She had only ever heard the sound of real battle once, on a summer's day in Exeter that had been filled with howls of rage and screams of terror—and with sights she would never be able to forget. It had seemed to her that the end of the world had come.

For some, it had.

And now similar battles were taking place somewhere far to the south, where the Danes must have begun their raiding in Wessex. She was grateful she wasn't there to hear them or see them. Still, she wanted news.

She wanted to know where Cnut was, or if he was still alive. There were many ways that a warrior could meet death, even aside from battle: from poisoned water or bad meat, from the bloody flux or some wasting disease, from an insignificant wound that festered and turned lethal. Cnut may even have drowned before his ship met with the others at Sandwich, and she would never know.

She scowled at that thought. She was wed to the son of the Danish king, she held vast estates in Mercia, yet she must depend on men for nearly everything, including news of events going on in the world beyond her gates.

And how men liked to hoard such news! They kept it from their women, seeking to protect them from the horror of what was happening in the wider world. As if women needed or wanted such protection! When a battle was lost was it not the wives and daughters who would be raped or dragged off to some worse fate by the victors? How did ignorance protect them from that?

She wished that she had been born a man so that she would not have to look to them for so much. It was what she hated most about being a woman. That, and the task of childbearing.

She peered speculatively down the length of her body. As yet there was no outward sign of the babe growing within her. But the child was there, she was certain. She was sick every morning, and she had missed her courses for two months now. Cnut had been gone for four, so it was going to be a near thing.

Luckily men were half-witted and easily deceived when it came to the details of pregnancy. She would claim it was Cnut's. Alric may not believe her, but he would not be fool enough to admit to fathering her son. And it must be a son. Even if she bore a girl child and had to replace it with someone else's brat, she would give Cnut a son.

No, Alric did not worry her. Tyra, though, looked at her sometimes with that cold, knowing stare. What was behind it? If the cunning woman harbored suspicions about Alric, she might be compelled to share them with Cnut or with Swein.

But Tyra, she reminded herself, could prove nothing. If questions should ever be raised about the child's father, what weight could the claims of a slave carry when her mistress denied them as lies?

No weight at all.

A shout from the guard tower drew her attention, and a moment later the gate opened. She was relieved to see Alric ride in, and not Thurbrand or, worse, another boatload of Danes.

She had sent Alric to her cousin in Lindsey weeks ago, with messages for Aldyth and her husband. She was eager to hear his news of events taking place in the south, but she had no wish to greet him under the eyes of the shipmen—eyes that were, she suspected, just a little too sharp.

She hurried into the hall and was waiting when he strode through the entryway and tossed his mud-stained cloak to a servant. His eyes met and held hers, and she felt, as ever, the little thrill of excitement that he could arouse in her with just a glance.

But from today she must be more circumspect with him. Her pregnancy and the presence of those shipmen in the yard dictated that. She wanted to give no one an excuse to raise questions about the child's father. That Tyra might suspect something was bad enough. She would have to keep Alric at a distance.

He came swiftly to her side and she held out her hand. Alric placed a lingering kiss upon her palm, and she guessed he would venture further if she allowed it. She was tempted to do so. It had been many weeks since he had been here and touched her thus, and the arguments she had used to steel herself against him nearly crumbled into dust. But she drew her hand away and stepped back a little to make a space between them.

He raised an eyebrow at her.

"A chilly greeting, my lady," he said. "Have I done something to cause you displeasure? Has one of those louts I passed on my way in usurped my place in your heart?"

She placed a warning finger against her lips, glancing past him to make sure that no one overheard them.

"Those men are a gift from King Swein, sent here to protect me while my husband wages war in the south." She seated herself on the bench against the wall and gestured for him to join her. "Twenty extra mouths to feed and twenty pairs of eyes to watch my every move. Alas, you and I must pay the price, for a time at least." For a very long time, probably, but she would tell him about the child later.

"So I may look, but I may not touch," he murmured. "A cruel fate, lady. Send me away again soon so I will not be tempted beyond my strength to resist."

She laughed. They were pretty words, but Alric had resisted her for years when her father and brothers were alive. He would do so again when necessity demanded, and she had no doubt that he would find some willing wench—or several—to satisfy his appetites. And that was another advantage to being a man.

A servant brought them ale, and when he had gone she set her cup aside and turned to Alric.

"Tell me what news you bring from the south. I know that the king called out his army but no other word has reached this godforsaken place."

"The king gathered his forces at Salisbury last month, that much I know for certain. There were rumors of a battle, but I could not discover if it really took place."

"So you know nothing more than I do." She stood up and began to pace. It was maddening that she should have no more information than a common alewife.

"I know that Godwine of Lindsey took far fewer men to the levy at Salisbury than he should have."

She spun to face him. "Men actually refused to take up arms?" That would have been like a knife thrust to the king.

"They took to their heels rather than march south to fight, and not just in Lindsey. I would hazard that all across eastern Mercia there were men who had no great desire to risk their lives for lands not their own, and for a king who no longer has their trust."

She sank to the bench again, thrilled by the possibilities this raised.

"So our efforts to turn men against the king have been fruitful," she said.

"They have indeed. And if Æthelred could not raise a host that outnumbered the Danish army, I doubt very much that he would have hazarded a pitched battle. The slaughter would be too great. If it had occurred we would have heard something by now, even here."

She nodded, reassured by his words. Æthelred saw himself as doomed. It would take very little pricking to weaken his confidence. Besides, he was a coward. He would not fight if he could find a way to sidestep it.

"What news of my cousin?" she asked. "Did you speak with Aldyth or her husband?" Siferth and his brother, Morcar, were the most powerful of her kinsmen, and they were bound by oath to avenge the deaths of her father and brothers—deaths ordered by the king. If there was to be a true uprising against Æthelred, her kin must set it in motion.

Alric took a long pull from his ale cup before setting it on the bench beside him.

"I did not meet with the brothers," he said, "and the news I have of them will give you little joy."

She scowled at him. "Out with it then," she said. "Do not taunt me."

"You are not the only one courting your kinsmen," he said. "Since last I spoke with them some six months ago, they have entertained both of the king's elder sons. The king, too, has favored them. At Bath in September he granted them several estates that once belonged to your brother Wulf. When I arrived at your cousin's manor, Siferth and his brother had already left to join the king's host. I cannot say where their allegiance might lie—with you, with the ætheling Athelstan, or with the king."

His words were like a splash of icy water. She felt as if the cold from outside had crept into the chamber, into her bones even. She shuddered, picked up her cup, and took a deep swallow.

"You are right," she said. "That is ill news indeed."

"Lady"—his voice was a seductive growl as he leaned to whisper in her ear—"they are men of wealth and property. They are in the king's eye. They cannot hide in the forest like lesser men. They cannot even make their way to you here for fear of drawing the king's men after them and putting you at risk. Eadric has been nosing around Siferth's estates searching for you, and your cousin is terrified of him. You cannot press too hard for their support. Not yet."

She was forced to admit to the truth in his words, although they did little to reassure her. Siferth and Morcar, like all of Æthelred's nobles, had much to gain by joining the winning side in the power struggle that was taking shape within the realm. And they had much to lose if they made the wrong choice. As yet she had nothing to offer them or others like them except the promise of future reward from an enemy king. They did not even know of her marriage to Cnut, for she had been sworn to silence until Swein and Cnut were prepared to make their bid for England's throne.

But she was tired of waiting, tired of living like an anchorite in this forgotten corner of Æthelred's kingdom.

She ran her finger around the rim of her silver cup and considered what she could do to bring about the downfall of the king and so end her exile. What would happen if she should go to her cousin, seek refuge there until her confinement? Siferth was oath-bound to give her his protection. If she were to tell him that the child she carried was Cnut's son, what then? Could she not compel Siferth to forsake Æthelred? The men of Lindsey and the Five Boroughs would follow Siferth's lead, and that should be enough encouragement to draw Swein to England by next summer.

She tapped her fingers against the cup. There was Cnut to consider. He would forbid it, would claim that it was too soon. But Cnut, if he was alive, was in far-off Wessex. He could not stop her.

Swein's shipmen, though—out there in the yard—they would try to keep her in Holderness. She would have to make her preparations for the journey without alerting them to what she was about. It would take time—weeks, perhaps—but it could be done. And when all was ready, a great feast for the Danes and a liberal hand with the mead would allow her to slip away. She would take her own men, loyal to her alone, to guarantee her safety on the road; and she would leave word for Catla that she was making for Jorvik, in case that lout Thurbrand should try to find her.

Once more she set her cup aside and turned to Alric, placing a hand upon his arm.

"How many days," she asked, "will it take us to reach my cousin's estate in Lindsey?"


**London**

The queen's chamber was crowded almost to bursting, and Emma, searching frantically for her daughter, found her in the arms of a stranger. The young woman's white breast glimmered in the candlelight, and Godiva's tiny hand patted the bare flesh while she sucked greedily, wide eyes fixed on the face above her.

Emma threw off her cloak as she strode across the room to claim her child.

"Give me my daughter," she said.

The wet nurse looked up, startled, but she made no move to relinquish Godiva.

"The babe was hungry, my lady," she said. "She was crying for ever so long—"

"Just give me the child," Emma snapped.

Obediently the young woman slipped her finger into the voracious little mouth at her breast. Godiva began to howl, fists flailing, clearly outraged at being plucked from the one thing that gave her pleasure.

Emma snatched up her screaming daughter and carried her into the tiny chamber where Edward once had slept. Margot followed, as Emma had known she would, with a servant at her heels. Without a word, Margot took Godiva from Emma's arms, dandling the protesting infant while the servant assisted Emma with her gown. Moments later Emma was seated with her daughter at her breast.

Margot dismissed the servant, then stood with her hands folded in front of her.

"When I did not hear Godiva crying I feared the worst," Emma chided, although Margot's disapproving stance seemed to imply that somehow *she* was the one at fault.

"You must not blame that young woman," Margot said.

"I do not," Emma said, calmer now that Godiva was safe in her arms. "I blame you. How could you give her to another when you know that I need the child as much as she needs me?"

"Her need is for sustenance, my lady," Margot said, "not necessarily for you."

Feeling as if she'd been slapped, Emma had to bite back a bitter retort.

"Emma," Margot said, "you are a queen in peril, in a city that is likely to be under attack very soon. You belong to all of London, not just to this child. There are many, many people who will make demands on you, and they will draw you from your daughter's side. It is happening already. If you cannot attend her when she has need of you, your child will suffer far more than you will. I promise you, your mother did not permit you to suffer in such a way."

Emma swallowed the knot in her throat.

"My mother was wed to a man who had need of her at his side, who sought her counsel—not one who shut her out."

"Yet there are many in this city who welcome your counsel, and you have a duty to them," Margot insisted, her voice gentle now. "If you do not place your daughter into the hands of someone who can provide for her every need, you will be constantly torn between caring for your babe and caring for your people."

Emma closed her eyes. She did not want to hear this now, and especially not from Margot. She could ignore the advice of others, but Margot was the only person left to her whom she trusted utterly. And now she wanted her to be wrong.

"Leave me," she said. "We will speak again presently."

Alone with her daughter, Emma shifted the child to her other breast. The baby was already growing heavy with sleep. Emma could feel the tug and pull of Godiva's mouth slow as the child slipped into a doze, a little pearl of milk forming at the corner of her mouth. She had to rouse the child to suck some more just to relieve the heaviness of her breast.

She knew that Margot spoke the truth, but she could not bring herself to make the sacrifice that was being asked of her. She had nursed Edward for a full year before the demands of her position had forced her to give him over to another, and even then it had nearly broken her heart to do it. Godiva, barely four weeks old, was at the center of her life—as she should be, for daughters belonged to their mothers in ways that sons could not.

But she had not reckoned on the arrival of a Viking fleet and the urgent demands upon her that would result from it. Overseeing the city's response to the refugees and the sick, offering comfort to the stricken and reassurance to the despairing—these were the tasks of a queen. The Londoners would turn to her to lead them in their intercessions with God, as she had today. She must be free to move about the city, and she could not take Godiva with her.

She gazed into her daughter's sleeping face, at the tiny bow of her mouth and the round, fat cheeks. For a moment she could only marvel at the tenderness that gripped her. She had once feared that because she had given her heart to her son, there would be no love left for another child. How wrong she had been.

She knew what was best for her daughter but, God forgive her, she could not relinquish her to another. Not yet. Not so soon.

"I cannot give you up, little one," she whispered, grazing her finger against the soft skin of her daughter's cheek. Then she sighed and kissed the tiny nose. "But it seems that I must learn to share you," she said.

She would welcome that young woman as one of her attendants, and between them Godiva would have two mothers to nurse her, at least for a little while.


November 1009

Three days after the last of the Danish warships had sailed from Wight, their prows bent toward some objective that none could know for certain, Athelstan, with the king's permission, had at last set out for

London. He took with him his brother Edrid, twenty of his mounted hearth troops, and thirty Middlesex men on foot who had accompanied him from London in September. It took six days to reach the Thames Bridge, and by then he knew where the Danes had gone. Smoke hovered above the eastern horizon, and the bridge into London was choked with Kentish folk seeking refuge from the shipmen who were already raiding as far west as Greenwich.

He had sent a message ahead to London's bishop requesting a meeting, and when he entered his hall on Æthelingstrete he found a party of city leaders waiting for him. After dispatching someone to the palace to advise the queen that he would attend her before day's end, he turned to the men who were gathered around a trestle table in the center of the hall. He greeted each of them, gestured to them to sit, then took a place on the bench beside Bishop Ælfhun.

"When did the first ships arrive?" he asked.

"More than ten days ago," the bishop replied. "They've set up camps on both sides of the Thames, and they've been plundering any vessels that enter the river's mouth. We'll see no goods from the Low Countries while the Danes squat beside the river, but our landward supply routes north, east, and south are still open."

"Our ships are still in place on the river?" Athelstan asked.

"Yes, still moored in three lines at Earhith, and that was a good decision, my lord. They've met the Danish ships twice now, and turned them back both times. The main body of the land force, though, has moved to the north shore, within striking distance of London. Our defenders continue to man the walls as you instructed. We've added more men as newcomers enter the city but, truth be told, the number of those seeking refuge has increased our burden rather than lessened it. The queen has been meeting daily with city leaders to deal with at least some of the difficulties that we've been facing."

Difficulties, Athelstan thought grimly. What a polite way of describing the provision of food and shelter, setting up a system for disposing of human and animal waste, and keeping peace among fractious countrymen in crowded conditions and wretched weather. Difficulties that, if not resolved, would lead to pestilence and death. Judging from the crowds he'd seen today trying to get into the city, the difficulties were only going to get worse.

It was well after nightfall when he set out at last for the palace. Despite the growing number of people inside London's walls, the city was quiet due to watchmen stationed outside each church to enforce the curfew.

It was almost too quiet. It was as if the city itself was holding its breath, waiting for an axe to fall.

When he passed St. Paul's, the voices of the brothers at prayer floated into the clear night, the Latin verses of compline echoing in the alleys around the massive stone church, and he caught snatches of the psalm.

*My ravenous enemies beset me . . . crouching to the ground, they fix their gaze like lions hungry for prey.*

The psalm was unfamiliar, but it seemed an appropriate choice, given the enemy camped farther downriver. He hoped that the lion was not yet ready to pounce.

Inside the palace gates a servant scurried up to take his horse. Athelstan could see light glimmering from the high windows of the queen's apartment, and he moved in that direction but the lad stopped him.

"If you are come to see the queen, my lord, you will find her on the ramparts," he said.

"So late?" Athelstan asked.

"It is her habit to go up to the tower each night. I think she looks at the enemy watch fires, to see how close they've come."

He found Emma at the northeast corner of the wooden tower, barricaded against the cold by a heavy cloak and hood, her figure lit by a nearby torch. She was looking out over the marshes that spread beyond the city walls to the north and east as if she were held spellbound by whatever she saw in the darkness beyond.

He placed his hand over hers on the parapet, and as she grasped it in silent welcome he followed her gaze into the distance. Hundreds of fires glowed out there, pinpricks of light marking the enemy camp. They were, he guessed, less than a day's march away. A larger blaze burned amid the smaller ones, and he studied it for a moment, trying to puzzle out what it was.

"Barking Abbey is burning," Emma said, answering his unspoken question. "The nuns are safe, for they have been sheltering at the bishop's estate here in the city. They brought with them everything that they could carry—books, relics, vestments—anything of value. But they could not bring it all." She sighed. "This will be a blow to the abbess. She has been praying that they would spare her church, at least. I wonder, will anything out there be left standing when they are finished?"

There was no despair in her voice, only frustration and anger that seemed to match his own.

"We should have prevented this." It was Eadric's doing, all of it. Every life lost, every village ravaged could be laid at Eadric's feet. "My father should never have allowed Thorkell and his army to return to their ships. You heard what happened at Salisbury?"

"That Eadric advised the king to avoid a battle, and that you and he nearly came to blows. Yes, that much I know. How the king and Eadric intend to rid us of this enemy I have not been able to discover."

"I should have murdered Eadric," he snarled, "and rid us of one enemy, at least. As for those bastards"—he jerked his chin toward the distant fires—"we have to meet them on the field of battle and come away the clear winners. But to do that our leaders must be of one mind, and right now that is impossible. We are our own worst enemies." He took both her hands and turned her so that he could look into her face, its features sculpted in the flickering torchlight. The last time he had seen her she had been ripe with pregnancy. Now she looked drawn and tired. Stretched. Yet still she was beautiful. "How is it with you, lady?" he asked. "And with your daughter?"

"We are well enough," she replied, then she frowned. "You spoke of Eadric; has he gone with the king to Worcester?"

Ah. So she knew where the king planned to spend the Yule. Then she must know of his youngest sister's imminent nuptials as well.

"To witness my sister's marriage to Ulfkytel," he said, "yes. Surely Wulfa has asked the king to allow you to be there with her."

"Has asked and been refused," she replied. "The king is still angry with me, despite my efforts to appease him." Her voice was bitter. "He asked me to intercede with my brother Richard, to request Norman help after so many of our ships were lost in the spring. I did so, but Richard very regretfully declined. He has his own more pressing concerns that demand ships and men. So I have earned the king's displeasure once again and remain an outcast from the court. In any case, Worcester is too far away—too long and difficult a journey for my daughter. Even with an enemy army outside our walls, she is safer here." She turned to look again at the fires burning on the horizon. "How long, do you think, before they march upon the city?"

He squinted up at the clear night sky, riddled with stars.

"If the weather holds," he said, "it will likely be within a few days."

"Can we beat them?"

"No," he said, frowning at the campfires so numerous that they mirrored the stars up in the sky. "But we can keep them outside the city until they grow weary."

"And then they will strike somewhere else, someplace less able to withstand them."

"Unless God intervenes," he said, "and keeps them weather-bound until the spring."

Before the next dawn a storm blasted in from the east accompanied by lightning and thunder so biblical in their fury that Athelstan wondered if the abbess of Barking Abbey had called down the wrath of Saint Ethelberga on the men who had savaged her shrine. The storm lashed London for three days, and on the fourth day, when the rain had ceased, a nearly impenetrable fog crept up the Thames Valley to lie like a dead thing upon the river and the city. It mingled with the smoke from the city's dwellings, making it impossible to see across even the narrowest of lanes. Londoners were accustomed to the noisome vapors, but those unfamiliar with the city had to be warned away from the river, for even the rushing sound of the water was deadened, and one careless step might lead to a watery death.

All that day the wet, cloying mist smothered London and the surrounding countryside, and if there was an army out there, it hadn't been seen or heard. Athelstan's scouts reported that the enemy remained in their camp near Barking. At a meeting with London's war council, he speculated that Thorkell might not risk moving his men in the fog across the unfamiliar, sodden moor that lay between Barking Abbey and London.

"But he might send a smaller force against us under cover of the fog," he cautioned, "to test our defenses and catch us napping. Our men on the walls must remain wary."

In midafternoon, with Edrid at his side, Athelstan walked the ramparts between the Aldgate and the Bishopsgate. This, the council believed, was where Thorkell would focus any attack. The enemy would likely wait until the fog lifted, but there was no guarantee of that. Sentries stationed on the wall had to remain alert, no matter how exhausted they might be from long hours of keeping watch in the impenetrable mist.

Athelstan spoke a word of encouragement to each man he passed. At the same time he listened for the usual clamor of activity from the streets below. But London was hushed, for the fog muffled every sound. Even the church bells ringing the hours were muted, as if their tongues were made of clotted wool. It was not the weather alone, he knew, that had silenced England's greatest city. The knowledge that an enemy could be but an arrow's flight away, waiting to strike, was a burden that each citizen carried like a dead weight. Fear was as palpable as the droplets in the mist.

As he and Edrid approached the wide platform above the Bishopsgate, a cloaked figure appeared almost immediately in front of them.

"I hope to God," a gruff voice growled, "that you haven't rationed all the ale in this damned city. I've been riding for days and I could use a drink."

"Edmund!" Athelstan cried, reaching for his brother's arm and clasping it in greeting. "God alone knows how you found your way here through this infernal swill, but you are most welcome. I thought that you were on your way to the king at Worcester. Did you get lost in the fog? Did you bring any men with you? Wait. Let us get out of this murk so we can talk in comfort."

When they were seated at a scarred table in the watchtower beside the Aldgate, he repeated his questions.

"I was summoned to Worcester, yes," Edmund replied, "but I left

Winchester before the summons could be delivered." He grinned. "At least, that is what Ealdorman Ælfric will swear to when the king asks for me. I think Ælfric would have come with me, for Emma had sent him word of the army perched on your doorstep. But unlike me he could not bring himself to ignore a summons from the king." He paused to toss back some ale, then said, "As for men, I've brought nearly twenty of Ælfric's best warriors with me—you will know most of them—as well as arms and supplies. We would have been here sooner but the storm slowed us and then we nearly had to crawl the last ten miles. *Christ*, how long has it been like this?"

Athelstan rubbed the back of his neck, aching from the weight of his mail shirt. "It started this morning and God only knows when it will lift. I cannot decide if it is to our advantage or not. The king's levies may have returned to their homes for the winter, but Thorkell's men have been making a nuisance of themselves in Essex and Kent. We have been able to do little to hinder them except to provide refuge for those trying to escape them."

"You think they'll attack London?"

"They are camped less than a day's march to the east, so I would be surprised if they did not try. I hope to give them little joy for their efforts, though. Our walls are firm, and there has been no sign of siege engines so far. Anything heavy would get bogged down out there on the moor, especially in this weather." He frowned. "They have had plenty of time to build small catapults, though, and there are likely men among them with the skill to do it. If they can cobble something together with sufficient range, they might lob enough stones at us to shatter our ramparts and get through. Still, the palisades are high and the ditches outside the walls will keep them at a distance. I think our worst threat will be from fire arrows. We've organized teams all over the city to deal with them, and certainly the weather has lessened that danger for the moment."

"They might lay a siege," Edmund said, frowning. "They were able to surround Canterbury back in August."

Athelstan shook his head. "We're protected by the river," he said. "We've placed ships across the Thames at Earhith and two more lines of them just east of here, downriver from where the city wall meets the water. They can't get to us with their own vessels unless they somehow break through all three lines, and our navy—well, what's left of it— won't make it easy for them. They can't surround us and they can't sur- prise us. Canterbury, if you recall, was attacked at night with no warning, and had no opportunity to bolster its defense with seasoned warriors. London has been preparing for weeks."

Edmund stroked his short, dark beard thoughtfully. "As you say, the Northmen are fond of striking when their victims aren't looking. So what are they up to while we're not looking?"

"In this damned fog," Athelstan said, "it could be just about any- thing. I've got men watching them from the hills above their camp, but for the moment they seem to be staying put."

He saw that Edrid, seated across the table from him, was frowning, chewing on some idea that he seemed reluctant to voice.

"Out with it, Edrid," Athelstan encouraged him.

Edrid set down his ale cup and said, "Ealdorman Uhtred told me that a good commander always thinks like his enemy. So how would you at- tack London, if you were Thorkell?"

"A heavily fortified city like this?" Edmund asked. "I wouldn't even try. I'd go around it. Hit someplace else that was less well defended."

Athelstan considered the question, thinking back to the last time the Danes had brought down a fortified English town.

"At Exeter," he said, "they used stealth. They found the hidden en- trance into the city and sent in a small raiding party to open the gates from the inside."

Edmund shook his head. "That couldn't work here. There are no se- cret entrances into London."

"True," Athelstan agreed. "And every gate has a dozen men on guard at all times, day and night. When they open at dawn, anyone who wants entry has to make a thorough accounting of himself, and if he even smells foreign he's turned away."

"What about the river gates?" Edrid asked. "Those are far easier to breech."

"But our ships have barricaded the river," Athelstan said again.

"Unless the Danish ships stage a full-on naval attack, they can't get through."

"What if they don't use ships?" Edrid asked. "What if they use small boats—wherries, say—that hold only one or two men? Wait for the incoming tide, slip a score of boats into the water, and you'd be carried right past the blockade. At night, in this fog, nobody could see them; couldn't even hear them."

Athelstan looked at Edmund, who was staring back at him, horror blooming in his eyes.

"Sweet Holy Mother of God," Edmund whispered.

"They could do it," Athelstan said. "They wouldn't even need to attack the river gates. The wall along the water is low enough that they could scuttle over it like rats."

"Let's say they make it over the river wall and into the city; where would they go?" Edmund asked.

Athelstan did not hesitate. "The Whitgate," he said, "in the eastern wall, close to the river. If I were planning this, I'd have more men waiting outside there, ready to storm in once the first group attacked the guards and opened the gate."

"But how would the men inside the city find the Whitgate?" Edrid asked. "Even if they know it exists?"

"Thorkell's men must have taken a dozen merchant ships in the Thames estuary over the past weeks," Athelstan said. "Most of them would be piloted by men who could navigate blindfolded along London's bankside and all the boatyards and alleyways below the bridge. I don't doubt that Thorkell could find at least one man who could be persuaded to guide a force into the city in exchange for his life."

"Could they do it tonight?" Edrid asked. "Could they put together such a plan so quickly, using the fog as cover?"

"Every seaman in Christendom knows about London's fogs," Edmund said. "They may have worked out the plan months ago, hoping they would get a chance to use it. Athelstan, can you be certain that Thorkell's army still lies up at Barking? Could the bastards have moved toward the city without your scouts knowing it, or without us hearing it?"

"In this damned swill I cannot be certain of anything," Athelstan said. "They won't attack until the morning, though. They'll want their men to be fresh."

"What about the men slipping in from the river?" Edmund asked.

"They would have to wait for the tide to turn in their favor."

"The tide was flooding when I crossed the river just after midday," Edmund said. "Could they already be in the city?"

"I don't think so," Athelstan said, trying to think as Thorkell would and working out a plausible plan in his head. "They would not try to enter the city in daylight, even with the fog. They'll come in the fourth watch, I expect, when the tide starts to flood again." He clapped Edrid on the shoulder. "Good work, brother," he said. "And for your reward you can sit up with us beside the Whitgate tonight."

He shouted for his hearth troops and sent runners to all the city commanders with orders to double the men on the wall. Then he led his brothers and their company of warriors through the silent, murky streets toward the Whitgate.

If Edrid's conjecture was right, they would see battle before dawn.

The light in Emma's bower had been dim all day in spite of the high window and the extra candles she had called for. Now it was nearly dusk, and like the other women seated around her, Emma squinted so that she could better focus her eyes on her task—in her case the stitching of a long seam in the side of a plain linen scyrte. In times of war, her mother had taught her, delicate embroidery work was an affront to God and to the men who risked their lives for their lord. The wounded needed warm, serviceable garments to replace torn, ripped, bloodstained linen that often had to be cut away from mangled flesh. So for many days now, all over London, women had been seated at their looms or bent over strips of linen or wool, making their own preparations for battle.

When a servant entered to announce that Father Martin had arrived and was begging an audience, Emma looked up in alarm. The priest was supposed to be attending Edward in Ely. What would make him journey here, especially now, with an army camped just outside the city walls?

She nodded to the servant, called for wine, and glanced at Margot. Gray eyes met hers with gravity, their message clear.

*Stay composed. There are many eyes upon you. Whatever happens, do not forget who you are.*

With an effort of will Emma lodged her needle in its fabric, set the scyrte aside, and folded her hands to steady them. Margot rose and came to stand beside her.

Father Martin, his cloak already discarded, the hem of his robe wet and muddy, hurried into the room and dropped to one knee before her.

"Edward is well," he said even before she had a chance to ask after her son.

A weight lifted from her heart at these words, but as she gave him her hand and bade him sit, she searched his face for some clue to his mission. It had been seven months since he had accompanied Edward to Ely, and Martin looked little changed, although there were lines of weariness and worry about his eyes.

"Something is amiss, though," she said. "Tell me what it is."

"There is pestilence at Ely, my lady," he said.

One of the women in the chamber cried out, and although Emma quelled her with a glance, she, too, was alarmed at this.

"Go on," she said.

"Many have fallen sick, and some have died, young and old alike. Peterborough Abbey has been struck as well. Abbot Ælsi deemed it unsafe for Edward to remain in the fens, so the prior and I were charged with escorting him to the royal manor at Headington. Eight days ago we set out, accompanied by all of Edward's Norman guards, and we made it as far as Northampton when bad weather forced us to take shelter." He paused for breath. "Your son begged us to bring him here to London, but when the prior explained that he was bound by holy vows to obey his abbot's command, Edward accepted his fate. You would have been proud of him, my lady." He gave her a wry, tired smile. "Nevertheless, I am here at Edward's request to beg you to meet him at Headington, although I warned him that it may not be in your power to do so."

She imagined Edward, angry at being thwarted in his wish to return to her, striving to be a brave ætheling when he was simply a little boy who wanted his mother. Her heart ached for him.

"I fear you will have to disappoint your young lord when you return to him," she said. "He must look to Wymarc to console him in my absence." She saw a shadow fall across Father Martin's face, and her heart lurched again. "What is it?"

"Robert fell ill on the morning that we left Ely. His mother stayed behind to care for him and for the others who were suffering."

She felt Margot's hand upon her shoulder, and she reached up to clasp it, to steady herself against this news.

Margot asked, "What is the nature of the pestilence?"

"It begins with head pain and fever, followed by a painful cramping of the stomach. The body rejects all nourishment."

"The flux," Margot muttered. "And those who are weak at the start will waste away, while the strong, like Robert"—Emma felt a reassuring squeeze at her shoulder—"will mend. Still, sending Edward away was a wise course of action. Father, did you hear any rumors of sickness as you came south?"

"None."

Margot nodded. "It might be a disease wrought from the foul air of the Fenlands," she said. "The pestilence may not thrive outside the mires of East Anglia"—she drew a heavy breath—"yet I mistrust this fog that has come upon us here in London." Her gaze seemed to lose focus, and she murmured to herself, "The airs are thick and fetid, and I fear they are laced with evil humors. Mary Thistle might ward off whatever is coming, and I had best begin brewing it." She beckoned to a servant. "As if we did not have enough troubles to vex us." She was shaking her head as she hurried out of the chamber.

Father Martin watched her leave, then turned to Emma.

"Is she well?" he asked.

Emma sighed. "Yes, but the years are taking their toll, I fear, and she is burdened with the care of us all. Her mind is wonderfully lucid, although when she fixes on an idea she forgets all else."

Her own thoughts still lingered on Wymarc and Robert, and on the events at Ely. She questioned the priest for more details, garnering from him a clearer understanding of the part that Wymarc had played in tending the sick and in urging the abbot to send Edward to safety.

"Edward will find Edyth at Headington," she said, "where she is awaiting the birth of her child." What kind of welcome would he receive from his half sister, who had only ever regarded him with resentment? A chilly one, she suspected. Likely Edward would have need of a friend. "For Edward's sake, Father, I would have you return to him as soon as you can—tomorrow if you feel up to the journey."

She would be sorry to see him go so soon. She had missed him these past months, for he had been more than her spiritual adviser. He had been her confidant, her supporter, and her friend.

Edward's need, though, far outweighed her own.

"And what should I tell your son?"

What message could she send that Edward would understand? She recalled Margot's words a few days before, that she risked being torn between the needs of her daughter and the needs of the people of London. Yet here she was, torn between the needs of daughter and son.

"Tell Edward that his new sister is too young yet to travel, and that I cannot leave her behind. Tell him that I will come to him as soon as I can."

It was only a few days' travel to Headington. As soon as Godiva was strong enough, in just a few more weeks, she would grant Edward's plea and go to him. Reassure him that all would be well. That much, at the least, she could do for her son.

But for Wymarc and Robert, she thought bleakly, she could do nothing. Pestilence did not bow to the commands of a queen. It was a ravenous beast that fed on all in its path, young and old alike. Despite Margot's reassuring words, she was afraid for Wymarc and her son, but she could not see how to help them except to commit them to God. Their deliverance rested in His hands, not hers.

# Chapter Twenty-One

November 1009

London

Long before dawn Athelstan had placed his men among the workshops and storage sheds scattered near the Whitgate in an area between the Lorteburn and London's eastern wall. It was part of the king's royal shipyard, and there were numerous places for men to hide amid the outbuildings and the upturned hulls of ships awaiting repair.

From his position in a gap between two sheds, Athelstan could not see the city wall that rose some distance away to his left, but he knew that armed men stood on its ramparts, one man every five feet all the way down to the wooden tower at the water's edge. He had warned them that because of the torches posted at intervals along the palisade, they would be targets if there were bowmen among the raiders.

"Keep your shields up and your heads down," he had told them. "You men on the ground, hold your attack until you hear my command. Stay alert and do what you can to stay warm."

Time passed slowly as they waited among the shadows, and Athelstan stood pressed against the shed to avoid the steady drip from the eave's wet thatch. He had taken a position that was farthest from London's wall, facing a muddy path that ran west from the Whitgate toward the burn. He could make out little of what lay on the other side of the path except vague shapes that were likely piles of scrap wood, coiled rope, and tuns of pitch. As he strained his eyes and ears to make out any movement, he went over the layout of the Whitgate in his mind.

Like every other gate into the city, it had an outer and an inner door separated by a tunnel roughly nine feet long that bored through the width of the wall. The doors were made of solid oak, reinforced with iron crossbeams—part of the increased fortifications he had ordered this past summer. That effort was paying off now, for once the stout doors were locked from the inside, it would be no easy task to break through them.

Unlike the other gates, which were wide enough to allow carts and wagons through, the Whitgate was narrow, barely wide enough for a man, and so low that one had to stoop to go through it. On the outer side there was no bridge across the defensive ditch below the wall, merely a narrow stone landing and an even narrower flight of stone steps that led down along the wall and into the ditch itself. If there were men out there, waiting to climb those steps and enter the city, they were standing knee-deep in water, mud, and refuse.

That, at least, was a cheering thought.

Some instinct made him turn and look north toward the Bishops-gate. At first he could see nothing but fog and the dim shapes of houses in the streets behind him. Then a rain of stars appeared.

Fire arrows.

So, the attack had begun. He imagined the Danish force gathered on the moorland between the Bishopsgate and the Aldgate. How many men? The bulk of Thorkell's army, surely, to keep the Londoners' attention focused away from the river. If he and his brothers were right, there were more men just here, on the other side of the Whitgate, waiting for it to open from within.

He drew his sword slowly, so that it made no sound, and he strained his eyes to gaze into the dark that was fading now toward morning. Nothing moved.

*Christ*, where were the bastards? They should have been here by now. A sudden black doubt clouded his mind. What if he had been wrong about the Whitgate? What if even now there were armed men farther west along the river, making their way toward one of the other gates, gutting anyone who got in their way?

Then he saw a disturbance on the path, tendrils of mist twisting and swirling, dark shapes gliding like phantoms in the predawn. They made no noise, and he guessed that they had sacrificed their ring mail for stealth. It would have worked had Edrid not guessed their plan. A spear's length in front of him, a man emerged from the shadows followed by other dark shapes that slipped past where Athelstan stood pressed against the shed. He was itching to move, poised to intercept the swordsmen, but he wanted no enemies at his back when his trap was sprung.

At last, when he'd counted ten heartbeats and no other shapes had appeared from out of the fog, he darted from cover. He roared the name of the king, the signal for his men to attack, and the nearest of the shadows whipped around to face him, sword at the ready. The stroke came from above, but Athelstan ran into it, meeting it with his shield and throwing his foe off balance. He kept driving forward, slashing sideways, sword biting deep into leather and flesh that yielded and fell. He dragged the blade across the man's throat and ran on, sprinting toward the wall, where the clash of weapons and the shouts of men now filled the air.

The shipmen, hopelessly outnumbered by the defenders who had sprung at them from all sides, had turned to attack the English with a ferocity born of desperation. Athelstan, hearing the crunch of axe on wood from somewhere near the wall and knowing that their efforts would be for naught if the gates were breached, ignored the battle in front of him and made for the bastard attacking the oak door. As he neared the wall he saw Edrid run up the palisade steps and then, to his horror, saw his brother throw himself down onto whatever was below him. The axe was stilled briefly, then the blows began again.

Cursing, he tried to make his way to Edrid, cutting savagely at a squat, toad-faced shipman who got in his way. Then a bull of a man in a leather jerkin stepped into his path, his sword arm raised to strike. Athelstan brought his shield inside the arc of the brute's stroke, ramming its edge into the shipman's shoulder and plunging his sword at the man's middle. He felt his blade slice against a rib, and in the same instant he saw Edmund spring at the shipman from behind to bury his sword in the big man's back.

With that stroke, the skirmish inside the wall was over, yet the rhythmic beat of axe on wood continued, and Athelstan realized that the Danes were still trying to get through the wall from the other side. He looked toward the ramparts and saw defenders clustered above the landing. Some were heaving stones the size of a man's head into the outer ditch. An instant later the sound of the axe was stilled.

He searched wildly for any sign of Edrid. His men, most of them blood-spattered and winded from exertion, were stalking among the fallen Danes to finish off any who still lived.

He saw Edmund and ran to him, gripping his arm.

"Edrid is down," he said. "Help me find him."

"He's here, lord," one of his men, Birstan, called.

Athelstan, with Edmund at his heels, went over to where Birstan was crouched on the ground beside Edrid's body.

"There is no blood, lord," Birstan said, "but I cannot wake him. He's alive, though."

"You men"—Athelstan motioned to two of his hearth troops—"take him to All Hallows, along with anyone else who needs care." He turned back to Birstan. "Did we lose anyone?"

"A few wounded is all," Birstan said, "and more work to do, judging by the look of things."

Athelstan followed his gaze northward, where fire arrows continued to rain over the wall to the accompaniment of distant shouts and screams. He nodded.

"You take twenty men," he said to Birstan, "and scour the area between here and the river. Make sure that there are no more water rats hiding near the hythes or trying to make their way into the city. You men"—he pointed at the guardsmen assigned to this section of the wall—"strip the enemy dead of their arms and anything else of value and put it in the guardhouse for sorting later. When you've finished with them, dump their bodies over the wall." He grimaced. "Let Thorkell and his northern vermin see how London treats uninvited guests. The rest of you will come with me to reinforce the men at the Aldgate."

But he did not set out immediately. Instead he watched with Edmund as Edrid was gently laid upon a shield.

"He will come around," Edmund said. "He has just taken a bad knock to the head."

"I hope to God you are right," Athelstan muttered, watching the men carry his brother away. "I do not want to have to tell the king that he has lost another son."

Edmund grunted. "I do not want to tell him that we lost London to Thorkell." He clapped Athelstan on the shoulder. "Come on. We cannot do any more here, and we are needed elsewhere."

Athelstan nodded, and together they led the men up toward the Aldgate, their shields held high against the arrows that continued to rain down on the city.


## December 1009
## Greetham, Lindsey

Elgiva stood beside her mount, her stomach twisting with anxiety as she waited for permission to enter Siferth's great hall. She was weary, her limbs heavy as stone, and she was eager to be within doors. But the men set to guard the hall's entrance were regarding her companions with suspicion. The snow that had threatened all morning began to fall in thick, wet flakes as Alric, who had been negotiating with the armed door wards, came to her side.

"I'm to escort you within, my lady, and Tyra with you. Your hearth men, though, must stay in the stables, under guard."

She nodded. She had been half afraid that they would turn her away before she could even speak with her cousin.

Inside the screens passage a gray-bearded steward gruffly demanded their names and business, then left them under the eye of four burly guards while he informed his mistress that Alric and his sister, Ealhwyn, from Jorvik, requested shelter for the night.

"You should have given him my true name," she muttered to Alric. "I am safe enough here in my cousin's hall."

"You are south of the Humber now, my lady," Alric replied, "and even in your cousin's hall you would not be safe should your true name be spoken. Rest assured your cousin will know well enough who is at her door."

Impatiently she drummed her fingers against the screen beside her as she peered around it to watch the servant's slow progress toward the dais. Lord Siferth, they had been told, was still with the king at Worcester, and that was just as well. She was confident that if he were here she could win his support for Swein's bid for England's throne, but it was a relief not to have to begin such an endeavor today. She was tired, and the discomforts of early pregnancy had turned out to be even worse than she remembered. Seven days of winter travel had taxed her more than she had anticipated. The potions that Tyra had brewed for her had done little to ease her queasy stomach and aching limbs, and now she wanted nothing more than a cup of warm wine and a cushioned seat by the fire.

The steward arrived at last at the top of the hall where she could see her cousin, flanked by two older women, pacing back and forth with a squalling child in her arms. That would be Aldyth's son. A little tremor of envy snaked through her, but she would have her own son soon enough.

Her cousin seemed too occupied with her screaming brat to pay the old man much heed, and Elgiva could see no sign that Aldyth understood who was asking to see her, when the old man turned and beckoned to them.

"Stay here," she said to Tyra, "and speak to no one."

She nodded to Alric, who led the way through the noisy, crowded hall.

Aldyth's folk were busy with winter chores: A group of men were repairing leather straps on bridles and hauberks while others were using whetstones to put a fine edge on knives and swords. Three women were seated at looms, while a group of girls oversaw a clutch of small children who tumbled together in an enclosure away from the central fire. Several women sat in a circle, each with a spindle and distaff, and several more had pulled trestle tables away from the wall and were preparing to lay a meal.

By the time they reached the dais Aldyth had handed her son to a servant and now she stepped forward to greet them. Beneath her linen veil her thick, dark hair was plaited and knotted atop her head so that she looked even taller than Elgiva remembered. One shoulder of her rich, dark-green woolen cyrtel was blotched and wet with her son's tears—or something worse. Elgiva pursed her lips, assessing the value of Aldyth's gown, the jeweled pins that held her headrail in place, and the embroidered hangings that draped the wall behind her. There was wealth in this hall—gold that Swein and Cnut could put to good use. She smiled at Aldyth, who returned it with a look so cool that Elgiva felt her stomach clench with anxiety again.

"You and your—your *sister*—are welcome, Alric," Aldyth said, although there was no note of welcome in her voice. "I am eager to hear what errand brings you so far south."

She gestured for them to follow her, and she led them into a small, private space behind the embroidered draperies. Two intricately carved chairs faced each other there, illuminated by an oil lamp suspended from an iron chain. The moment that the draperies closed behind them, Elgiva felt her cousin's fingers grip her wrist like the talons of a hawk.

"Who knows that you have come to me?" Aldyth hissed.

Taken aback, Elgiva wrenched herself free from her cousin's long, agile fingers.

"No one knows," she snapped. "I traveled here in secret. Until today I did not even wear a woman's gown. I am not a fool, cousin. You have nothing to fear."

"Only someone with nothing to lose has nothing to fear." There was just the hint of hysteria in Aldyth's voice. "I have been afraid ever since your father was killed. Even my husband is afraid."

Elgiva looked from her cousin's white, angry face to the two chairs. She chose the larger one, sat down, and shrugged off her cloak. She flicked a hand at Alric, who placed himself where he could watch the hall lest someone come close enough to overhear their conversation. Raising an eyebrow at her cousin she asked, "Is that why Siferth trails after the king like a whipped dog? Because he is afraid?"

Aldyth stiffened. "The king commands his presence. Siferth has no choice."

"There are always choices," Elgiva said. "Sit down."

Her cousin hesitated, clearly resentful at being given an order in her own hall. Then she drew the second chair forward so that it angled toward Elgiva.

"You are mad to come here," Aldyth said. "They are still searching for you. What is it that you want?" Her brown eyes glinted with anger.

Cow eyes, Elgiva had always thought them—large and liquid and warm. But now they were hostile and a little wild. This was not the cousin she remembered. Aldyth, six years her junior, had ever been mild and sweet-natured, biddable and eager to please. There was nothing sweet in her expression now. Or mild. Something had hardened her. Was it marriage or was it fear that had done it? Fear, she guessed. Most likely fear of Eadric, the king's butcher.

Well, that made common cause between them. And now she must find some way to use her cousin's fear to her own advantage. She leaned forward and placed a firm hand on her cousin's knee.

"It is Eadric who frightens you, is it not?" she asked in a low voice. "Aldyth, he murdered my father. He drove me into hiding, and yes, I know that we are not safe. But I am not your enemy. What has he done to you that you are so afraid?"

Her cousin's face went pale, and her lips narrowed into a thin, straight line. She turned away from Elgiva for a long moment, and when she turned back there was anguish in her eyes. She clasped her hands in front of her and began to rock back and forth, staring into the middle distance, breathing hard as if she could not get enough air.

Elgiva wondered if perhaps it was Aldyth who was a little mad.

After a few moments, though, her cousin seemed to recover her wits and her breath, and she began to tell her story.

"Eadric was here, only a month ago," she said. "Siferth was away, and Eadric had far more men with him than my husband had left behind to protect me. At first I made them welcome. I had nothing to hide, and I thought that when they found no trace of you, they would leave us in peace."

She paused, took another gulp of air, and went on.

"They did not leave. Eadric made himself master of my hall, and his followers searched every farm and village within a day's ride from here. Men were tortured and women beaten, all of it pointless because there was nothing to find. On the last morning that he was here Eadric came to my quarters with his bullies and ordered the girl tending my son to go out of doors and to take the child with her. His men would see to them, he told me, while I answered his questions. And I did what he wanted. I answered everything he asked me—so many questions—and all the while I heard my babe crying and the girl screaming and screaming and it would not stop." She shut her eyes, putting her hands over her ears as if she could hear the sounds again.

Elgiva remained silent, waiting. There was more to the story, and Aldyth needed to rid herself of it.

Her cousin drew another long, desperate breath.

"They raped Jenna. That was her name, Jenna. They stripped her and savaged her like wild dogs. I do not know how many there were. Ten? Fifteen?" She spoke in a rough, husky whisper now. "She was only twelve summers old, little more than a child. She could not speak when they were through with her, and she was so badly hurt that we could do little for her. She died during the night." Aldyth raised her eyes to Elgiva's. "I do not know what they did to my son. I will never know. There were no marks on him but—"

Her voice trailed off. Elgiva recalled the wailing child she had seen when she entered the hall, then she pushed the memory away. The only child that mattered was the one that she would bear.

"Did you tell Siferth what happened?"

Aldyth shook her head.

"Eadric warned that it would be unfortunate for Siferth to hear news that might distress him. He might even come to harm." Her mouth twisted into a grimace. "He smiled when he said that. Eadric can smile even while he does his filthy work. I think he is the devil come to life."

No, not a devil, Elgiva thought. Just a man drunk with power. She stood up and studied her cousin, who looked more sick and weary, even, than Elgiva felt.

"A time is coming, Aldyth, when Eadric and the king will pay for their crimes against our family. I will have my vengeance on them for the murder of my father and brothers, and you and Siferth will help me get it."

Aldyth gazed at her with dark, suspicious eyes.

"What do you mean?"

Elgiva placed her hands on the arms of Aldyth's chair, and their faces were only inches apart.

"Three years ago my father betrothed me to an enemy of the king. Because of that act he was murdered and my brothers killed, but there were other men in the north who knew and approved of their intentions, although they escaped the king's vengeance. I believe that your husband was one of them. What Siferth does not yet know is that the marriage took place. I am the wife of Cnut Sweinson," she said in a fierce whisper, "and even now I am carrying his child." She saw the understanding blossom on her cousin's face. "Soon the Danish king and his son will claim my properties and the allegiance of my kin, and when that time comes, Æthelred had best look to his throne."

She studied Aldyth's face to read her response, but to her surprise her cousin pushed her away.

"You are a liar!" Aldyth cried. "My husband would never betray his oath to the king."

"Don't be stupid!" she snapped. "Any man would if he thought he could gain lands and influence as a result. And even if Siferth is innocent as a newborn lamb, your close kinship to me will make him suspect in Æthelred's eyes. It already has, or he would not keep Siferth so closely at his side, nor would Eadric have dealt so harshly with your people. You have no choice except to help me!"

Aldyth covered her mouth with her hands, and Elgiva wondered if she would weep. But her cousin lowered her hands and glared at her.

"A moment ago," Aldyth said, "you told me that there are always choices. Were you given a choice, Elgiva, when you wed this Danish prince?"

Elgiva scowled. Aldyth knew as well as she did that women were rarely consulted when it came to marriage.

"My choice," she hissed, "lay in what I would do next. I could either crawl into a hole and die, or I could one day become a queen." She sat down again, clutching the arms of the thronelike chair, steeling herself against the griping in her stomach that seemed to worsen under her cousin's cold gaze. "I have chosen the latter course."

Aldyth's mouth twisted, as if she'd tasted something sour. "And what is it that you want of me?"

"Refuge—until my child is born next summer. You are my closest kin, Aldyth. I would have my child born here in your hall, not among strangers."

"Here!" Aldyth bolted upright, panic flaring in her eyes again. "But what if the king discovers that you are here—"

"How will he discover it? Eadric was here only a month ago and found nothing. He is not likely to come back, and nor will anyone know that it is your cousin who bides with you over the winter. They will know me only as Ealhwyn, from Jorvik. At the very least allow me to stay until Siferth returns. If your husband commands me to leave, I will go." And that, she was certain, he would not do.

She watched Aldyth, and could almost see her weighing the risks in her mind. Both the English king and the Danish king would be ruthless in their vengeance. Which one was most likely to win?

Finally Aldyth said, "Swein's path to the throne will not be an easy one. Æthelred will resist. His sons and many of his nobles will fight for him out of kinship or out of fear." She leaned forward. "You seek my help. Tell me: Do you expect me to give it out of kinship with you or out of fear of the Danish king?"

Elgiva shrugged. "I desire only that you help me, Aldyth," she said. "I do not in the least care why."

When the household gathered to eat, Aldyth led them in prayer, petitioning God's blessings on the food and on a tedious and lengthy list of folk that included a guest who had apparently died the night before.

"I hope that not all of my cousin's guests go from her hall straight to God," Elgiva murmured to Alric as they took their places at the board.

"You need not worry. One of the grooms told me that the dead man was with a group of monks from Peterborough who sought a night's shelter here. He was already sick when he arrived, and his brothers were forced to leave him behind. Unless you are sick, you have nothing to fear."

He nodded to the servant, who was offering to ladle fish soup, the standard Advent fare, into his bowl. Elgiva clenched her mouth tight and waved the servant away. Of course she was sick. She was pregnant.

She broke a piece from the small, brown loaf in front of her and ate it in tiny bites, for the pain in her stomach had worsened during her conversation with her cousin. It was not illness that plagued her, she knew, but misgiving. Aldyth, who had shown little enough enthusiasm upon learning the purpose of this cousinly visit, had shared news that only added to her anxiety.

Thorkell's army, which had ravaged for weeks unchallenged by Æthelred's fyrd, had come to grief when it mounted an attack on London. The Londoners had defended their city from behind its great walls, and the Danes had lost good men and gained nothing for their efforts.

She took a sip from her cup, but the fear that she had carried with her from Holderness turned the wine to gall in her mouth. For all she knew, Cnut might be one of the Danish dead.

"Tomorrow," she murmured to Alric, "you will set out for the Danish camp. I would know if I still have a husband living. If you find him, give him my greetings, tell him that I am with child, but make no mention of where I am." She had no wish to give Cnut an excuse to berate her.

Alric slanted a speculative glance at her.

"And if he is not living?" he asked.

She toyed thoughtfully with the bits of bread in front of her, worrying them to broken fragments. Then she gave a careless shrug, for she would not have Alric see how much that thought frightened her.

"Swein Forkbeard," she said, "has another son, has he not? One Danish prince, I think, is as good as another."

# Chapter Twenty-Two

December 1009
London

Athelstan arrived at the London palace in response to an urgent, early morning summons from the queen. He paused at the entrance to Emma's chamber and waited for the steward to announce him. The scene before him, like the one that had greeted him belowstairs, was one of frenzied activity—the men and women of the queen's household going swiftly about the task of packing up her belongings. Bedding, gowns, caskets of jewels, reliquaries, shoes, piles of embroidered hangings, blankets and small clothes for the child—all the armaments of a queen were being sorted into bundles and coffers.

Where did she think to go? Had the king relented and bid Emma join him at Worcester for Christmastide? His brother Edrid, recovered from his injury at the wall, had left for the king's court at Worcester more than a week ago, and he had been unencumbered by an infant and a large household. Emma might arrive there by Christmas, but it would be an arduous journey over muddy roads into Wessex and into Mercia, even if the weather held fair.

He frowned, acknowledging to himself the real truth of the matter. Whether the journey she intended was easy or difficult, he did not want Emma to leave London. Yes, her presence here kept him on a sword's edge between desire and despair. But maddening as it was to see her every day, unable to touch her or even to speak to her as freely as he wished—that torment was better than to see her not at all.

The steward beckoned him into the inner chamber, and here the packing was already completed. Coffers were shut and stacked. Emma sat at a small table while her clerk stood at her side holding a neat pile of what must be letters. A brazier along the far wall was the only other furniture left in the room.

As Athelstan entered, the clerk bowed himself out, leaving them alone. Emma rose to greet him.

"Thank you for coming so quickly," she said. "I need to—"

"Tell me that you are not going to Worcester," he said.

"Not to Worcester," she replied. "I go to Headington."

"Headington? To my sister?" Edyth was at the royal estate there, awaiting the birth of her child. "Is all well with her?"

She handed him a parchment and he read it with increasing astonishment. It was a letter demanding that Emma send Margot to attend Edyth's lying-in, couched in language so imperious and condescending that he would have expected Emma to burn it, not agree to it.

"It is presumptuous, is it not?" she asked, with a wry smile. "The king's daughter issuing commands to the queen? It shows how powerful Edyth and her husband have become. Or think they have become." She clasped her hands together and began to pace the chamber. "I have been forced from the king's side for nearly a year now, and in that time Edyth has insinuated herself into the role of queen. It cannot continue. I would risk the king's wrath and go straight to the court at Worcester if Godiva were not too young to travel so far. Instead it seems I must content myself with a river journey to Headington so that I may remind Edyth who is England's rightful queen."

He tossed the letter onto the table. He recalled now that Edward, too, was at Headington.

"And you will see your son, of course," he said. Emma did not fool him; it was Edward who drew her to Headington. There was nothing that Emma would not do for her son. Even her eagerness to resume her place at the king's side was all for Edward.

"Of course I want to see my son," she said.

He strode over to the glowing brazier, where he warmed his hands and did not look at her. He wanted to rebuke her for wanting to leave London—for wanting to leave him; but he did not have the right.

Was there any greater fool than a man who loved where it was not wanted?

"So what is it that you wish of me?" he snapped. He knew that he sounded cold and angry. Well, *by the cross*, that was how he felt. She would remove herself from his protection, far from his reach, and he could not help but resent it. He was only mortal.

"I must make a grand show of force and power when I descend upon Edyth," she said, "and I want your assurance that you will have no need of my hearth troops here. Is it true that the Danes have returned to the camp at Benfleet? Is London safe?"

He hesitated. He could lie. He could persuade her that he needed her Norman warriors, and that she would be courting disaster if she set foot outside the city's walls. But there was a trust between them that he would not destroy with a lie, even if it meant sending her away from him.

"My men and I shadowed the Danes all the way to Benfleet," he said. "I expect they will remain in their camp through the Yuletide."

"And then?"

He shrugged. "They will have to forage for food again, but I do not think that they will come to London. We have convinced them that they are wasting their time trying to break through our defenses. They tried stealth and were repulsed. Their attempt to fire our ships in the Thames met with no success, and their recent effort to lure us out of the city to give them battle failed as well."

He stared into the glowing coals, tormented still by that memory. A large band of armed shipmen, rabid with drink, had formed a shield wall just out of bowshot from the archers that he had placed upon the wall. They had hurled insults and curses, challenging the defenders on the ramparts to come out and face them in open combat. He had seen it for what it was: a last, desperate effort to get them to open the city gates. Knowing this, he had given strict orders that the gates remain shut.

When no one ventured out to meet their challenge, the shipmen brought forward a group of English men and women, their hands bound behind their backs, presumably taken captive somewhere along the Thames shore.

The poor wretches were forced to their knees while behind them their captors continued to shout and threaten. After a time, a Dane stepped up to one of the prisoners and casually sliced his throat. There were shouts of outrage all along the wall, and Athelstan, imagining the terror of the remaining captives who could only wait to die, very nearly gave the order to attack. He knew, though, that if he should do so, much worse would follow.

The city gates remained closed.

They were butchered one by one, so that the last to die, a woman, was forced to watch all the others die before her. They had wept, howled for mercy, begged for rescue, while he and his army had watched the grim spectacle from the safety of their walls.

The Danes had left the bodies to rot in the mud and the gore, and the next day the shipmen had decamped. When at last the Londoners went out to bury their dead, he had counted the corpses. There were thirty of them—exactly the number of the Danish attackers who had first attempted to sneak into the city in the fog, and whose corpses he had ordered tossed outside the wall.

He understood the message: *An eye for an eye.* After all, it was what war was all about.

He was suddenly aware of Emma standing beside him. She must have read his grim thoughts, for she placed her hand on his arm and her expression was soft with compassion.

"You could not have saved them," she said.

"I know," he murmured. "But I cannot forget them. There is a debt owing, and the shipmen must be made to pay it."

And on it would go, blood for blood on either side until the cost became too great for one side to bear.

"What will you do," she asked, "now that the Danes are gone from your gates?"

He drew in a long breath and released it slowly. There were so many ways to answer that question.

"We will sharpen our swords," he said, "and make ready to fight them again in the spring."

She nodded.

"God grant you victory," she whispered.

He gave her a long, sober look, took her by the hand, and studied their twined fingers. The words of a prophecy that he had long dismissed came back to him. *He who would hold the scepter of England must first hold the hand of the queen.*

He had believed once that it signified her son, a child whose tiny hand had clutched at his mother's fingers. Yet now Emma's fingers lay in his grasp, and he could feel the tension, sharp as a knife blade, that ran between them. If he tried to hold Emma, she would pull away, so for now he must let her go.

He released her hand, but he held her gaze for a moment as he said, "And God grant you a safe journey, my queen."

He had taught himself patience. His father would not live forever. Someday the crown—and the queen—must belong to him.


**December 1009**

**Headington, Oxfordshire**


Emma stood at the prow of the royal ship as it nosed toward Headington under a sky pregnant with snow. Four more vessels followed hers, all of them riding low in the water, for they were crowded with attendants, supplies, household goods, and armed men from Windsor and Cookham as well as from London.

As her ship glided toward the shore, Emma scanned the palisade that surrounded the royal manor, searching for her son's standard. But there was no ætheling's banner floating above the towers that framed Headington's gate.

Edward had left, then. The king must have summoned him to Worcester for the Yule feast or sent him elsewhere—somewhere beyond her reach.

She straightened her shoulders and lifted her chin a little higher, for she could not show any sign of disappointment or regret in front of Edyth. It would be like handing her stepdaughter a weapon with which to wound her, and Edyth had enough of those already. She would not hesitate to use them, for she would surely resent the display of queenly power that was about to be paraded before her.

Emma hoped that the ensuing hostilities would be conducted in private and would be relatively bloodless although, knowing Edyth, she guessed that neither outcome was likely.

Once ashore, she led her attendants up the gravel path and through the open manor gates. She saw that word of her approach had preceded her, for within the king's great hall a formal greeting had been prepared. Light glittered from the massive central hearth and from dozens of blazing candles and torches. The hall was filled with women—not only those of Edyth's household, but also many of the noble wives of Æthelred's court who had been invited to attend his daughter's lying-in. Edyth herself stood on the dais, hugely pregnant, yes, but magnificently gowned in a loose robe of deep blue wool, its hem and its long, wide sleeves embroidered with gold. Golden threads glimmered in the mantle that was flung around her shoulders, and her honey-colored hair was caught up in a white silken coif held in place with a golden band. She looked as regal as any queen.

Emma was not surprised. It was an old ploy—the lavish display of royal wealth to inspire awe among the nobility and thus secure their allegiance. But if Edyth believed that she could play that game against a crowned queen and win, she had miscalculated.

Slipping her cloak of white fox from her shoulders so that it fell into the hands of the attendant following behind her, she strode confidently forward, aware that the firelight in the hall would be reflected in the shimmering silk of her golden gown, in the loops of gold at her throat, and in the twisted gold circlet upon her brow. The women in the hall made obeisance as she moved through them, and she greeted many of them with a word or a touch that was met with glad smiles. When she reached the dais she stopped, her eyes on Edyth.

The girl was near the end of her pregnancy. Beneath the lovely coif and gown her face and body were swollen, and her exhaustion was written in the smudges beneath her eyes. Emma's heart contracted with pity as she remembered that other Edyth—the girl who had loved to listen to the singing of the king's scop with her head resting against Emma's knee.

But that young girl no longer existed, and Emma hardened her heart against her stepdaughter. Margot's words of caution, uttered years ago, hummed in her mind. *You must look to your own children. Try to mother the children of the king, and you will break your heart against stone.* Emma was here not for Edyth's sake, but for the sake of her own son and baby daughter.

She continued to gaze, wordless and unsmiling, into Edyth's resentful face, but the king's daughter made no gesture of reverence or even of welcome.

*Foolish girl,* Emma thought. *Do you not realize that you have already lost this ridiculous game?*

Standing beside Edyth on the dais, the aged wife of Ealdorman Godwine, Winfled, was making her obeisance and Emma saw the old woman tug at Edyth's gown. At last, face contorted in fury, Edyth bent her head and dropped her eyes. It was a sullen gesture, but it was submission nonetheless.

She responded by taking Edyth's hand and formally kissing her cheek.

"I thank you, Edyth," she said, her voice ringing through the hall, "for such a lavish welcome during this holy season." To Edyth she whispered, "Make some courteous reply, and then we will retire to your apartments. I would speak with you alone while my chambers are made ready."

Edyth's mouth gave a quick, resentful twist, reminding Emma that the girl had never been good at hiding her feelings.

Eadric, she thought, had not yet taught his wife how to dissemble. She would learn soon enough.

"As Queen Emma is weary from her journey," Edyth's voice was brittle as glass, "we shall dine together in private this evening."

Edyth led the way to the women's quarters, but when they reached Edyth's chamber it was Emma who dismissed the attendants, even Margot.

Edyth glared at her. "Your presence here, my lady, is completely unnecessary. I asked for Margot's assistance, not yours."

"As I remember it, you did not ask at all," Emma said. "You commanded." She made a circuit of the chamber, snatching up a thick woolen shawl from the bed and wrapping it around her shoulders before claiming a chair next to the brazier. Silk, she reflected, made a stunning impression, but it did little to keep out the cold. She studied the girl-woman before her, noting again the blue smudges beneath her eyes. "Your babe disturbs your rest, I think. Lie down upon your bed, if you wish. Your feet must be swollen. Mine looked like loaves of bread in the last month before Godiva was born."

Edyth ignored her suggestion and instead sat on a cushioned bench, leaning her head against the wall and closing her eyes.

"You wished to speak to me?" she asked, her voice sullen. "What is it?"

"I expect you can already guess what I am going to say, Edyth, but in case you do not, let me be perfectly plain. You may be a great lady now, the wife of the noble Eadric as well as the eldest daughter of the king, but you do not wear a crown and you never will. When you presume to command me, you presume too much. I am your queen, and you will give me the respect that is my due both within these walls and before the world."

Edyth opened her eyes and her face was cold. This, Emma thought, would be every bit as unpleasant as she had anticipated.

"Why should I respect you?" Edyth asked. "You are a queen with no power."

Emma looked at her askance. Edyth was old enough to understand how power worked, but did she really grasp all its subtleties? She said, "If the measure of power is how close one stands beside the king, then at this moment in time I am, indeed, powerless. But if power is measured by lands, by wealth, and by ties to men of influence, then I count myself powerful indeed." The archbishop of Canterbury, the bishop of Winchester, and Ealdorman Ælfric were even now interceding with the king on her behalf, and the bishop of London was on his way to Worcester to add his voice. She expected to be summoned to her husband's side before winter's end, but that was not something she need share with Edyth. Instead she continued, "You must understand that a queen's power, like that of a lord or an ealdorman, waxes and wanes like the moon and the tides. Nevertheless, it is not my power that deserves your respect, Edyth, but the choice that your father made when he wed me. Dishonor the queen, and you dishonor the king himself."

Edyth appeared unmoved. "Yet even my father regrets now that he chose to make you queen," she said.

That gave Emma pause. She did not doubt that Æthelred often regretted his decision to give her a crown, but he was not one to admit his mistakes. She thought it unlikely that he would voice that particular regret to anyone, least of all to his daughter.

"Has he said as much to you?" she asked, and was gratified to see the little frown of uncertainty that clouded Edyth's brow. "I would remind you, Edyth, that the king has given me two children, as well as income and estates to provide for them, and that he has named my son as heir to the crown."

"Edward will never wear the crown," Edyth spat. "When my father dies, Athelstan will take the throne, and all the nobles will support him. You will be sent back to Normandy, and your children with you."

Emma sighed. She would not be drawn into a pointless argument about events that might never occur.

"It must be a comfort to you to be able to read the future so clearly," she said. "I confess that, for me, it is a mist that I cannot penetrate no matter how hard I try. For now, therefore, let us concern ourselves with matters as they stand. The king still lives, and I am his anointed queen. However much it offends you to bend the knee to me, you have no other choice. You saw what happened in the hall just now. The only person humiliated in there was you, and it will happen again and again unless you recognize my authority, however unwillingly."

She waited for some response, but Edyth merely stared, stone-faced, into the flames. Emma took her silence as a small victory, and decided to broach the issue that was most on her mind.

"As you have mentioned your brother Edward," she said, "perhaps you can tell me if he has gone to his father in Worcester."

Still Edyth did not look at her, but she answered, "My husband and your son were summoned to the Christmas court. They set out two days ago. Eadric did not wish to leave me, but . . ." Then she seemed to gather herself from wherever she had been and looked straight at Emma. "They were here together for some time, though, and Edward developed a marked fondness for Eadric."

For the first time, Edyth smiled, a cold smile, for her words were meant to wound. And they succeeded. That Edward had fallen under the wily Eadric's spell was even more terrible than the realization that Emma had missed her son by only a few days. It made her want to weep with vexation.

"Ealdorman Eadric," she said slowly, choosing her words with care, "has charm that must appeal to all who meet him." Snakes, too, were charming in their way, and Edward was far too young to recognize the danger of such a one. She wondered if Edyth even saw it.

But Edyth was frowning now, and then the frown became a grimace. She clutched at her belly and looked up at Emma with frightened eyes.

"I think the babe is coming," she whispered.

For an instant the rancor between them fell away, and they were merely two women facing the miracle of life—and the very real possibility of imminent death. Emma stood quickly, called out for servants, and sent one of them for Margot. Once she was assured that Edyth was in good hands, she slipped from the chamber. Edyth had made it clear that she did not want her there.

There was nothing she could do for her stepdaughter now but wait and pray.

# Chapter Twenty-Three

December 1009
Worcester, Worcestershire

At the invitation of Archbishop Wulfstan, who had chosen to spend Advent and Christmas at his northern see of Jorvik, Æthelred had settled into Wulfstan's Worcester palace for the winter. Once the ecclesiastical apartments had been augmented by the king's royal furnishings they were comfortable enough to suit him, but the chapter house was little to his liking. He found the paintings of saintly bishops that glowered at him from the plastered walls oppressive. Lit from below by banks of candles and from above by clerestory windows, they seemed to regard him with stern dislike. On this day, much to his irritation, their disapproving expressions were reflected in the faces of the three high ecclesiastics who had summoned him to meet with them.

The Canterbury archbishop and the bishops of Winchester and London sat at a table that held an elaborate gospel book and an assortment of scrolls. Ælfheah had appropriated the bishop's throne, and Æthelred scowled at him from his somewhat humbler chair in the center of the chamber. The only witness to what he was beginning to regard as a trial by ordeal was Eadric, and if Æthelred had realized what his insufferable bishops would inflict upon him, even Eadric would not have accompanied him. For the better part of an hour they had been forced to listen to an endless litany of the sterling qualities of Queen Emma.

It was a travesty. He had appointed all of these men to their sees, yet they seemed to think that they could call him to account.

At first he had regarded Ælfheah's lean, spare, earnest figure with equanimity, but that had turned to ire as the archbishop, whom he had counted among his friends, pelted him with scriptural references to husbands and wives, then read to him letters from numerous prelates commending the queen to her husband's grace.

When Ælfheah looked to him for a response, he only just managed to control his rage. Through clenched teeth he acknowledged the wisdom of their counsel and agreed to embrace his queen and keep her at his side. Ælfheah, still grave but apparently satisfied, gave him a final blessing, then led his two fellows from the chamber.

The king waited until the massive oak door closed behind them, and until the monk who had crept in to retrieve the gospel book had lumbered away. Then, rising from his chair, he strode to the table and with one savage swipe knocked everything on it to the stone floor. Parchment rolls skittered along the pavers, candles in their silver holders clattered noisily, and still he felt his temper throbbing like a drumbeat in his head.

"You see how they school me to treat with my wife?" he snarled to Eadric, who had stood, deferentially silent, throughout the interview. "You are my chief counselor. Why did you say nothing in my defense?"

"One chooses one's battles, my lord king," Eadric replied. "Who am I to argue with the counsel of two bishops and the archbishop of Canterbury not to mention"—he gestured to the parchment rolls now scattered across the floor—"a host of abbots and a Norman archbishop as well? Your lady wife is eager to return to your side, judging from the arguments of the men she has persuaded to plead her cause. In any case, what does it matter if Queen Emma returns to your court? She is but a woman. Get her with child again, and you can send her into seclusion once more."

Æthelred grunted and slumped into the episcopal throne that Ælfheah had abandoned. He kicked one of the scrolls out from under his foot and gestured the ealdorman to a chair.

Eadric's words were true enough. What maddened him, though, was not the thought of Emma at his court, but the knowledge that she had so many damned allies. His first wife had lived in his shadow, where she belonged. Emma, though, courted his churchmen and ealdormen, garnered information, and corresponded with men of power. His mother had done the same, and her ambitions for him had led to the murder of a king. When he considered that, his ill temper turned to misgiving. What might Emma's ambitions for her son lead *her* to do?

"I already have one son who covets my throne," he muttered. "I do not want Emma's son slavering after it. I would keep her away from Edward."

"Send Edward back to Ely Abbey in the spring," Eadric said. "He need not even see his mother."

Æthelred frowned. "It will not do. The queen began to shower Ely with offerings from the moment that Edward arrived there. I'll wager that every altar in that church is adorned with gifts from the queen. She all but owns the prior. Who knows what lessons he might teach Edward about the acquisition of power? No, I dare not send the boy back there. He must go where Emma's hand cannot reach."

For a moment he considered sending the child to his wife's kin across the Narrow Sea, but he rejected that idea at once. Emma's brothers would raise the boy a Norman, then send him back in five years' time at the head of an armed fleet with orders to seize England's crown as his birthright. No, he could not send Edward to Normandy.

"Then give Edward to me," Eadric said.

Æthelred looked at his son-in-law. The candlelight threw up shadows that flickered across Eadric's comely face and made the dark eyes glimmer. The thin lips framed by an elegantly trimmed beard curved in a feral smile.

"To you?" he asked.

"Let me take him to Shropshire for fostering. One of my thegns has lands near Wenloch, and the college of canons there can provide tutors for the boy. You need not trust Edward to Ely, and you can wean him from that Norman priest who hovers over him like a mantling hawk." He paused and his black eyes narrowed. "Edward will be your son, not Emma's. Is that not what you want?"

Æthelred considered it. The plan had merit. Edward would be far from court, far from his half brothers and, most important, beyond the reach of his mother. Emma would not like it, but she could hardly complain. In any case, she had a daughter now upon whom she could lavish her maternal attentions.

Eadric, of course, would profit from the arrangement. Edward's welfare would be in his hands, and that would give him power not just over
Edward but over Emma as well.

He studied his ealdorman, who was watching him with glittering
eyes. This would mean more wealth, more influence for him. And why
should Eadric not have it? He had been a good and faithful servant and
would continue in that role. If he was well provided for.

"Yes," he said, nodding slowly. "Take Edward with you across the
Severn. And send word of this plan to Emma. I will not have her complaining to the bishops that I have hidden her son from her." He'd had
his fill of disapproving priests, and of Emma and her son. He called for
wine and, leaning forward, he raised the question that had been hovering at the back of his mind since Eadric had arrived at the palace gate
this morning. "Tell me what you have discovered about Elgiva."

Eadric's smile faded and he, too, leaned forward. "If the lady is north
of the Humber, then she is well hidden. My men have searched for her
from Beverley to Durham and have found no trace of her."

"What of Siferth's wife? Does she know anything?"

"Nothing, my lord. I went to her myself, and she denied all knowledge of her cousin. I am certain that she spoke me true."

Æthelred did not ask what made Eadric so certain. The methods of
persuasion that Eadric used had been proven effective, and the details
were unnecessary.

"I trust that Siferth's lady will not complain of you to her husband
and thus negate all the gold I have spent to gain his loyalty."

"The lady will make no complaint," Eadric said.

Æthelred stared for some time into his wine cup, weighing possibilities.

"So if it is not Elgiva who is stirring up disaffection in the middle
shires, then it must be Athelstan." His eldest son had ever been a trial to
him—stiff-necked, stubborn, and far too fond of his own opinions.
Would Athelstan challenge him for the throne? His son's mind had ever
been a mystery to him, so he could not say what he might do. "The
bishop of London claims that Athelstan has done well in defending London from the Danes."

"Surely that is good news," Eadric observed.

"It is not!" Æthelred snarled. "My son fights the Danes from behind London's high walls and claims a victory, while I look a coward because I refused to meet them in the open field. It is a measure of kingship to protect your people against a foe. My son is building a heroic reputation, and so I must wonder what else he may be building."

His words seemed to echo ominously in the lofty chamber. Eadric pursed his lips and met Æthelred's steady gaze, and the silence between them lengthened.

Finally Eadric spoke. "You are not alone in your fears regarding your eldest son, my lord. Few men will speak of it to you, but his disdain for your rule and his desire for the throne are there for all to see. Do not listen to his counsels, for they are not given with your interests in mind. Mistrust him. Fear him, even."

*Fear him.* Hearing those words, Æthelred felt a sickness of heart that became a physical pain, a heaviness in his chest that made him sweat in spite of the December chill. He pressed the heel of his hand against the pain and although it eased, its echo lingered.

He saw a movement in the darkness behind Eadric, a deeper shadow among the shadows. The ghost of his brother regarded him, eyes glowing with portent, his baleful, silent gaze a reminder that royal kin could rarely be trusted.

December 1009

**Greetham, Lindsey**

Elgiva opened her eyes, recognized the brightly painted carving on the rafters of her cousin's guesthouse, and shut her eyes again. She had vague memories of waking before this, lightheaded and too weak to sit up, each time with Tyra bending over her, forcing her to drink some foul liquid and, far above, the swirling dragons carved into the roof timbers. The dragons had slipped into her dreams, scorching her with fiery breath then winging her to a mountaintop to leave her there, naked and frozen. She had tried to convince herself that all of it was a nightmare.

There had been a lucid moment when she had begged Tyra to tell her that none of it was real. But Tyra was a truth teller, and she had insisted that what had happened was no dream.

She'd lost the child. Nothing else mattered but that. The days of horror as the pestilence felled the members of her cousin's household; her own fear when she realized it had caught her in its grip of slow, grinding pain; the terrible stench of shit and vomit and death; the blood, slick as sweat, that had fouled her shift and bedding. None of that mattered now because the child that had been growing in her womb was gone.

She might as well have died too, now that all her careful plans were in ruins.

When she opened her eyes again Tyra was there, helping her to sit up. *Dear God,* she was thirsty! She opened her mouth like a babe to sip the broth that Tyra spooned into her, and she noticed something she'd never seen before. Dangling from a leather thong about the woman's neck was an amulet of amber with runes scratched upon it. Had the amulet protected her? Was that why Tyra had not taken ill?

Someday she would ask. Today there were other things she wished to know.

"How long?" she murmured.

"Seven days," Tyra replied.

It had seemed far longer.

"What of Aldyth?" she queried. "How fares my cousin?" Not dead, she hoped. It would be much harder to draw Siferth into Cnut's camp if Aldyth was dead.

And then she almost laughed, choking on the thin broth, for with no son to strengthen Cnut's claim to England's throne, what did it matter? She lay back against the pillows for a moment to catch her breath.

Yet it did matter, she reminded herself, for she had been promised that she would be the mother of kings.

Tyra had not answered her, so she reached out and stopped the woman's hand with its laden spoon and repeated her question. "How fares my cousin?"

"She did not sicken," Tyra said.

Resentment flickered in her mind at Aldyth's good fortune.

"She was spared the worst of it, then."

"Hardly spared," Tyra replied. "The pestilence killed many of her people. Her son is dead."

She recalled the fretful child she had seen when she first entered Aldyth's hall, and the story that her cousin had told about Eadric's cruel men; recalled her cousin's lingering fear for her son. Perhaps it was just as well that the boy had not lived.

"What of my people?" Elgiva asked. "My hearth men?" There had been twelve in her company.

"Three of your men took sick," Tyra said. "Two died."

"And Alric? Has he returned?"

"We've had no word from him." Tyra pursed her mouth and dipped her spoon in the broth again. "That means nothing."

It was a statement of fact rather than an attempt to comfort her. More of Tyra's truth telling.

Weakly she waved away the broth and rested against the pillows again, trying to focus her mind. Alric had gone south to look for Cnut. He might have taken ill on his road, or he might not, and she had no way of knowing when—or if—he would return. She must simply wait.

Two days later Elgiva finally had enough strength in her legs that they could carry her beyond the guesthouse in search of her cousin.

"She is lost within her grief," Tyra had told her when, wishing to speak to her cousin, she had sent the slave to fetch her. "She has taken to her chamber, lady, and will speak to no one. It happens that way sometimes. When the need is great, strength can be found to shoulder whatever burden comes. But when the trial has passed . . ." She shrugged.

Elgiva found Aldyth in her chamber, huddled in a chair and staring into the glowing coals of a brazier. She placed a stool beside her cousin and sat down, dizzy and chilled from the effort that it had taken to walk the fifty paces from her own chamber across the manor yard to this one. She said nothing for a while, merely studying Aldyth, who did not acknowledge her presence with even a glance. Aldyth's hair hung loose and tangled, and although the blanket that Aldyth wore about her shoulders hid most of her black woolen cyrtel, the hem was torn and dirty. Elgiva recalled that her cousin's body servant was one of those who had died. She wondered when her cousin had last washed herself and changed her gown. She wondered what she could say to pull the woman out of whatever dark space she had withdrawn to.

She decided to say nothing. Not yet. Instead she went over to the coffer near her cousin's bed, opened it, and pulled out a hairbrush and a ribbon. She dragged the stool around so that she could sit behind Aldyth, and set to brushing her cousin's dark, dirty hair. She might as well have been grooming a horse for all the response it earned her. She did not stop, though, until she had teased out all the tangles. When she began to braid the long tendrils, her cousin spoke at last.

"I want you to leave as soon as you are well enough to travel."

Elgiva paused in her braiding. It was not what she had thought to hear, and she could hardly believe that her mild cousin would be so callous.

"I am your kin," she protested, "and your guest. Surely you would not turn me out of your hall in midwinter." She completed the braid, secured it with the ribbon, and stood up to confront her cousin. "Why do you want me to leave?"

"Because when my husband returns I do not wish him to find you here," she said dully, still staring at the fire. "He will ask questions, and there are too many things that I must answer for as it is."

That was true, she reflected. Aldyth would have much to explain. The pestilence. The new graves in the churchyard. The dead child.

"So you will tell him nothing of Eadric's visit here? Of the murdered servant girl? You will say nothing of me and of what I can promise you?"

Aldyth looked up with those cow eyes of hers. "I will tell him nothing that Eadric and the king may one day use against him." Her eyes were large and beautiful but vague, as if there were nothing behind them but mist.

"I am of your blood, Aldyth," Elgiva reminded her. "I have a right to ask for your shelter and you have an obligation to grant it, especially in times such as these." Her cousin could not hide behind that fog in her

mind for much longer. She must be made to understand the gravity of
the step she was about to take.

Aldyth's gaze went back to the brazier. "My first obligations are to
my people and to my king, not to you. I should never have welcomed you
into my hall. It was disloyal to the king, and this pestilence was sent to
punish me for my sin."

Elgiva wanted to slap her. Æthelred was a wicker king, an empty
thing of sticks and straw. What kind of God would punish people for
turning against such a ruler?

"Do you really believe that I am the one who brought the pestilence
down upon you?" she demanded. "Aldyth, there was sickness in your
hall before I even came here."

"Then perhaps it was your child that the pestilence was sent to destroy!" Aldyth stood up, no longer passive but angry, as if somewhere
inside her a fire had seared away the haze. "The Danes are burning our
towns and laying siege to our cities. They would destroy us, and you
would have me help them! I will not do it, nor will I allow you to drag
my husband into your schemes. He is oath bound to the king, and the
penalty for breaking that oath is death. I have watched my son die. I will
not condemn my husband as well."

"Yes, your son sickened and he died," Elgiva spat. "My father and
brothers died as well, only they were murdered by order of the king.
Whether you help me or not, Aldyth, I will see that king punished, and
you are mad if you think that you can hide from what is to come. One
day there will be a Danish king on England's throne, and those who have
not been his friends will be treated as his enemies."

"Then your new king will be no different from Æthelred! What is
there to choose from between them?"

Again she felt the urge to slap sense into her cousin. The difference
between the two kings was that one of them would lose.

"If Siferth supports Swein and his son," she urged, "the rewards that
come to you will be vast. You must see—"

"I want no rewards! I want my son back! There is no king on earth
who can give me that!" Aldyth collapsed into her chair, dropping her

head into her hands as she began to weep. In a strangled voice she said, "I want you gone from here before Siferth returns."

"And if I refuse to leave?" She could not leave without speaking to Siferth. He would understand the risks and rewards far better than Aldyth could.

Then her conviction faltered. Swein of Denmark had sworn that he would not displace Æthelred until she had given Cnut a son, a child meant to be the rallying point for the men of the north—and she had no son. Swein would not come now for another year at least.

"If you do not leave," Aldyth's voice was coldly poisonous now, "I will send word to the king that you are here."

Elgiva stared at her for an instant, the words ringing in the air between them. Then she slapped the cow-eyed fool. It was a backhanded blow, and her ring scored Aldyth's cheek, but Elgiva doubted that even that would bring her cousin to her senses.

She stormed from the chamber and left Aldyth to her terror and her tears.

A.D. 1009    Then after midwinter [the Danes took] an excursion up through Chiltern, and so to Oxford . . .

—*The Anglo-Saxon Chronicle*

# Chapter Twenty-Four

Edyth's apartment, lit by candles, torches, and a brazier that was impotent against the bitter cold of predawn, was in a state of turmoil. Emma was paying little heed to the fuss, although she was dimly aware of servants hauling bundles and boxes out of the chamber and occasionally colliding with one another as they went in and out. The wet nurse for Edyth's three-week-old daughter paced among them as she tried to hush her whimpering charge. A young slave was crawling about the rush-strewn floor, frantically scrabbling for the earrings and pins that had scattered when she dropped a jewelry casket. Edyth helped as best she could by standing over the girl and scolding.

Emma, though, was seated in a chair, cradling Godiva, who was fast asleep in spite of the chaos all about her. She studied the small, round face beneath its linen coif, and her heart was heavy with the knowledge that when next she saw her daughter, Godiva would not look the same. Infants changed from week to week, and she could not say how many weeks it might be until she held this one in her arms again.

Swaddled in her cocoon of blankets, Godiva felt heavy and solid against her breast. The child had thrived these past weeks as the wet nurse that Margot had found for her, Wynflæd, took more and more responsibility for her feeding and care. Wynflæd would have all the care of Godiva now, and that only made this parting so much the harder.

After a time, aware that the commotion about her had lessened, she looked up to find Edyth standing in the center of the chamber that was emptied now of traveling chests and servants. Wynflæd stood a step behind Edyth, wrapped in a heavy cloak and carrying an armload of Godiva's shawls and blankets.

"If we wish to reach Eynsham before nightfall," Edyth said, "we must leave soon."

Emma felt as if she had just been wakened from a dream—one that she did not wish to relinquish.

"I will carry Godiva down to the wain," she said. Wynflæd nodded and hurried to help her rise from her chair.

"You'll waken her," Edyth hissed softly, "and if she starts crying, then Æthelflæd will start and we'll have no peace."

"I doubt she'll waken, my lady," whispered Wynflæd. "I fed her well a bit ago and she'll sleep for a good long while now." She glanced from Emma to Edyth. Then, as if she could see the tension that shimmered between the two women, she said, "I'll just go down and get settled, by your leave."

Emma watched her go and thought, not for the first time, that Wyn-flæd had been a gift sent to her by God. Turning to Edyth she asked, "Will you spend the next two nights at Eynsham?" She already knew the answer, but she wanted to put off the moment of leave-taking, unable yet to bring herself to part with Godiva.

Edyth gave an exasperated sigh. "Yes," she whispered, "and we will stay longer if a storm blows in, or if one of the children appears sickly, or if God sends an angel down and warns us that we mustn't leave the abbey. My lady, if you do not trust me to care properly for the child, why do you not keep her here with you?"

Now it was Emma's turn to sigh, for she was still not convinced that she was right to send Godiva away. There were rumors, yes—of a Danish army on the march, of towns set afire in the east, of a new enemy fleet landed at Maldon. She had sent riders out to learn if there was any truth to the tales, but the men had not yet returned and she was still uncertain what to do. Edyth, though, had no doubts. She had determined to go to the king, to risk her newborn to the hazards of bad weather and winter roads rather than chance being caught here by the Danes. After two sleepless nights Emma had agreed that Godiva must go as well.

"Of course I trust you, Edyth," she replied. "It is just that it is hard to part with her. Surely you understand that." She looked down at the sleeping child. "I've had her for such a little time."

Edyth sniffed. "You make it sound as if you will never see her again." At Emma's reproachful glance she crossed herself and murmured, "Forgive me. I should not have said that."

Yet Emma could not dismiss the words. She asked herself yet again if she erred in sending Godiva away from her just now. The rumors may be groundless. Even if they were true, the Danish army would probably never come near Headington. They would stay close to the coast, for there would be great risk in journeying so far inland where they might be cut off from their ships.

But an army, she knew, was an unwieldy monster, incapable of rational thought. She still remembered all too clearly with what casual cruelty the Danes had murdered the men and women on the plain outside of London.

Yes. She was right to send Godiva away.

"You have the letter that you are to give to your father?" she asked.

"I do; and the letters for Edward and Father Martin. Emma," Edyth whispered urgently, "it is time for us to leave."

Emma nodded and followed Edyth down the narrow stair, reflecting that, had events not intervened, she would be going with her to Worcester. She had hoped to greet Wymarc there when she arrived from Ely with young Robert, whose recovery from the pestilence had been such welcome news. She had anticipated long conversations with Wulfa, newly wed to the king's thegn Ulfkytel.

More than anything, she hungered to take Edward into her arms, to once more have her son close by her side.

The moment that Archbishop Ælfheah had handed her the king's letter summoning her to court she had begun making plans for the journey—nearly two weeks, she had reckoned it would take, in wintertime.

But much had changed in the past few days, and the reunion that she had envisioned was not to be, for she found that she could not leave Headington yet. God's hand was at work, and she must bend to His will. One day, she hoped, His plan would become clear to her.

Outside the hall, thirty men-at-arms waited, some horsed and others on foot. The pack animals stood in a line behind the covered wain that held the nurses and children. Emma kissed Godiva lightly on the cheek, made the sign of the cross on her forehead, and handed her into Wynflæd's care. She blessed Edyth as well, and embraced her, although Edyth's response was stiff and forced. There had been no reconciliation between them these past weeks, despite Emma's efforts.

*There are some battles, my Emma,* Margot had told her, *that you cannot win. This with Edyth is one of them.*

Margot had been right, of course. Emma watched, regretful but resigned, as Edyth took her place inside the wain, and the procession moved out of the yard in the stark dawn light.

Chilled by the cold and by her own sense of loss, she went indoors. There were not many of her people about, for she had need of few personal attendants and had sent most of them with Edyth. Her hearth troops had stayed behind though, as well as grooms to care for the mounts, in addition to the attendants and slaves who made up the Headington household even when the king was not there.

She made straight for the chamber set aside for high-ranking guests, where less than a week ago Archbishop Ælfheah had been housed. Today a woman kept watch there over a still form that lay in the great, curtained bed.

Emma went first to the hearth to warm her hands, and the servant, seeing her, stood up.

"Has there been any change since last night?" Emma asked.

"She woke once, my lady, and took some broth, but it's barely enough to keep a mouse alive."

"I shall sit with her awhile now," Emma said. "Try to get some sleep."

The servant nodded and crossed the room to crawl beneath the bedding on a pallet there, while Emma took her place upon the stool. She reached for the pale, wizened hand that lay against the coverlet, chafing the palm gently, for the flesh was chill in spite of the room's warmth.

How many times had this hand come to her aid? Far more than she could possibly recall. She could remember clinging to it as a little girl, and she recalled its cool, dry touch against her feverish skin when she had some brief childhood illness. It had comforted her in grief and steadied her when she was frightened. It had guided her babes into the world and been ever at her service, even from a time before she could remember.

She sent her mind back over the past few months, searching for the moment when she first knew for certain that Margot was ill, but she could not find it. To be sure, her step had been less quick of late, and she had grumbled often at her own forgetfulness. But she had never complained of pain or even weariness, until one morning she had not been able to rise from her bed without help.

*I must leave you soon, my Emma,* she had said when Emma had been called to her side. *I have seen more than sixty winters, child, and I am weary.*

Emma had insisted that Margot would soon be well, and she had been cheered when her old nurse had nodded and smiled in agreement. Margot had kept to her bed, asking for pillows so that she could sit up and take some part in the household activities going on about her. Every day, though, she had seemed to grow somehow smaller, and Emma had read the truth in the lines graven on her face. Yesterday morning, Christmas Day, she had asked that Godiva and Æthelflæd be brought to her bedside. After blessing them for the journey they were about to take, she had complained of being tired. Emma had ordered a servant to carry her to this chamber so that she could sleep, but once here, Margot had begged to speak with a priest and they had been closeted together for some time.

After that, whatever strength had been supporting the old woman had seemed to desert her, and now Emma guessed that it was only a matter of time before her spirit ebbed slowly away.

As she held the familiar hand, the ancient eyes flickered open and Margot smiled.

"I am glad that you are with me," Margot whispered in the Frankish that had been her first language.

Emma replied in the same tongue, "I will never leave you."

December 1009

London

Athelstan paced while Archbishop Ælfheah delivered instructions from the king. He did not like what he was hearing, but he could hardly blame the messenger; Ælfheah was merely doing as he was bid. When the archbishop was finished, Athelstan turned to him and studied the face of this man who had been his adviser for as long as he could remember, and who had often interceded with the king on his behalf.

"So I am to remain here in London? I am forbidden to leave the city for any reason?" he queried, hoping that he had somehow heard it wrong.

They were in the great hall of the London palace and Ælfheah, seated at one of the trestle tables, gestured toward the sealed parchment that lay in front of him.

"No doubt there is more written there—the penalties if you should disobey. I have not read it."

"*Jesu!* He still mistrusts me. He is like to exile me next, or brand me an outlaw!"

"Then you must prove him wrong by obeying him to the letter," Ælfheah urged. "And as you are in charge of London's defense, his command that you remain here strikes me as neither unreasonable nor unusual."

But the king had made him a prisoner of London! He was forbidden from setting foot outside the city, even if he was needed elsewhere—and that was exactly the situation he was facing now.

"Archbishop." He rested his hands on the table, bringing his face close to Ælfheah's to impress upon him the import of what he was about to say. "A large host of Danes has left their camp at Benfleet. Half of their force remains behind to guard their ships, but the rest of the army has gone north. Five days ago they burned Hertford. I do not know where they will strike next, but there is nothing to prevent them from following Ermine Street northward to lay waste to every town and abbey between here and Stamford."

The archbishop's lean face had paled as Athelstan spoke. "Another winter campaign?"

Athelstan straightened, wishing that he had better news to give. "They are not content, apparently, to wait for spring before taking up arms again," he said. "Foul weather does not seem to deter them, and mark me, Archbishop, they do not fear us. Why should they? We've made no effort to stop them."

"Have you sent word to the king?"

"I have, but my message will not have reached him yet, and I cannot wait another week for his reply. The men of London are already gathering arms and supplies, and as soon as we are ready I intend to lead them north. At the very least we can harry any raiding parties who might try to break away from the main force. With any luck we might even reduce their numbers, perhaps even find a likely place to bring them to battle. You can see why I chafe at this order from the king that would keep me penned up here inside the city."

"Let Edmund lead the force that you would send, then. If you ignore the king's order—"

"Is it the king's order?" he snarled. "Or is it Eadric's?"

Ælfheah grimaced. "Both, I expect."

"I thought as much. So even you, Archbishop, cannot wean the king from the counsel of his pet vulture."

Ælfheah's expression was grave, and he looked suddenly weary. That was no wonder, Athelstan thought. Asking the archbishop to separate the king from his beloved ealdorman was asking much indeed. Even the pious Ælfheah could not perform a miracle.

"I have tried to reason with the king," Ælfheah declared. "I have counseled him against placing his trust in Eadric, but I cannot reach him. Your father is sore afraid of something—I know not what. Some nameless dread is eating away at him."

"He sees visions," Athelstan said. He had once seen his father's face—a mask of horror—when the king was in the grip of a waking nightmare. "Portents of danger he calls them. If they have driven him to place his trust in a man like Eadric, then they must be from the devil himself." He began to pace again, his mind so filled with misgiving that he could not keep still.

"You must not judge your father so harshly," Ælfheah reprimanded him. "He carries the burden of a kingdom upon his shoulders, and the Danes are an ongoing scourge upon this land that greatly troubles him."

"It is my father who is the scourge upon England." He glanced at Ælfheah, saw the apprehension in the man's eyes, and sighed. "Have no fear, Archbishop," he said. "Despite what my father believes, I do not intend to relieve him of the burden of his crown." Although, he thought, it may one day come to that. He scowled and tried to massage some of the tension from his neck. *"By Christ*, though, I would like to rid us of Ealdorman Eadric. My father, my brother Edwig, my sister Edyth—they are all of them besotted with the man." He should have listened to Wulfnoth, should have made some move against Eadric before the debacle at Sandwich. Instead Wulfnoth was in exile and Eadric's influence and power had only increased.

"Edyth is bound to him in wedlock," Ælfheah protested. "She has no choice but to take his part."

Athelstan frowned. He did not like being reminded that his sister was wed to a man he so despised. "It will go hard for her when my father dies," he murmured, almost to himself, "and she will be forced to choose between husband and brother." When the throne was his, Eadric would be exiled, and Edyth could stay or go—he did not care. Then he faced Ælfheah again, for now that they were speaking of Edyth he could pose the questions he had wanted to ask from the moment the archbishop had arrived. "Did you see my sister at Headington on your journey here?" The more important question he offered as an afterthought. "Did you see the queen?"

"I did, for the king entrusted me with messages for Emma. To speak to her on his behalf, to give her pledges of his affection. Both your sister and the queen are to join him at Worcester. When I left Headington five days ago, preparations for the move were already under way, although—"

He stopped short, and Athelstan turned to see what had distracted him. Edmund had come into the hall and was striding purposefully toward them, his face grim.

"Forgive me," Edmund said, "but my news is urgent. The Danes have raided St. Albans and are making for Berkhamsted."

"Berkhamsted!" Athelstan stared at Edmund in disbelief. "They are headed west, then?"

"West," Edmund said flatly. "Our men captured one of their scouts and managed to drag some information out of him. He may have been lying, but I do not think so." He paused and frowned, as if reluctant to share what may be misinformation.

Athelstan, impatient, snapped, "What, then?"

"Thorkell intends to torch Oxford, to avenge the Danish folk who were massacred there on St. Brice's Day."

"God have mercy," Ælfheah whispered. "That burning was seven years ago. Does the vengeance never end?"

"Not in this world, Archbishop," Edmund answered. "No injury is ever forgiven—no outrage forgotten."

"So if they're making for Oxford," Athelstan said, "they'll likely go through Aylesbury."

Edmund nodded. "And from there to Headington, where there is a bridge across the Cherwell."

But Athelstan was already thinking about what needed doing, and now he turned to Ælfheah. "Edyth and the queen, you say, are on their way to Worcester?"

"Edyth, certainly, intended to leave Headington quite soon," Ælfheah replied, but now his face had gone gray. "One of the queen's Norman attendants, though, fell ill just before I set out for London. You know the woman—the healer, Margot. Emma would not leave her, and she planned to remain with a small household at Headington."

Athelstan cursed. That put the queen and her people directly in the path of the Danish army.

He called for messengers to bid his war leaders join them, for they must be consulted and new plans laid out. Some hours later, after debating the best course of action to take, the men sought their beds at last. As Athelstan stalked from the hall he snatched up the letter that Ælfheah had delivered from the king. He would read it later, if only to discover what his punishment would be for disobeying his father's command to remain in London.

# Chapter Twenty-Five

December 1009

Headington, Oxfordshire

I t was late afternoon, and Emma guessed that outside the palace walls the winter-bright day must be fading to dusk. In this chamber, though, all daylight had been banished—the shutters pulled tight and only a few candles burning in the darkness, as if to remind those present of the greater darkness that awaited them all. It comforted her that of the few folk remaining within the palisade, most of those who could do so had gathered here, not at her bidding, but out of respect for the woman who had been healer and counselor to her household for so many years.

Only once before had she kept a deathbed vigil, watching alone at the side of the twelve-year-old son of the king. Her sorrow then had been for the child who would not see manhood, for the promise of youth that would never be fulfilled. This time was different. This time her grief was all for herself.

The familiar, beloved face of her old nurse beneath its white cap was more pale even than the pillows that cushioned her head. Margot lay in a deep slumber, yet even so Emma half expected her to sit up and scold her for wearing only one shawl and for covering her hair with such a thin headrail.

*I was in a hurry, Margot,* she would have excused herself, *and you were not there to find me something more to the purpose.*

Margot's gray hair was just as Emma had often seen it in the early dawn—neatly braided in two long plaits that lay atop the bedclothes.

But her forehead bore the cross of ashes, and her hands the linen gloves that marked the dying. She had been sleeping just so most of the day; now, though, each breath had become a labor. The voice that had advised and sometimes admonished Emma would soon be stilled forever, and already she missed that wise counsel.

To her right, at the foot of the bed, the priest read psalms from a little book by the light of candles placed on either side of him. Emma wondered if Margot could hear him, and if she would understand prayers of comfort murmured in Latin. She wished that the priest would be silent so that she could whisper to Margot in the Frankish tongue, but death had its rituals that must be honored. At such a time as this, the presiding priest ruled, even in the halls of the king.

As she watched the rise and fall of Margot's breast, the intervals between each shuddering breath lengthening every time, it occurred to her that although she and the others here had come to pray and to witness, in the end death was a private thing, a journey that could only be made alone. In that, it was not unlike the task of giving birth.

Memories of the midwife and healer for whom childbirth had been the central miracle of life flowed through her mind like water in a stream. It had been Margot who had comforted and reassured her when her first babe had miscarried in a wash of blood, Margot who had eased her fear that there might never be another child. When she had labored for so many hours to bring Edward into the world, Margot had alternately cajoled and bullied her, forbidding her to despair, using her voice and even her body to support her when the pain seemed too great to bear. Margot had coaxed Godiva into the world, and but a few weeks ago she had placed the squalling, red-faced Æthelflæd into Edyth's arms. She had been a miracle worker in their midst, and Emma knew that she would feel this loss more than any other she had yet faced.

She closed her eyes to plead for acceptance of God's will, dimly aware that the chamber door behind her had opened and closed. As she tried to find the words to beg for the spiritual aid she sought, a man's voice whispered urgently in her ear.

"Our scouts are reporting that there are horsemen approaching from the east, my lady. We cannot say yet who they are, but they may be outriders from the Danish army. Unless they pass us by and make straight for Oxford, they will be here within the hour."

A current of alarm swept through her, and in an anguished instant the remembered sights and smells of carnage assailed her. What was she to do now? A message had come three days ago warning that the Danes were driving west from Berkhamsted; but the Chiltern Hills and days of hard walking through snow and sludge lay between there and here. She had not reckoned that the Danish army could cover that ground so quickly. She had counted on a week's grace at least, and so had not instructed her people to flee.

Could she have made so grievous an error, and must all of them pay for it?

She drew her shawl closer about her, assailed by a sudden, painful memory. Years before she had ignored the advice of someone far wiser than she was and had ventured beyond the walled city of Exeter with an escort that was too small to keep her safe. They'd been surprised by an enemy force in a narrow lane from which there was no escape, and every man with her had been butchered. If God had forgiven her for that, she had not forgiven herself, and she had vowed never again to be responsible for such horror. But *sweet Virgin*, she could not see how she could have chosen, this time, to do anything other than remain at Margot's side.

"The city has been warned?" she asked. Many in Oxford had fled, but there were some, like her, who had pressing reasons to stay behind, or who simply had nowhere to go.

"We've sent riders, yes."

"And the palace guard?"

"The archers are on the palisade."

"Then there is nothing more to be done. Thank you for bringing me word."

She heard the door open and shut again, but as she began once more to pray for acceptance, for courage, and, most of all, for wisdom, she was weighing her options. Should she alert her small household to the danger bearing down on them? What would it accomplish? If the army was in sight, it was already too late to try to escape. Better to face danger here, within the palisade with armed men atop the walls, than to be caught in the open, running.

Lost in her anxiety about what the next hour might bring, she was abruptly brought back to the present, for to her astonishment, Margot opened her eyes and smiled.

"*Madame,*" Margot said.

Emma leaned forward to touch her arm, and then realized with a start that Margot's eyes were not looking to hers but were gazing on the empty space beside her. Seeing what? she wondered. Or whom?

"*Madame,*" Margot said again, on a long sigh this time as her eyes closed once more.

The priest had gone silent, and Emma held her breath, waiting for Margot's next inhalation—but it did not come. The priest began the familiar Latin of the Pater Noster and other voices, too, took up the prayer. She did not add her voice to theirs, for she felt too sharp a sense of loss to speak. It seemed to her that she needed Margot now more than ever, when the world was about to collapse about them, and there was likely to be injury and pain, and deaths far less peaceful than this one.

She watched as Margot's gentle face, lifeless now, seemed to fall under a shadow, and she felt her throat knot with a grief that she was afraid she hadn't the strength to overcome. She closed her eyes against her fear, and when she opened them again she saw a thing that sent a prickling up her spine. A white mist rose from the body and hung above it briefly before fading into the darkness.

Mute with wonder, she looked to the others in the room for some sign that they had seen what she had. Every head, though, was bowed in prayer. She alone had witnessed that final departure—Margot's soul released from its earthly vessel, for she was certain that was what it was. She tried to find some comfort in this mark of God's grace, but she could not. Her sense of abandonment pressed upon her like a cross that she was forced, against her will, to bear.

She knelt in silence for a little longer, praying once more for the strength to confront whatever trials lay ahead, but the sound of shouting filtered through the walls and again her prayer was cut short. She could tarry here no longer. Her duty now was to the living, to help them face, and if possible evade, approaching danger.

As she stood and turned to leave the chamber she heard heavy footfalls in the outer passage, and the door was thrust open. She tensed as armed men spilled into the chamber. Behind her there was a rustling of leather and wool as the mourners stood up, reverence and solemnity shattered. Someone began to whimper, and there were mingled cries of fear and protest.

In front of her another man pushed his way through the door—a man whose cloak was trimmed with fur and fastened at the shoulder with a gold clasp. His gaze swept past her, and she saw him take in every detail—men and women, priest and candles, the bed that had now become Margot's bier.

She looked up into his stern face, into eyes the color of marsh flowers—the same bright blue as her daughter's. All of the king's children had blue eyes, but only Godiva and Athelstan shared that heart-stopping brilliance. Now Athelstan's eyes met hers briefly before he addressed the household members clustering behind her.

"You must all be ready to leave within the hour," he ordered. "Make whatever preparations are necessary and assemble in the dooryard as quickly as you can."

He had barely finished speaking before the men-at-arms began herding everyone from the chamber. Emma found that the priest was suddenly at her side, livid with outrage.

"My lady, we cannot leave one of God's chosen unburied, without the proper rites ordained by—"

"She will be buried here, Father, next to the chapel," Athelstan said, putting his hand upon the priest's shoulder and drawing him aside, "but it must be done quickly. Eadmer," he called to one of his men, "you and two others assist the priest in whatever is necessary, but do not take any longer than you have to." He turned to Emma and said, "My lady, I would speak with you."

His hand was at her elbow, and she felt his sense of urgency as he propelled her across the passage and into a much smaller chamber. She had time for one quick glance back to the bed where Margot's body lay before the door was shut.

In the central hearth the remains of a fire smoldered, giving off little light and even less heat, but she was still too numb with grief to take any notice of the cold. Athelstan, though, she could not ignore. He stood solidly in front of her, exuding impatience and what she guessed was controlled fury.

"How close are they?" she asked.

"Close enough to strike tonight." His voice was brittle with anger. "You should have left two days ago. Did you not receive my message?"

She looked away from him then, unable to face the accusation in his eyes.

"I did not believe that they could get here so soon." Or was it that she had not wanted to believe it? Be that as it may, she'd had no choice and she would not allow him to chastise her for the decision she had made. She met his cold gaze and said, "I could not leave Margot here to die alone, Athelstan. I could not do it."

"And what of your daughter?" He was still angry, his voice laced with reproach.

"I sent her with Edyth." At least he could not upbraid her for that. "They will have reached Minster by now, unless something has delayed them at Eynsham Abbey. I had thought to follow them tomorrow, but I see that I must leave tonight."

"Tonight you must go to London, not Eynsham."

She frowned, searching his face in the meager light. "To what purpose?" she demanded. "The king has given me leave to join him at Worcester, and I have no wish to return to London." At Worcester they would all be waiting for her—Godiva, Wymarc, Wulfa, Father Martin, Edward. She longed, more than anything, to see Edward, and he was at Worcester.

"That road is too dangerous," he said. "Thorkell's army is massing just north of here, and he likely has men ranging as far west as Eynsham. The only safe route away is south, and you need to get behind stout walls—"

"It is not safety that concerns me," she snapped. "It is making my way to the king and to my children."

"My lady," he said, his voice as coldly polite now as the expression on his face, "it is pointless to argue. You will journey south toward London tonight. You owe that to your people. I think you would not want to put them in harm's way if you can help it."

She drew a long breath, acknowledging the truth in his words. She had made the choice to stay with Margot, and she could not fault herself for that. But to willfully lead her people toward danger would be unforgivable—the act of a petulant child, not a queen.

Steeling herself against disappointment now as well as grief, she closed her eyes and nodded.

"Then tonight I will go to London. But not until Margot has been laid to rest." Surely she could finish that task, at the least.

She felt him grasp her shoulders then and when she looked into his face, his brow was no longer furrowed in anger.

"Emma," he said gently, "I am sorry about Margot."

It was the tenderness in his voice that undid her. She had withstood his anger and disapproval, had been as strong in the face of Margot's death as even Margot would have demanded. But now he had deprived her of her stony shield, and the tears that she had kept at bay overwhelmed her.

His arms came around her, but even as she wept against his shoulder, she knew that this was not the time to mourn, that she must stem her tears.

"Your people will be waiting for you out there," he said, his voice tender, rallying her. He took her head in his hands and grazed her cheeks with his thumbs to remove all trace of her weeping. "They will be looking to you for courage."

She nodded, so racked with emotion that she dared not try to speak. She could only gaze mutely at him with gratitude as she prepared herself to face whatever the next trial would be. But he did not release her. Instead he pressed his mouth to hers, and for a moment she clung to him, returning his kiss, hungry for him even though, after too brief a time, she forced herself to pull away.

Why must it always be like this—the demands of duty placed above all else? Yet she knew the answer well enough. Duty, loyalty, honor—all of that came with the vows she had taken when she had bent her head to accept a crown.

Moments later he was ushering her out of the room, and the weight of her responsibilities settled heavily upon her shoulders once again. That burden, though, would be lighter, she assured herself, now that Athelstan was there to share it. The orders that he had given were swiftly obeyed and soon Emma, swathed in her traveling cloak, stood at Margot's graveside. She had tucked a cross of garnet and gold into a fold of the shroud—a defense against evil spirits and a pledge that Masses and prayers would be said for the repose of her soul, that she would not be forgotten. She watched, dry-eyed, as the makeshift coffin was lowered into the earth and Athelstan's men set about the hard task of filling the shallow grave with wet, clinging mud.

When the priest closed his book, still scowling his disapproval at such a hasty burial, Emma murmured a final farewell: "May the Lord defend you from all evil, and may the power of Christ Most High reside within you."

Then, along with the priest, she joined the group that had gathered outside the hall. There were not enough horses for all of them. Some would have to walk, but all the belongings had been loaded onto the animals so that the walkers could travel light. She nudged her horse over to where Athelstan, astride his own mount, was speaking intently to one of her Norman guards.

Around them, the day was falling into twilight, and as she looked toward the river she saw mist settling on the water. Several men bore torches to light their road, but she fretted that they would be of little help should a heavy fog set in. There was still no sign of their enemies, and as she was marveling that so mighty a host could approach in such silence, Athelstan swung his horse about so that he was facing her.

"My man Eadmer will lead you," he said. "The road is muddy and treacherous, though, and your people will be weary. Go slowly and rest often. You should be at Dorchester by dawn. I've told your men to keep armed riders at the back of your line, in case any of the Danes take it into their heads to move in your direction, although I don't think that will happen. Tonight their goal is Oxford. What they will do tomorrow is anyone's guess, so do not linger in Dorchester. Rest a few hours, and then carry on to Cookham. Try to get to London by week's end if you can."

She blinked at him in surprise.

"But where will you be? I thought you were coming with us."

"There are still some who need to be assisted out of Oxford. Not many, thank God. Your men spread the alarm in good time. We cannot save the town, though, if the Danes are set on burning it. I've not enough men. All we can do is shadow them, keep people out of their way, and keep the king apprised of their movements. Edmund is gathering a force in London, and if I see an opportunity we'll bring our own army forward and try to force a battle. That's the last thing they want, though, and they'll take pains to avoid a confrontation." He smiled grimly. "It's an endless game of cat and mouse—one we never seem to win."

He turned in his saddle and signaled to Eadmer, and the company began to move along the London Road.

"I will see you in London," he said to Emma. "Go with God."

He reached out to her, and for a moment their hands met, until he released her and turned his horse toward Oxford.

"Go with God," she whispered, watching the bright head until it faded into the twilight.

Then she guided her mount in the opposite direction, careful of the folk about her who walked in the gathering shadows. They were not a large company—some twenty-odd, she guessed. And although she knew each of them by name, she could not dismiss the sense of desolation that engulfed her.

All those she loved were behind her, somewhere in the darkness that had descended upon England.

**A.D. 1009**   [Oxford] they burned, and plundered on both sides of the Thames. Being fore-warned that there was an army gathered against them at London, they went over at Staines; and thus were they in motion all the winter, and in spring, appeared again in Kent, and repaired their ships.

—*The Anglo-Saxon Chronicle*

# Chapter Twenty-Six

March 1010

Aldbrough, Holderness

Elgiva sat on the floor of Catla's bedchamber, hands clasped about her knees. Two arms' length in front of her Tyra knelt among the rushes, frowning intently at the rune sticks scattered in the space that had been cleared between the two of them. Elgiva flicked her gaze between Tyra's face and the rune-marked pieces of bone, with an occasional glance to where Catla, her belly huge with child, lay asleep on the bed against the far wall. Thurbrand's wife would soon present him with another son, according to Tyra, who claimed knowledge of such things even without consulting her gods.

It was just the three of them in the chamber, although Elgiva could hear Catla's other two brats howling about something out in the dooryard while their nurse's voice brayed protests. Except for their distant screeching, all was quiet. Even the looms set against three of the chamber walls were stilled, the weavers having joined the rest of Thurbrand's people and her own in the fields. The sowing would go on for several more days, moving from one plowed strip to the next until the seed ran out. With luck the weather, like today, would stay dry. If not, they would work in the rain and come inside at sundown wet, chilled, and grumbling even more than usual. When the planting was done she would have to throw a feast. The men would get drunk, and in the autumn half the women would be in the same condition as Catla was now.

And if her own belly were still flat then, she would envy them and silently curse them all.

"Well?" she whispered to Tyra.

But the Sámi woman made no reply. Oblivious to everything but the rune sticks, she began to chant softly, words that Elgiva did not understand although the mere sound of them—eerie and in some strange tongue—made her flesh crawl.

She contained her impatience. Scrying the future, it seemed, could not be rushed. Someday she would ask Tyra to discover how much longer she must stay trapped in this dismal place. She wondered if the Sámi woman knew some magic that would spirit her away from Holderness.

She had forgotten just how tedious this existence was, had even thought of Holderness as a haven when she was making that miserable, bone-cold journey north from her cousin's lands.

Aldyth's cruelty in forcing her to leave in midwinter—so unexpected from one who had once been so cowed by her—still rankled. She had lingered at Greetham as long as she dared, hoping to see Siferth, hoping that Alric would return with news of Cnut. But her cousin had been as cold and relentless as the wind blowing across the empty wolds, and she had managed to draw only one concession from her.

"Tell Siferth that I was here," she had begged Aldyth, "and bid him send word to the king that I died in the pestilence that took your son. It will keep Eadric from hounding us."

Aldyth had agreed, but there was no way of knowing if she would actually do it.

At last, on a chilly, sunless day when Tyra said that the omens were good, she had left her cousin's hall. Two days later Alric had caught up with them. Cnut was well, he'd reported, and had been pleased to learn that she was with child. How it had galled her to send Alric back to him with word that she had miscarried.

So much depended on the birth of her son, and her disappointment at having to return here, childless, had been a grim burden that she carried with her the whole length of that awful journey. Nor had her homecoming been any cause for celebration. The night of her return Thurbrand had stalked into her hall bellowing like a bull, raving at her for having slipped away from him last fall. He was so fearsome that she had snatched a knife from the table to fend him off, but one of Swein's men had stepped between them and Thurbrand had had the sense to back down.

That had been two months ago. Alric had returned since then, but she had sent him hastening south again, to gather what news he could of Siferth and of events at Æthelred's court.

How she envied Alric his freedom to come and go as he pleased. She longed to get away from here—to go to Winchester or London or Canterbury. The Easter court would soon be meeting at one of the king's great halls, and Emma would be there—gowned in silk and seated on a chair with embroidered cushions, instead of crouched among the rushes astride a straw-filled sack.

Still, she thought smugly, the Easter court would hardly be a joyous gathering. Thorkell and Cnut had made certain of that. They had led their shipmen almost unchallenged through the Thames Valley throughout the winter. An army had gathered outside of London to bring them to battle, but the Danes had crossed the Thames and deftly avoided a confrontation. Thorkell's men had torched village after village as they made their way back to their ships, and how it must have enraged Æthelred and his sons to watch that trail of smoke snaking across the sky, far beyond their reach.

Served them right—the wicker king and his straw sons. She would take her own vengeance on them one day. Perhaps, she thought, concentrating once more on Tyra, this Sámi cunning woman might even help her.

Tyra had closed her eyes and was running her hands lightly across each fragment of bone, fingering them, touching whatever power emanated from the scored ivory. Then her eyes opened, focusing with such needle-like sharpness on Elgiva that she shuddered.

"Two sons," Tyra said, in a voice so strange it seemed borrowed from some other world. "Both will grow to manhood. Both will leave this middle earth before you."

*Both will grow to manhood.*

Her sons, then, would not all wither in the womb as the last child had. She need not despair. That her own life would be longer than theirs was hardly a surprise. If a woman could survive childbirth, she might well outlive her sons.

Most men's lives ended with a sword stroke, while women simply died of boredom.

At least, they did if they lived in Holderness.

Tyra had closed her eyes again, slumping against the bed frame as if she were a poppet made of rags and straw. The power that had been within her had withdrawn, and she looked haggard, her face so pale that even her lips were white.

"Tyra," Elgiva hissed softly, "you cannot rest yet. You must tell me when Cnut will return, and when I will bear him a son."

She saw Tyra's chest move as she heaved a sigh, but the Sámi woman neither opened her eyes nor made any reply. Elgiva clenched her fists with impatience, but she knew better than to press Tyra any further. The woman was exhausted and all her power fled. More questions would have to wait.

For a long moment she gazed thoughtfully on that drawn and pallid face, gnawing on an idea that she had been considering ever since the first time she had seen the cunning woman's hands play across the shards of bone with their mysterious markings. Slowly she moved her stiffened limbs, repositioning herself so that she was on her knees, mimicking the slave woman's stance when she had been reading the runes. She leaned forward just as she'd seen Tyra do it, fingering the small, scored rods, hoping to feel some kind of power emanating from them.

She felt nothing. She lacked the skill to make the runes speak to her. Until she gained it, they would be nothing more than bones. She sat back on her heels, and when she looked at Tyra again, the Sámi woman was eyeing her.

"You have lusted after my power for many months now, have you not?" Her voice was normal again, no longer filled with magic. "Why is that, lady?"

*Because*, Elgiva thought, *you are a truth teller, and any secrets that you learn about me through your skills might not remain secrets.*

Instead she said, "You would not be so weary if you could share the burden of soothsaying with another."

Tyra grunted. It may have been a laugh, but Elgiva could not tell.

"Look at me," Tyra said. "Each time I use the power, there is less of me afterward. Is that what you long for?"

She had never considered it in that light; had never thought that in using such a power, she might be used in turn. But what did it matter? The power was worth the risk. And besides, Tyra had just told her that she would have a long life. She would outlive her grown sons.

"I want to learn your skill," she replied.

"The learning is but a small part of it," Tyra said. "It is a gift, lady, that is granted only to those of the Sámi blood. If you are not born with the power inside you, even the most skilled gerningakona cannot teach it to you."

Elgiva scowled, but she did not argue. She well knew that Sámi women were like the Old Ones who hid in the hills of Western Mercia. They could trace their lineage back to a strange, mystical race. They had powers of perception that normal people did not have, and they communed with beings that were not of this world. Her old nurse had gone to see such a one, years ago. Groa would never reveal who it was she spoke with, but she had repeated the soothsayer's words many times.

*Your children will be kings.* She could hear Groa's voice again as if it whispered in her ear—the only voice that ever came to her from beyond the grave. Her father and brothers were dead, too, but if they spoke to her she could not hear them. Was it because Groa had been pagan? Did her spirit still linger here in this world?

Like Tyra, Groa had come from the far north. But if Groa had known the old magic, she never let on.

She had known other things, though—how to mix potions that could cure or harm, how to recognize herbs and put them to use. She had even known some powerful charms. Surely these were arts that could be taught, whatever race a woman might spring from.

"What of your skill in herbal lore and healing magic?" she asked Tyra. "That knowledge does not reside in blood and bone. I would have died at Greetham had you not saved me with your potions; and that amulet that you wear—it protected you from the pestilence, did it not? These are things I wish to learn, and I would have you instruct me." Even if Cnut came to her tomorrow and made her great with child, she would still have to spend many months here in Holderness, waiting for the birth. The days and weeks had to be filled somehow, and skill in the knowledge of herbs and potions might prove useful in the days to come.

Tyra looked at her steadily—one of those narrow-eyed, penetrating looks that always made Elgiva uneasy. She kept her own gaze just as steady as Tyra's, though. This woman could not read minds, she insisted to herself, only faces. Tyra could not know what thoughts were in her secret heart. Besides, Tyra was a slave. She had to do what she was told.

"I am Swein Forkbeard's slave," Tyra said, and Elgiva, startled, was forced to question whether the woman might, in fact, be able to read thoughts. "He ordered me to do your bidding, lady, and so I will do as you command me."

The woman's hard, narrow gaze continued to pin Elgiva, until finally she was the one who had to look away.

Two days later Elgiva walked beside Tyra across a waste field, some distance from the hedge that marked the boundary of her lands. It was a bright morning, although the ground was muddy and her skirt now wet and filthy from her passage through knee-high weeds that were not, she was learning, all weeds. Already Tyra carried a basket containing roots that would ease coughing and several stalks of a fern that would expel worms.

*Jesu*, she hoped that she would never need that remedy.

Recognizing the shoots of healing plants in the spring and their flowers in summer was only part of what Tyra had promised to teach her. Preparing the leaves or seeds or roots in the proper manner would be the next step, but that, Tyra had said, would come later.

There was a great deal that she must learn. She wondered if a year would be long enough. Or two. Or even ten.

Just ahead of her she spied a familiar plant—delicate, fernlike leaves that she remembered from the meadows near her father's manor. She bent to pluck a stem, but Tyra slapped her hand away before she touched it.

"What's wrong?" Elgiva asked. "That is feldmore. My old nurse used the seeds to brew a remedy for my father's head pain when he'd had too much wine."

"Nay, lady. Feldmore grows only in dry soil. This plant loves the moist ground, and even this early in the season it is much taller than feldmore. This is hymlice. All of it is poisonous. If you give a man a drink brewed from even a few seeds, he will not live to drink anything again. Study it well so that you will recognize it, but do not touch it."

Elgiva stared at the plant. Such a simple, weak-looking thing, yet it was deadly. She made note of the place where it was growing, memorized the shape of the leaves, compared them to her memory of feldmore, and she looked up only when Tyra touched her arm.

"There are men coming this way," Tyra said.

Shielding her eyes from the sun Elgiva made out two figures on horseback moving along the narrow track that led from Thurbrand's holding.

"Someone come to fetch you for Catla's lying-in, perhaps," she said.

"Nay, lady. That is your man come to you. And the other, Alric, is with him."

She felt her heart give a little leap, although Tyra, she told herself, must be guessing.

"Even you cannot see so far, Tyra," she said.

"They'll be wanting food and drink, and most of your people are in the fields." Even as she spoke, Tyra was cutting diagonally back across the meadow in the direction of the hall.

Elgiva glanced after her, then walked forward to intercept the horsemen, staring into the blinding sun, not yet certain that Tyra was right. When one of the riders dismounted and came toward her with a familiar, loping stride, she began to run. In a few quick heartbeats, Cnut was gathering her into his arms.

They passed the next hour or so—she did not bother to reckon the time—alone in her chamber. Before her husband had taken any food or drink, he had taken her twice, and it was only after all his needs had been met that she could sit at his side in the nearly empty hall and ask all the questions that only he could answer. Alric sat across the table from them, nursing a cup of ale.

"How long can you stay?"

Out of the corner of her eye she saw Alric hunch his shoulders, like a man expecting a hailstorm. She guessed that she was not going to like what she was about to hear.

"One week only," Cnut said. "The winds were against us, and it took us far longer to get here than we had hoped. We have a mission to complete in East Anglia, and only a little time to accomplish it."

One week. During that time they would couple frantically, then part for months perhaps. Once again he had come when she was least likely to conceive. Perhaps she could convince him to take her along on this mission, whatever it was. Now, though, she sensed, was not the time to bring it up.

"What will you do in East Anglia?" she asked.

"Break Æthelred's hold on England, I hope. Alric picked up some useful news during the time he spent in Lindsey. He was there at your bidding, I am told."

His black eyes fixed on her, and she bridled beneath that hard gaze. He had warned her not to meddle in men's affairs, despite the fact that they were her affairs as well.

"I sent him to gather information, nothing more," she lied.

"And it was well done," he said soberly, "I will give you that. Not like this other business—the journey you made to your cousin. In that, you disobeyed me, and worse, you put yourself and all our preparations in danger. If Thurbrand had taken it into his head to beat you senseless for it, he would have been within his rights."

She had not tried to make a secret of where she had spent those weeks last winter. Too many people had been with her, and one of them was Tyra, the truth teller.

"I lost the child," she said, her voice acid. "Do you not think that was punishment enough? Now, will you tell me of this plan of yours or not?"

Her husband met her gaze for a long moment, then reached for his ale cup and gestured to Alric to speak.

"I was able to learn that the king's thegn Ulfkytel has been ordered to gather an army to bring against our force that is camped at Benfleet. He will be drawing his men from East Anglia, but that lot are sheepherders first and warriors second. They'll not be lured into any shield wall until after they've finished shearing their flocks."

"Ulfkytel will not have his full force until late in May," Cnut said with a slow smile, "which means that we can strike first, and with a much larger force."

She thought about that. A pitched battle, she had once overheard her father say, should be avoided whenever possible unless your own men far outnumber the foe. In this case the Danes would have the numbers on their side. Even so, the English would be led by Ulfkytel. She had never met him, but she knew of him.

"Ulfkytel is someone to be feared, my lord. He led his East Anglians against the Danes once before and nearly won."

"Nearly will not be good enough," Cnut said, "and we will have the advantage of surprise as well as numbers. Until now, Thorkell has taken pains to avoid a direct confrontation with the English, so Ulfkytel will not be looking for us to strike at all. The timing, though, is the key. We want them reeling at the first blow. A few frightened men who break and run can determine the course of a battle."

"But they will be fighting to protect their own lands," she said. "Even if they are afraid, they might hold their ground."

"Some may," Cnut said, "but there will be some among them whose kin live across the Danish sea, and others who escaped the butchery on the Feast of St. Brice some years back and who still dream of vengeance. We have sent our men among them—traders mostly, men like Alric here who listen well but say little. We will approach them again in the next few weeks, and we will not go empty-handed."

She saw how the plan would work. He would give them silver, and plant them among Ulfkytel's force. They would turn and flee, drawing others with them so that a force that was already outnumbered could be cut down to near nothing.

"Seek out Thurkytel," she advised him. "He has lands near Ipswich. His father and brother were with my father at Shrewsbury and died there with him. He will have no love for Eadric or the king. Alric knows the man."

She did not say that she had sent Alric to Thurkytel three times in as many years to nurture his hatred of Æthelred. She was a woman, and she was not supposed to meddle, yet it was her meddling that had laid the foundations for this plan of Cnut's, even though he did not know it and would likely not thank her if she told him. Yet by her reckoning, he owed her a boon, and she saw no reason why she should not ask for it.

She waited until the next night, when they were both breathless from bed play and she was cupped within the shelter of his arm. The chamber was lit only by the flickering light of a dying fire, but she could see his face clearly, the high brow and the long, straight nose—so sharp it looked as though it had been sculpted. He was staring into the darkness above them, and she knew she must speak now, while he was languid with pleasure and most likely to grant her request.

She ran her tongue against his ear then whispered, "Take me with you tomorrow. I will make certain that you do not regret it. "

He combed his fingers through her hair, tugging playfully at a thick curl.

"I cannot," he said. "You would distract me, and that might be dangerous. I want no distractions."

"There will be women enough there to distract you, I think." She turned her face against his hand and nipped the flesh below his thumb. "That is why I wish to attend you. Will you make me beg?"

"Beg all you like," he said, grinning, "but you will remain in Holderness. You are safe here."

"Safe!" She snorted. "And bored as well. I hate it here. It is cold and damp and ugly." And then another thought struck her. "May I not go to Jorvik, then? I could be your eyes and ears there."

"Jorvik is no less damp and ugly, and I will not be able to visit you as easily there. And do not imagine that you will slip away from my men again. That is a trick that only works once."

Visit her as easily! She hardly saw him at all.

"You are just like my father!" She threw herself back on her pillows. "You would keep me mewed up for your own purposes, like an eyas. Why not just seel my eyes and put jesses round my ankles?"

"Your eyes are too fine to be seeled," he said. "But I will give thought to the jesses. Would silver chains suit you? Or perhaps you would prefer gold."

She gave him a clout on his shoulder, but he laughed and covered her body with his, and although at first she struggled against him, he had the measure of her. His mouth and hands against her skin made her forget everything but the pleasure he aroused in her.

At least, for a time. When he lay asleep beside her she reckoned the number of days and nights that they would spend together, and the number vexed her. Cnut was young and virile, and he gave no heed to the passing of years. But she was older than her husband by five winters, and every year mattered to her.

How many winters were left to her, until she was too old to breed and would no longer be of use to him?

Two sons, Tyra had said she would have, but in five days her husband would set sail, taking Alric with him, and leaving her again with her womb empty. She would be surrounded by women and guarded by Danish shipmen whom she dared not trust, and so would have no man at her side. No man in her bed. She might as well be locked up in an abbey.

She turned to gaze at Cnut. His face was a mere shadow in the darkness, but he was like his father—a force as solid as stone. She could not move him to do her bidding, and she hated him for that just as she had hated her father and brothers. Like them he wielded a power over her that she could not rebuff.

Not until she had a son.

She pressed her hand against her belly, caressing the soft flesh, certain that despite the pleasure Cnut had taken in her body, her womb would not quicken. Not now.

And she hated him for that as well.


**April 1010**

**London**


On the Friday before Holy Week a special Mass was celebrated at St. Paul's, beseeching God's mercy upon the realm and pleading for victory over England's enemies. Emma attended, along with many of the king's thegns and their wives who had made their way into the city for the Easter court. Æthelred and his retinue had not yet appeared in London but were expected any day. Athelstan and Edmund, to the dismay of both Emma and Archbishop Ælfheah, had left the city with their hearth guards the day before.

Emma had tried to dissuade Athelstan from disobeying his father's command to remain in London for the Easter court, but all her arguments were futile.

"My staying," he had said, "serves no purpose other than to proclaim my submission to the king. What is the point of that? He mistrusts me no matter what I do. Edmund and I can be of far more use in East Anglia with Ulfkytel, readying the levies for battle, than we can by staying here and offering advice to my father that he will not take."

"But he charged you with London's defense," she had protested. "You cannot just walk away from that."

"I can, because the city is well protected. *Jesu*, it is bursting with armed thegns and their retainers. I have turned over command of the London fyrd to Ealdorman Ælfric, and the king and Eadric will be here with more men in a matter of days at the most. In any case, I have already disobeyed my father's command by journeying to Headington in January. I did it again when I led an entire army outside the city walls to head off Thorkell, for all the good it did. How many times can he punish me for the same offense?"

"It is not the punishment that you must consider," she had persisted. "It is how he will construe your actions."

"Emma, he will condemn me no matter what I do." He took her hands in his and gazed at her so earnestly that her heart broke for him. "I am afraid that the only way for me to win my father's esteem is to die for him."

"Do not say that," she had protested, alarmed by such a malediction.

He had smiled ruefully at her, and kissed her palm. "Believe me, I do not intend to take that route into my father's affections."

She had not been reassured. It seemed to her that the future lay before them like some great beast waiting to pounce, and she could not contemplate it except with dread. Ever since Margot's death she had feared that every leave-taking would be as final as that one had been.

Unable to banish her misgiving, she had clung to Athelstan's hand ever so briefly when he came to bid her farewell. She had remained dry-eyed as she watched him walk away, but the terrible certainty that she would never see him again wrapped itself about her like a shroud.

When the Mass at St. Paul's was ended, she returned to the palace, guiding her horse through a heavy mist that had settled like a pall upon the city. Inside the palace gates, she and her attendants were forced to make their way around a dozen or so packhorses that stood in front of the hall. Servants were busy relieving them of their burdens and, seeing this, she knew that the king had arrived at last.

She dismounted, hastening to her apartments. The children would be waiting for her there—Godiva in her nurse's arms, Edward probably settled on the bench, poring over a book with Robert beside him. Or the boys might be inspecting the alcove prepared for them, might have already discovered the carved ships and horses waiting there.

Sweeping past servants and men-at-arms, she climbed the stairs that led to her private chamber and went inside—only to find it empty but for the king. Æthelred had apparently been there for some time, for he had shed his traveling clothes in favor of a long, green woolen gown that he wore over a white linen cemes.

"Where are the children?" she asked.

Only then did she see that the coffer that held her private correspondence was open and its contents strewn haphazardly on her worktable. He was absorbed in reading something that he did not like, for he was scowling.

She swallowed her resentment at finding him pawing through her letters and held her breath, waiting for the answer to her question.

"My daughters will join us in good time for next week's Easter court," he murmured, not looking up from the letter in his hand. "Sit down."

She did not move.

"What about Edward? Is he not with you?"

He looked at her now, his eyes cold.

"Edward is in Shropshire, and Edyth's daughter as well. I have weaned Edward from that Norman priest you set over him like a shadow and have sent him to foster parents. He will be as safe with them, you may be sure, as he would be in Rouen"—he waved the parchment he'd been reading—"as your brother here suggests."

Stunned, almost weak with disappointment, she sought the cushioned bench that lined the wall and sat down. She kept her back straight and her chin high, though, for she did not wish him to perceive what a blow he had just dealt her. It had been a full year since she had seen Edward. How much longer must she wait? Would he even remember her when he looked upon her again?

Her hands trembling with anger and cold, she slipped off her damp cloak.

"Was it Ealdorman Eadric who counseled you to send the children away?" Of course it was. Why did she even bother to ask?

"It is far better counsel than what your brother is urging—that you send your children to him in Normandy." He looked up at her then, and she read the anger there, behind his eyes. "He has suggested nothing of that to me. The only missives I get from him are complaints that I am causing you grief by keeping you from my court. Is it true, Emma? Do you pine for my company, sweeting?"

His tone was sarcastic, baiting her. As she refused to answer him, he answered himself.

"No. I see that it is not my company you seek, but Edward's. How disappointed you must be. Did you hope to accompany your son across the Narrow Sea to your brother? Are you so afraid of the Danish rabble sweeping across England that you begged Richard to give you shelter?"

"All of England is afraid, my lord," she said. In the streets of London the fear of what the summer might bring was as thick as the Thames fog. "But I did not ask my brother to shelter my children in Normandy, I assure you. Nor do I think that fostering Edward at so great a distance as Shropshire is a wise move. As your heir he should stay closer to the court. I can understand your desire to protect him from our enemy, but when word gets out that you have sent him so far away, it will hardly reassure your people—"

"I did not send Edward north to protect him from the Danes," he snapped, "but to keep him away from you."

He was purposely goading her, and she did not know why.

"And who, pray, will explain that to the frightened people of London?" she demanded. "Will you post a writ to claim that you sent your son away because you were afraid of what he might learn at his mother's knee?"

"Your tongue is too sharp, lady," he said. Yet there was a note of satisfaction in his voice, as if he was pleased to have finally sparked an angry response. "If the bishops could hear you now they would not wonder that I wish to keep you from my court."

Ah. There it was. His bishops had sided against him in her favor, and he did not like it. She should have guessed that he would use Edward to punish her for besting him. What a fool she had been to think that he would allow her son anywhere near her.

She took a deep breath to cool her anger, for it would do her little good. He would use it as an excuse to send her away again.

"My lord, I am your consort and queen. Never have I given you cause to reproach me, yet you will not trust me even with the upbringing of our son."

"No. Nor would I trust your brother. I would not see Edward turned against me as his elder brothers have been." He looked past her, into the middle distance, and his eyes grew vague. "Athelstan and Edmund have left London at the head of armed troops, against my express instructions that they remain within the city. I have not yet discovered where they have gone, but I fear the worst."

She stared at him, thunderstruck. He would think the worst of his own sons, in spite of other, far more obvious, explanations. Perhaps Athelstan was right. Perhaps the only way to earn this king's esteem was to die for him. Yet someone must try to reason with him.

"Athelstan and Edmund have gone to East Anglia, my lord, to aid Ulfkytel in gathering the army that you ordered him to bring against the Danes. They kept their destination secret because you wisely insisted that no one must know what Ulfkytel is doing."

His gaze snapped back to her, suspicion written in every line of his face.

"And how is it that you know all this?"

*Because I am your queen,* she thought. *It is my business to know such things even if you would keep me ignorant.*

She said, "I was one of several who was privileged with the information. The others were the bishop of London, Archbishop Ælfheah, and Ealdorman Ælfric."

He scowled. Apparently the list of those who knew of the æthelings' plans—a list that did not include him—did not sit well.

"I suppose you believe that this excuses my sons for disobeying my command."

"I believe that they are not planning any action against you, my lord."

For a time he said nothing, merely gazing at her thoughtfully, as if he would uncover other secrets that she might be keeping hidden from him. She kept her face carefully blank, for she did have one secret that he must never learn—a hopeless, inescapable yearning for a man who was not the king.

At last he stood up, glanced once more at her brother's letter, then tossed it back onto the table.

"Richard's concerns are baseless, of course, and his offer of refuge for the children pointless. When you write to him, tell him that what I need are men who can stand with us against the Danes. It's a pity that he is so reluctant to offer that kind of assistance." He strode toward her and grasped her chin, forcing her to look up at him, into eyes as fathomless as stones. "Now that I have accommodated the bishops by bringing you back to court, I would have you attend me tonight. Surely your champions will wish to see you with child again as soon as possible."

"My lord, it is Lent," she protested, flinching from his touch yet unable to escape it. "Abstinence is—"

"If you think it a sin to lie with your king, that is between you and your confessor. But sin or no, you will attend me tonight and every night as it pleases me." He released her and started for the door, then paused to add, "We might send the girl to Normandy, I suppose. She is too young to be of any use here."

After he was gone, his words echoed in her mind, filling her with apprehension and rage. She could see what he hoped to do. She could even glimpse, to her disgust, what it was that drove him.

He wanted her pregnant again so that he could remove her from court without having to defend his action to the bishops or to her brother. That was policy.

He would mold Edward in his own image, using him in whatever manner suited his purposes. That was vanity.

He would make the Danish raids an excuse for taking her daughter from her, sending Godiva across the Narrow Sea, perhaps forever. That was pure spite.

He could accomplish all of it, if he wished. He had the power. But he had made a grave error in allowing her to see what was in his mind. There were ways of circumventing his power, and he would discover that a queen was not without resources. For the time being, at least, she had episcopal support that he dared not oppose. His threats, for now, were mere words, but they were words that could be shared and thus made impotent.

She watched her servants enter the chamber in the wake of Æthelred's departure. How many of them were the king's spies, and which of them had brought him the coffer of letters that she had kept so carefully locked away?

It did not matter. Soon she would have most of her trusted household members about her, including Father Martin. With their help she would see that certain of the king's magnates were made aware of his threats.

Æthelred would not find her a willing victim, and she would do her utmost to make sure that he did not use her children as weapons against her.

A.D. 1010   This year came the army, after Easter, into East Anglia . . . where they understood Ulfkytel was with his army. The East-Angles soon fled. There was slain Oswy and his son, and Wulfric, son of Leofwin, and Edwy, brother of Efy, and many good thanes, and a multitude of people. Thurkytel Myrehead first began the flight; and the Danes remained masters of the field of slaughter. There were they horsed; and afterwards they took possession of East-Anglia, where they plundered and burned three months; Thetford also they burned, and Cambridge; Oxfordshire, Buckinghamshire, and so along the Ouse till they came to Bedford, and so forth to Temsford, always burning as they went.

Then all the privy council were summoned before the king, to consult how they might defend this country. But whatever was advised, it stood not a month; and at length there was not a chief that would collect an army, but each fled as he could: no shire would stand by another . . .

When the army had gone as far as they would, then came they by midwinter to their ships.

—*The Anglo-Saxon Chronicle*

# Chapter Twenty-Seven

December 1010
Gloucestershire

Emma had been told that the view from Ciresdune was beautiful, and as she stood on that hilltop and gazed into the distance, she had to agree. The scene below her, though, was deceptive, for it made her almost believe that England was at peace.

She had walked a little away from her companions, and now she turned around slowly, taking in the fields and forests of Mercia and the distant hills that marked the northern edge of Wessex—all of it covered with the glittering veil of a recent snowfall. It was as if God's finger had touched all the burned and broken things in this land and made them whole again.

But she knew that was not so. In the spring, or perhaps sooner, the snow would disappear, and the ruins that lay beneath would be revealed—broken villages and broken lives.

Broken trust. The people of England had placed their trust in their king, and he had failed them. It had not been for want of trying, but it was failure just the same.

She drew in a deep breath of the clear, chilly air. Above her, the sky was a brilliant blue, awash with sunlight. She tried to find hope in all this dazzling brightness, but she could not. The knowledge of all that had been lost in the past months was too oppressive.

"I am afraid," she said, admitting the truth to herself as well as to Wymarc and Father Martin, who had come here with her.

They joined her now at the very crest of the hill. Father Martin folded his hands, resting his chin upon them before he spoke.

"Everything has its season, my lady," he said. "This, it seems, is the season for fear and for weeping."

"You have been afraid before, Emma—we all have." Wymarc placed a reassuring hand on her arm. "Yet we are safe here, for now at least."

Emma gave her a grateful smile, for her friend was ever one to find some trace of gold even in a world of gloom.

"It is not for myself that I am afraid," she said, "but for my children and for your son. I am afraid for the king's children and for the English out there who are facing a bitter, cheerless winter. I can foresee no happy resolution to the trials that they are facing—that we all are facing. As hard as I look for it, I cannot discover any hope within my heart."

"Then do not look within," Father Martin urged. "Look to God. And ask not for hope, but for courage and acceptance."

Likely there was wisdom in those words, she told herself, yet she could not quite bring herself to trust them. He would have her bow to God's will, yet she could not accept that England's ravaging was the will of the Almighty. It was the will of men, and it came with all the cruelty that men could inflict on one another. Sometimes it made her so angry that her prayers were not petitions for mercy but howls of rage.

She could say nothing of this to Father Martin and Wymarc, though. They must each of them find whatever comfort they could. It was true that there were many things for which she should thank God. Her own household had been with her now for some months—Godiva and her nurse, Wymarc, Father Martin, and many of those who had escaped with her from the Headington palace and who wished to remain at her side.

They had come with her to the king's winter council in this far western corner of England, a place as yet untouched by the enemy and the havoc that they had wrought. The king's daughters and their husbands had arrived already. Ælfa's retinue included her little girl, who was two winters old now. Hilde, too, had made the long journey with them from Northumbria, accompanied by a young retainer of Uhtred's named Godric, who had sought and been granted her hand in marriage. Their wedding feast would throw some welcome joy upon the Christmas gathering.

Three of the æthelings, though, had yet to answer the king's summons, and that added to her dark mood. Even now she peered into the distance, first north then south, half imagining that she might catch some sign of them. It was foolish, of course. She was too far away to make out the road that Edward would take from Shropshire or the route that would bring Athelstan and Edmund from London.

It was Athelstan's absence in particular that filled her with misgiving. He was not yet reconciled with his father, had not even spoken with Æthelred for a full year. He had kept the promise that he had made to her in London before Ringmere, though—had not died in battle to please the king. He had been wounded, though, an injury that had been slow to heal but had done nothing to appease his father's wrath at his son's disobedience. The king demanded word of him daily and glowered when he could learn nothing. They knew only that he had left London and should have arrived here already—only he had not.

She imagined a hundred things that could have delayed him, but the most likely, it seemed to her, was that his bitterness toward his father might have goaded him into ignoring the king's summons altogether. She prayed that she was wrong. She prayed that he would come, and soon. His father needed every clear voice of reason left in the kingdom if he was to find a way out of the strife that had engulfed them this past summer—strife that would surely begin again in spring unless something was done.

And if Athelstan did not obey the summons, then his father would see it as the act of an enemy.

Even Edward had been sent for, although the king, wishing to keep her son from her side, had resisted doing so at first. She had won that battle—had presented her arguments with cool deliberation, one after the other, garnering support for each from the churchmen who advised the king. Eadric had argued against her, but when he recognized that she had the more powerful faction on her side, he reversed his opinion. Eadric apparently preferred to change his allegiance rather than lose, no matter what the conflict.

And there was so much conflict now within the royal halls! She and Æthelred lined up arguments between them like shield walls, and she sometimes wished that, years ago, before her brother had sent her across the Narrow Sea to bear arms against a king, he had thought to school her in the arts of war.

When they returned to the king's hall, riding past scores of tents that sheltered the small army of retainers accompanying the members of the witan, she saw that a new banner had been raised above the entry gate.

Edward had come.

She looked at Wymarc, who met her gaze with glistening eyes and a bright smile. Robert, too, would be among Edward's company. Both of their sons had arrived.

The cloud of fear and tension that had hovered over her for months lifted. She quelled the urge to hasten into the royal apartments to find Edward, for he must pay his respects to the king first, and she had no wish to be reunited with her son beneath Æthelred's disapproving gaze. She would wait in her quarters for Edward to appear, as she knew he must. Æthelred could not hope to keep them apart, even though he might desire it.

After what felt like an eternity her son at last entered her chamber, and she wanted to weep at all the changes that two years had wrought. She remembered him as a plump, sunny little boy who had loved to curl up in her lap while she told him stories. Now he was six winters old and he stood before her tall and straight, but stiff and unsmiling. His hair was still fair and fine, but the curls that she had so loved had been shorn away, making his thin face look thinner still.

He was the image of her sister, Mathilde, she thought with a pang, right down to the hollow cheeks and narrow mouth.

Edward made no move toward her. He offered a stiff bow and merely gazed at her in silence, studying her just as she was studying him.

He wore a silver-gray tunic embroidered with golden thread, and under it a saffron scyrte. He looked every inch the heir to a throne, the expression on his face so carefully composed that she thought he must have been made keenly aware of his standing as first among the æthelings.

Would he have any idea how perilous a privilege that was? Edmund would be livid at seeing his half brother robed so extravagantly, especially when the rest of the court was in mourning.

She guessed that this was Eadric's doing, intended to cause strife among the brothers. Edyth, too, would likely have had a hand in it, for she had of late taken a great interest in Edward. Her once staunch defense of Athelstan's claim as the king's heir had been cast aside the moment that she finally resigned herself to permanent enmity between her husband and her eldest brother. Should desire for the crown ever bring Athelstan into conflict with Edward, the support of Edyth and her husband would go to Edward.

*Dear God,* she prayed, *please do not let it come to that.*

And then she dismissed the king's other children from her mind and focused only on this silent boy before her. Was Edward shy? Or was he searching his memory for some image of her?

Leaving her chair she knelt in front of him and gathered him into her arms. He suffered her embrace, but clearly it was unwelcome. It was as though she'd wrapped her arms around a child made of stone. When she sat back on her heels to look at him, he returned her gaze with cool politeness.

Had he learned, at so early an age, the trick of hiding his thoughts and feelings? It had taken her far, far longer.

Once more she wanted to weep.

"Do you remember me, Edward?" she asked.

"You are the queen," he said promptly in a high, clear voice. It was a politic answer, and very correct.

It was not at all what she had hoped for.

She drew him to a bench and for some time they spoke together— she asking probing questions, he providing answers that revealed very little. Eventually a servant came to fetch him, to ready him for the evening meal, where he was to sit at the king's right hand. When he left her, Edward bowed once more, as stiff and formal as when he first entered the chamber.

She watched him walk away, his back straight and his chin high.

That much, at least, he had from her, although he could not know it. He had been her son once, her darling, her world. Who, she wondered, her heart riddled with grief, did he belong to now?

## December 1010
## Near Saltford, Oxfordshire

"I think we must have taken the wrong turning at the last crossroads," Edmund said. "We should have been there by now, surely. Are you certain that you know where you're leading us?"

Athelstan merely grunted. He knew where he was going. He glanced behind, at the half-dozen men and packhorses that traveled with them, assured himself that there were no laggards, then looked to the path again.

A thin blanket of snow covered the ground, pale in the winter light. The sky was the color of dirty slate, and a late-afternoon breeze bit forehead and cheek, sharp as a blade. Until now Edmund had voiced no complaint nor said much of anything at all. Athelstan had been grateful for his brother's companionable silence, but he knew that Edmund's patience would not last much longer. Nevertheless, they rode for some distance before Edmund spoke again.

"Athelstan, we must be lost. You cannot possibly know where this stone circle is. It's been—what—nine years since we were there? And we had a guide then, not to mention the minor point that we came at it from a completely different direction."

"We're on the right path," Athelstan replied, using the tone of command that brooked no argument.

For a time Edmund relapsed into a brooding silence, and then, as Athelstan had expected, he put it all together. "You've been to see her since then, haven't you." It wasn't a question. "*For Christ's sake*, why? You said she was a fraud. Why go back to consult her again? And why are we going now?"

Why. He had never spoken to anyone about what the seeress had said to him on that first occasion, or ever breathed aloud the even more ominous prediction she had made when he saw her next—that he and his brothers would walk a bitter road.

He had tried to convince himself that she was a fraud, that a man would be a fool to take her dire prophecies seriously.

But three of his brothers were dead, and for the past year, not just the sons of Æthelred but everyone in England had been walking a bitter road. After the slaughter at Ringmere had destroyed much of Ulfkytel's army and sent those left alive running for their lives, the Danes had sorted themselves, as far as he had been able to make out, into five groups, some horsed, some on foot. They fed on food stolen from the mouths of English children. They forced English men to watch while their wives, sisters, and daughters were raped. They stole whatever loot they could grab, and depending on the mood of the shipmen and their leaders, they torched what they could not carry. From East Anglia to the Fosse Way, and from the Thames Valley to the Fenlands, for seven months England had been brutalized and burnt.

Through it all he had been ordered to stay within the walls of London, under threat of banishment should he disobey. He had railed against this punishment, but Edmund had called him a fool.

"What do you imagine that you would do even if you could quit London?" Edmund had demanded. He had gestured to Athelstan's bandaged left leg, slashed and broken at Ringmere. "It will be months before you can walk or ride a horse. You are no use to anyone until that's healed, so stop complaining that you're being ill used."

Once his leg had healed it had taken weeks to regain the strength necessary to ride or to stand and wield a sword properly. During that time he had chafed at Edmund's reports of English levies defeated in one shire after another. The Viking decision to split their force had made it impossible to anticipate where they might strike next and so raise a defense. For England, the summer had been one long string of disasters. The kingdom was verging on ruin, walking the bitter road that the seeress had foretold. Even he did not know what he expected to gain by consulting her again. She had never spoken him good fortune, and he feared that whatever she might tell him today would be no better. Yet he felt compelled to find her, to look once more upon the face of one of the Old Ones as she stood there in the midst of the stones. Perhaps he just wanted reassurance—that if her ancient race still survived in this land, his own people were not doomed.

Edmund, obviously irritated by the long silence, broke it with a string of curses. Then he demanded, "How many times have you spoken to the cunning woman?"

Athelstan hesitated, for once he admitted to it, Edmund would want to know more.

"This will be the fourth time," he said at last. "And no, I will not tell you what she said to me."

Edmund cursed again, but there were no further questions.

In the distance ahead of them Athelstan could now make out the sentinel stone on the ridge, its shaft pale against the sky's lurid darkness. When they drew up beside it he searched the hollow for the black-clad figure. The stones were there, jagged and dark against the snow. But this time, for the first time, she was not waiting for him.

He frowned, searching the stones and then looking carefully among the oaks that surrounded the ring. Where her small cottage had once stood—a thing of wattle, daub, and thatch—there was only a jagged mound of snow beneath trees whose bare limbs were blackened and burnt.

"The Danes must have struck here, too," Edmund observed. "*Christ*, how did they find it? This is the middle of nowhere. Athelstan, if she truly had the Sight, she would have seen what was coming and fled. We're wasting our time, and it will be nightfall before long. I would like to sleep in a bed tonight, even if it is only in a raw, half-built hall, which is all that we're likely to find after this summer's horrors."

But Athelstan was only half listening, already urging his horse down among the oaks that surrounded the standing stones, making his way toward that mound that he could see on the other side. He hoped that Edmund was right and that, unlike so many others, she had taken warning and managed to slip away. She would have had little enough to carry with her, certainly nothing that a shipload of Danish raiders might covet.

When he reached the blackened trees he dismounted and strode over to the mounded snow. Some of it had already melted away, so that he could see some of the collapsed, charred timbers beneath. Edmund joined him, and together they dragged away what was left of the snow-limned posts that had anchored the small building.

When he saw what they'd uncovered, he recoiled, cursing, although he'd been half expecting it. It was similar, he imagined, to what must lie among the countless other ruins that had littered England this past summer—dead bodies with staring eyes, partially burned corpses, figures so mutilated that none could tell if the dead were men or women.

Here the fire had not burned hot enough to turn bones to ash. He was staring at charred, decaying flesh, and holding his breath against the stench of it. She lay where she had fallen, crushed probably when the roof beam had collapsed on top of her.

Had they locked her in and set the place ablaze? *Jesu*, he hoped it had not been like that.

"Now what?" Edmund asked, his face grim. "We cannot bury her. The ground is too hard."

"We have to do something," Athelstan said. From what he could see of the corpse, some burrowing creature had already found her. They couldn't leave her like this. "She lived among the stones. Surely we can find enough of them here to cover her."

He gestured to his men, and they walked a wide circuit, gathering the largest rocks that they could carry, using them to build a cairn over her where she lay, there beneath the oaks.

And all the time the last words that she had spoken to him rang and rang in his ears until he thought that they would make him mad.

*I see fire*, she had said, *and smoke. There is never anything else.*

Was it her death she had foretold with those words? Or was it England's?


December 1010
Kingsholme, Gloucestershire


When the æthlings arrived at the royal estate two days later it was near dark. Athelstan, with Edmund right behind him, strode into the chamber assigned to them and found Edwig comfortably settled on one of the beds. His brother had a wall of cushions at his back, one booted foot atop the linens and, as usual, an ale cup in his hand.

"Drinking alone?" Athelstan snapped, irritated at the very sight of Edwig. His brother had become Eadric's devoted shadow, and it was difficult to tolerate him anywhere, much less share quarters with him.

He crossed the room to sit gingerly on the edge of a bed and stretch out his legs. He was tired, his wound still pained him, and he did not think he had the patience to deal with a besotted Edwig.

"No one to drink with," Edwig said, slurring his words so that Athelstan wondered just how drunk he was. "The king has called a privy meeting, and I was not invited."

Edmund had gone straight to the glowing brazier, but now he regarded Edwig with interest. "A meeting about what?"

"Peace terms," Edwig snorted. "Archbishop Ælfheah's just come from Kent, where he's been meeting with that bastard Thorkell." He waved his cup—a salute to the Danes, Athelstan supposed. "The king has gathered his closest advisers to his bosom so that Ælfheah can tell them just how much peace is going to cost us."

"So what are you doing here?" Athelstan demanded. Drunk or not, Edwig was an ætheling and he should be with the king.

"Banished." Edwig grinned. "Caught with my breecs down in the chamber assigned to the archbishop."

Edmund's face registered disbelief and disgust all at once. "*Christ*, you're a fool! What were you doing? Swiving some serving wench in the archbishop's bed?"

"She was willing," Edwig protested, "and the chamber was empty! How was I to know Ælfheah would barge in and nearly faint at the sight of my sweet, bare ass?" He gave a high-pitched, drunken laugh.

Edmund looked at Athelstan. "Shall I hit him? If he's unconscious, we won't have to listen to him."

"From the look of him, he'll be unconscious soon enough. And I want to hear what he knows about that peace proposal. Edwig! What were the terms that the king offered to Thorkell?"

"Usual rotten terms." Edwig appeared suddenly more sober. "Twenty-four thousand pounds of silver and provisions through the winter. They're to take themselves off when the sea lanes open and vow never to come back."

"It will take more than twenty-four thousand pounds to accomplish that," Athelstan spat. "Thorkell has us on our knees, and he knows it."

"But that is a huge sum!" Edmund protested.

"He will demand more, though," Athelstan said, "and the king will be forced to give it."

Edwig sat up and swung his feet to the floor.

"Athelstan is probably right," he said, swaying slightly. "But be of good cheer. There is some welcome news. Our northern friend Morcar has found the Lady Elgiva."

"The devil he has," Edmund said. "Where is she?"

Edwig raised his cup in another salute. "Dead and buried in a church-yard in Lindsey."

Athelstan caught Edmund's eye, and he suspected they both had the same thought. Had Elgiva been murdered by order of the king?

"How did she die?" Athelstan asked.

"Pestilence. God's hand at work," Edwig said, mockingly pious as he sketched the sign of the cross. "She went to her cousin—what was her name? Siferth's wife? The tall one with the big eyes?"

"Aldyth," Edmund murmured. "Her name is Aldyth."

Edwig snapped his fingers. "Well done! So, Elgiva visited her cousin Aldyth last winter, took ill, and died along with half of the household. The cousin kept it to herself all this time, and Siferth only recently dragged it out of her. He seems to have taken sick now, so it was Morcar who brought the news. Too bad for Siferth, because the king rewarded his brother with a pretty piece of land up in the Five Boroughs."

"As if he needed any more land," Edmund observed. "He and Siferth own nearly everything up there as it is. Now all the lands that once be-longed to Elgiva will fall to them as well."

"Lands that they will have to pay taxes on," Athelstan reminded him. His father was adept at exchanging land for silver and gold—one of his few talents.

"And taxes there will be," Edwig agreed, getting up unsteadily to pour himself more ale. "The king will likely scrape every penny he can get from every single English hide to make the Danes clear off."

"His thegns will howl at that," Edmund said.

Edwig laughed again. "Yes, they will, miserable cowards! Wait until you see the king's hall. It's like a kennel full of snarling dogs. They yip at each other about the best way to stop the Danish bastards, but not a one is willing to lift his sword against them. The king curses them, curses the devil, even curses God—although not when there are priests about." He took a long pull from his cup, spilling ale as he staggered back to the bed. "He cursed poor Ulfkytel for losing that battle up at Ringmere. Swore that our sister was wasted on an East Anglian who didn't have the sense to die when he lost his battle; even threatened to take Ælfa back and give her to someone else." He waved his cup again. "Your coming, my lords, will be most welcome, I promise you—fresh meat for all the hounds to fall upon. Be prepared to lose a little blood."

Athelstan scowled and got to his feet. He'd heard all he wanted to hear from Edwig.

"Thank you for the warning," he said, and turned to Edmund. "I think it's time we let the king and his dogs know that we're here."

# Chapter Twenty-Eight

December 1010

Kingsholme, Gloucestershire

Æthelred studied the man who stood before him—archbishop, royal emissary, longtime counselor. He looked from Ælfheah's weary face to the golden cross at his breast and the crosier that he leaned upon, with its inlay of silver and gilt.

*Sweet Christ!* If the man had flaunted such ornaments when he met with Thorkell, the Danes would have doubled their tribute demands and thought themselves cheated even then.

Uneasy, he shifted his gaze from the archbishop to the others who were gathered in the hall—his kin and closest advisers. Edward, the heir, was seated below the dais on his right, arrayed in gold that rivaled the archbishop's gilding—Edyth's work, he guessed, and foolish.

Opposite Edward, on the left side of the hall, Emma was clad in a dark gown more fitting to the occasion, her only concession to ornament a silvery veil that hid her bright hair. His daughters sat beside her, their faces drawn and their eyes avoiding his. He had wed them to powerful men; likely they feared some impending clash between their husbands and their father, as well they might. But he had lavished gold on them all their lives, and if they wished to prove their gratitude, they would know on which side their loyalties should lie.

He swung his gaze to the æthelings' bench. The two eldest were still missing. Was their absence a blessing, he wondered, or a portent of trouble yet to come?

The prayers beseeching wisdom had been said, and now he felt all the eyes in the hall settle on him, looking to him to signal the archbishop to speak. He hesitated, searching Ælfheah's face for some hint of the message that he carried from the enemy. He could read nothing, and as he nodded to Ælfheah to begin, he saw Athelstan and Edmund enter the hall and take their places.

So, they had come at last, his disobedient sons. He wanted to ask what business had detained them, but Ælfheah's voice, filling the air with the force of a sermon, claimed his attention.

"Thorkell has quartered himself for the winter at Rochester, my lord," Ælfheah said, "much to the dismay of the townsfolk. I met with him there and presented your terms to him. Your offer of winter provision has been accepted, and in order to honor your pledge and ease the hardships imposed on the citizens of Rochester, I have already directed that stores from my own lands be sent to him."

Æthelred nodded approval. Had the archbishop not given the shipmen the food, they would likely have stolen it in any case from somewhere else. Still, it would take far more than what Ælfheah could provide to feed thousands of men for the next three months. More would have to be sent—a heavy burden on the southern shires, and they would not welcome it.

"Will they take the tribute we offered," he demanded, "and leave England?"

This was what he was impatient to know, but something in the archbishop's eyes warned him that he was not going to like what he was about to hear.

"The Danes have rejected the twenty-four thousand pounds of silver I offered them, and have demanded instead the sum of forty-eight thousand pounds."

The throbbing of blood in his ears all but drowned out the cries of outrage that filled the chamber.

Eadric's voice came to him through the din. "They are mad!"

"Not mad," he murmured when he was able to speak. "They are devils."

They meant to break him, meant to incite rebellion. They had already pillaged most of the northern shires, burned crops, stolen from poor and wealthy alike. The burden of tribute, like that of provision, must fall upon Wessex, and Wessex had been hard hit the summer before.

"Our people already resent the taxes they have paid to fortify towns and equip our armies—all of it in vain. You know as well as I do, Archbishop, how the men of England are likely to greet a demand for more taxes. What answer did you make?"

"That I would return with your response in the week after Epiphany."

*Good Christ.* Had the fool no notion of how to use the winter months to their advantage? Far better to make the Danes sit in their cold winter camps and ponder what the English might be planning than to give them a prompt reply, whatever the answer might be.

"Why did you not specify a date for our response more distant than early January?" he growled.

"I tried, my lord, but it was Thorkell who named the date, and he threatened more violence if we do not meet it."

Thorkell. The very name filled Englishmen with terror. Yet Thorkell was mortal, and greedy. That weakness could be used to bring him to heel. Such a thing had been done before.

"It will be no easy task to gather so much tribute, should we even agree to their demand. We must play for time." He leaned forward in his chair and raked his eyes across each man in the chamber. "I will tell you the answer that I have in mind to send back to Thorkell. I would not grant his request outright, for I would not have him see me as so easy a mark. Even if I am forced to meet his demand in the end, I would be remiss if I did not try to bargain with the bastard. We will fill their bellies to prevent their ravaging, but there is no need to fill their ships too quickly with our coin. What say you? As desperate as this game is between us, it is still a game and we must play to win."

There was a murmur of voices, of men consulting one with another. He studied them, reading doubt on some faces and despair on others. When he saw Athelstan get to his feet to speak, he cursed softly. His son rarely agreed with him on anything, and he could tell from the whelp's frown that he would raise some objection. He sat back in his chair and waited for it.

"I urge you, my king," Athelstan said, "to give the Danes what they demand so that we rid ourselves of them as soon as may be."

He stiffened, suspicious. This was an unexpected plea from one usually so eager to resort to arms. What kind of twisted policy was behind it?

"You surprise me," he said. "In the past you have been the first to object to any concession to the Danes. As I recall, it has ever been your counsel to fight."

"We did fight, my lord. We lost. Some in this room were there. Many who were there are dead now because the Danes are better armed and better trained. Yes, I still think that we should fight them, but not until we are stronger than we are now. Our people are disheartened, our towns burned, and our women raped. We are a beaten kingdom, my lord. If we toy with them, and they come against us—"

"I am not beaten," he snarled, "no matter what you believe. I am determined on the course that I will take—to reject the Danes' demand and offer them something less. They will either agree or hold fast, but at the very least it will buy us time."

He paused and swept the room once more, meeting each man's gaze and finding acquiescence but for his two eldest sons. He directed his next words to them.

"I agree that we need well-trained warriors, and although I once swore that I would never again hire Danes to protect my kingdom, the time has come to test that policy once more. Archbishop," he said as he now looked to Ælfheah, "did you make such an offer to Thorkell?"

"Forgive me, my lord, but I did not," Ælfheah said.

The words struck him like a blow. He had counted on Ælfheah to broach the idea of a future alliance with the Danish warlord. All his strategy depended upon it.

"Why not?" he demanded.

"Because Thorkell is only one Danish leader, my lord, among three, and I was prevented from speaking with any of them in private."

He nodded. "They do not trust each other then. That is all to the good." Ælfheah's mission might not be such a disaster after all, if he had gleaned some useful information. "What else did you learn?"

"Thorkell has the greatest number of men," Ælfheah replied, "more than forty ships manned by disciplined Jomsvikings. The second largest force is led by his brother, named Hemming. His host is made up of pagan Norsemen, and I judge that there is little love between the Norse and the Danish shipmen. Thorkell and Hemming, though, are closely bound by a kinship not easily broken."

Æthelred grunted. The good archbishop was forgetting his Bible. Cain and Abel had been brothers, too, and it hadn't stopped one from murdering the other. Ambition, greed, even a beautiful woman could sunder the closest of kin. He glanced at his sons. Would that he could read their hearts and discover what jealousies and injuries were writ there.

"What of the third warlord?" he asked.

"His force is the smallest—only twenty ships by my reckoning. He is young, of an age with your own sons, but men say he is a seasoned fighter and that his warriors are the best armed of the lot."

"The young are known to be reckless," Æthelred growled. "Mayhap this cub could be persuaded to defect from his allies if we could find a way to present the idea to him." As he spoke, the expression on Ælfheah's face darkened. "I see that there is something about this young war leader, Archbishop, that you do not like. Why? Who is he?"

"He is called Cnut, my lord. He is the son of Swein Forkbeard."

The name Forkbeard hung in the air like the echo of a curse, and as if it had been a summons, he felt his brother's sickly shade invade the hall.

*By all the devils in hell*, he thought, *why do you continue to torment me?* He did not know if it was his dead brother, or Swein, or the devil himself that he addressed. It did not matter. He hated and feared them all. There was a heaviness filling his chest, and when he lifted his eyes to search the silent room, he found his brother's face, a massive bloated thing, hovering above his sons.

What in God's name did it want? Were his sons to be Edward's victims or were they to be his instruments, wielded like swords to destroy England?

"I curse you," he whispered under his breath. Then, gathering what voice he could, he roared at it. "You do not rule here! Get out!"

To his relief the thing dwindled in size to almost nothing, but relief turned to horror when the fetch rushed at him, sending pain rippling through his chest. As if from some great distance, he heard the shouts and clamor of men.

The king's wild cry sent Emma rushing to his side, but Archbishop Ælfheah was there before her, grasping Æthelred's shoulders to prevent his slumping from the great chair. She knelt down beside the king, calling for wine as she gently slapped his cheeks and saw, with relief, his eyes flicker open. Someone handed her a square of linen, and she wiped the spittle from his mouth and chin before holding the wine cup to his lips.

He will not die, she reassured herself. This has happened before. He will recover.

But she wished that there were not so many witnesses.

The king swallowed a little of the wine, then pushed the cup away.

"That will do," he said weakly, scowling.

He was still pale as a winding sheet. She glanced around at the cluster of nearby faces and guessed that the fear she saw there must reflect her own. When Æthelred had begun to fall, she had thought that the whole kingdom was about to crumble. It was not as grave as that, praise God, but how would he explain what they had all just seen and heard— a king gaping and shouting at some invisible presence?

She could only imagine what doubts and fears must be going through the minds of those crowding around him now. Indeed, the whispering had already begun.

"Archbishop," Æthelred said, still breathing heavily, "I thank you for your service." He waved a dismissive hand. "Leave me now, all of you," he commanded, his voice gaining enough strength to quell the buzz of voices in the air. "Eadric, Hubert, you will stay. I would draft a response to the Danes that we can present to the witan tomorrow."

She watched, astonished, as family and counselors acquiesced to his command. There were confused and worried looks among them, to be sure, but even in this weakened state Æthelred wielded enormous power over those close to him. He could even, she realized, make them question what their own eyes had seen.

She looked for Edward among those filing out of the hall and found that Edyth had taken charge of him, guiding him away with an arm about his shoulder. He did not glance back toward her, nor had he once looked to her during the council session.

He had no need of his mother.

Her heart contracting with pain, she turned her attention back to the king, who was flanked now by Eadric and Hubert.

Æthelred was eyeing her with an expression of surprise and displeasure, apparently irritated that she was still there.

"I would have you wait for me in my chamber, lady," he said gruffly. "What I do here now is not your concern."

She studied his face, still pale from the fit or visitation or whatever it was that had stricken him. His hands on the arms of his chair were clenched, as if to steel himself against pain.

"My lord," she said softly, "can this business not wait until tomorrow? I fear that you are ill."

"Then you are mistaken." He glared at her, and his voice was filled with menace.

She read the threat in his eyes. He would not admit to even the merest hint of illness. In speaking of it before Hubert and Eadric she had made a grave error.

Bowing to his will she left him, stepping from the warmth of the hall into the frigid chill of a moon-bright December night. The yard was deserted but for Athelstan and Ælfheah, who stood conversing together, their cloaks pulled tight against the cold.

Athelstan's eyes met hers, and she felt her heart contract once again. Here was another who gave her cause for concern. It had been many months since last she had seen him, and in that time he seemed to have changed beyond measure. He was travel weary, yes, but in his face she read, too, echoes of pain and unspeakable loss. The list of noble dead at Ringmere was a long one, and among them were his friends and kin. All of England was reeling from that slaughter, but he had witnessed it. How could he not be damaged by it?

Ælfheah turned then and, seeing her, held out a welcoming hand. She placed her own in his, and he kissed her ring with grave courtesy.

"How fares the king?" he asked, his eyes dark with concern.

"He insists that he is not ill," she said. "Whatever was troubling him has passed."

"He is frightened of shadows," Athelstan snapped.

"Have more compassion, my lord, I beg you," Ælfheah said. "He spoke rough words to you in the hall just now, but do not let that turn you against him. Your father is sore beset by his enemies, and he has little patience even for those he loves."

"Your belief in my father's affection for me is touching, Archbishop. Forgive me if I cannot share it."

"No!" Ælfheah's voice rang with censure. "I will not forgive it! Athelstan, you must curb your anger, especially now when your father has great need of—"

"Whatever needs the king may have, he does not look to me to answer them. He will not listen to me and you know why as well as I do."

The resentment in his voice was familiar to Emma, but now there was new bitterness and even pain threaded through it. Had he but known it, he sounded very much like his father. "Athelstan," she said gently, drawing his gaze to her, "that he doesn't wish to listen does not mean that he cannot hear you."

"The queen is right," Ælfheah agreed. "You do not know what is in his mind, or how he may reflect upon your words when he is alone and at peace."

"Is my father's mind ever at peace?" Athelstan demanded. "I have not seen it."

Ælfheah huffed impatiently. "You have been sundered from the king for too long, Athelstan. What do you truly know of him now? Yes, he harbors suspicions against you, I know that. But you must forgive him. Seventy times seven times Our Lord commands us to forgive. I beg you to grant your father that grace, especially now in this time of great turmoil. He needs his sons by his side, but he needs you most of all. You must not abandon him."

"I pledged him my oath when I came of age, Archbishop, and I have never broken it."

"Yet you have been tempted, my lord."

Athelstan looked as if he'd been slapped, and she came to his defense. "Temptation is not a sin," she insisted.

"Yet man is weak, and ofttimes the worst folly appears in the guise of wisdom and valor," Ælfheah replied. "For that reason, Athelstan, I ask you to repeat your oath of fealty now, to me."

There was an angry light in Athelstan's eyes that frightened her. "Do you mistrust me, Archbishop, as my father does?"

"You have all my trust, my lord," Ælfheah assured him. "And if the king should ever question your loyalty in my hearing, I wish to be able to tell him that you swore to me, before God, that you are his true man." He clasped the golden cross that hung at his breast and held it toward Athelstan.

She held her breath. Athelstan's anger, she could see, was only barely restrained. She half expected him to curse and stalk away.

Instead, he surprised her. He reached for the cross.

"I pledge fealty to my lord and father, the king, for as long as his reign shall last." His voice was strained, but the words were clear.

She began to breathe again as Ælfheah grasped Athelstan's shoulder.

"One day," the archbishop said, "you will make a great king, perhaps as great as Alfred. Trust in God, and do not despair." He turned to her. "You, my lady, have witnessed his oath as well, and you will, I trust, take his part should the need arise."

"I will," she assured him.

"Then I am content," Ælfheah said. "My lord, I shall trust you to see the queen safely to the king's quarters. I would beg that honor for myself, but I am weary and very cold."

He sketched a cross in the air, murmured a blessing, and bid them good night. She watched him stride slowly away, perceiving in his hunched shoulders and hesitant pace the exhaustion that he had kept at bay in the presence of the king.

"I wonder," Athelstan murmured, "if my father recognizes that man's worth? How tireless he is in the service of his king?"

"I suspect that he does not," she replied. Any more than he recognized the loyalty of his eldest son, strained though it may be.

Together they set out for the king's lodging, making their way across the slippery mud of the yard. After only a few treacherous steps, though, she was forced to clasp his arm for support, and just that merest touch set her to trembling. How was it, she asked herself, that no matter how much time and distance came between them, her yearning for him still burned so strong? She could not snuff it out. It was as if her blood and bone understood what she sought to deny—that some part of her must always be a part of him.

She glanced at his face, for the moon was full and high, and in its light she could see that his mouth was set in a hard line and his brow was furrowed. She sensed his anger—at his father, at the Danes, perhaps even at her, she could not say. She wished that she could ease it by telling him all that was in her heart. She could not. Moments ago he had pledged yet again his loyalty to the king, and that oath compelled them both to silence.

She drew in a long breath and considered the many questions she wanted to ask him—about the battle at Ringmere; about his injury; about the long, weary time he had spent in London; about the despair she had read in his face when he had pleaded with the king.

She rejected them all and asked simply, "Will you stay at the king's side now?" Which meant the same as, *Will you stay by my side?*

He was silent for a time. Three steps, she counted. Four.

"I will stay," he said at last, "until the king bids me leave." He paused and then added, "Or until you do."

He had heard it, then—the real question behind her words. And he had given her the answer she had hoped to hear.

"You know that I will never bid you leave," she said softly. "I have always counseled you to stand beside the king."

They had arrived at the entrance to the royal chambers. Now he turned to her, his face grim in the shadowy light.

"And if my father casts me out, Emma? If I am exiled, what will your counsel be then?"

She looked up into eyes that pinned her with a fierce, bruising gaze. She wanted to sweep the question aside, to insist that Æthelred would never banish his son. But it would be a lie. She knew the king; knew that if he felt threatened he might indeed send Athelstan away.

"You must never give him cause, Athelstan," she pleaded. "Just now you swore to the archbishop that you would be loyal. That was well done. Ælfheah will be able to defend you, and your oath will—"

"That oath will not earn me the king's trust, no matter how many times I repeat it. You demanded a similar pledge from me once, do you remember? I have kept it. I have not raised my hand against my father. But I will ask you now the same question I put to you then. When I am free at last to reach for England's throne, what assurance is there that it will be mine for the taking? I have seen our enemy's strength, and it is enough to daunt even a seasoned warrior. As for the king, you saw what happened in the hall just now. The very mention of Swein Forkbeard's name brought him to his knees. All England is on its knees!" His mouth twisted into a grimace. "Think on that, my lady, and then, if you can, tell me again that the oath I swore tonight was well done."

He waited for no response from her, but stalked back toward the hall. She was left with his harsh words echoing in her mind, adding the weight of his fears to the dread she already carried in her heart. She stood there for a long time, bathed in moonlight, chilled by the cold and by something far worse as she pondered not only what Athelstan had said, but everything that had passed in the king's great hall. Ælfheah's words, especially, came back to her with sudden clarity, and a name flickered into her mind that she had not heard for many years.

Cnut.

He had been a youth with fiery hair and his father's black eyes, no more than fourteen winters old, she guessed, when she had struggled to break free from him on a shingled beach awash with moonlight. Athelstan had come to her aid then, but she had never revealed, even to him, that her captor was King Swein's son. Had she done so, Cnut would surely have been delivered into Æthelred's hands; and because she could not be certain of his fate after that, she had kept silent.

What delusion had been in her mind that night? Had she believed that an act of mercy on her part might work some change in Cnut, who had been England's enemy from the moment he was born? Had she truly been that foolish?

*The worst folly appears in the guise of wisdom and valor,* Ælfheah had warned. It seemed to her that those words pertained far more to her than to Athelstan. An act that she had believed courageous and merciful had in fact been the greatest of follies. Cnut was now a man and a warrior, and he was come again to prey upon the English. Who could say what horrors the people of England would face—had already faced—because of a choice that she had made on that lonely beach when she had thought herself to be so merciful and wise?

# Chapter Twenty-Nine

January 1011
Redmere, Holderness

"It was not some enemy's hall that they plundered and destroyed in Northamptonshire! It was mine!" Elgiva, still enraged by news that had reached her a month before, stalked back and forth in front of Alric. She had kept her fury bottled inside for weeks, and it was a relief to loose it at last. "I am Cnut's wife and so the daughter of their king. My holdings should have remained untouched by those hounds!"

"The raid was at night, my lady, and none of them could have known that the hall belonged to the wife—"

"They should have known! My steward opened the gates and submitted to them, and then they gutted him! Explain that!"

Alric shrugged and she wanted to slap him.

"Likely they were drunk," he said.

"Drunk? Of course they were drunk. They were besotted with lust for rape and murder. I've seen such things with my own eyes." Had seen it, and had tried for years to wipe it from her memory. Even now it came back to her—the glint of sunlight on steel, and butchered flesh where once there had been a woman. She cursed.

"It was Hemming's men who plundered your lands," Alric protested. "He makes no attempt to control them—merely sets them loose, like wolves, and lets them slake their bloodlust on anyone in their path."

She turned on him, still furious, for were not all men ravening beasts—Danes, English, Normans, all of them? Not a one of them was any better than his fellows.

"And what did my husband, who so prizes discipline, do when he learned of this?"

"He could do nothing, lady. Nothing. Hemming is Thorkell's brother. The three of them are warlords, and they do not berate each other or their men for ravaging enemy lands."

"I am not the enemy!" The argument had come round to the beginning again. She threw herself into a chair, exhausted. Disgusted.

"Cnut does not trust Hemming," Alric offered. "He would like to be rid of him and all his shipmen. Thorkell won't hear of it, though, and there's an end to it."

No, that was not the end. If Cnut would do nothing about Hemming, then she would.

"Where is this Hemming now?" she asked. Cnut was at Thurbrand's steading, and Alric had brought word that he would be with her on the morrow. "Is he with Cnut?"

"No. He and his brother stayed in the south, enjoying the comforts of the bishop's palace in Rochester. You will not, I fear, have the pleasure of meeting Hemming."

"I would find it no pleasure, I promise you," she said, "but I thank you for what you have told me. You have given me much to consider." Hemming did not know it, but he had sparked a blood feud between them. She would make him pay for ravaging her lands, although it would not be anytime soon. She must be patient, but when she took her revenge she would enjoy it all the more for the wait.

Two weeks later Elgiva lay awake in the near darkness, unable to sleep, sifting through a wilderness of thoughts and impressions. The presence of Cnut and two shiploads of Danes had thrown her entire household into a frenzy that had never ebbed. During the daylight hours she had scarce had a moment alone with her husband. Thurbrand had summoned men to meet with him from as far away as Lincoln, and Cnut had ordered her to keep to her own quarters.

"Your presence in Holderness must remain secret," he had told her. "I do not wish to wake one morning and find an English army at our gates."

"The king's army has had little success of late," she reminded him, "and Wessex is far away." And, she hoped, Æthelred believed her dead.

"Northumbria is far too close, though," he argued, "and Uhtred would welcome an excuse to pillage Holderness. He is like a sleeping bear and, as you know, an old enemy of Thurbrand's. It would be unwise to rouse him."

And so, although she did not like it, she had kept to her quarters and away from the private councils conducted in the hall. At night, though—and the nights were long and sweet—she had Cnut to herself.

She turned on her side to look at him. He, too, was sleepless, his face pale in the dim firelight, his gaze pinned to the roof beams, oblivious to her.

She did not like it when any man was oblivious to her.

She sat up, pulled the thick fur covering from the foot of the bed, and wrapped herself in it before leaving Cnut's side. As she had hoped, her withdrawal from the bed had caught his attention.

"What are you doing?" he asked.

"I'm pouring us some wine. Something is troubling you, and if you will not speak of it to me, at least the wine will make us both drowsy."

She poured two cups from a jug that she had set there earlier in the evening, still untouched because their bed play had distracted them. They'd been too drunk on each other to bother with wine, for this was their last night together. On the morrow he would sail south again, to Rochester and his fleet.

As she returned to the bed he sat up, and she admired the lean beauty of him and the way the firelight turned his hair and beard to copper. Their sons would be beautiful. This time when he left her, he would leave a boy child growing in her womb. She was certain of it.

She handed him the cup and watched for his reaction as he drank.

He looked at the cup, then at her.

"I've never tasted wine like this. What have you done to it?"

"Tyra and I have been mixing honey and herbs into the wine," she explained. And unknown to Tyra, she had been using some of the methods that she had learned from the Sámi woman for certain purposes of her own. She tasted the wine. "This is our best effort so far, I think.

Honey, ginger, and cinnamon." And nutmeg, to make a man more potent, but she saw no need to mention that. The spices had been costly, but she hoped they would be worth the price. "Do you like it?"

He brought the cup to his lips, his eyes on hers, swallowed, and nodded.

"I like it well," he said.

She smiled, pleased, and handed him her cup to hold as she crawled back onto the bed beside him.

"It has magical qualities," she said. "After one cup you will unburden yourself of all your troubles, and then your wife will take you into her arms and make you forget them."

"You need no spells or magic to learn what troubles me," he said. "You need only ask."

She settled herself, cross-legged, beside him, the fur around her naked shoulders and the wine cup in both hands.

"Is it something about King Æthelred's second gafol offer that concerns you? Surely you did not expect him to immediately agree to your demand for forty-eight thousand pounds, did you?"

He frowned and looked into his cup, thoughtful.

"Æthelred thinks to play a game with us, thinks to outwit Thorkell. He is mistaken. The English king has lost already, although he does not yet know it."

The words sounded like one of Tyra's prophecies, and they made Elgiva shiver.

"He has offered you thirty thousand pounds," she said. "Are you saying you will not accept it?"

"No, of course we will not. They have given us until Easter to make our reply, but I think we will not wait that long."

"So you will tell them no and demand—what?"

He leaned over and kissed her ear. "That is a secret."

She ran a finger around the rim of her silver cup, not looking at him, not wishing him to see her displeasure. Second only to men ignoring her, she disliked it when they kept secrets from her. But she would not pursue it. She wanted no quarrels tonight. She must keep him here in her bed so that he would leave her with a son.

"Will you tell me what is troubling you, then?" she asked.

He drained his cup and put it aside.

"I find that I am yoked to a madman," he said, resting back against the pillows and clasping his hands behind his head, "and I cannot seem to disentangle myself."

"Hemming, you mean." She bit her lip. She must not rail at him about the burning of her hall as she had railed at Alric. It was hard, though, to keep the words from spilling out.

"Hemming is a man of little wit and even less judgment," he said. "He and Thorkell have the same blood in their veins, yet one is the exact opposite of the other. Thorkell is everything that Hemming is not, but he will not listen to a word against his brother. Believe me, we have argued about Hemming more times than I care to list."

"My lord," she said, "you must find a way to rid yourself of this Hemming." She peered into his face, waiting for him to look at her, and when he did she continued. "If the limb of a tree is diseased, you have to cut it off, or so Tyra has instructed me. If you are not ruthless with Hemming, you put your entire venture at risk."

"That is my greatest fear," he agreed, "that Hemming will make some foolish move that will shatter my father's plan for England's conquest— about which Hemming knows nothing. Yet for now, I need him. And aside from that, we have sworn oaths to each other. If I break my oath, commit some treachery against him, I will lose all standing, even among my own men. And Thorkell would surely seek revenge for his brother's sake. No, it is not to be thought of. Still," he said, frowning, "I am uneasy about Hemming."

"Do you fear that he may turn against you? Surely not! You are Swein's son. If he should strike..." She stopped, for was not Hemming's ravaging of her lands a blow against Cnut, albeit a subtle one?

As if he read her mind, Cnut took her hand and kissed it.

"The burning of your hall was a blunder, not a planned strike." He frowned. "It is an excellent example, though, of Hemming's witless leadership. Had Thorkell or I or even Alric been near, it would never have happened. I can do nothing about it now, but someday, I vow, I will build you a palace where your great hall once stood."

He slipped her cup from her hand and tossed it to the floor. Gathering her into his arms, he kissed her deeply, his fingers moving purposefully to her breasts and to her woman's parts. But if the sweet wine and the touch of skin on skin had driven Hemming from his mind, it had not worked so on her. She was bound by no oath, and she had a score to settle.

The next morning, early, Elgiva went in search of Alric. When she found him, she drew him aside, away from the crowd of shipmen in the hall and into one of the curtained alcoves, where they were hidden from prying eyes.

"Something must be done about Hemming," she whispered. "Cnut wishes to be rid of him, but he can do nothing because they are oath bound." She arched an eyebrow at him. She was taking a risk now, but she did not think it was a very great one. "I am not bound by any oath, and I would repay Hemming for his assault upon my hall. I need help, though. Are you willing?"

"I have no great love for Hemming," Alric said, "and you have but to command me to have your will done. You know that."

"Understand me," she said. "I am asking for a life, and I will pay you well." She opened her hand to show him the ruby in the center of her palm. "There will be another such stone for you when the deed is finished."

He took the stone, his eyes glistening. Then he took her hand and kissed her fingertips.

"I would do it for love, lady," he said, "but I thank you for the gift." He kissed her palm and then gently bit the flesh below her thumb, his eyes never straying from hers. "How do you wish it done?" he whispered.

She looked into his eyes and wondered what he had meant by the word *love*. They had known passion together, and even now his mouth upon her hand roused a hunger for him that made her breath catch in her throat. But it was not love. Reluctantly she drew her hand from his and reached into the purse at her belt, pulling out a clay vial stoppered with wax.

"Pour this bit of liquid into Hemming's ale cup. Use it all." She guessed that it was very potent, but she wanted to be sure that it would have its intended effect. Tyra had taught her how to make potions from dried leaves of all-heal and nettle root, and it was a simple matter to do the same with the root of the hymlice. The difficulty had been to do it in secret, away from the all-seeing eyes of Tyra. "Have a care," she said, placing her hand against his cheek. "I would not have you discovered."

He nodded, took the tiny flask, and slipped away. She waited several minutes before she followed, stepping from the alcove into the hall's central chamber.

On the far side of the hall Tyra was packing bundles into one of the supply coffers that would go with Cnut's men. She looked at Elgiva with an arched brow and a glance so knowing that Elgiva felt a wave of foreboding wash over her.

But Tyra knows nothing, she told herself. And by the time that Hemming is dead, what she thinks she knows she will have forgotten.

She left the hall and went in search of Cnut, to bid him farewell.

# Chapter Thirty

March 1011

Wherwell Abbey, Hampshire

It was nearing midday, and as Emma stood with Wymarc in the abbey's cloister she glanced up at the square of dull sky visible above the central garth. The morning's steady rain had lightened for the moment to a shimmering mist—a welcome respite, she thought, however brief it may be.

She dropped her gaze to her daughter and stepdaughter, who were both squatting beside a huge puddle in the convent yard. Unconcerned by either the damp air all about them or the wet grass beneath, both girls were absorbed in the progress of a bit of wood that bobbed on the puddle's surface. Standing a little to one side, Godiva's nurse kept a close eye on her charge, not yet two winters old, who now dropped to her hands and knees and seemed about to follow her makeshift boat right into the shallow lake. Eleven-year-old Mathilda, though, was just as watchful as the nurse. She dangled another bit of wood in front of Godiva, who gave a squeal of delight and, sitting back on her rump, promptly lost all interest in the escaping vessel.

"Mathilda reminds me of her elder sisters when they were that age," Emma said to Wymarc as they resumed their stroll. "On the brink of womanhood, yet still a child."

Now, she thought, all three of the king's eldest daughters were wed, while Mathilda would soon take the vows that would shut her behind convent walls forever. For the first time in a decade, at Emma's urging, the sisters had been reunited for the upcoming ceremony.

"I wonder which of the king's daughters will have the easier life path," Wymarc said, "those wed to great lords, or this one, who will be wed to Christ?"

"If one is not well suited to it, the path will be a difficult one, no matter how easy it may appear to others," Emma replied. "Can you imagine Edyth as a nun?"

Wymarc laughed. "No," she said. "Even to be abbess would not satisfy Edyth."

Even to be an ealdorman's wife did not satisfy Edyth, Emma thought. She had hoped that Edyth would make plans to leave the court after the upcoming Easter council at Winchester, which was what her sisters intended. But Edyth had made it clear that she would remain at the king's side. No doubt she would continue to second whatever poisonous advice her powerful husband murmured in Æthelred's ear.

Neither an official adviser nor a queen, Edyth nevertheless wielded influence as Eadric's wife and the king's daughter, and she was poised to step into the role of queenlike adviser should Emma stray from court for any reason—to visit her estates, to see her son, or to go into seclusion while awaiting the birth of another child.

She turned her eyes again toward her small daughter, wondering if the Almighty would bless her with more children; wondering if, in that event, she could manage to cling to what little influence she had with the king. On occasion she won a skirmish, like this lengthy stay here at Wherwell. Despite Edyth's objections she had persuaded Æthelred that the king's daughters should spend the better part of Lent with Mathilda, beseeching God's mercy upon the realm.

It was a realm that had great need of prayers. And if there was any truth in the veiled warning from her mother that had come but two days ago, the kingdom had need of far more than prayers.

*I would not have you relinquish your duty to your husband and king, but I urge you to make for yourself and your household a place of refuge. Choose some stronghold near the sea, I beg you, so that should the need arise, you can send your children to safety.*

The words, as she had read them, had seemed to burn in her mind, as if they had been written with fire. What did her mother know or suspect that she would send her such counsel? How much time did she have to prepare for whatever calamity was hinted at in the letter, and how was she to gather her children about her if such a thing occurred?

Edward was already far beyond her reach, for Eadric had sent him back to the estate of his foster parents, across the Severn. She had seen to it that Wymarc's son, Robert, accompanied him, and she had sent Father Martin north as well to watch over the boys from the small monastery of St. Peter at Shrewsbury. But they were all of them many days' ride away.

She would have to warn Father Martin and give thought to what her mother had advised. She held two fortified estates near the coast, at Exeter in the west and at Ipswich in the east, both miraculously spared during last summer's Danish raids. Preparations would have to be made; her reeves alerted in both places to be prepared for her arrival at any moment, unheralded but with a large retinue in attendance. There must be a vessel and crew always at the ready.

A sudden peal of laughter rang out from the central yard, and she stopped to gaze again at Godiva and Mathilda. Even if she should provide a refuge for her children and her household, what of Mathilda? Unlike her sisters, she had no lordly husband to protect her. Would convent walls and the garb of a nun keep her safe?

The rain that had been threatening began to drum on the grass, and Godiva's nurse scooped her up. Emma, watching them run toward her, opened her arms to comfort her now wailing daughter. Perching Godiva on her hip she had taken only a few dancing steps with her when they were interrupted by the porteress.

"There are king's men in the outer court, my lady," she said, "and Lord Edmund has requested audience with you and Lady Edyth. He and the abbess await you in her chamber."

Emma felt a surge of alarm and saw it reflected in Wymarc's suddenly pale face. Edmund would never ask for her unless forced to it. They rarely spoke, and she had long ago given up all hope of earning his good opinion. He must have come on some urgent royal business.

A dozen dire possibilities ran through her mind, but she kept her demeanor calm as she kissed Godiva, delivered the child to her nurse, and with Wymarc at her side followed the porteress into the wing that housed the abbess's chamber.

She could hear Edyth's voice as she neared the door, and she halted a moment in the entryway.

"I knew that my father would send for me," Edyth was saying. "I can be ready to leave within the hour."

Edmund stood facing Edyth and the abbess, and he seemed to fill the small chamber. He was a big man, taller than his brothers and broader in the chest and shoulder. He was garbed for war in a coat of mail, and the thick padding beneath it and the ankle-length woolen cloak that he wore over it made him seem even larger. He had thrown back the hood of his cloak, revealing the dark hair that set him apart from his brothers and sisters. There was no mistaking, though, the high brow and straight, aquiline nose that he shared with Edyth. Dark he may be, but Edmund was no changeling. He was Æthelred's son.

She stepped into the chamber, and Edmund turned to her.

"My lady," he said with a curt bow. "The king sends his greetings, and commands that you and my sisters attend him at Winchester. We are to set out tomorrow at first light."

The unease that she had suppressed stirred again.

"What is the reason for the summons?" she asked.

Although it was her question, he directed his answer to Edyth. "The Danes are on the move. They have left Rochester, and because we do not know what they intend the king would have all of you inside the city walls."

The expression on his face was carefully blank, and she read his purpose. He did not wish to cause alarm. Nevertheless, she guessed that this move by the Danish hird must be Thorkell's response to the king's attempt to bargain with him: more slaughter to show the English that this was not a game, as Æthelred had termed it, but deadly serious.

"What about your sister Mathilda?" she asked. "Does the king wish her to wait upon him as well?"

But it was the abbess who came forward to answer her.

"Mathilda is no longer the king's daughter, my lady," she said. "She belongs to God, and she will face whatever is to come with her sisters in the Lord." She turned to Edmund. "If there is nothing else, Lord Edmund, the porteress will show your men where they are to sleep."

The words were not yet out of her mouth before Edyth was hurrying toward the door.

"I will tell the others that we will be leaving in the morning," she called over her shoulder.

Emma was not sorry to see her go. Edyth saw this as merely a heaven-sent opportunity to return to court. She did not recognize it for the disaster that it was.

She looked to Edmund, whose face still gave nothing away, although his glance moved uncertainly now between her and the abbess.

"How bad is it?" she asked. Perhaps he would reveal the rest of it, now that his sister was gone. "Please tell me."

He hauled in a breath, running a hand through his hair in a way that reminded her of Athelstan.

"It is bad enough," he replied, addressing the abbess now. "The Danes have pushed south into Kent and Sussex. They've burned Hastings, and when I left Winchester this morning there was no clear indication yet of where they might strike next. Best bear that in mind, Abbess. The prioress within the walls at Nunnaminster will offer you and your good sisters shelter. You need but ask." At last he turned from the abbess to face Emma, and there was something in his eyes that filled her with foreboding. She reached for Wymarc's hand. "I am charged to tell you, my lady, that Ealdorman Ælfric's granddaughter is dead."

An image of Hilde sprang into her mind, dressed in her bridal gown with a wreath of bay leaves on her head. Another image followed on its heels, of Hilde mounted on a horse at her husband's side as they set out for Sussex and the estate that was part of her dowry. Sussex, where a Danish army was ravaging, unopposed.

She felt Wymarc's arm steal about her waist as though to steady them both, but she kept her eyes on Edmund even as her thoughts flew to Ælfric. How would he bear the loss of his grandchild? How was she to bear it when Hilde had been like a daughter to her?

But the question that formed on her lips was one she voiced almost against her will: "What happened?"

"What do you think?" he snarled. "The Danes swept through Sussex like a windstorm and she was caught in their path. She died with her husband, likely in some manner so vile you cannot even imagine it."

The sob that had been building in her throat broke free, and beside her Wymarc gave a strangled cry. Hilde was but an innocent girl. In all her brief life she had harmed no one. Why had such a brutal fate been meted out to her?

And even as the thought formed in her mind she sought the crucifix on the wall, where the suffering Christ hung, dying.

*No one on this earth, Lord*, she thought, *deserves such a fate. Why do you allow it?*

"What will the king do now?" she asked, and her voice was sullen. What did it matter, really?

"What he should have done in the first place," Edmund snapped. Even through her despair she could hear the censure in his voice. "He will do what my brother urged—send them the forty-eight thousand pounds of silver that they demanded. He has no other choice. He never did."

A.D. 1011   This year sent the king and his council to the army, and desired peace; promising them both tribute and provisions on condition that they ceased from plunder. They had now overrun East Anglia, Essex, Middlesex, Oxfordshire, Cambridgeshire, Hertfordshire, Buckinghamshire, Bedfordshire, half of Huntingdonshire and much of Northamptonshire; and to the south of the Thames, all Kent, Sussex, Hastings, Surrey, Berkshire, Hampshire and much of Wiltshire. All these disasters befell us through bad counsels; that they would not offer tribute in time, or fight with them; but, when they had done most mischief, then entered they into peace and amity with them.

—*The Anglo-Saxon Chronicle*

# Chapter Thirty-One

"By all the gods, what a stench!" Elgiva hovered in the open doorway of the brew house, her hand over her nose and mouth for fear she might gag. "What's in there?"

The ceorl standing beside the cauldron and vigorously stirring the steaming brew paused in his task to look up at her with a blank, stupid gaze.

"It's naught but honey and water, my lady," he protested. "The smell of the honey is strong, to be sure, but not bad, I think."

He was young, this fellow, his dark beard still thin although he was tall and brawny enough for the task he'd been set. She'd seen him about the yard and the stables, and she liked the look of him. Just now his bared arms glistened with sweat from heat and exertion, and his sinewy shoulders and broad chest strained against the fabric of his thin summer tunic.

She wondered how skilled he was with a sword. She was likely to need men who were good in a fight before long. Right now, though, she envied him that light tunic and those bare arms. She was wrapped in three layers of linen, and she was far enough along in her pregnancy that she felt like a sow.

Reluctantly she pulled her eyes from the lad and looked to Tyra, standing at a nearby table, for confirmation that what she was smelling was only the mead beginning to ferment.

Tyra looked up from the huge basket of flowers and herbs in front of her and slapped her assistant on his bare arm.

"Keep stirring, man," she ordered, "or you'll find yourself back in the smithy instead of the kitchens." She nodded to Elgiva. "Likely it's the bairn in your belly that's causing the mischief, my lady, not the scent of the honey."

It was true that she'd been sickened by odors all through this pregnancy, more so than ever before—a sure sign, she'd been told over and over, that she was carrying a boy.

*Boys are right bastards even in the womb*, was a general saying among the women of Holderness. As if to prove the point the baby gave a sharp kick, and Elgiva winced. She stepped out of the brew house and away from the nauseating fumes just as the gate ward shouted that a large company of men was approaching.

"Ten horsemen," he called, "and the rest on foot. They've just unfurled the raven banner."

She paused to draw in as deep a breath as her cramped lungs allowed. The raven was the badge of both Cnut and Swein, but surely it had to be Cnut who was beneath that banner. She had sent word to him months ago that she was with child, begging him to come before the winter set in. Now here he was, even sooner than she had looked for him. There must be news! Perhaps his father was poised to invade England at last.

Her babe seemed to tumble inside her, and she clapped a hand to her belly. Yes, this was surely a boy—and as unsettled by his father's arrival as she was.

She hurried across the yard and went into the hall, calling for servants to fetch food and ale.

By the time the newcomers stepped through the open doorway and made their way toward the dais, the torches in the hall were blazing and she was clutching the brimming welcome cup. In the flickering light, though, she could see that the man who led the party was not Cnut.

The silver drinking bowl felt suddenly too heavy in her trembling hands, and the child within gave another vicious kick. Cnut must have stopped on his way to consult with Thurbrand. It would not be the first time that he had done so. Likely he had sent these men ahead to apprise her of his coming.

"You bring me word from my husband, I think," she said. "When will he be here?"

"Not for some time, my lady."

She didn't like vague answers, and she scowled at the man.

"Why?" she snapped. "Is he hurt? Where is he?"

"He sailed for Roskilde some weeks ago. Before he left he charged me—"

She muttered an oath and slammed the vessel onto the table beside her, not caring as ale sloshed across the table and onto the floor.

Damn all men, she thought, and damn her wandering husband most of all.

She turned back to Cnut's man and glared at him. She was tired and hot; her back ached as if she'd been broken in two and then stitched back together; and now here was news that was as unwelcome as it was unexpected. He glared right back at her, his contempt for her so obvious she wanted to cuff him. Yet he had brought her news, and unpleasant as it might be, she would hear all of it.

"You men," she said to his companions, "there is food and drink. Sit you down and eat. You," she said to their leader, "come with me."

She led him to one of the alcoves at the side of the hall and eased herself onto the bench at the table there, nodding to him to sit opposite her. She waited while servants brought him food, studying him in the charged silence that lay between them.

She knew this man vaguely—one of Cnut's retainers. She tried to remember his name, Ari or Arni or—Arnor. That was it. Arnor. He had to be well past thirty, with a humorless face that was weathered from a lifetime spent at sea. His beard and hair were still dark, though, as were his eyes. Just now he was filthy from travel, and he smelled far worse than the vat of boiling honey in the brew house.

She watched him wolf down a hunk of cold meat and take a huge swallow of ale before she spoke.

"What message did Cnut ask you to give me?" she asked.

He set down his cup, belched, and wiped his mouth with the back of his hand. "He bid me say that he will come as soon as he is able."

She snorted. How many times had Cnut sent her that message? Twelve? Twenty? A hundred? She was sick to death of hearing it. She looked at Arnor, waiting for the rest of it. There had to be more, but the brute seemed in no hurry to share.

"What else?" she asked, irritated and impatient.

He picked up the brown loaf in front of him and ripped off a chunk before answering.

"That's all of it," he said.

He didn't look at her. He seemed far more interested in his food than he was in her, and she had to struggle to keep her temper. All of Cnut's Danes treated her like this—as if she were a nithing, as if she were Cnut's hostage instead of his wife. It did not matter that she had learned to speak their language or that without her meddling, as they called it, the battle at Ringmere would have been a rout instead of a victory. The Danes still treated her as if she were an inconvenient necessity, someone to be guarded, not trusted—an outsider. It was what she disliked about them the most.

The shipmen understood bribery well enough, though, and so did she. If she wanted any information from the locked coffer of this fellow's thick skull, she was going to have to pay for it.

She pulled some coins from the purse at her belt and pushed them across the table toward him.

"Why did Cnut go to Denmark?" she asked. "Did Swein send for him?"

He eyed the coins for a moment, hesitating, then he lifted his gaze to her. There was something malevolent in his eyes. It was far more than dislike, and something she had never observed before. All her life men had looked at her with hunger. Even Cnut's men, who made no secret of their distrust of her, still betrayed their lust in quick, covert glances. What made Arnor different from all the rest?

Much as she would like to know, this was hardly the time to address the question. All she wanted from him was information about Cnut, and the silver should buy her that.

She cocked an eyebrow at him and said, "Well?"

He responded by using his knife to sweep the coins into his own purse. He said, "Our Cnut had a bit of treasure he wanted to see delivered safely to King Swein."

Ah. She should have guessed that silver would send him scurrying to Denmark. Swein's coffers must be empty again, and he would look to Cnut to refill them.

"Has Æthelred paid the gafol, then?"

Once more Arnor was slow to respond, seeming to weigh his words as if they were as precious as Æthelred's gleaming silver.

"Only a quarter of it. He has asked for more time to raise the geld, so there's to be a quarter payment again at the end of September and the last of the forty-eight thousand pounds of tribute will be delivered in the spring. Getting these stiff-necked English to pay what they've promised us is like trying to raise sail in a tempest," he grumbled.

Yes, she thought. It was almost as difficult as prying useful information out of a tight-lipped, stinking Dane. But she was not so much interested in where Cnut was as when he was likely to make his way here.

"When will I see my husband in this hall?" she demanded. "Before he returns to Rochester?" King Swein the greedy would certainly insist that Cnut be in Rochester for the next gafol payment, but that was weeks away.

"He may not return to Rochester at all."

Now he'd surprised her, and she stared at him, astonished.

"What do you mean? Why not, if there is still tribute to be paid him?"

"There's a nasty storm brewing at Rochester," he growled. "I've sent to Cnut, warning him to keep his distance." He leaned forward, resting his elbows on the table to point his knife at her. "Look you, Cnut hadn't been gone a single day before that Canterbury archbishop came nosing around like a dog in heat."

Archbishop Ælfheah. She had never liked him. He was far too fond of Emma, and far too in love with his God.

"What did he want to do?" she sneered. "Baptize them?"

He used his knife to spear a hunk of meat and raise it to his mouth. "Whatever it was, it led to a quarrel between Thorkell and his brother

Hemming, and next day Thorkell sailed with more than half his ships, all of them loaded with treasure. My guess is he went to his family lands at Ribe."

Now she was the one who leaned forward, for this was worrisome news.

"Do you mean Cnut and Thorkell have both left Rochester? And it's Hemming who is in charge of all the shipmen still in the camp?" Cnut had feared that Hemming was half mad and liable to do something ill-considered—something that might ruin Swein's carefully laid plan to wrench England from Æthelred's grasp.

"Aye. What's more, he's been meeting almost daily with that arch-bishop. Hemming's men don't like it. They're not overly fond of priests, and seeing Hemming befriend one makes them about as happy as cats in a sack." He reached for his cup and took a long swallow of ale, but she was aware that he was watching her even as he drank, looking to see what she made of all this, she supposed.

She took a few moments to mull it over, trying to put the pieces to-gether. What would Archbishop Ælfheah want with Hemming? Not to convert him, surely. Hemming would never suffer that, although he might enjoy gulling Ælfheah, toying with him the way a falconer uses a lure to bring a merlin from the sky. But even that entertainment would pall quickly.

She reviewed everything she'd heard about Hemming and all that she remembered of Ælfheah, and then she had it, and it made her feel sick again. Ælfheah must be urging Hemming to turn against Thorkell and Cnut, to throw in his lot with the English. And if Hemming pledged himself to Æthelred, he would bring all his own shipmen with him and perhaps whatever men Thorkell had left behind as well.

The thought of it made the bile rise in her throat and she swallowed hard to keep the nausea at bay.

Hemming had to be stopped—should have been stopped already. She had given Alric the poison to dispatch him months ago. What was he waiting for?

"Where is Alric?" she asked. "Did he sail with Cnut to Denmark?"

"Been wondering when you would ask me about that prick." Arnor set down his cup and turned to spit on the floor. "Alric is Hemming's dog now; sits at his feet and translates what passes between him and the churchman. Whatever is going on there, your precious Alric is right in the middle of it. Makes a body wonder," he said thoughtfully, wiping his blade on what was left of the bread, "if Alric might even be the one who is at the bottom of it"—he lifted his eyes to hers—"mayhap at your bidding."

She watched the candlelight glint dangerously along the blade of his knife and she felt a ripple of unease.

"Do you imagine that I would conspire with Hemming and Ælf-heah? Pah! If Alric is licking their boots, it's none of my doing."

"Yet Alric is your man," he said with a sardonic smile, "so how else do you explain it?"

How, indeed? Had Alric transferred his allegiance from her to Hemming? If he'd been enticed by some recompense more valuable than rubies, it might explain why Hemming was still alive.

She considered telling Arnor what she had charged Alric to do. Somehow, though, she didn't think that confessing to a scheme to poison the Danish warlord was likely to reassure him. Besides, her commitment to Cnut was obvious to anyone with eyes.

"I cannot explain it, nor do I need to," she said. "I am Cnut's wife and big with his child. I do not have to defend myself against your baseless suspicions."

He shrugged. "You say the child is Cnut's, but I've heard tell that there are men hereabouts who have spent far more time in your chamber than Cnut ever has."

Once again she wanted to hit him, but the knife was ready in his hand. She had no wish to give him a reason to use it.

"You must have straw for brains to make such a foul accusation in my own hall," she snarled. "Get out, and take your shipmen with you."

She waited for him to get up, but Arnor didn't move, except to reach for the pitcher and pour more ale into his cup.

"I'll sail to Rochester soon enough," he said, "to see which way the wind is blowing. But these men"—he gestured in the direction of his companions—"will stay here. You and your child—Cnut's child, if you like—will have need of more men. For your protection."

He looked at her with cold, glittering eyes, and the threat in them was plain enough. He would leave behind more Danish thugs to guard her, and their first concern would not be her protection.

"As I said," he went on with an evil smile, "there is a storm brewing. I think we would not want to have you swept away."

September 1011

Rochester, Kent

It was hot. Athelstan ran a finger around the damp, clinging neckline of his linen smoc and muttered a silent curse at the fate that had brought him to this wretched place. He glanced for what he guessed must be the thousandth time toward the Medway. A group of Danish shipmen were out there in the searing afternoon sun, muscling bulky sacks of silver into a large pan for weighing, then muscling them out again.

They were nearly finished now, thank God. Twelve thousand pounds of coin and hack silver hauled out of the holds of English vessels, inspected by a gang of Danes, weighed, and stacked inside a storehouse set well above the tide line. It had taken three days.

He had watched it all, one of a handful of English nobles—and of what passed for nobles among the Danes—charged to be official observers. Today they had broken bread together to mark the completion of this second payment of the gafol, their tables sheltered from the harsh sunlight by a broad canopy.

Still, it was hot. And his anger at being forced to dally here beneath Rochester's walls to bear witness to this spectacle made him hotter still.

"Have the bastards humiliated us enough, do you suppose?" he snarled.

Beside him his brother Edrid grunted a wordless reply. Archbishop Ælfheah, who was seated next to that ox, Hemming, at the top of the table, didn't hear the question, but from the grim set of his face Athelstan guessed that the archbishop, too, had stomached about as much of this as he could take.

The Danes had demanded that the dozen English nobles and prelates who had delivered the silver should wait here, forced to watch while the shipmen inspected and weighed every pound of the English gafol. He didn't know what he hated more: their glee as they pawed through the enormous treasure, or their obvious satisfaction at doing it before the eyes of the Canterbury archbishop and two of Æthelred's sons.

"By Christ, I want to leave this place," he muttered. "That's the last of the silver weighed. The tide is ebbing, and I see no reason to prolong this any further, especially as our host looks as though he's beyond caring whether we are here or not."

The potent beor had been flowing freely today, and Hemming had clearly downed far too many cups of it. His huge body slumped against one side of his chair, and his small eyes, framed by thick brows and an unkempt beard, had fluttered closed some time ago. A string of drool seeped from the corner of his gaping mouth.

And this man was to be their ally! What a colossal mistake! Ælfheah had been adamant that of the three Viking warlords, this one was the least governable, the one most likely to turn against them if given even the slightest provocation.

Yet the king had insisted on going ahead with this mad scheme.

Of course Hemming can't be trusted, he had argued. He's abandoning his Danish allies, isn't he? He's already an oath breaker, and so what? We merely have to keep him happy and give him no reason to abandon us in turn.

So the delivery date for this second gafol payment had been moved forward to take advantage of the absence of Cnut and Thorkell. God alone knew where they had gone. Hemming, though, claimed that when they returned, they would find that the Danish ships they'd left behind would be ranged against them from the Thames mouth all the way to the Isle of Thanet.

"Do you think we can trust him?" Edrid asked.

"No!" Athelstan growled. "I cannot see what's to prevent him from taking the silver, hauling up anchor tomorrow, and sailing as far from England as a steady wind will take him."

"But there's to be an even larger payment in the spring if he keeps his word to us," Edrid protested. "He'll want that silver as well, won't he?"

"A bird in the hand, Edrid," he replied. "Why not take the silver now and be done with it? What does he have to lose? He can turn his back on England, let his brother and Cnut split the gafol we've promised to deliver next spring, and have a good laugh at us for believing that he would defend us against his own kind."

He cursed again, wishing he knew if that was indeed what Hemming was thinking.

He eyed the man who stood behind Hemming's chair—no Dane, but a Mercian who knew the Danish tongue and was acting as translator between Ælfheah and the warlord. Who was he, and who did he answer to?

He would relish holding a knife to that fellow's throat and putting a few searing questions to him. He must know a great deal about these Danes. Surely he had some inkling of what was going on in Hemming's pisspot of a brain. He might even be persuaded to reveal the names of others who, through bribery or threat, had tied themselves in some way to the Northmen. There had to be more of them. *Christ.* How many more? How many Englishmen had lost faith in their king after two years of slaughter and destruction?

He saw that Ælfheah, who seemed to have determined at last that it was pointless to remain here any longer, was getting to his feet. Every Englishman under the canopy, as well as the few Danes who could still stand, rose with him. To Athelstan's relief no one bothered to take their leave of the besotted Hemming.

At the wharf, he and Edrid bid the archbishop farewell. Ælfheah would sail south to Canterbury while they made for the Thames and London. Their leave-taking was brief, for they were all of them eager to be on their separate ways.

While the oarsmen maneuvered their ship into the river, Athelstan looked back toward the shore. A lone rider emerged from the shadow of the city wall and set out toward the bridge that crossed the Medway and led north to London.

"Is that the Mercian?" he asked Edrid.

His brother looked to where he pointed just as the horseman halted to say something to the guard at the bridge.

"It is, yes," Edrid agreed. They watched as he kicked his horse into a gallop and crossed the span. "I wonder where he's going in such a hurry."

"Yes," Athelstan said. "So do I."

Athelstan had cause to remember that moment two days later when a flurry of rumors reached London that Hemming was dead. An English noble, it was said, had slipped into Rochester and gutted him in the night. Another tale blamed the death on a Rochester whore who had smothered Hemming while she was in his bed; another that the Canterbury archbishop had cast a curse on the Dane that had made him sicken, his bowels turned to water. However Hemming had died, it was always the English who had killed him.

"If Hemming is dead," Athelstan told Edmund, "it was none of our doing. The most likely explanation I can think of is that he drank himself to death."

Yet the image of a rider hastening across Rochester's bridge kept returning to him. Could the Mercian, Alric, have somehow been responsible for the warlord's death? And if he was, had he done them a favor or had he brought more trouble down upon their heads?

Ten days later, he had the answer. Canterbury lay in ruins, and Archbishop Ælfheah was a prisoner of the Danes.

# Chapter Thirty-Two

"What are you going to do?" Emma raised the question the moment that Æthelred stepped into the bedchamber.

For hours she had been waiting for him, nervous and agitated because she knew what detained him. A single hostage, an abbot, had been released from Canterbury and had arrived at the palace just after dark, accompanied by three Danish warriors. The king had been closeted with his advisers and with the Canterbury priest ever since.

Now it was late, well into the night's second watch, and instead of answering her, Æthelred ordered the body servant who entered the room a step behind him to bring more candles.

"And put more charcoal on the brazier, then leave us." To Emma he said only, "Wine."

She went to a table where a flagon and cups stood ready, poured the wine, and brought it to him. He took a long swallow but still did not reply to her query. The servant did the king's bidding while Æthelred paced the chamber in moody silence. She watched him, waiting for him to speak and hounded by apprehension.

For two days the grim outlines of the attack upon Canterbury had swirled through London's streets. The cathedral and its precincts had been burnt and the city pillaged. The king's hall and the archbishop's palace had been destroyed and Canterbury, as she had known it when she first came to England, was gone. What she did not yet know was how many lives had been lost.

What she could not guess was what the king proposed to do about it.

A direct assault seemed unlikely. The Danes had taken Canterbury by stealth, arriving on the Feast of Roodmas when the cathedral had been jammed with worshipers venerating the relic of the Holy Cross. Few men had been left to watch the city gates, and the enemy had wagered that they could enter almost unopposed. They had won their wager. Now, though, Canterbury's stout walls would be well defended by Vikings, and the watchers would be vigilant. Any attempt to retake the city by force would cost many lives and would probably be futile.

She could imagine no other recourse except to offer more tribute. But the king was already pledged to deliver another twenty-four thousand pounds of silver in the spring—the last of the forty-eight thousand that had been promised them.

What if treasure, though, was not the prize that the Danes were after?

The warning that her mother had sent at Easter, hinting of some calamity about to strike England, had been racing through her mind since she'd first heard of the attack. Was the assault on Canterbury only the beginning of some greater wave of destruction?

She continued to watch as her husband paced, the silence broken only by the hushed movements of the servant. When he slipped out of the chamber, she repeated her question: "What will you do?"

Still he did not answer her, but only strode to the table where the flagon stood and poured himself more wine.

Perhaps he had no answers to give.

"I should never have sent Ælfheah to negotiate with the Danish warlords," he said. "I'll send no more churchmen to parley with my enemies. They are worse than useless."

"You sent Ælfheah because you deemed him trustworthy," she reminded him.

"And look where it has led! Despite his efforts the Danes ravaged Kent and Sussex in March, and now they've taken Canterbury. The devil hound them to hell."

She was standing beside the brazier, watching him, and she could not find it in her heart to do anything but sympathize with his frustration and outrage. The Danes had bested him on the battlefield and at the bargaining table. Now they had broken faith with him by pillaging Canterbury. It was a monstrous crime, and London was rife with rumors of what horrors they might commit next.

"Have they given any justification for breaking the truce?" she asked.

"They say it has naught to do with the truce. They claim that Ælfheah murdered Hemming, and this attack is their revenge." His pacing had taken him to the window, and he drew the leather curtain aside and stared into the darkness. "They've taken more than two hundred hostages," he said. "Ælfheah and the bishop of Rochester are the most prominent, but Canterbury was filled with nobles and high-ranking clergy when it fell. Abbots, priests, monks—*Christ*. They've even imprisoned the nuns."

With the drawing of the curtain the night air invaded the room and Emma felt a sudden chill. But it was his words, not the breeze, that made her shiver. What would happen to the women while they were in Danish hands? *Sweet Virgin*, it might already be too late. She went to where he stood near the window embrasure.

"The women must be freed," she urged, "before—"

"The Danes will not let them go without some recompense," he said savagely. "Surely you know that."

Yes, she knew it only too well. The taking of hostages was a favorite tactic of the Danes. Books, relics, innocent victims—anything and anyone could be captured and held for ransom. Seven years ago the price on her own head would have been half of England had Swein Forkbeard managed to get her to his ship as he had intended.

"How much do they want?"

"We do not yet know," he said, turning from the window, "but the ransom of an archbishop and a bishop will be costly. They have bid us send three envoys unarmed into Canterbury to meet with their leaders and learn their demands. Three Danes will remain here as pledges that our men will not be harmed."

So it was treasure that they wanted, after all. "Who will you send?"

If it were up to her, she would send Athelstan, but the king would never agree to that. He had no confidence in his sons.

"Eadric will go, with two of his thegns. I would trust no one else."

Eadric. Of course. She turned away from him, frowning into the night, her gaze drawn to the distant glow of a single torch that flanked the palace gate. She did not share his blind trust in Eadric. The man was silver-tongued to be sure and would likely be a skilled negotiator, but she doubted that the good of the king or of the realm would be his first concern. And who could say what secret alliances Eadric might secure with the Danish host, given such a golden opportunity?

"Ealdorman Eadric is a wise choice as lead envoy," she said slowly, searching for an argument that did not tell against the man but might persuade Æthelred to rethink his decision. "It puzzles me, though, that you would send two thegns with him rather than men of his own rank. Should not the representatives of the king be chosen from among the highest nobles in the realm?"

He was silent for a time, his brow knitted, and she began to hope that he might, for once, heed her words.

"The Danes that we are dealing with are thugs," he growled at last. "Their actions do not deserve the kind of courtesy you would offer them."

"The Danes hold Canterbury and two hundred of your subjects! Surely their welfare is what is at stake here."

"And who would you have me send, lady, to lick the boot heels of their captors? That is what it amounts to, is it not?"

"Yes, my lord. I fear you are right in that, and it is to Eadric's credit that he is willing to do it. But surely he deserves the support of men of equal status. Another ealdorman at the least, and although you do not wish to send a churchman, I beg you to reconsider. Most of the men and women imprisoned in Canterbury are God's servants. Surely they will be in need of His consolation during this time of trial. Did none of your bishops offer to go?"

He barked a humorless laugh. "All of my counselors now in London offered to go—two bishops, two ealdormen, and three of my sons. Their esteem for Ælfheah is admirable." His tone was bitter.

How he must resent this show of support for the archbishop, she thought. He must wonder if they would respond in the same way had he been the one captured.

"Do not begrudge them an opportunity to be of service, my lord," she said, "to you as well as to Ælfheah. Send your ablest men to barter for his release. For if you do not, your ministers may fear that, should they find themselves in similar peril, you will do even less for them. Their trust in you will be strained."

For a time he said nothing, and she waited in tense silence, aware that he was weighing her words against his own fears and resentments and suspicions.

"You are like the rest of them," he said at last. "You have a fondness for the archbishop."

He set down his cup and rubbed his face with his hands. She could see how exhausted he was and she wondered how long it had been since he'd had a peaceful night's sleep. Not in all the years that she had been wed to him, she would hazard.

"You have a fondness for the archbishop as well, my lord," she said. "I think that, more than anything, you are angry with him because he was among those taken captive."

"I am angry that I must haggle with these Danish vermin! And yes, I blame Ælfheah for not finding some way to escape before the city fell. Instead he tried to negotiate with the devils. He's a damned fool." He expelled a long breath. "But I would not have it said that I made light of Canterbury's ordeal. I will send another ealdorman to accompany Eadric. Now that I think on it, as most of the ransom payment will be drawn from ecclesiastical coffers, the bishop of London should participate as well. Canterbury, though, is in ruins, and a loss not just to the Church, but to all England; for that I will always blame Ælfheah."

The next day Emma watched from the steps of the king's hall as Eadric departed for Canterbury in the company of Ealdorman Ælfric and Bishop Ælfhun. Seven days went by, and there was no word from them, nor any lessening of the frightening rumors that leaked into Emma's apartments from the streets of London. One of the worst claims to reach her was that the archbishop had been allowed to die of thirst. She tried to dismiss it as groundless, yet she knew that such stories often had some basis in truth, and there had been talk, as well, of pestilence in Canterbury. Could Ælfheah have succumbed to disease?

She had no answer, and there was another worry on her mind now, too, for she was convinced that she was with child. It should have been a time of rejoicing, but the grief and uncertainty surrounding the fate of the Canterbury hostages weighed upon her, and she feared for her unborn babe. She had miscarried in the past, and Margot was not here to help her if it should happen again.

Godiva was her frequent companion now, and on the eighth day after the delegation had left for Canterbury they sought refuge out of doors from the uneasiness within. The day was fine, likely one of the last of the season, Emma guessed. The fruit trees in the palace orchard, already denuded of apples and plums, were ablaze with autumn color, and in spite of the sunshine, a chilly breeze hinted of cold weather to come.

Emma sat on a blanket with Godiva in her lap, Wymarc at her side and a number of her women nearby. When her daughter held up a small hand, the prelude to a favorite game, Emma laughed and obediently clasped it. She mimicked nibbling the tiny fingers, eliciting squeals of delight from Godiva. A moment later, though, her daughter began a new game, scrambling away to gather an armful of gold and russet leaves that she distributed among Emma's household.

Watching her two-year-old walk stolidly away from her, bestowing each leaf as if it were a missive of great import, Emma called to mind the meaning of Godiva's name—God's gift. It was a reminder that a mother could not cling to her children, for what God bestowed He might take away again all too soon. It was the pattern of life, and she had already tasted its bitterness when Edward had been taken from her. Remembering this, she yearned to clasp Godiva to her breast, to hold time and the world and even God at bay.

A movement near the gate drew her eyes in that direction, and when she saw Ealdorman Ælfric approaching she pushed herself to her feet and hurried to meet him. Some of her attendants made to follow at first, but she stopped them with a gesture, and they fell away like a scattering of autumn leaves.

"What news do you bring from Canterbury?" she asked. Hungry for whatever he could tell her she led him to a bench and sat down beside him.

"It is heavy news, my lady," he said, taking her hand in his big paw. "Eadric and the bishop are making their reports to the king even now, and I was given leave to bring word to you."

He paused then, and she tensed as a dozen fears assailed her. She waited for him to tell her that Archbishop Ælfheah was dead or so gravely ill that he could not live.

But Ælfric fixed his gaze upon Godiva, and Emma suspected that his thoughts just now were all of his granddaughter Hilde, whose death at the hands of the Danes was still a fresh wound. Unwilling to press him, she studied his face with growing concern as she marked the changes that grief had wrought upon him.

She had never been certain of his age, knowing only that he was one of the king's elder counselors. In these last months, though, ever since Hilde had died, Ælfric's anguish seemed to have withered him. His face was grown so thin that spare flesh hung in folds beneath his eyes. His hair and beard, once the color of steel, had gone pure white.

Finally, her eagerness to hear what heavy news he would impart forced her to break the silence.

"Is Ælfheah dead then?" She watched his face, dreading the answer he would give.

He looked as if startled out of a daze. "No, he is not dead, although many in Canterbury were killed or savaged." He shook his head. "The city and the cathedral are in ruins, and I doubt that we will ever know how many lives were lost. The archbishop, though, is far too valuable to kill, not while our enemies have a hope of claiming a ransom for him. They are demanding three thousand pounds for Ælfheah alone, although there are scores of other hostages as well. When the Danes have finished with Canterbury, it will likely be wrung dry of everything of value."

"All because they blamed Ælfheah for the death of this man Hemming?"

Ælfric nodded. "They claim that Ælfheah poisoned Hemming when they were at table together. The archbishop has protested his innocence, of course, but they do not believe him, or at least they say that they do not."

"They must let him go, though, when the ransom is paid," she said. "What is being done to gather it? I will contribute. I have jewels that will go some way toward meeting the Danish demand."

He squeezed her hand.

"There will be no ransom paid," he said. "Ælfheah has forbidden it."

She stared at him, thunderstruck.

"He cannot forbid it," she protested. "He must be set free. The kingdom has need of him. Dear God, the king has need of him!"

"Emma, he is the archbishop of Canterbury, so yes, he can forbid the payment of any ransom."

"But why? It is unthinkable. Someone must speak to him and—"

"I did speak to him. I tried to reason with him, but he is determined that he will not submit to the Danish demand. He insists that if the ransom is paid it is the same as admitting guilt in the matter of Hemming's death. He will not allow it. And as to the price on his head, he says that Canterbury has paid and paid again. He will not ask his people to sacrifice any more."

"But if others pay, and not the people of Canterbury! Or if the king should withhold the last of the tribute until Ælfheah is set free—"

"If the king should do that, the Danes will strike yet another city, and then another, and there will be no end to it. Æthelred cannot interfere in this matter! It is between the archbishop and the Danes, do you not see that? The truth is"—and here he took another deep breath—"I do not believe that Ælfheah wants to be released."

Once more his words astonished her. "Did he tell you that?"

"In a fashion, he did. My lady, you know Ælfheah, and you know that he sees God's hand in everything. He sees this imprisonment as an opportunity to bring God's Word to the enemy army, and perhaps even to negotiate a lasting peace with them. He wants it, Emma. He embraces it."

She felt numb. Yes, she could see that Ælfheah would try to minister to the Danes. And she could even grant that the king must allow it because he had no choice.

But while Ælfheah was preaching to their enemies, it meant that one less voice would be offering wise counsel to Æthelred. It was a heavy price to pay, and for what? What if Ælfheah's efforts among the Danes were unsuccessful? What if they grew restive again in the coming months until the last of the gafol was delivered? Whatever the Danes may claim, the attack upon Canterbury seemed to her a violation of the truce agreement that they had made with Æthelred.

"What assurance do we have that they will not break the peace again?"

"None," he replied. He took hold of her hands and held them, regarding her with an expression so filled with concern and affection that it brought tears to her eyes. "That is why I wish to raise a matter with you that has been preying on my mind for many weeks."

"My lord," she said, "we are friends of old. You have but to speak, and you know that I will listen." It must, she thought, have to do with the king, and she hoped that Ælfric had some useful counsel to offer.

"It was at my urging, my lady, that your brother agreed to send you here to England to wed Æthelred. I feel as responsible for your safety as if you were my own child. No," he said, as she began to protest, "hear me out, I beg you. England is far too treacherous a place now for you and your children. The Danish army that is camped in Kent is lawless. It is a mindless beast with no head and no heart, and we cannot foresee what atrocity it may commit next. I beg you to take refuge with your brother in Normandy, at least until the gafol has been paid and this menace has left our kingdom. And do it swiftly, before the winter sets in and the sea passage becomes treacherous."

She was silent, turning his words over and over in her mind. Whenever she allowed herself to dwell on the horrors committed at Canterbury, her instinct was to gather her children and flee. But that was the instinct of a mother, and she must think first as a queen.

She had been urged to flee before this—to go where she would be safe. But she was bound to the king and to this kingdom by solemn vows, by the demands of duty, even by political expediency. What message would it send to the people of England who were struggling against invasion, famine, and disease if she were to abandon them?

She clasped Ælfric's hands tightly, knowing that his plea came from his regard for her. Nevertheless, she would not be moved by it.

"I thank you, Ælfric, for your counsel. But you know that I cannot leave England. My duty is here." She glanced away from him to Godiva, who was dancing in a pile of leaves. "And the king has already said that he will not allow my children to depart."

A silence hung between them for a moment, and then he said, "Not even your daughter?"

She looked at him then, and the expression on his face was one of grief at the pain that his question must bring.

She cast her mind back more than a year, recalling Æthelred's words that had seemed such a threat at the time. *The girl can go to Normandy. She is of little use.* She had repeated that conversation to Ælfric, seeking his aid in keeping her daughter at her side.

She had not forgotten the king's words, merely buried them. Was it the queen in her that had done that, or the mother? And what kind of mother would allow her daughter to remain at risk when she had the means to send her to safety?

"My lady," Ælfric said, his voice insistent, "in the streets of Canterbury I saw children who had been torn from their parents' arms and kept in filthy hovels to await ransom. I saw the bodies of children who had died in burning buildings or had been trampled by—"

"Stop!" she cried. "You have said enough, my lord. I need hear no more."

She stood up and walked a little away from him, her mind in turmoil. She had not yet told the king that she was pregnant, but when she did, he would likely take Godiva from her, as he had taken Edward, and place her where it suited him. Far better to send the child to Normandy where she would not only be safe, but where she would hear her mother spoken of with affection instead of with poisonous lies. Yet any trip across the Narrow Sea would be treacherous, and as Ælfric had pointed out, the fair weather would not last many days longer.

"How are we to get her away?" she asked, her gaze still focused on her daughter. "There are still enemy ships blocking the entrance to the Thames." That seemed to be the only difficulty. Æthelred, she knew, would not hinder Godiva's departure.

Ælfric had stood when she did, and now he came to her side.

"They have moored their vessels along the Thames's southern shore," he said. "If Godiva takes ship at Benfleet she'll not be hindered, and she can reach Bruges in a day if the weather is fair. From there it will be easy sailing along the coast to Fécamp."

She made no reply to this. Her own voyage along the whale road from Fécamp to Canterbury as Æthelred's promised bride had been anything but easy. Nevertheless, she could see no other choice.

She reached for his hand.

"Will you accompany her?" she asked him. "Will you make certain that she arrives at my brother's court safely?"

"You need not even ask, my lady. Of course I will do it."

Comforted by this, she beckoned Wymarc. There was much to do to prepare for Godiva's journey.

The day of leave-taking came in early October. With her daughter's hand clasped in hers, Emma approached the two vessels that would carry Godiva and her attendants to Normandy. It was midmorning on the feast day of Guardian Angels, and although the breeze off the water was cold, the sky was clear, empty but for the seabirds that wheeled overhead.

Only Godiva and Ælfric still remained ashore, and Emma knew that she could not delay their departure any longer. She bent down beside her daughter and gathered her, bundled as she was in layers of linen and wool, into her arms for a final embrace. She had explained this parting to Godiva the night before, but even so she could not be sure how much of it the child understood. After whispering a blessing, she gave her a final kiss, then watched as Ælfric hoisted her into his arms and carried her up the boarding plank. He placed Godiva in the arms of her nurse as the plank was hauled over the gunwale and stowed.

Left on shore with Wymarc at her side, Emma saw her daughter reach a hand toward her, and she felt tears knot her throat. She whispered, "I do not think that I can keep from weeping."

"It will be harder for her, Emma, if she sees you cry," Wymarc said.

She nodded. Wymarc was right, she must not cry. For a few moments longer, as the ship struck out from shore, she watched until her vision began to blur. Then, turning away, she took Wymarc's arm and began walking back toward the village of Benfleet, her mouth clenched tight against her grief.

Godiva's sudden, piercing wail rose above the rush of the breeze and the cries of the gulls. It seemed to wrap itself around her heart and wrench from her the tears that she had tried so hard to contain. But she did not stop walking, and although the temptation to do so was strong, she did not look back.

# Chapter Thirty-Three

November 1011

Redmere, Holderness

Elgiva stood beside her bed and lifted her hands to admire the sinuous vines worked in silver and gold along the borders of her wide sleeves. She could not even begin to imagine the worth of this gown, woven of deep-blue godwebbe, with its gilding at sleeves and neck and hem. Swein Forkbeard was a generous gift giver, she would grant him that.

He'd sent other gifts as well—the silver fillet at her brow, three of the bejeweled chains around her neck, the golden girdle and jeweled knife at her waist, and even the leather shoes that she wore—her rewards for giving Cnut a son at last.

Well deserved, as far as she was concerned, and just in time. At today's gathering of Cnut's supporters, she would appear before them not as merely the Lady Elgiva of Northampton, heiress to vast lands in the Five Boroughs and mistress of the hall, but as the gorgeously attired bride of a Danish prince.

Tyra held out a small coffer containing golden ornaments, and as Elgiva selected several bracelets to wear, Catla entered the chamber, trailed by the usual flotsam of children in her wake. Elgiva waited for her cry of admiration at the sight of the gown, but Catla didn't even glance at her. She was too busy fussing over Cnut's son, lying asleep in his nurse's arms.

Stupid woman, Elgiva thought. All babies look the same.

Except, she corrected herself, Swein Cnutson was far handsomer than any of the creatures that Catla had produced.

She waited until Catla finally settled herself on the bed with her youngest brat.

"Well?" she asked.

Catla studied her, then frowned and began to chew nervously at her lower lip.

She is jealous, Elgiva thought, irritated. But she's too cowardly to say so.

"Out with it, Catla," she snapped. "Am I flaunting too much gold for my lord's hall? Are you afraid that the sight of me will drive his men mad with desire?"

She was only half in jest. She wanted his men to be inflamed by the sight of her. That was the point.

"Does Cnut know that you will be in the hall for the gathering?" Catla asked, her voice little more than a whisper. "Thurbrand says that women are not welcome, that they will be discussing men's business."

Elgiva snorted. "Cnut's business is my business," she said. Many of the men who would be there had once been her father's thegns, men who would harbor resentments against the king and Eadric. Cnut had not asked that she be there, but he would not be fool enough to dismiss her, not after she entered with Cnut's son—the grandson of Ælfhelm and of Swein—in her arms. And if Thurbrand didn't approve, he could go hang. "Where is Thurbrand now?" she asked Catla.

"He is talking with Cnut and some others who came with us."

"What others?" Then looking down at her waist she said, "Tyra, fasten that girdle more tightly or it's like to slip off and trip me." To Catla she said, "Who came with you?"

Catla had turned her attention to the child on her lap, who was attempting to dive headfirst onto the floor. "Two Danish ships landed today at the mooring below our steading," she said absently. "Cnut's men. You'll know them. They've been here before—Arnor, Eirik, all that lot."

Elgiva froze. So Arnor was back! He had been away for so many months that she'd begun to hope the bastard was dead.

Likely he had messages to deliver to Cnut before the larger meeting began. And if he had brought news from the south, she wanted to hear it. Besides, she had a score to settle with Arnor.

"That will do!" she said to Tyra, although there were still bracelets and rings aplenty in the coffer. She spun around, pleased by the musical, jingling sound of gold on gold, and she pointed to the nurse who held her swaddled, sleeping son. "Come with me."

Walking close beside the buildings to avoid the slick mud in the middle of the yard as well as the score or so men gathering there, she made her way to the hall. Bypassing the wide, main door she slipped through a smaller entrance at the back leading to a narrow, private chamber that Cnut claimed for his own whenever he was in Holderness. As she had expected, she found him seated there, with Thurbrand standing to one side and a servant close by. Arnor straddled a bench in front of Cnut. The shipman's face, she noted, was marred by a yellowish bruise around one eye and a nasty cut on his lower lip that was not quite healed. An accident, she wondered, or a brawl? She hoped it had been painful, whatever the cause.

When she entered, Arnor abruptly broke off whatever he'd been saying, and every face turned to her. She offered no greeting, but walked straight to Arnor.

"Bring the child here," she called to the nurse, who stood hesitating at the chamber door.

The girl scurried to Elgiva's side, and the babe, disturbed by the cold and the movement, began to whimper. Elgiva pushed the girl toward Arnor, who recoiled as if he'd been struck.

"Nay, the bairn will not harm you," she said. "He's no knife yet to dangle before your eyes, although I have one." She touched the bejeweled hilt of the knife at her belt. "But I would have you look closely at him." She drew back the blanket to reveal the fine down of red-gold there, a match to Cnut's hair and beard. "Do you still insist that this is not Cnut's son? I warn you. His father has already acknowledged him, and all the women on this holding were present at his birth." She said to Cnut, "This vermin threatened me when last he was here and claimed that you had not fathered my child. I want him to admit to his lies, and I demand—"

"Be quiet!" Cnut interrupted her. The baby was squalling now, and Cnut motioned to the nurse. "Take the child away. Elgiva, I would hear

Arnor's news. Sit you down and be silent, or get out. You," he barked at the servant, "get your mistress a chair."

Now she felt the tension in the room. She had been too intent on facing down Arnor to notice it before. Whatever news the shipman had brought, it had fouled Cnut's usually genial temper. She sat down next to her husband and swallowed her anger, but she could not resist casting a surly glance at Arnor. The lout raised an insolent eyebrow in response, and she had to suppress an urge to demand that someone blacken his other eye.

Cnut said to Arnor, "I've heard at least four different tales today of how Hemming died. Do you know the truth?"

She drew in a quick breath. So Hemming was dead!

She looked at Cnut, but she could read no joy or even relief in his face. Instead he appeared worried by news that should have filled him with satisfaction. What was wrong with the man that he could not recognize a gift when it was handed to him?

She turned her attention back to Arnor, who was speaking of an agreement that had been forged between Hemming and Archbishop Ælfheah. Then he gave an account of Hemming's death at table and of the attack on Canterbury that followed some days later—all of the events months old, yet they had heard no whisper of them until now.

She had been right about Hemming, she thought with satisfaction. He would have turned against both Cnut and his brother if he hadn't been stopped. He deserved to be dead and his mischief buried with him. That Alric had dispatched him in a manner that cast blame upon the archbishop was a masterstroke. It could not have gone any better. Perhaps she should reward him with yet another ruby for that alone. She wanted to ask for more details of Hemming's death, but given Cnut's mood, she dared not interrupt.

"What of Thorkell?" Cnut asked. "He must have returned to Rochester by now. Did you speak with him?"

"Oh, aye. We spoke," Arnor said, "although he did most of the talking. He does not believe that the archbishop killed Hemming, my lord." He ran a knuckle along the cut on his lip. "He blames you."

Hearing this, Elgiva felt the tiniest flicker of unease. Beside her, Cnut froze, then leaned forward, eyes wide with shock.

"How? I was in Denmark!"

"Aye. But our friend Alric was at table with Hemming when he died, and he's not been seen since."

"Alric!" Cnut repeated.

"I don't believe it!" Elgiva could not keep silent. If Alric was tied to Hemming's death, her role in it might come out, and Arnor already harbored suspicions about her. She had no idea what Cnut would do if he discovered that she had ordered Hemming's death, and she had no wish to find out. "Husband, you cannot believe that Alric would—"

"Hold your tongue, woman!" Thurbrand snapped, glowering at her. "It is what Thorkell believes that matters."

"I'm to give you a message from Thorkell," Arnor said to Cnut. "I'm to say that he knows Hemming is dead by your command. That there is bad blood between you now, and should you ever come within his reach, your life is forfeit." He fingered his jaw. "It is not a message I'll soon forget," he said. "I've fewer teeth than I once had, compliments of Thorkell's men."

Thurbrand sucked in a breath. "If Thorkell has become your enemy, Cnut," he said, "then whoever killed Hemming has done you an ill turn."

Cnut's face was furrowed now with concern. "Hemming was poisoned, you say," he murmured. "Is that a certainty?"

"So Thorkell says, and he had it from men who were present at the feast and close to Hemming's table," Arnor replied. He fixed accusing eyes on her. "Poison is a woman's weapon."

Cnut was studying her now, as well, with questions in his eyes.

Beneath his steady gaze, the golden chains around her neck felt tight, and she found it difficult to swallow. They were all looking at her, and she licked her dry lips, searching for some way to turn their suspicions elsewhere. It would do no good to rage against Arnor, for Cnut would side with his trusted shipman, even against his own wife. Thorkell, though, might suit.

"There is no proof that anyone murdered Hemming," she said. "Thorkell claims you did it, my lord, and we all know that is false. I'll wager that even Thorkell knows it. Consider what he gains by accusing you. How many thousands of pounds of Æthelred's silver that has been pledged to you will now go to Thorkell instead?"

There was silence for a moment, and then Thurbrand muttered, "By the gods, she may be right. Your father has never trusted Thorkell. Perhaps he has been wise in that."

"Thorkell has powerful allies," Cnut said, "and my father's fear is that he may one day make a grab for Denmark's throne. I disagree. I do not believe that Thorkell wants a kingdom."

"What does he want, then?" she asked.

He shrugged. "Who can say? Gold? Power? Renown?"

"He may well want the throne of England," Thurbrand suggested. "How does he factor in Swein's plans for unseating Æthelred?"

"Thorkell's part is done. His role, although it was never spelled out to him, was merely to weaken England's resistance. That much is accomplished. Next summer, before the English can recover their military strength, my father will lead his invasion. Thorkell is welcome to be a part of it, but he is not necessary."

"Then Thorkell no longer matters," she said, breathing a little easier. "You do not need him."

"Perhaps not now," Cnut said, "but who can say what lies ahead? And it matters to me," he said, getting to his feet and beginning to pace, "because he has been my friend. He would not accuse me unless he believed I was guilty. He must think that I have broken my oath, both to him and to Hemming, and that is a grievous thing."

"You set far too high a value on loyalty," she scoffed.

He looked at her coldly. "Loyalty is a rare commodity, Elgiva. How am I to convince men to trust me, to follow me into battle, if they believe that I might one day betray them?"

Thurbrand grunted. "Women have no understanding of the greater affairs of men," he said. "Send your lady away, Cnut. She has no place here."

She opened her mouth to protest, but Cnut spoke first.

"The men are already gathering in the hall," he said, and she realized that she had been hearing the buzz of voices for some time. "You know your part, Thurbrand," Cnut went on. "Get in there before some fool discovers a grudge and starts a fight. I'll join you shortly. Arnor, go with him. We will deal with Thorkell and his threats later."

When they were gone she went to stand before Cnut. She had come through this little crisis about Hemming's death unscathed, and now they must both prepare to meet with the great men of northern Mercia. She ran her hands along the embroidered dragons that graced the sleeve of his tunic and admired the ornate silver belt buckle and the intricate inlay work of his scabbard and sword grip. He wore no crown upon his head, but the golden brooch that fastened his fur-lined cloak was the size of a man's fist, and that was gold enough for now. She would be proud to stand at his side, for he carried himself like the king that he must one day be.

"This meeting will be a great success," she said. "I do not doubt that the men of Holderness and the Five Boroughs will pledge themselves—"

"What do you know of this business between Airic and Hemming?" he asked, pinning her with dark, suspicious eyes.

She looked at him, feigning wide-eyed innocence—a look she had mastered long ago.

"I know nothing more than you do, husband," she lied.

He grunted, but she could not tell if he believed her.

"And have you had any word from Alric in the past six months?"

"No." That, at least, was the truth.

"Tyra tells me that you have learned how to prepare a great many herbal infusions. Elgiva," he said slowly, "have you been toying with poisons?"

"No, husband, I have not." It was another lie, but it rang true even to her ears. Thank the gods she had managed to keep her potions secret from Tyra the truth teller.

For a moment he just stared at her, studying her face as if he would peel back skin and bone, and read what was in her mind. It made her shiver.

"It worries me," he said, "that Alric fled from Rochester when he did. It marks him as guilty."

"Can you not put yourself in his place?" she demanded. "Imagine yourself an Englishman seated at table beside a Danish warlord. You suddenly realize that your host is, inexplicably, dead." She gave an exasperated sigh. "Cnut, you told me yourself what Hemming's men were like. Wouldn't you flee, for fear they would murder you and ask questions later?"

"That is a possible explanation," he said, his face grave, "although it seems unlikely."

He lifted his hand to run his knuckles lightly along the side of her face, to finger the fine linen of her headrail, to graze the back of her neck. She searched his eyes for some sign of what was in his mind, willing him to kiss her, for then she would be certain that he had believed her. But he did not kiss her.

"Elgiva," he said, and there was steel in his voice, "I will wager that the men in there will think you the perfect ornament to my hall. They will want to devour you with their eyes and lose themselves in imagining what lies beneath your gown. But I am the one that they must heed, not you. So you will accompany me in there with Swein in your arms, you will welcome the men warmly, and then you will return to your chamber."

She pulled away from him, stricken. "I will not. Most of these men are here because of their kinship to me, and I want to be—"

"Listen to me!" She had little choice, for he grasped her by the shoulders and gave her a rough shake that made her teeth rattle. "Thurbrand controls his woman by beating her until she is bloody," he snarled. "I'll not stoop to that, Elgiva, but I will not have you arguing with me at every turn. You will obey me even if I have to lock you in your chamber with only bread and water until you learn to do as you are told. You have an important role to play in a carefully designed plan, and you will do it without questioning me. I have left you on your own for too long, and although you are mistress of this hall, I am its lord and you answer to my wishes, not to yours. Now go and get our son."

He turned her around and pushed her toward the door.

She gritted her teeth to keep from saying aloud the curse against all men that rose to her lips. There would come a time, she vowed, when she would not have to bend to the will of every human creature that strutted across the land with a cock dangling between his legs.

Before she reached the door he called her name again, and she halted, waiting for whatever would come next.

"If I find that you have lied to me about Alric," Cnut said, "I promise that I will do far worse than beat you."

With his words ringing in her head she stepped into the cold, slamming the door behind her.

"Then I will make sure," she muttered as she made her way across the yard, "that you never find out."

A.D. 1012   This year came Ealderman Eadric, and all the oldest counselors of England, clerk and laity, to London before Easter; and there they abode, over Easter, until all the tribute was paid, which was forty-eight thousand pounds.

—*The Anglo-Saxon Chronicle*

# Chapter Thirty-four

April 1012

Windsor

Æthelred struggled to open his eyes, grimacing against the pain that nagged the right side of his body at head, shoulder, and ankle. He was propped against a multitude of bed cushions in a chamber where candles cast fitful light, and where the gaping blackness beyond the high, narrow windows proclaimed that the hour was late.

His right foot, tightly bound between two lengths of thin wood, lay atop the bedclothes, throbbing like the very devil. As he scowled at it, a long shadow in the shape of a man crept across the bed, and what had been a vague pain at his temple soared into agony.

With an effort he turned his head toward the shadow's source, frightened—uncertain if he was awake or still in the clutch of nightmare.

"*Christ*," he gasped, "Wulfstan." The ache in his head lessened, and despite the heaviness that seemed to press on all his limbs he was wide-awake now. The leech, he remembered, had given him a potion to ease his pain, and the draught must have sent him to sleep. For how long? he wondered. "What day is it?"

"It is Good Friday," Wulfstan replied, stepping closer to the bed and sketching a cross above Æthelred's head.

So he'd been lying here, in and out of dreams, for two days. He studied his Jorvik archbishop, whose face and beard were starkly pale against the smudge of his black traveling cloak.

"Should you not be in London?" he grunted.

"We should both be in London, my lord. I was on my way there when I learned that you were lying here abed." Wulfstan lifted his hand, and a young man in monk's garb emerged from somewhere out of Æthelred's sight to place a chair at the archbishop's side. Wulfstan sat down and said, "Edyth bade me welcome, and told me of your fall."

"I did not fall," he snarled. "My infernal horse threw me."

They thought him careless and inept, but they had not seen what had happened, there on the London Road, for he had been alone. His heralds had ridden ahead and he had outstripped the hearth troops riding behind when his mount had balked suddenly, mid-stride, stamping and snorting, ears a-twitch. His skin had been crawling with premonition, but he could see nothing amiss until the air around him had seemed to thin and stretch so that each breath became a struggle. In that breathless moment Edward's form had taken shape, luminous as candlelight, beckoning him toward London. The horse went mad with terror, rearing and plunging, and though he struggled to keep his seat, all feeling in his hands had fled, and the reins had slipped away. He'd known nothing after that until he awoke, his face drenched with his own blood and his body racked with pain.

He had been neither heedless nor negligent, but he could not defend himself; he could tell no one the truth of it, least of all the archbishop.

"So you will stay here rather than attend your court in London?" Wulfstan's voice, laced with disapproval, needled him back to the present. "What pains you the most, my lord? Your injuries or your pride?"

"What do you think?" he muttered. "The leeches told me it was only by God's grace that I didn't lose an eye." And if that was true, it was the only favor that God had shown him in years. He touched the strip of linen that bound a noisome poultice to his forehead, where there would be a scar, he'd been told, above his right brow.

Edward's mark upon him.

"I think it must be your pride that's ailing, for you look well enough to attend your council if you wish it." Wulfstan's shrewd gray eyes glittered with reproach. "I understand that the last of the tribute payment is to be turned over to the shipmen in London after Easter. However much you may wish to distance yourself from that ordeal, you would be unwise to do so. *Take up your pallet and walk*, says the Lord."

Æthelred shifted on his pillows, uneasy under Wulfstan's penetrating gaze.

"The Lord is not here, Archbishop, and my leeches have forbidden me to walk or to ride. Would you have me carried helpless through the streets of London to be laughed at and mocked?"

"I would have you be a king, and not shirk from your duty. You are neither wounded nor sick, my lord. You agreed to meet the enemies' demands, and your place is in London to see the final payment carried out."

"My place is wherever I choose to be!" His brother's fetch had beckoned him to London, and that was a summons he would not heed. "Eadric will act for me."

"Eadric is no king, nor ever will be. If someone must act in your place, then appoint your son to it."

His son! Yes, it would please Athelstan to give the nobles of England a taste of what they could expect with a vigorous young man on the throne.

But he was not fool enough to give his son that opportunity.

"Eadric is my chief ealdorman," he said, "and the witan looks to him for leadership. Athelstan must wait until I am dead to take his place upon the dais." He narrowed his eyes at Wulfstan. "Did Athelstan urge you to press this suit with me?"

"He did not. I speak to you at Christ's urging. Take heed, for He tells us that every kingdom divided against itself will be brought to desolation." Wulfstan leaned toward the bed, his features softening. "My lord, you have the means to repair what is broken between you and your son, and if you—"

"My son must bend to my will however distasteful he finds it! If he cannot do so, I have other sons—one even that I have not seen as yet. Emma's child awaits his christening in London. I trust you will attend to it. He is to be called Alfred—after a king, you will recall, who purchased peace from the Danes when forced to it. Just as I have."

"And this peace that you have bought will last how long, think you?"

Wulfstan scoffed. "Until the next shipload of devils makes its way across the Danes' Sea?"

Æthelred scowled at him. "Cease your harping, Archbishop. I could do nothing else, and you know it. Yes, I have ransomed England with silver, and I will do it again if I must. Your churchmen who were captured at Canterbury purchased their freedom with coin speedily enough. I see no difference."

For a time the archbishop made no reply, and Æthelred began to hope that he'd silenced the old man, until Wulfstan spoke again.

"Ælfheah did not pay," he said.

No, his old friend had not paid, and was likely to find himself sold as a slave among the Rus if he did not meet the shipmen's price soon.

"Ælfheah is a fool!" he snapped. "He may be God's anointed, yet still he lies at Greenwich in the keeping of devils. Would you have me hand them England as well?"

"I would have you commit yourself to God, as Ælfheah has done!"

"That is an archbishop's office, not mine!" *Christ*, his head ached. Would no one come to rescue him from this implacable priest? Where was Edyth?

"It *is* your office, as God's anointed king! Can you not see that the Lord's hand is at work in this strife? For two years we have been victoryless, and God's anger lies at the root of it. Your people turn away from Him! All through your northern shires the crossroads are laden with offerings to false gods. Heathen beliefs have sullied your kingdom, and until we address that evil and the disloyalty it breeds, we shall remain weak while our enemies grow ever stronger. The trouble lies not with your sons, my lord, but in the wickedness of Godless men."

Æthelred was silent for a time, sifting through the archbishop's words. Wulfstan's preoccupation with petty offerings to heathen gods did not concern him, for they were church matters, best dealt with by the priests.

Disloyalty, though; that was an evil that demanded royal action.

"Treachery has ever found a foothold in the north," he mused. "It is like a fire smoldering in thatch. You can smell it, but it is near impossible to find the source until it has become a blaze, and by then it is too late.

I had hoped that in naming a new ealdorman for Northumbria I had put out that fire."

"I make no complaint against your ealdorman," Wulfstan said. "Uhtred is God-fearing, and he honors his oaths. But the walls of his fortress are high, and the rumblings of discontent can seldom be heard through stone and mortar. It is your lesser lords who will have heard the things that I have—rumors of meetings held in secret, and of Danish ships lurking along your northern shores. Instead of lying here wallowing in your suspicions, do as I have said! Get you to London and discover what your northern thegns can tell you."

Æthelred exhaled a long, exasperated breath. Wulfstan was only confirming what he already knew. The rot that had begun with Ælfhelm and his sons had not been checked by their deaths. What he needed to discover now was how far the rot had spread. To question his northern nobles, though, would be useless, for he could not trust their answers.

"Nothing awaits me in London, Archbishop, but wrangling and humiliation, half-truths and outright lies." And something even more sinister, he feared. "I want none of it. But I will give thought to all that you have said, and when next I meet with my council we will address the evil in the north. And now"—he raised his hand to stem any further discussion—"you will leave me, for I am weary."

He closed his eyes to further signal that the interview was ended. Moments later, when the scrape of a chair and the sound of retreating footsteps told him that Wulfstan was gone, he opened his eyes again, for sleep was impossible now. His mind kept toying with the archbishop's words. *Meetings held in secret. Danish ships prowling the northern coast. The trouble lies not with your sons.*

Yet he could not be certain that his sons were blameless. The links that Athelstan had forged in his youth to the men of the northeast had grown ever stronger with the passing of years; and Eadric had warned him that Athelstan was not to be trusted.

Had there been pledges exchanged between his son and the northern lords? As yet he had no proof of it, but there was no denying the corruption that was spreading through his kingdom. Before he could cut it out, though, he must determine how far it had spread, and how close it had come to his own family.

As for London, some horror was waiting there—of that he was certain. His brother's ghostly beckoning guaranteed it, and no power on earth—not even an archbishop—would move him to go there to meet it.

**Sunday, Easter Octave, April 1012**
**Middlesex**

Athelstan rode with a small company toward Stebunheath, where his men were keeping watch on the movements of the enemy fleet. The last of the gafol demanded by the Danes had been delivered midweek, and by treaty agreement every Viking ship must raise sail by sundown today. Despite the thick fog that had settled on the Thames, the dragon ships were already on the move, or so he'd heard. He wanted to see it for himself and discover, too, if there was any news of Archbishop Ælfheah, who by all accounts was still a prisoner of the Danes.

When they were as yet some distance from the outpost, Edmund, who had been riding ahead with Edrid, slowed his mount and fell in beside Athelstan.

"I've just learned that you've put Godwin in charge of the posting out here," Edmund said. "I thought you intended to find a place for him on one of your Sussex estates."

Athelstan had to bring his thoughts around from the imprisoned archbishop to Wulfnoth's son.

"Godwin had no wish to stay in Sussex after his mother died," he said. "He's looking for a chance to prove himself, and I'm willing to give it to him—for his father's sake. If it hadn't been for that meeting we had with him at Corfe, Wulfnoth would not have been exiled and might even still be alive today. We owe his son something." The news of Wulfnoth's drowning off the Hibernian coast was only a few weeks old, and it had come hard on the heels of the death of Godwin's mother. He was parentless and landless now, and he was in need of friends.

"Agreed," Edmund said, but he was frowning. "You'd be wise to keep him away from London, though, while Eadric is holding court there. God-win blames Eadric for his father's banishment after that mess at Sand-wich, and if the two of them come face-to-face there's likely to be trouble."

Athelstan scowled. *Jesu*, when he'd been forced to watch Eadric play-ing king at the Easter court he'd been tempted to commit murder him-self. He could hardly blame Godwin, who was younger and had even greater reason to hate Eadric, for wanting to do the same.

"I'll see to it that Godwin stays out of London," he pledged, and Ed-mund nodded.

When they arrived at the lookout, Athelstan could see ships under sail—too many even to count—making their way downstream toward the Thames mouth. For nearly six months the vessels had been moored along the river's southern bank while the shipmen who manned them had set up their camps to the east of Greenwich. Peering into the shred-ding fog he could tell that the Vikings' fortifications were no longer the vast scar across the landscape that they had once been. A great number of their tents were still in place, though, and there must be forty ships, he guessed, still lining the opposite shore.

"It looks like some of them are in no hurry to leave," he observed to Godwin, who had come forward to greet him.

"I'm surprised that any of them made it to their ships this morning," Godwin said. "They kept a bonfire going all night long, and they were making enough noise to wake the dead."

"Likely they were celebrating their triumph over us," Edmund said.

"If they were feasting, it ended in a brawl," Godwin told them. "From here it sounded like Gog and Magog let loose upon the world."

Athelstan stared hard into the distance, and it seemed to him that there was some kind of activity taking place on one of the hythes beside the largest of the ships.

"Edrid," he said, "your eyes are better than mine. Can you make out what is happening over there?"

His brother shaded his eyes against the sunlight just now beginning to break through the fog.

"They're loading something onto the ship, but there are too many men clustered there for me to make out what it might be."

"Treasure?" Edmund suggested.

"It may be," Godwin agreed. "That ship is flying Thorkell's banner. How many pounds of silver do you suppose his vessel can hold?"

"All the silver in England, if Thorkell had his way," Edrid said.

Athelstan was only half listening to them. He swept his gaze over the ships that were still docked across the river and decided that there were far too many to suit him. And he could see men moving among the tents now—once again, far too many.

"I count at least forty dragon ships still moored over there," he said. "Edrid?"

After a few moments Edrid answered, "Forty-five."

Athelstan nodded. "Which means that there are more than a thousand men still in that camp, and they don't look as though they're planning to leave anytime soon. I don't like it."

They watched in silence for a time as the vessels from upstream continued to sail past them, making for the open sea. Athelstan kept his eyes on Thorkell's ship. He had half a mind to cross the river and nose around. But the nearest ferry was an hour's ride east at Renaham, and from there another hour's ride back to Greenwich. Still, it might be worth it to send someone over to have a look.

He was about to give the order when Thorkell's vessel, every oar manned, was maneuvered into the Thames with its prow facing upriver. Seeing this, he muttered a curse that was echoed by every man around him.

"The bastards are going to London," Edmund snarled.

"They cannot mean to break the truce!" Edrid said. "Not with a single ship—sixty men at most. They'd have to be mad to attempt it."

Athelstan scowled and shifted uneasily in his saddle. "It doesn't smell right, though," he said. "And it wouldn't be the first time they've bypassed city walls through some kind of treachery. It's how they brought down Canterbury last year." *Jesu!* Was it about to happen again?

Gesturing to three of his hearth guards he said, "You men ride for the ferry at Renaham. I want to know what went on in that camp last night, and why those vessels are still moored at Greenwich. And be careful! We may have a truce with the Danes until sundown, but I don't trust them to keep to it and nor should you. Discover all that you can, but stay in the shadows. Report to me tonight in London."

Edmund was shaking his head, his expression grim. "They're rowing with the tide now. Whatever they're planning, we'll never reach London in time to—"

"That's no reason not to try!" Athelstan snapped. They would need a larger force than this, though, to take on sixty Danish shipmen. They would have to gather men along the way and it would slow them down, but he could see no help for it. *Christ!* He wished he knew what Thorkell was up to. "Godwin, I'm taking your men—all but three. If you see any more movement of men or ships toward London, light the warning beacons, then make for the city."

He chafed with impatience while horses were saddled and mounted. At last, with a final glance toward the river where Thorkell's vessel was long out of sight, he led his men swiftly westward. All his instincts howled that this move by Thorkell was exactly what it looked like—a ploy to gain entry into London. It was the one city that had successfully repelled the Danes again and again. How they planned to take it now he could not imagine, but with every passing moment his conviction grew that they meant to break London at last, and that Edmund was right. He hadn't a prayer of getting there in time to stop it.

# Chapter Thirty-Five

Sunday, Easter Octave, April 1012
London

There was silence in the tiny chamber where Emma, seated with her infant son in her arms, looked down into eyes that were the same brilliant blue as her daughter's. She sang to him—one of the Norman lays she had learned in her girlhood and that she had sung to Godiva and to Edward.

When his eyelids drifted shut she watched the child for a time in the silence, admiring what she could see of him amid blankets, swaddling bands, and a woolen cap. From the moment that she had first looked on this babe she had loved him, and she marveled at the miracle that was a mother's heart, where there was room enough for each of her children, no matter how many God might send.

Unlike his brother and sister, though, Alfred had never been hers alone, even for a little while. She had given him immediately into the care of others, for she had duties to perform, and journeys she intended to take—at the very least to her estates in East Anglia and Rutland to see for herself what havoc they had suffered at the hands of the Danes. The child would come with her, of course, but she would not be able to respond to his needs. Even now there were letters awaiting her attention, requests from petitioners that she must grant or deny. Reluctantly, she kissed him once more, placed him, still asleep, in the arms of his wet nurse, and left him.

In her outer chamber the women of her household were gathered around an embroidery frame set beneath a spill of midday sun that made the reds, greens, and blues of their silken threads gleam with jewel-like brilliance. Nearby, close beside the warmth of the brazier, Father Martin was bent over a table. In front of him lay a stack of letters and at his elbow two large books. Emma went to his side and ran her fingers over the fine leather volumes.

"These are the books that Abbot Guillaume has requested for the abbey at Fécamp?" she asked.

"Yes, and there is a third, as well, my lady, that is not yet finished," he said. "The abbot at the Old Minster has written that it should be completed in a matter of weeks."

She nodded. "Let us wait, then, and send them all at once."

She drew her mother's most recent letter from the pile on the table and sat down to read it again, for it was filled with news of Godiva. Her daughter, it seemed, was happy. She was prattling in French now, no longer the silent and frightened little girl she had been when she had first arrived in Rouen. She had become the great pet of her cousins, and she was fascinated by Richard's daughter Eleanor, born just after Christmas.

*Be assured, though, that she has not forgotten you. She prays for you each night.*

Emma wondered if that was true. Did her daughter pray for her, or did she merely repeat words that were prompted by her nurse? Godiva was not yet three winters old. How much would she even remember of the mother she had last seen six months ago on a windswept shore at Benfleet?

Emma closed her eyes, filled with a desperate yearning to see her daughter, to have not just her sons but all three of her children with her. She had never meant for Godiva to be away for long, and the enemy army that had been the cause of her daughter's exile would be gone by day's end. In a few months the good sailing weather would arrive. Perhaps then, by midsummer at the latest, Godiva could come home.

She heard the chamber door creak open, and she looked up and saw Wymarc's son, Robert, there. He was a sturdy boy of eight now, and his face had the same genial good looks as Hugh, the father he had never met. He glanced toward the circle of women, found his mother, and offered her a quick smile; then, clearly on a mission of some import, he hurried to kneel at Emma's feet.

Patricia Bracewell

She was glad to see him, for glimpses of Robert and Edward, dwelling in the household of Ealdorman Eadric during this London sojourn, had been infrequent. Just now Robert's face was flushed and he was breathing hard. Something had brought him here at a run.

"I see that you have news," she said, setting her mother's letter aside and giving him her full attention. "What is it?"

"A dragon ship has put in at the hythe nearest the eastern wall, my lady. The shipmen have asked to speak with you or with Lord Athelstan, but Ealdorman Eadric has forbidden them to come any further into the city." He paused to grab a breath. "He purposes to meet them at All Hallows Church. Edward is to go with him."

She frowned.

"Did Eadric send you to me?" she asked.

"Nay, lady. I came of my own accord. I thought that you would wish to know."

She nodded. Indeed, she did wish it; neither was she surprised that Eadric would withhold this news from her. In Æthelred's absence the senior ealdorman had been granted a king's authority, and it was no great leap for him to assume the power of a queen as well—especially a queen only newly released from childbed.

A far more disturbing question was what the shipmen wanted.

She flicked a glance at Father Martin, who was looking at her, his brow arched in speculation. "This may have to do with Archbishop Ælfheah," he suggested. "Perhaps he has at last agreed to allow his ransom to be paid."

"Pray God you are right," Emma replied. It still chafed her that when Eadric had supervised the final gafol payment to the Danes, he had not raised the issue of the archbishop. If there was to be some negotiation for his release now, she did not wish to leave it in Eadric's careless hands.

"Was anyone else summoned to attend this parley?" she asked. "Lord Athelstan and his brothers, or the bishop of London?"

"He sent for no one, my lady. The other æthelings, as far as I know, are all without the city. Eadric and Edward, along with a company of men, are already in the yard preparing to set out for All Hallows."

So if she was to be a party to this parley, she must move quickly.

She ordered hearth troops summoned and horses saddled, then slipped into the woolen cloak that a servant had fetched for her.

"Wymarc, you will attend me. Father Martin, please send someone to alert Bishop Ælfhun. If this is about Ælfheah, he will want to be there."

As she and Wymarc hurried down the outer stairway that led to the yard, Wymarc observed, "Eadric will try to stop you from going with him, Emma. I hope you're ready for an argument."

"I'm looking forward to it," she replied. "Eadric has usurped far too much authority these past weeks. It's time someone reminded him that he's not the king." As Wymarc had warned, Eadric was not well pleased to see her. He strode toward her with his hands raised to prevent her from joining the gathering company.

"My lady," he said smoothly, "the king would not wish you to involve yourself in—"

"The king is not here, Lord Eadric," she interrupted him. "I hope you will not presume to tell me what I can and cannot do."

She made to brush past him, but he clasped her arm to halt her.

"You are under my protection and you will do as I say." There was a subtle threat in the silky voice, and the smile he turned on her was cold.

She said nothing but looked pointedly at his hand clutching her arm.

Two of her Norman hearth men drew near and, seeing them, Eadric loosed his hold on her and stepped aside with something approximating a bow.

"Who is it that wishes to speak with me?" she asked, sweeping past him so that he was forced to fall into step behind her.

"It is the Danish leader Thorkell," he said, "along with whatever crew he's brought with him—fifty shipmen if not more. They make a formidable force, and they are dangerous men."

"All men are dangerous, my lord," she snapped. "What can you tell me of this Thorkell? You met him when you turned over the last of the gafol, I believe."

"He is as brutal and merciless as every other Dane, and near as powerful as King Swein. He is in league with Swein in some way, although he has denied it. I don't believe him. Thorkell is a liar, and he knows just enough English to make his lies appear truth. It's likely he intends to make some further demands of us and threaten more murder and pillage if we do not agree."

Demands for what? Would this Thorkell have come himself to barter for Ælfheah? Perhaps, if the stakes were high enough. The original price for the archbishop's release had been three thousand pounds, but it was possible that now an even greater sum would be asked.

Or, if Thorkell was as devious as Eadric claimed, he might have some darker purpose altogether, something that none of them could discern.

*Some darker purpose.* Her mother's voice slipped into her mind, and she was a child again, listening to a cautionary tale about the treachery of men. *Your grandfather William did not discern his enemy's darker purpose, so when the parley was requested he willingly agreed to it. By mutual consent they left their weapons outside the church; but some days before, his enemy had concealed a sword within, for he was shrewd as well as treacherous. The sword, alas, did its work, and with a single stroke William's reign was ended.*

There were two lessons in that story: Always know your enemy's intent, and never put your life into his hands.

In going to meet Thorkell, was she ignoring the lessons that her grandfather had bought with his life?

They had reached the horses, and a groom helped her mount while Eadric continued to protest and she continued to ignore him, her mind still on her grandfather's fate. She glanced at Edward. He was tall for a lad of seven winters, and in the saddle he looked every bit the young warrior, right down to the knife that was sheathed at his belt. He wore a simple woolen tunic and mantle that were a far cry, thank heaven, from the brilliant raiment that Edyth, still at Windsor with the king, would have chosen for him. Despite his modest garments, though, he carried himself as one who knew very well that he was an ætheling and that it was his right to be a witness to this meeting.

In spite of that, and remembering her grandfather's fate, she was tempted to order him to remain behind.

Edward returned her gaze with nothing more than a solemn nod, as if to remind her of the vast gulf that had grown between them. She could imagine how much wider that gulf would grow if she should forbid him to accompany her. He was a king's son, and he would resent being treated like a child. In his place she would feel the same; so she said nothing to him about staying behind.

Besides, she assured herself as she returned his nod, this parley could only be about Ælfheah. There would be no darker purpose, no weapons, and no danger.

When they reached All Hallows, they found that a small crowd had gathered outside. It was Sunday, and they would be curious, Emma supposed, as to why armed men had surrounded their little stone church, keeping them from their worship.

"How many of them are in there?" Eadric asked one of the guards at the door.

"Only six, my lord," was the reply. "We've posted twice that number of our men inside, keeping watch."

"You've taken all the weapons?" he asked.

"Yes, lord." The guard jerked a thumb toward an array of knives, swords, and even a bearded axe that rested against the church wall. He opened his mouth as if to say something more, then seemed to think better of it, for he clamped his lips shut and stepped aside.

Emma saw no point in crowding even more men into the building, so she ordered her hearth guards to remain outside. Then she followed Eadric, now divested of his own sword, into the church, with Wymarc and Edward just a few steps behind.

The interior was dim, and while Eadric stopped to speak to one of the Englishmen ranged along the wall on either side of the door, Emma paused to allow her eyes to grow accustomed to the gloom.

At the far end of the church she could see the Danes clustered together beneath one of the high windows, separated from the English by the length of the nave. They were clad in the mail tunics that marked them as warriors. Whatever their business here, they were nervous. She sensed their restlessness in their shifting movements, could hear it in the quiet rasp of metal rings grating one against another.

She could hear as well the murmur of a single voice, and she traced the sound to a priest who knelt before the altar. He was facing the nave, whispering prayers over something that lay on the floor before him.

When she realized what it was, arranged there on the paving stones below the altar step, she was suddenly afraid. Her fear pushed her forward until she was gazing down at a length of soiled linen. Once it had been an altar cloth. She knew it well, for she had stitched some of the golden roods at its hem with her own hands, and with her own hands she had offered it to the Canterbury archbishop—a gift from the royal family. Now it was a shroud, and with a sinking, hateful certainty, she bent down and drew a corner of it aside.

What she saw made her press a hand to her mouth to still the keening wail that rose in her throat. She knew it to be Ælfheah, although his face was so terribly damaged she scarcely recognized him. One side of his head was nothing but a pulpy mass of crushed bone and raw flesh, while the other side bore a score of wounds from what must have been a multitude of blows. Someone had cleansed his face and bound his shattered jaw closed with a strip of linen, yet there was no mistaking the cruel death that he had suffered.

A swelling rage engulfed her, and from somewhere beyond it she heard Wymarc weeping and Eadric shouting to the men at the door to allow no one inside.

She lifted her gaze from Ælfheah's body to glare at the Danish leader—a huge man with an ugly scar on one cheek and a head shaved bare except for a long tail of hair that hung down his back. He was watching her with wary eyes beneath thick, dark brows.

He was right to be wary. Ælfheah's blood cried out for vengeance and every impulse urged her to take it—to call for slaughter here in the sight of God. Yet she could not do it, for she had taken upon herself the burden of royal responsibility, and these men had come here unarmed and under truce.

"I have honored your request for parley," she said, her voice breaking despite her efforts to control it, "but I did not think to meet with such a display of treachery as this."

The big man took a step toward her, and she tensed, ready to deflect an assault. There was movement behind her—Eadric, she guessed, reaching for the sword that he did not have.

But Thorkell dropped to one knee, as did all those with him.

"Not my treachery, my lady," he said, stumbling over the English words. "I tried to save him!" He grasped a silver cross that he wore on a leather thong about his neck, and it struck her that it, too, like Ælfheah's pall, might be one of the spoils from Canterbury. "I swear to you," he said, looking at her with eyes that did not falter from her own, "I swear that I offered all my silver to save him. But they wanted blood. I could not stop them!"

"They were your men!" she cried. "Under your command! You expect me to believe—"

"Nay, they were none of mine! They were my brother's men, and pagans." His face was dark with anger, and he spoke haltingly, his words a mixture now of tortured English and Danish. "Since Hemming's death they answer to no one. They were mad drunk with wine and bloodlust, howling to their gods to grant them fair winds." He grimaced. "Your priest was their offering."

*Blot*, he named it—spitting out the Norse word for blood sacrifice as if it fouled his mouth to speak it.

For a time she was speechless, stunned into silence as she imagined what Ælfheah must have endured at the hands of his captors, reluctant to accept that this man was not one of those responsible. She did not want to believe him. She wanted someone to blame, to punish. Yet in his defense she heard again Ælfheah's words at Gloucester almost as if he were whispering in her ear.

*There is little love between the Norse and the Danish shipmen.*

And on the heels of that memory came another, of Ælfric's description of the army at Canterbury.

*It is a mindless beast with no head and no heart.*

Eadric, who must have heard all that Thorkell had said, even if he had not understood every word, spoke into her ear, "It is true that he was not among the men we bargained with at Canterbury. But remember, this man is a skillful liar."

Emma recalled what Eadric had said of Thorkell—that he was a liar, and devious, and greedy. But the same could be said of Eadric, and so she did not know what to believe.

She looked to the sanctuary for help, to Ælfheah, lying beneath the altar cloth that she had embroidered and had herself given to him.

As if he read her thoughts Thorkell murmured, "Ælfheah treasured that gift because it came from your hand. Two seasons he was among us, and I learned to call him friend. But, God forgive me, I could not save him."

Stricken by his words she looked at him and saw that the anger in his face had been transmuted into grief.

She forced herself to swallow her rage, for she had to believe him. What other choice did she have? He had come here weaponless, empty-handed but for the body of a man he swore he had tried to save.

She drew in a long breath and lifted her eyes to where the light, seeping through the high, narrow windows, had begun to fade.

These men must leave the city, and soon. Once word spread of Ælfheah's death, the people of London would demand vengeance, and more blood would be shed.

She made up her mind what to do, and prayed that she was making the right choice.

"Rise," she ordered, "and go to your ship. Your pledges demand that you be gone from England before today's sun sets." She could not wish him well, though, and felt no gratitude that he had brought Ælfheah's body to London. Her horror and despair were far too great for that. "Lord Eadric, assign some men to see that the Danes reach their ship unharmed."

Eadric moved to Thorkell's side, but the big man ignored him and made no move to rise.

"There is a second pledge, lady, that I must honor," Thorkell said.

"What pledge?" she demanded sternly. Now that she had made the decision, she wanted him gone.

"That I would place myself and my men into the service of your king, should he wish it."

Surprised, she flicked a glance at Eadric, and she read cunning and speculation in his face. She could guess what he was thinking. Whoever carried word of such an offer to the king would be in high favor indeed, for Æthelred had long wished for just such an alliance. But could Thorkell's words be trusted?

The story of her grandfather's murder at the hands of an enemy who proffered peace came back to her again. Her mind raced to Edward, standing just a few steps from her. Was there some threat here that she could not discern? But the Danes were unarmed. The only thing that Thorkell clutched was a cross, and now she wanted to believe he spoke the truth.

"You swore this to Ælfheah?" she asked.

"He feared for you and for your children, and begged me to offer you my protection. I gave him my oath."

And now she recognized what this truly was—Ælfheah's bequest to her, a final act before he faced his death. Whatever dangers lay ahead in the months and years to come, Thorkell and his fleet could be the key to the safety of her children.

She kept her eyes on the big man's face, but she knew that Eadric was watching her, watching Thorkell, itching to intervene.

"This may be a trick," he hissed. "I told you, he is Swein's man!"

"No!" Thorkell spat. "No longer!" His face was flushed and angry again. He spoke not to Eadric, but to her, and she believed he spoke the truth.

Whatever alliance he may have made with the Danish king had been severed. Even so, other Viking leaders had broken with Swein in the past only to rally to his side again when it suited them to do so.

"If Swein should one day bring a fleet against England," she pressed him, "what then? What guarantee can you give that you would not betray us?"

He stood up, clutching the cross at his breast. He reached for her hand and placed it around his so that the cross was clasped by both. Bending his head to hers, he spoke for her ears alone—and in Danish. "I swore so to Ælfheah, who told me to trust you and no other. Now I swear so to you, by our Savior's cross." His eyes locked on hers. "You must take heed, for Swein is indeed coming—and it will be soon."

She stared at him in shock, and he gazed back at her confidently, certain that she had understood him.

The promise that Ælfheah had made to her years before echoed in her mind.

*Give me leave to reveal your secret if I see the need to do so.*

But Ælfheah was not the only one who had known her secret. Swein, too, had known that she spoke her mother's tongue, and Thorkell had once been Swein's ally.

She would have questioned him further, but a desperate shouting and pounding erupted at the back of the church, and as she turned toward the sound, the door crashed open.

Athelstan stormed in, armed men following in his wake, and his face was such a mask of fury that she almost did not know him.

Thorkell's men scrambled to their feet, but she moved to the altar to shield Ælfheah's body, afraid of what Athelstan might do if he saw it. She was too late. He was already striding toward the altar, and he swept her aside as if she were made of straw. He gave the ruined face only one swift glance before swinging around and drawing his sword.

She followed him, clutching his sword arm as he placed the point of his blade at Thorkell's breast.

"No!" she cried.

In the same instant she saw one of the Danes snatch Edward, pull the boy's knife from its scabbard, and press it against his throat.

# Chapter Thirty-Six

Emma heard the unmistakable whisper of more blades slipping from scabbards, and she knew that the nave behind her was bristling now with English swords. Far more terrifying to her, though, was the frightened face of the Dane who held the knife at Edward's throat.

*Sweet Virgin*, if there were to be a slaughter here, Edward would be the first to die.

"Athelstan, stop!" Her cry collided with Eadric's bellowed command to sheath swords.

No one heeded them. She felt Athelstan's arm tense beneath her hands, his sword still threatening.

Thorkell stood motionless and silent, glowering at Athelstan, who smiled grimly and jerked his head toward Edward.

"If you think that I care about the life of that boy," he said, "you are much mistaken. Kill him or let him go; it makes no matter."

Cries of protest erupted from some in the church, while Eadric spewed a string of invective. At the same time Emma, still keeping a firm grip on Athelstan's arm, spoke in Danish to the man who was clutching Edward.

"No harm will come to your leader," she said, praying that he would disentangle her words from the din around them. "Do not kill my son."

The shipman's wide, startled eyes flashed to hers, and the hand holding the knife trembled. She kept her eyes on his bewildered face while

Athelstan and Eadric shouted at each other, their voices echoing through the church.

"This is madness!" Eadric roared. "These men came here weaponless!"

"These men are Danes," Athelstan threw back at him, "and all Danes are liars! They swore peace and then they sacked Canterbury. They swore to leave England, yet there are a thousand of them still camped at Greenwich! They are truce breakers, and if there is madness here, it is you who are mad for trusting them! Emma!" She dragged her eyes from Edward's captor to Athelstan's face. He was glaring at Thorkell, and she saw no mercy or pity or any thought of Edward. Only rage. "Have you forgotten the innocents butchered before London's gates?" he demanded. "Have you forgotten what they did to Hilde? Whatever they have said here, you cannot believe them!"

His words were knife strokes to her heart, for she remembered all of it and more. Too much blood had been spent for far too long, but this madness had to stop. She would not see Edward added to the list of the dead.

Her decision made, she took a breath, steeling herself for what she must do. Keeping her eyes fixed on Athelstan's face, she released his sword arm to grasp the naked blade.

Athelstan flinched, and searing pain shot through her palm, but she did not let go. His shocked eyes snapped to hers and he swore at her, but when she forced the sword point down and away from Thorkell, Athelstan did not resist her pressure.

She placed herself in front of the Danish leader, still clutching the blade.

"These men are under my protection," she said, and now it was her voice that echoed through the church. "Anyone who wishes to do them harm must kill me first!"

And then, because she could think of no better way to assure the Danes that she was their ally, she shouted the words again—this time in her mother's tongue.


Emma's cry was greeted with a profound silence. Every man there, Athelstan guessed, was mazed by the flood of Danish words that had just spilled from the lips of an English queen.

He flicked a glance to Emma's bleeding hand and then back to her face. She was glaring at him with fierce, unyielding eyes, and he was baffled by her willingness to protect such a man as this.

"What lies has he told you that you would defend him?" he cried.

*Christ!* What misguided conviction had possessed her? With a single step she had placed herself at the mercy of the Danes. They needed no weapons. They could use Emma and her son as shields and make any demand they wished. He would be powerless to stop them.

Before Emma answered him, the big Dane snarled a command, and Athelstan readied himself to make a rush at Edward, certain that the bastard who held him was about to slit his throat. Instead the brute released the boy, thrusting him away unharmed before tossing the knife into the shadows behind him.

He saw Emma draw a deep breath, almost a sob, but she did not step away from the man she was shielding, nor release the sword.

"Thorkell has told me things that you have not heard, my lord." Her voice was commanding—and ice-cold. "You are in no position to judge if they are truth or lies."

A sudden chorus of cries rang out from the back of the church, and chancing a quick glance over his shoulder Athelstan saw the bishop of London shoving his way forward.

"In the name of God, what is happening here?" Ælfhun elbowed his way to Emma's side, and casting a horrified glance at her bloody hand, he gently pried it from the blade. "Put your weapons down!"

Athelstan made no move to obey, nor did his men. He continued to clutch his sword, his eyes on Thorkell, alert for the slightest flicker of threat.

"Archbishop Ælfheah lies there murdered!" he spat. "And the queen would defend his murderers!" This was all a ruse; it had to be. Emma had been beguiled by lies, promises—he did not know what. "These shipmen would gain entry into the—"

"These shipmen," Emma cut him off, "have come to us weaponless, bearing the body of our archbishop and an account of his death. Their leader wishes to speak with the king. It is not for Lord Athelstan or for any of us to determine the truth of their story. Only the king can do that."

Athelstan stared at her, helpless with rage at her blindness, for how could this be anything but some trick that would lead to disaster?

"They have cozened you, lady! Do not fall prey to their lies, I beg you, for they will betray us!"

And then he despaired, for she was looking at him with eyes of stone. She would not listen to him. Whatever this Thorkell had said to her, she believed him.

Eadric, too, moved to stand beside her, and now there were three of them shielding the Danes from the English. Emma had wrapped her bleeding hand into a fold of her cloak.

"Put your sword away, my lord," Eadric snapped. "Have you not spilled enough innocent blood already?"

"Blood has been spilled all across England, Eadric," he snarled, "by these men and others like them. Or had you not noticed?"

From just behind him Edmund hissed into his ear, "Leave it. You are wasting your breath here."

But he could not leave it.

"What of the dragon ship out there? What of the fleet that still lies at Greenwich? My lady, do you mean to welcome all our enemies into London?"

He had meant it as a taunt to make Emma think twice about what she was doing. To his surprise, she frowned, then held a brief, whispered exchange with the Danish leader.

He glanced at the faces of Eadric and the bishop, and he read their uneasiness at not being party to what passed between the queen and the Dane. Yet neither man made a protest, and it dawned on him that the balance of power in this chamber, perhaps even in the kingdom, had shifted the moment that Emma had seized that naked steel.

And surely Emma knew it.

"The Danish ship," she announced, "will return to Greenwich. Eadric, I would have you send some of your men with them, to keep watch on their doings. Thorkell has agreed to this. He and his companions will be escorted to the palace by my house guards, where they will await the king. Word of Ælfheah's death must not stir beyond these walls until the Danes are safe within the palace, lest some misguided soul seek vengeance." Her defiant eyes met his. "Does that satisfy you, Lord Athelstan? Will you and your men put away your swords now?"

The very air seemed to crackle with tension. He could order his men to slay the Danes, slay even Eadric, and that would be one less enemy to deal with. But he could not guarantee the safety of Emma and the bishop if it came to a bloodbath. When all was finished, whatever the outcome, he would have to face the king's justice, and he was not prepared to lead his brothers in rebellion.

Which left him no choice. He sheathed his weapon and signaled to his men to do the same.

"I am not satisfied in the least, my lady," he said. "And mark me, you will have cause to regret what you do here today."

That night in his London hall, Athelstan sat scowling into a half-empty wine cup as his brothers recounted what had occurred after he'd stalked out of All Hallows.

"The bishop must have summoned every clergyman in London to escort Ælfheah's body to St. Paul's," Edrid said. "The queen and Eadric led a line of mourners that stretched across half the city."

"And is that not an unholy alliance," Edmund snarled, "the queen and Eadric? I have warned you for years that Emma is not to be trusted. Now that she's whelped a second son, she is near to achieving the power that she's been lusting after since she first set foot in England. *Christ!* She would strike a bargain even with the devil if—"

"Leave it, Edmund!" Athelstan barked. He had nearly managed to erase the image from his mind of Emma glaring at him with hatred in her eyes and with Eadric at her side. He did not need it thrown in his face.

"Listen to me!" Edmund was shouting now and clearly not willing to let it go. "Eadric and Emma will urge the king to forge an alliance with Thorkell without questioning whether the vermin can be trusted. You know that! And because Emma speaks the Northman's tongue—and that is something she has craftily hidden until now—*Christ!* What a liar she is!" He stopped for breath. "Because of that, she is likely to be given a seat at the king's council. Think you there will be room for us there when Emma, Eadric, and Thorkell have the king's ear?"

Athelstan took a long swallow from his cup, then slammed it to the table and got to his feet, goaded by the suspicion that Edmund could be right.

Emma was no fool. She must have recognized that if Thorkell pledged his service to the king, her knowledge of Danish would no longer be a liability but an advantage. Why else would she have revealed such a thing after hiding it for so long?

But Edmund had not finished. "The king will surely accept Thorkell's offer of ships and men," he went on, "but not without great cost. He will have to tax his nobles yet again and they will not thank him for it. Few of them will be comforted, I think, by the sight of a Danish fleet settled on our shores."

Athelstan was only half listening to him, for he was seeing again the scene in the chapel—Emma trying to block the sight of Ælfheah's shattered face, Emma grasping the blade of his sword, Emma stanching blood with a fold of her cloak. And then, abruptly, another memory intruded, of young Edward held fast with a knife at his throat.

He had urged the Dane to dispatch the boy, hoping to gull him into thinking he had hold of a useless hostage. *Jesu.* Had Emma believed him?

"Athelstan!" Edmund's voice recalled him to the present. "The men on the king's council will resent Thorkell. They will balk at having to pay for his fleet, and their discontent might suit our own purposes. We could—"

He rounded on his brother. "What purposes, Edmund?" he demanded. "Would you counsel me again to rebel against the king? How many times must I tell you that I will not walk that road?" He had given Ælfheah his word on that. Even the archbishop's death did not release him from his vow. "You would have me seize the throne, but where would I look for allies? In the north Elgiva and her brothers are dead; those of her kin who remain have been showered with lands and offices to bind them to the king."

Edmund was on his feet now, the two of them facing off against each other.

"You cannot mean to stand aside and do nothing," Edmund protested. "You cannot believe that Thorkell can be trusted!"

Athelstan shoved past his brother. He was not certain what he believed. At All Hallows he had been convinced that Thorkell's appearance in London had been some ploy to get inside the city's defenses. Now he was not so sure. Thorkell's fleet still lay at Greenwich, their sails furled and bound, no threat to London. The men he had sent there for news had reported that, far from being responsible for Ælfheah's death, Thorkell had gone to great lengths to try to prevent it.

What had the Dane said to Emma there in the church that had made her trust him? He did not know, but something had convinced her that he would keep his word.

"I do not know what to make of Thorkell," he said. "But I will not make any move that would fracture this kingdom."

Edmund cursed. "The kingdom is already fractured," he snarled, "and has been since Eadric murdered Ealdorman Ælfhelm."

Athelstan turned to glare at him. "And what do you think would happen if we do as you suggest: make alliance with disgruntled northern nobles and raise our banners against the king?"

Edrid stood up and moved to Edmund's side. "Athelstan is right," he said. "The king would use Thorkell and his shipmen as a weapon against anyone who dared oppose him. It's too big a risk."

"We must be patient," Athelstan insisted. "The balance of power at court is shifting beneath our feet. Ælfheah is dead and we cannot know who will replace him. Thorkell will negotiate some kind of alliance with the king, but we can't even begin to guess how much influence he will have. Eadric still holds the king's favor, and with both Edwig and Edward under his thumb—"

"Edwig is no use to him," Edmund objected, "drunk or sober."

"We cannot be certain of that," Athelstan cautioned. "Every ætheling is throne-worthy. There is no telling what use Eadric may have in mind for our brother." He frowned. "I think he will use his hold on young Edward to exert pressure on the queen. And she is more likely to have the king's ear now, with two sons to her account."

"So the court is a vipers' nest," Edmund spat. "Can you think of no better strategy than to merely avoid being bitten? I put it to you again: What if this Thorkell cannot be trusted? What if he turns on England, betrays us to our Danish enemies from within?"

Athelstan ran an unsteady hand through his hair, troubled by Edmund's words. His brother, God forbid, could very well be right.

"Let us pray that does not happen," he said. "But if it does, Edmund, and we are not united behind the throne, when the Danish hammer stroke falls, England will shatter like glass." He drew a long breath. "It is but another reason why we cannot break with our father."

He looked at Edrid, who nodded his agreement. He looked to Edmund, who gazed back at him, his face still dark with whatever black conjectures were running through his mind.

Finally, Edmund ground out reluctantly, "As you wish. We will not break with the king." Then he glowered at Athelstan and added, "Not yet."

Athelstan heard the warning there, but for now he was satisfied. He turned away from his brothers and stared into the flames of the hearth, calling to mind the very last words that the seeress had said to him.

*I see fire and smoke. There is nothing else.*

If that prophecy was true and England was to be tried by fire yet again, he hoped to God that he would not have to be the one to set it alight.

A.D. 1012   Then submitted to the king five and forty of the ships of the enemy; and promised him, that they would defend this land, and he should feed and clothe them.

—*The Anglo-Saxon Chronicle*

# Chapter Thirty-Seven

April 1012

Windsor

Emma stepped from the gloom of the king's great hall into the fading light of late afternoon. The palace yard swarmed with priests, royal messengers, hearth guards, and kitchen slaves—all of them members of the king's household who populated this Windsor manor. She paid little heed to them as she turned her steps toward her own apartments, for she was still sifting through the events that had taken place in the hall over the past few hours.

Inside her chamber, Wymarc and Father Martin rose quickly to greet her, and Wymarc hastened to slip the cloak from her shoulders.

"It is done," Emma told them. "The king has accepted Thorkell into his service. There is to be a formal oath-taking at the midsummer assembly."

So much had happened in such a very little time! Eight days ago she had stood in All Hallows Church raging at the Danish warlord over Ælfheah's shattered body. Three days later she had mourned with all of London as the archbishop was laid in his tomb. Today she had arrived here to serve as interpreter between the Dane and the hastily assembled king's council until an agreement had been hammered out between them.

Today's meeting, though, had left her restless and uneasy, and her discomfort was compounded by the throbbing in her wounded hand.

Wymarc seemed to read her thoughts, for she appeared at her side with a cup of wine.

"It will ease the pain in your hand," she said, "and help to restore you.

The meeting could not have been an easy one. I imagine the king was not well pleased that Thorkell insisted that you be there to speak for him."

"No," she replied, "he was not pleased. Nor did he offer a warm welcome to his new ally, although I suppose that is only to be expected. What I did not anticipate, though, was that today's council session would be so ugly."

"There was opposition to the alliance, then," Father Martin said.

"There was a great deal of opposition, yes," Emma replied.

"And Lord Athelstan?" Wymarc asked. "Did he oppose it?" Emma knew that she was remembering Athelstan's rage at All Hallows.

"He was not there," she said. "None of the æthelings were there." They had not been summoned, she had been told, and it was just as well. The meeting had been hostile enough without them. "The king himself said very little," she continued. "It was Eadric who directed everything."

Eadric, who had hastened to the king with his version of the events at All Hallows even before Ælfheah had been laid to rest. Eadric, who had embraced the Danes and their forty-five dragon ships like a lover.

"Today I saw a side of the ealdorman that I have never witnessed before," she said. "He was no honey-tongued flatterer, using half-truths to persuade and cajole. He was a bully. He abused any man who spoke against him so savagely that he may as well have walked into the hall with a cudgel."

In spite of that, many men had opposed him, for they were bitterly against the king's alliance with the Danish warlord. She had been hard-pressed to translate all the rapid, angry exchanges for Thorkell's benefit, even as she suspected that he understood far more of what was said than he was inclined to reveal.

"It is strange that the king would trust anyone else to handle the negotiations, even Eadric," Father Martin observed. "Could it be that the injuries from his fall still plague him? He is not a young man."

Emma considered it. She had seen the sinister gash across his brow, and she had been told that he needed a staff when he walked. But if he had been in pain he had hidden it well. She was familiar with Æthelred's black moods, and it was not pain that she had discerned in his glowering silence, but a seething rage that he barely managed to keep in check.

She was about to speak of it when a servant appeared with a summons for her from the king.

"There must be some mistake," Wymarc protested. "She has only just come from the hall. She's not even had a chance to catch her breath."

But the servant was adamant. The king was in his chamber, and the queen was to attend him there.

"It appears that Æthelred is about to break his silence," she said as Wymarc helped her with her cloak.

Her friend's brow was clouded with concern, for they both knew what this was about. Emma squeezed Wymarc's hand to reassure her, but as she followed the king's man, her heart was hammering.

She found Æthelred seated in his great chair, his bandaged foot stretched out in front of him. His only attendant, Hubert, was reading aloud from what appeared to be letters, but when she entered the chamber the steward's high-pitched voice abruptly ceased.

As she approached the king he pinned her with a black look. Yes, she thought, this is going to be unpleasant.

As it was clearly a formal interview, she made an obeisance. He did not bid her rise, though, and she realized that he wanted her on her knees before him, like a penitent at the feet of an angry God. But she was no sinner come to ask forgiveness. She was his queen, and she had done nothing for which she needed to repent. She met his gaze and, despite the rage that she read there, she stood up, defiant, regarding him with practiced calm as she waited for him to speak.

"I see that the office you performed at the council today has swelled your sinful pride, lady," he snarled. "How it must have amused you all these years to keep me ignorant of your excellent command of the Danish tongue so that now, at long last, you could make me look ten times a fool. If you think that I am pleased to discover that my queen can parley with my enemies so effectively, you are much mistaken."

"My lord, until now I saw no advantage to you in revealing something that might raise suspicions that I could somehow be a Danish—"

"It is not your task to determine what is and is not to my advantage!"

"It was not to *my* advantage, then," she said. A bitter memory assailed her, of the beating she had suffered in the early days of their marriage.

She had upbraided him for ordering the slaughter of Danes settled in his kingdom, and he had left her battered and bleeding. But to dwell on that would make her angry, and anger would not serve her today, so she thrust the memory aside. "Now that Thorkell has given you his pledge," she continued evenly, "my knowledge of his language can be of some service to you. Use it or not, my lord, as it pleases you."

"Oh, I will use it," he sneered, "for you have insinuated yourself into Thorkell's confidence, and he will trust no other. But do not profess that you are acting for my benefit, Emma. I know you too well. Thorkell is but another name to add to your list of allies, for you continue to labor under the mistaken belief that you have some claim to power at my court. This is not Normandy, lady, although I do not doubt that you wish it could be."

"My lord, you wrong me if you believe that I covet power for my own sake," she said evenly. "I seek only to protect my children."

He barked an angry laugh. "And do you think I would accept the word of one who by her own admission has been lying to me for ten years?" He glared at her, his eyes filled with malice. "If I had my way you would find yourself across the Narrow Sea, stripped of titles, lands, crown—of everything, I think, that you hold most dear." Leaning forward, he spoke in a voice laced with threat. "Enjoy your tiny sphere of influence while you may, but I'm warning you: If you use your newfound power against me I shall repay you sevenfold. There is a reckoning coming, Emma. Forget it at your peril."

No, she thought. She was not likely to forget it.

When he dismissed her, she made him another graceful obeisance and left the chamber with a purposefully measured tread. She was still England's queen, and despite his threats, nothing he could do would change that. Not now, for she had given him three children. They must be her shields against him.

She was trembling, though, for the interview had troubled her greatly.

She did not return to her chamber, but climbed the steps that took her to the walkway along the palisade. The daylight was fading, and the cloud-filled sky had a sullen cast to it. Below her the royal hythes that had been bustling at midday were deserted now, and the Thames flowed silent, its surface swept clean. For a time she stood there, looking to the river for a serenity that eluded her.

Æthelred claimed that she had allies—a sphere of influence, even— yet it seemed far otherwise to her. Granted, Thorkell supported her, but every man at today's council session, whether churchman or royal thegn, had been injured in some way by Thorkell's army: lands burned, churches pillaged, daughters raped, sons slain. They had good reason to hate and fear Thorkell, and to be suspicious of the queen who had befriended their enemy. She had seen the hostility in their faces; she could not hope to find allies among them now.

Casting her mind back to All Hallows, she questioned the decisions she had made there. Had it been wise to throw in her lot with the Danes? Was it truly what Ælfheah would have wanted? She was still uneasy in her mind about that, although in Thorkell she had gained a protector for herself and her children; a protector for the realm, come to that.

But Thorkell was not one who could give her wise counsel, and there were few now that she could turn to for advice. How she grieved for the counselors whom she had lost! Margot, Hilde, Ælfheah—they lived now only in her memory.

And there was another loss, too: Athelstan. She had trusted him, had loved him as she had loved no other man. But at All Hallows he had set himself against her, would have sacrificed Edward for the sake of vengeance. It was a betrayal that filled her with anguish still, and added to the weight of her fear for her son.

And as she counted her losses, the king's dire words came back to haunt her.

*There is a reckoning coming.*

She knew him too well to consider it an empty threat. As he saw it, they were locked in a game of power and control, and he had some move in mind to make against her. Of that she was certain, although she could not see yet what it might be.

*If I had my way you would find yourself across the Narrow Sea, stripped of everything that you hold most dear.*

Would he send her away from England? Was that to be his weapon?

No, he would not dare. He would fear her brother's swift and harsh response. But if the king should try to drive her away, should make her life here so hateful that she would willingly choose to cross the Narrow Sea, what then?

She drew in a long breath. What then?

All around her the darkness was falling, but in the gloaming the Thames had become a shining silver ribbon. She looked from that glimmering line to the downs, their countless shades of green still beautiful even under a darkling sky. In that vast sweep of field and meadow, of river and forest and sky, she found the answer to her question, and she found, too, a balm for her troubled soul.

She could not deny her Norman blood, nor would she sever the family ties that bridged the Narrow Sea. But long ago she had pledged herself to an English king and to his people. Come what may, that was not a pledge that she would lightly disavow. Her family now was English, not Norman, and her destiny must be here.

Despite all that a king could do, she belonged to England.

# Author's Note

The entries in *The Anglo-Saxon Chronicle* spanning the years A.D. 1006 to A.D. 1012 are grim reading. A litany of woe, they describe the turmoil and bloodshed in England caused by successive invasions of ever larger Viking armies that eventually scoured nearly every shire.

In that account of battles and of repeated, futile attempts by the English to rebuff the enemy, there is no mention of Queen Emma. This is not surprising. The chroniclers were recording the major events of Æthelred's reign some years after they occurred, and they had no interest in the activities of royal women. Where Emma was and what she was doing in this period must be a matter of conjecture. There are clues, though.

Emma's name on the witness lists of four of the dozen or so charters of Æthelred that have survived from this period confirms her presence at some of the meetings of the witan. Why she witnessed some charters and not others is impossible to say. Historian Pauline Stafford, in her book *Queen Emma & Queen Edith: Queenship and Women's Power in Eleventh-Century England*, suggests that Emma's main concerns at this time would have been children and family. I have followed her lead and have used the dates that she has surmised for the births of Emma's daughter and younger son. But I also have had to address the issue of why there were so many years between those births. Æthelred's children by his first marriage appeared to have arrived annually. That he sired only three children with Emma suggests several possibilities: There may have been miscarriages in between; Emma may have chosen to nurse her infants, which would have delayed conception; king and queen may have been separated by military actions or by choice. I have used all of these in my story because, quite simply, we do not know what really happened.

Emma's close relationship with Archbishop Ælfheah is conjecture on my part, but it is based on Ælfheah's twenty-year tenure as bishop of Winchester before his appointment to Canterbury. Emma, indeed all the members of the royal family, would have had a personal acquaintance with him at the very least. After his death, Ælfheah was immediately revered as a martyr. Looking ahead to A.D. 1023, when Ælfheah's remains were ceremoniously moved from London to Canterbury in a procession that included many nobles and ecclesiastics, it was Queen Emma, not the king, who accompanied the saint on that journey. This may have been no more than good royal public relations and a display of religious devotion; but it may hint, too, at a personal bond between Emma and the archbishop, and I have played with that idea in the novel.

The events at All Hallows and Emma's role there are fictional, although Ælfheah's capture, imprisonment, his refusal to allow ransom to be paid, and his brutal death are all documented. It is also true that on the day after his murder the archbishop's body was brought to London along with an account of how he had died. Shortly after that, according to *The Anglo-Saxon Chronicle*, Thorkell and forty-five of his ships submitted to the king "and promised him, that they would defend this land, and he should feed and clothe them." It is no great stretch to think that these two extraordinary events were somehow linked, but the details, including the reason behind the attack on Canterbury, are unknown. I have made them up to suit my story.

One cannot help but wonder what was going through the mind of King Æthelred during these difficult times. In the twelfth century, William of Malmesbury would describe him as lazy, among other things. Modern historians opine that he was given poor counsel and that, at best, he wasn't up to the task of fending off the Danes. There is no question, though, that the king was troubled by unrest from within his borders as well as from without; the debacle with the fleet in A.D. 1009 underscores that. The chronicles do not specify what accusations were made against the nobleman Wulfnoth at Sandwich; that was my invention. But Æthelred's flight, the astounding decision to send eighty ships to capture Wulfnoth's twenty, and the destruction of the fleet are all documented. The loss of those newly built ships must have been a massive blow to the king and the entire nation.

Æthelred was not so much *unready* as *unlucky*. As the Anglo-Saxon poet claims in "The Wanderer," *Wyrd bið ful áræd*: Fate is relentless. According to William of Malmesbury, Æthelred's ill fortunes were tied to the murder of his half brother, King Edward. He was haunted by that murder, and there were yet more killings that followed that one.

According to a twelfth-century chronicler, King Æthelred ordered the murder of Ealdorman Ælfhelm, and the deed was carried out by Eadric, who at some point was given the nickname Streona (the acquisitor). What crime had Ælfhelm committed that he should be punished with death and his sons blinded? We can only guess. Historians have seen it as a symptom of palace intrigue of some kind. I think his crime was huge, and I've put Ælfhelm's daughter, Elgiva, right at the heart of it.

And here I must explain something about Danish marriage practices, as well as define the term *concubine*. In eleventh-century England, Denmark, and Normandy, a concubine was a secondary wife, and it was acceptable for a man to have a wife and a concubine at the same time. More important, the children of a concubine, if they were recognized by their father, would have inheritance rights. As you may imagine, the Church frowned upon this, and under its pressure this practice would eventually disappear. That would not happen for some time, though, even in England.

It was also claimed that the Danes practiced a kind of marriage by abduction—snatching a bride and legitimizing the relationship with a dowry after the fact. It is unclear if this sort of thing actually happened, or if later Christian writers were simply piling more dirt upon the already infamous reputation of the Vikings. Factual or not, this practice was certainly in my mind as I wrote the book.

That Elgiva was Cnut's concubine is a certainty. Many years later there would be rumors that Elgiva, desperate to give Cnut a son, passed off someone else's child as his. The truth about that remains a mystery, but Elgiva, as I've imagined her, could easily have attempted a stunt like that.

The date that is usually accepted for the beginning of Elgiva's liaison with Cnut is A.D. 1013, but that is conjecture based on the fact that Cnut was known to have been in England that year. I have brought them together much earlier, in A.D. 1006. We don't know where Cnut was between A.D. 1006 and A.D. 1013, and we don't know where Elgiva was sheltered after her father's murder, so I've filled in those blanks with my own story based on the very few facts (and rumors) available. The wedding-night scene in Holderness, by the way, sprang from my imagination, not from any documented evidence about Viking traditions.

Regarding the sons of Æthelred by his first wife, we know more about Athelstan and Edmund than about any of their brothers. We can be certain that they were wealthy; they owned estates, weapons, armor, horses, and they had retainers and attendants. It appears that the relationship between Athelstan and Edmund was a close one. We do not know how their brothers Ecbert and Edgar died, only that in a given year their names disappear from the charters.

There is, of course, no record documenting what the æthelings felt toward their stepmother, Emma. The eldest brothers would probably have been about the same age as she was, so it's doubtful that they would have regarded her as their mother. The passion that I have imagined between Athelstan and Emma, I admit, is pure fiction. I fell in love with them both, and so I made them fall in love with each other. There is, however, historical precedent for a marriage between a king's son and his widowed stepmother. In A.D. 858, the newly crowned West Saxon king Æthelbald married his father's young, widowed queen. She was a Frankish princess named Judith, who had married his elderly father two years before. There is probably a great deal more to that story than the chronicles reveal.

As this novel ends, though, Emma is not a widow—not yet. She is a queen and a mother, with three children to protect and nurture. And as bad as things were for Emma and for England between A.D. 1006 and A.D. 1012, in the book that will follow, things will get even worse.

# Acknowledgments

My thanks once again to my tireless agent, Stephanie Cabot, for her encouragement and shrewd advice, and to the helpful team at the Gernert Company, especially Ellen Goodson and Anna Worrall. I'm grateful to my terrific editor at Viking, Emily Murdock Baker, for loving this book as much as she loved the first one; and to everyone at Viking Penguin who helped with the novel's production. Special thanks to Matt Brown, yet again, for the wonderful maps of England and London.

Thanks to Gillian Bagwell and Melanie Spiller for spending two years of their lives reading and rereading the manuscript as it grew and giving it as much loving attention as they gave their own work; to Leslie Keenan and Mary Wieland, who read the novel in bits and pieces and offered sage advice without ever discovering how it would end; and to Christine Mann for plowing swiftly through the second draft and making suggestions for draft number three.

I am indebted to David Levin, pathologist with Washington Hospital in Fremont, California, for fascinating discussions about mortal illnesses and burnt bodies; and to Craig Johnson of the Oakeshott Institute, who helped me envisage a battlefield and taught me something of swordplay; he has had far better students, I'm certain, but none more grateful. A humble thank-you as well to the anonymous knight at the 2013 International Congress on Medieval Studies at Western Michigan University who explained what happens when a sword blade is grabbed bare-handed.

Once again I have depended upon the work of scholars for my understanding of events in late Anglo-Saxon England, especially the following: Pauline Stafford's *Queen Emma & Queen Edith: Queenship and Women's Power in Eleventh-Century England* and *Unification and Conquest*; Ryan Lavelle's *Æthelred II*; Ann Williams's *Æthelred the Unready*; M. K. Lawson's *Cnut*; David Hill's *An Atlas of Anglo-Saxon England*; N. J. Higham's *The Death of Anglo-Saxon England*; Ian Howard's *Swein Forkbeard's Invasions and the Danish Conquest of England, 991–1017*; and Gale Owen-Crocker's *Dress in Anglo-Saxon England*.

Most especially, my love and thanks to Lloyd, Andrew, and Alan.